4:20 MILER

4:20 MILER

Claudell James

iUniverse, Inc.

New York Lincoln Shanghai

4:20 MILER

iUniverse books may be ordered through booksellers or by contacting:

iUniverse
2021 Pine Lake Road, Suite 100
Lincoln, NE 68512
www.iuniverse.com
1-800-Authors (1-800-288-4677)

ISBN-13: 978-0-595-37199-0 (pbk)
ISBN-13: 978-0-595-81598-2 (ebk)
ISBN-10: 0-595-37199-X (pbk)
ISBN-10: 0-595-81598-7 (ebk)

Printed in the United States of America

CHAPTER 1

▼

The heavy humid air flowed reluctantly from the earth as the lifting fog revealed a slight figure, a boy, traversing a narrow dirt road, running. As the landscape changed from brown to green; the boy began to prance with more eagerness as to the sight. He cast his eyes upon the road seeing it would grow from long troughs of liquid mud to surfaced thoroughfares and again mud. Kasper Wise moved sluggishly down the muddy country road. It had rained most of the previous day so he ran in the middle of the little narrow path avoiding the puddles on the edge.

"I don't need to slip and strain a leg muscle," he thought, being very selective of every foot placement. Kasper, however, was going to cover his six miles on this morning and nothing would cut this goal short. He had been running hard mileage for six months now and there were still two months before the track season.

"Got to keep my mileage up, with Saturday and Sunday, I'll get sixty-five miles in this week…I ought to try and get a couple more miles each of those days. Then I'll hit seventy miles!" he mumbled to himself, as he often does. "Coach says we'll have a time trial just to see where we're at…got to be under four-forty…if I can, maybe low four- thirties…and with speed work by the end of the season hopefully mid-four-twenties!" Kasper was a dreamer. Nevertheless, he felt that if he did not set his goals no one else would.

Smart, articulate in math and his beloved physics, Kasper and his two brothers had spent most of their young lives in Germany. Their dad had been a supply driver with the US Air Force. Now retired, Jayce and family lived in Central Ohio where he had extended family. Kasper's mom Beth, a German, met and married Jayce during those years in her country. Beth, a Bavarian country girl, had been resistive in coming to America to live permanently until her arrival in the country setting of this central Ohio County. Beth had no desire for Jayce's urban heritage of the big city. Kasper, a small child, born with a deformed right leg and respiratory problem was the oldest of the Wises' three boys. Due to his almost constant medical problems and equally his confinement at home with leg braces and his small stature, most observers assume that he was the youngest of the trio. Brother Eli was one year younger but two inches taller, while Greg two years younger was equal in stature as his senior brother.

The boy's first school in Ohio was Marlborough Union a large Division 1 school. How the young sickly Kasper got into such a vigorous sport as long distance running was quite an anomaly of circumstance. During his sophomore year at Marlborough, Mr. Larson, the football coach and his Health teacher had asked Kasper to come out for wrestling. The wrestling team needed some smaller kids to workout with the varsity. "Bo" Larson was a high-pressure type who could not understand kids who did not participants in sports. He would tell family and colleagues off campus, "I don't like kids who are not in sports, can't stand them. They're the ones who are always back talking you, undisciplined, disrespectful…" However, Bo Larson was fond of the little fuzzy headed, withdrawn, and taciturn Kasper. Having been in the army and stationed in Germany as well; Coach Larson found himself impressed by the little Kasper who spoke with a German accent when he did say something. Bo remembered Kasper's description of his education in Germany.

"We didn't go to the schools on the Air Force base," Kasper said, "Mother is German, and her childhood home was nearby. We lived with my mother's parents, mostly, an attended mom's old school. Dad and mom were always going off to temporary assignments, sometimes in other countries in Europe."

The frail Kasper was delighted to tryout for wrestling, although he never dreamed of making the team. "Workout and build up some muscles on those bones," Larson suggested to him. Thinking maybe this would help the youngster's absence of self-esteem. After the pushups, leg-lifts and running Kasper found himself exhausted, but delighted of this accomplishment. Another person may say he accomplished little; this was of no matter, Kasper thought he was a real athlete. He started seeing some muscle development and his endurance increased. The team ran four laps on the stadium track and finished up with running up and down the stadium stairs. Kasper would run to exhaustion. He cared more about his conditioning than the wrestling matches that followed and the thrashing he would experience.

"Six minutes fifteen seconds", Kasper reflected back to that day he ran his first time trail. "Man was that hard!" It was his first 1600-meter run. The boy had timed himself without another soul in sight. "How can anybody run a mile in less than four minutes? Those guys must be super. They have to be born with that ability." Kasper was sure of that back then.

Today running down the center of a muddy road, Kasper felt different. "The fantastic is realizes by brute force," he thought. "That's where I am. I've come a long way since those stadium drills. This run will give me nine miles total today."

Focusing ahead, he knew it was about time for that hill to show up. His arms started pumping a bit more, his breathing labored in the run now. He crested the little peak, then lengthened his stride and allowed himself to float down the leeward side saving energy. The boy could see his home as he made a right turn and made his last demand for pace. "Got to always finish hard," he reminded himself in the fast finish of the last forty meters to the front yard.

"Four-thirty will not get you anywhere in Division 1, but I may be able to beat somebody in Division 2," he thought.

The previous Autumn Kasper and brothers had transferred to Lakeport High, a small school that had the middle and high school in the same building. "Hittsville, here I come," he had said his first day at the place. "Now this is home," he submitted presently.

"Did you beat the Kenyans in the stretch?" That was Kasper's brother, Eli. Eli was sarcastic and seldom serious about matters, quite contrary to Kasper's nature. He approached and sat besides his still gasping Kasper on the porch. "I'll run with you Saturday. Lets' do some speed work, some intervals. That long slow stuff I can't handle," Eli added in a more serious tone.

"Sounds good," Kasper, replied. "But yea, I always try to run it in hard; got to get ready for the fast finishes." Then he thought on then He said to Eli, "Realistically, I am not going to count on running someone down in the stretch as slow as my four-hundred meter times are. That is for you Eli. If you get strong enough to stick with the leaders, you can do'em in."

"Come on let's knock-off those ten algebra and physics problems, "Eli suggested, "Then we can catch a couple movies on TV tonight, guy."

"Sounds good to me," Kasper agreed. He had made a deal with Lakeport's coach Thorpe to complete ten algebra and physics problems five days a week. Kasper's grades had been unimpressive at Marlborough; he just did not apply himself. He did not know what he was to do with his life, but mostly he hated being "over here" in America. "Wish we had stayed in Germany," he was always thinking, "everybody so clannish here. In Germany, we all had the same culture;

everybody's family had similar histories…nobody asking you, "'Where you're from or how come you talk like that?'"

At Marlborough Matt Thorpe had been an assistant coach for the track team and an Algebra teacher. Kasper had been one of his students in the algebra class. Thorpe liked and admired Kasper and his brother Eli. The boys were respectful, but stayed to themselves. Other students saw them as foreigners. However, what bothered Thorpe was the outright hostility Kasper experienced at Marlborough, when the boy went out track. Now, Kasper would finish last in the two-mile runs required at the start of practice. After this run, Kasper would struggle throughout the reminder of the workout. However, he made a habit of running a series of 200-meter intervals, to complete the practice after everyone else left the track. The head coach Wiley Smith did not care for Kasper. Kasper had made a point of suggesting that he would improve more with his short runs than with the long 400, 600, and 800-meter runs. Kasper made the point that, because of his inherent physical disabilities; running short intervals would: "enhance my development in a more expeditious manner." He had read about this method in running magazines and articles. It required little imagination to gage the reaction of Kasper's statement issued to the old coach. Coach Smith had thirty years at the helm of track and field in this old rural community. Add to this Kasper's status as a foreign minority, Coach Smith's dislike of Kasper might be predictable.

This was a point in character that rubbed people wrong with Kasper. When he did speak-up about something, he too often reminded people that he had learned the proper answer somewhere or read of it in some text. "That's a strange means of dealing with the subject, but then I guess that's the way you Americans see things," he would sat to close the encounter with this diatribe. Such encounters were Kasper's way of puffing up his own self-esteem; otherwise, he had little say in school encounters and affairs.

It was in these social setting and environs that led to a pleasing departure for the Wise family from Marlborough after Matt Thorpe took a head-coaching job at the small Lakeport High school. Thorpe seized the opportunity to recruit the Wise boys. He suggested they should consider moving to a school where the boys could get a fresh start.

"I like the work ethic I see in Kasper, and I want Eli and Greg to come out for track. It's going to be difficult to get a full team for track at this little school." Thorpe had told Jayce Wise. Thorpe had always had his eyes on Eli. Lanky and taller than Kasper, more athletic in stature and demeanor, "Eli looks to be a two minute half miler, if I can get him to make the effort Kasper does," he surmised.

ᚱᛚᚼᚠᚼᛃᛃᛪᚼᛘᛃ�075ᛪᚼᛪᚼᛪᚼᚼᛃᛪᚼᛪᚼᛃᚼᛪᚼ

Its' early spring, the first faint shoots of green were breaking out upon the elms and the sticker spearheads of the chestnuts were just beginning to burst into their five-fold leaves. Kasper, Cousin Danny, Eli, and the youngest brother Greg ran together in silence for the most part, as befits four young fellows who know each other intimately. The runners had circuited the border of Thorpe's farm, a distance of five miles. It was nearly four in the afternoon before they arrived back to the Thorpe house.

"Someone came looking for you boys," said Holly Thorpe, coach Thorpe's mother, as she opened the door to the sweaty pack, "There's been a young red-headed fellow, had a missing left arm, asking for ya'll. He struck me as a nice kid, just like you boys." Eli glanced reproachfully at Kasper. "Told you we should have gotten back, we left so late!" he said. "Terry Luke said he would drop by. He wants to start running with us." Eli directed his explanation to Mrs. Thorpe.

"Well, we can stop by Jimmy Luke's place on the way back home," Kasper suggested, as he walked into the living room. "We need Terry. He is no 'handicap' he's a Luke and he's been playing on the soccer team. The boy has got enormous natural speed." Kasper reminded them. "He will dust me any time in a four-hundred meter run."

"He's faster than me too," Danny interjected.

"A definite asset, we are in most classes together," interjected Eli, "I have raced him out on the field; he sticks with me neck to neck."

"Let's head over there now before he leaves," suggested Danny somewhat anxious.

Danny a first cousin had been living with his uncle's family since they moved to Lakeport. Danny's dad was in jail and his mother was seldom in his life at all. He had been living with Uncle George Wise. Twelve years senior to Jayce, George was in poor health. He had to take advantage of his brother, begging him to take Danny to live with them. Jayce and wife Beth, readily agreed, delighted to take the boy into their home and enrolling him at Lakeport High. Danny was rail skinny. He like most of the Wise family and clan was short and they all were of a thin stature. Understandably self-conscious concerning his father, jailed for drunk driving; Danny seemed withdrawn to most who observed him, not so with his cousins. He was pleased to match up with his German educated clan, who spoke with a foreign accent and where studious and athletic as well. Danny reasoned he had an opportunity with the Wises's at making a success of himself in something.

"Thanks Mrs. Thorpe, we should get going now," said Kasper, in his genial way. "It was great running around your farm; thank you for having us. May I ask how we can help you with something, before we leave?"

"I don't need you boys for a thing. You get along now and find that young fellow. I would like to see him with you all next time you are out here. He seemed nervous like he wasn't sure you boys would want him around." She paused contemplatively. "Wonder how he lost his arm?"

"Jimmy told us he was in a car accident with his mother when he was about seven; however, he's been on the soccer team." Emphasized Danny, "Terry's quite athletic you know."

"Oh, how terrible; he must have gotten over the trauma and is getting on bravely with his life," Mrs. Thorpe added.

The crew took its leave, climbed into the old pickup and headed out toward the opposite side of the Crimshead Lake area that bordered Lakeport near the location of the Luke family residence.

"If Terry joins us now," Kasper said as he drove, "there's enough time before the season to get him in shape. Then we'll have five middle and long distance men." He reminded the two smiling.

As they continued, Kasper reflected on the circumstances that brought this crew of runners at this place and time of events. Coach Thorpe took a lot of hazing from other coaches at Marlborough Union when he took the job at Lakeport and then persuaded the Wise brothers to follow. He liked the small town atmosphere and the people like the Luke family, "I am pleased I am not coaching at Marlborough anymore," he surmised to himself, although he still held teaching positions with Marlborough.

Coach Thorpe was not disappointed; he with little sarcasm inquired as to the wisdom of taking on the 'brood of little misfit.' However, Thorpe had a crew of ambitious boys who thought they could run their way to a college scholarship. Kasper and his brothers had already started running long runs on the dirt roads about the countryside. He would see them everywhere it seemed. Kasper had told him he was determined to make the track team; all the time though Thorpe knew old coach 'Wiley' didn't want any of the Wise brothers out for his team.

A thin rain began to fall as the load of boys turned from the road then into a narrow deeply rutted lane, with hedges on either side. Kasper pulled into a short driveway facing the small home. Before they came to a stop, Jimmy and the red-headed Terry appeared on the porch.

"Hey dudes," greeted Jimmy Luke, "figured you guys would drop by. Been cranking out the miles, huh?" If there was such a thing as a street wise, tough fellow, troublemaker, and jock rolled into one individual; well, such a person would be Jimmy Luke.

Like Kasper and Danny, he was a junior, but a provisional one in his case. Poor grades did not allow Jimmy to participate in any extracurricular sports. This year Jimmy was completing his last two years at the county career center, where he majored in the automobile mechanic program. Jimmy wanted to drive tanks in the Army; so this 'hands on' training was motivating for a young man, who otherwise showed seriousness of no matters, and certainly none concerning academics. However, at Central Career Center, Jimmy came back after the first week wanting to quit. "Man! I still gotta take Advanced Math and English 2. That crap is hard!"

Danny was with him that day and asked him, "Why did you sign-up for such classes in the first place?"

"The Army recruiter told me if I wanted to get into tank school, those courses are recommended. He said I'd have an advantage over others applicants with courses like that on my transcript," said the humbled Jimmy.

Danny thought briefly and replied. "That makes sense now if you think about it. If you want to drive a tank, you must understand many scientific concepts that go into range finding, navigation, optics. You'll have a computer that does all that, but you can't be some bone-head who thinks all that is just magic."

"Yea, but what about English 2," Jimmy shot back, "Now, what the heck is that got to do with tank driving?"

"You've got to read manuals and stuff, Jimmy," Danny suggested. "Plus you may get changes to your manual that you didn't learn in training; so you have to be good enough reader so you can interpret and make the necessary changes in procedures. You are going to have complicated navigation procedures, changes in ordinance size maybe; and all this Jimmy will be in the metric system. Shoot man! You are going to have to read complicated stuff."

"Huh."

"They ain't going to select some guy who just barely passed courses to graduate. Every time there's a change; they'll have to send a set of cartoon cards to him," Danny was being funny now, "The cards would be numbered, with a picture of Daffy Duck throwing switches."

Both boys chuckled. "Okay, I get the point. "Ha, ha, ha…"

Coach Thorpe was Jimmy's 'Santa' as well. Jimmy had to review all his assignments with the coach. With short, but consistent after school tutoring and 'blitz' study sessions after practice, Jimmy made his best ever grade report. Thus, he remained eligible to apply his sprinting to complement the distance men on the team. Thorpe wanted this boy's swaggering confidence on this team. Jimmy would provide the catalyst to inspire the group to success. The coach at little Lakeport thought he had a wild chance of besting the predictions of his chums at Marlborough. They had said that the little school could not muster enough talent to take on the wealthy big city schools in Division 2.

"Jimmy, invite the boys in," exclaimed an elderly woman extending her arms in an attitude of entreaty.

"We'll like to just sit on the porch, if you don't mind, ma'am," Eli said, "gotta be going soon.

"Well, I'll bring out some lemon aid, ya'll go ahead, make yourself comfortable." Sophie Luke retreated into the house.

"I just wanted to find out what times you guys go out to run," Terry explained meekly, as everyone gathered on the steps and about the porch.

The afternoon proceeded with instructions, methods, and the joys of these running gatherings. It ended with Terry's assurance he was not frightened at such vigor. Instead, he disclosed a great desire to undertake a place among these fellows.

"Everyday, after class, we dress in the lockers then stretches a bit and then we take off down the road two miles to Mrs. Thorpe's place. There we complete a selection of two-hundred meter repeats on a slight graded hill. Then it's maybe a three mile run on the road paths that undulate through the property," Kasper detailed the routine.

"A lot of times though," interjected Danny, "we'll run through the corn rows. It's rough going, but it packs muscles on the legs."

"You can say that again! You have to lift your legs and rotate the arms, if you are to keep moving. It makes you tough," commented Eli.

"Yea, you don't have much choice," Danny said in a tone and demeanor that showed he did not care for that exercise.

"How many miles you guys run everyday?" asked Terry. There was a shot but potent pause.

"Ah, we might get seven or eight when went we go out to the Thorpe farm," said Kasper carefully, but most days its like about four to five miles of intervals. Now Danny and I, we complete a four mile run early in the morning; now you and Eli will be our middle distance men, so Thorpe will ask that you run just three morning runs a week with us."

Kasper had tried to present the practices as relaxed, non-stressful exercise, but to no avail. "You guys be getting it," Jimmy intervened, to clarify to true nature of what his cousin Terry was getting into. "Most people around here see you guys booking it! Rain or shine hot or cold...ya'll be motoring!" He finished in his jollying manor with irritated the ever serious Kasper, nonetheless.

CHAPTER 2

▼

A day later, a week later, a month later it was all the same to the consuming gasps of breaths with endless sweating and exhausted air lack oxygen. Their demanding lungs would consume the life giving air of an indoor stadium in the matter of a few hours. Each day bought the routine that the burden of which they had voluntarily accepted.

"Thirty-three," Thorpe yelled as Kasper, Danny and Eli slowed with Terry and Greg trailing as they finished. "Good job. Walk and shack it out, "bout ninety seconds to go." Having slowed to a walk, they turned around and faced the dirt path, their chests still heaving from the effort of the run. "Seven down, five to go…one minute."

The pack started walking toward the start point, a rock on the side of the trail. Coach Thorpe watching from fifty meters away with an arm up in the air would start his stopwatch as the lead of the pack approach the start. With a drop of the arm, he would start the timing. They required only seconds to gain speed, it would last another thirty-five seconds, the target time. The coach would stop the timing as he observed the first runner crossing another natural marker, a tree stump. It was an important stump located exactly 200 meters from the starting rock.

A hand drop, 'snap' sounded the stopwatch and off they went. "Long strides, high arm rotation, keep 'em high!" yelled Thorpe, as they swept over the dusty trail. Halfway through the run Danny, then Eli, over took Kasper in the last meters. Kasper's lack of speed showed here, however this would change as the extent of the workout lengthened. Then the strength and background endurance would prevail over the fast-twitch muscle structure of 'speed', thus Kasper looked the 'master' near the end of these workouts.

"We are doing well," summarized the coach at the end of the session as he looked at the time-log history of their time-splits over the runs. You guys have dropped one and a half to two seconds on average in the last four weeks."

"Hey, that translates to about twelve to fifteen seconds for the sixteen hundred meters," suggested a heavy breathing Kasper.

"We'll see soon enough," Thorpe replied with caution in his tone. "Wednesday…time trail. Monday and Tuesday, we just stretch and shake the kinks out and rest. We need to see where everyone is. Danny, Kasper! Do not be running any twenty miles on the weekends. We need to start pulling off the high mileage men; we got to go for speed this time of the season, fellows." This plethora of surmise and conjecture and warning about the fitness of his runners required some drips of reality. Time trials will give some answers.

"It's forecasted to be pretty nice next week," Eli said, not knowing anything else to say; while like his pals he thought that coach Thorpe was feeling some urgent need to have some performance so he could place a bet with himself.

"We need something to chew on. And the trials will enable me to plan the relay events we have before us." He explained. "I want to enter us in Division 1. I need some times to submit by next weekend."

"Wednesday," Kasper muttered, after holding his concerns from the initial revelation. "I thought we had a couple more weeks."

"I'm trying to get us in a meet in Indiana. It is a big meet. We can match-up with the big schools. If you can get some good performances, you will be more confident when we match up with the locals. You're going to surprise yourselves and take note: what ever you do at the time trial you'll do better in a meet after a good rest and the adrenaline flow you will experience in competition," Thorpe pointed out with confidence and reassurance. Released now, the boys would string out and jog back to the school along the grassy trail bordering the road. Little traffic interfered this time of day, so they enjoyed the fresh smells from the fields, the butterflies, birds chirping, and occasionally they would gather some gleeful energy to chase a rabbit that caught their attention. Passing through an apple grove and some low hanging trees was the last obstacles to the school campus, where a hot shower climaxed the training session. These natural diversions were a necessity for the relaxing they sort both mentally and physically.

An hour later the quartet of Kasper, Danny, Eli, and Greg were wrangling through a set of physics problems. As Kasper suggested methods of finding solutions, Greg and Elli listened and occasionally interjected a question, as to the reasons for such approaches to the problems. Danny seldom interrupted, however he absorbed all arguments with utmost interest and intensity. Unlike the brothers who sometimes argue vehemently, Danny did not have the confidence to question one of Kasper's suggestions, this due to his limited and poor schooling he acquired from the city.

These study sessions would start with the discussions of the examples in the section of study and then move to the end-of-the-chapter problems. Kasper and crew would complete nearly all of these problems; more impressive, they in recent weeks, between class notes and Kasper's perusing through other references, the group was able to solve the problems on their own. They sort neither Thorpe nor teachers at school for assistance.

"Everybody understand?" Kasper asked, "Power is the rate of doing work. Work is force times parallel distance pushed. The units are the *Newton-meter*, which we call the *joule*. Divide this by the time in seconds it takes to complete this work and we have power! We get joules per second and we call this a watt. The unit of power is watts.

"You sound like you really are on top of this stuff," Danny commented feeling inadequate. "And you say at Marlborough you were just getting by?"

"While you guys are always praying for your color TVs, laptops, and pretty girls, well, I've been praying for wisdom," Kasper responded with a grin. He hesitated before continuing. "This stuff comes together the more you look at it." Hesitation again then laying down his pencil; everyone figured Kasper had some off topic revelation to disclose. "I got to tell you guys something. In January, while looking at the Notre Dame brochures. I saw a posting for a physics scholarship. There is an exam for this scholarship scheduled in mid-June for high school juniors so I am going to take it then." His colleague's eyes demanded explanation. "The brochure warned that these problems are at a rigorous level of aptitude. Proficiency in upper level algebra and calculus is necessary if the applicant is to realize a reasonable likely-hood of success, which is why I have been working extra to complete as many problems as I can. But I am scared; I don't think these problems are hard enough to get me ready for an exam that has calculus problems with physics." Kasper had the full attention from his mates now.

"Yea, I've heard about that scholarship," Greg broke in. "It's been around a few years Kasper."

"They will offer full all tuition paid scholarships to fifteen to twenty students from this tri-state area. I am going to be studying for it these days," clarified Kasper. "But I've still got to take the college entrance exams in August."

"Well, I've got to take 'em as well," added Danny rolling his head, not the least bit confident.

Eli shifted his eyes at the others with annoyance. "Sounds good guys but hey, I have other class work to look at. Besides, I am not going to be some physics-math type like you guys." With that, Eli made his exit from the group.

"Yea, lets' knock it off. You guys probably got other work to do." Kasper suggested. With that they scattered in different directions gathering materials they must peruse to complete the evening assignments.

Kasper had some other assignments likewise, but he did not care. He had to stay on physics. He was soon slumped over his cluttered little desktop, a couple physics books among a disarray of loose papers with various degrees of problems scribbled on mostly crimped papers; some incomplete partly scratched-out. Nevertheless, Kasper rummaged through them and finally fixed on one sheet. Captured by a particular physics problem that he could not get in agreement with the given solution, Kasper pondered alone. He had reviewed the fundamental concepts of this matter in several texts and re-checked his methods against examples presented, but to no avail.

"Use the law of gravitation and the measured value of the acceleration of gravity to determine the average density of the earth." The problem demanded.

"Density is equal to mass per unit volume. Volume of the earth….four-thirds, pie, times the radius of the earth squared…..the law of universal gravity is the formula. $F = GmM_E/r^2$…and the measured value of g acceleration is…9.8 m/s^2…think, think…" Kasper demanded of himself, "Got to find some connections that tidy up things. Let me see, what is the force?…aha! Force on a mass on the surface of the earth is mg…ok! Then I set this expression equal to the gravitational force…hey! Then I get an expression for g." Accomplishment seemed within his grasp. "This is equal to the right side of the gravitational equation." He lost his grasp, "but how so you get an expression for density?" Kasper looked at his scribble of numbers. Suddenly he stuffed the page in a book and slammed it shut. "Enough of this tonight," said the tired boy anticipating an early before school run.

Coach Thorpe waited, his eyes fixed on the five figures gathered before the start line on the Griswold Junior high school track. Katie Cummings a petite blond and the junior class secretary at Lakeport High was the track team's statistician. Katie logged the times of all training runs on a clipboard. She was never it seemed, without her beloved clipboard. Her long straight yellow hair flowed from under the Ohio University cap that she always wore when she was keeping statistics or not inside the school for that matter.

"I am ready when you are, guys," said Thorpe impatiently. He rubbed his hands together then retrieved the starter pistol from his holster. The group spread itself out in a single line. Kasper looked toward the coach to tell him to ready the stopwatch.

"Come on guys, let's see who's tough!" Katie called after them. Katie also was the team's number sidelines fan, not always pleasing to a tiring runner in the mist of struggling efforts, she had a biting sense of humor to pelt the boys with occasionally. "Don't you guys take too long now; I got a red-headed dude taking me to the movies this afternoon; never been out with a red-headed fellow before."

Jimmy and running mate, Roy Jerome was cracking up in laughter trackside Jimmy loved Katie's one-line punches; he was not articulate enough to drop humor as Katie so it was usual that he broke up if Katie let go with a line. The boys took the jest that they should get going and moved to the start position. They had learned to take Katie's humor in 'stride'.

"Let's see about all that hard work, fellows," said Jimmy attempting to ease the fears he knew they had, while still wearing a big grin on his face.

Bang! The gun sounded. Kasper surged forward to the lead of the group. Entering the first turn Danny smoothly moved one stride behind Kasper; then Eli, Terry, and Greg trailed within four strides of each other. Thorpe's heart beating excitedly, but he had not tried to guess the outcome. He was more nervous than his runners were of this trial run and predictions would have made him tenser than present.

On the backstretch, the boys raced with long strides and flowing arm movements. As they started into the second turn two hundred meters out, the first three boys synchronized stride rotation. "Thirty-four seconds," said Katie glancing at the watch. She had all their names lined in separate rows on her clipboard. She would credit the first three with a thirty-four, thirty-five seconds for the two lagers. Accomplished at gauging times of moving runners to cover a distance, one dare not criticize Katie's logs.

Into the curve, "They look good," Thorpe thought. "This could be a state final race considering my state of mind right now." Terry and Greg were behind two strides. Kasper looked relaxed but Danny and Eli appeared to be 'set and waiting'.

The group rolled out of the turn and ran gracefully into the straightaway. They all looked comfortable on this sixty degree, but gusty afternoon. Stoically moving they approached the first four hundred meters. "63, 64…67" was the time called as they passed the white line of the start point and entered lap two.

"Relax, relax, and watch your stride. Concentrate men!" Floating smoothly their feet barely making a sound, they rolled to each stride with deliberation. Breathing was slow and each air intake sunk deep into their lungs. "Terry, Greg, run your own race!" demanded Thorpe not wanting the pair to attempt to stay up with the veterans and being crushed by the pace, and ending the run poorly.

On the backstretch again, Kasper's rotation was evidently slower. Danny and Eli complied with the signal and sucked in a bit closer, eyes fixed on the heels before them. "People you're 'bout 1:42 at six-hundred meters….Terry! Eli!…1:45!" Coach called again.

Negotiating the second turn then heading into the stretch, Danny pulled-up nearly even to Kasper; who responded by quickening and lengthening his stride, towing the pack pass the eight-hundred meters, "2:18, 2:19, 2:22…," Thorpe bellowed. Then, "2:23, 2:24," he called as Terry and Greg passed the halfway point.

As the runners bore down the backstretch for the third time, the trio was as tight as in the first lap. However, strain appeared on Eli's face trying to keep up with the strong steady gait of Kasper. "Kasper should start pushing it now," thought Thorpe observing the struggle. "He should utilize his strength to get away from the speed behind him."

"Time is compressed, watching a race," thought Thorpe. "They seem to coming around so quickly." Thorpe's heartbeat was as fast beyond normal, "3:28, 3:29, 3:30, 3:31…!" called Katie as he watched the procession past. They hugged the long turn; but Danny moved pass Eli and pulled up to Kasper's side as the turn ended and the stretch began. Stubborn Eli clamped onto Danny not allowing him to pull away. Terry and Greg were still together thirty meters in arrears.

"Get back up there Terry, Alex," commanded Jimmy walking along the bordering rail of the track. Roy followed, silent with curiosity not having seen the boys train as much as Jimmy.

"There he goes," Thorpe exclaimed as Danny's arms went into a higher reach, his legs lifted and he was pass Kasper; but then Eli followed Danny and passed Kasper. "Let's lay it down, guys! You can beat 4:40!" yelled Thorpe. Danny leaned into the turn. Eli with more strain and effort attempted to maintain his position. As they straightened out of the last turn, Kasper went wide. Moving now in the second lane, Kasper followed Eli as Danny led. Eli tiring was now losing a foot every stride to Danny. Capitalizing on his brother's demise, Kasper pumping furiously pulled up to Eli's shoulder and with legs lifting higher, he pulled away and set his sights on Danny.

"All the way in now, rotate, rotate…" Jimmy called after them.

Danny started searching for the finish. Head leaning back too far, he just allowed himself to float across the finish, exhausted just holding off a forward leaning Kasper. Terry fought-off Greg to finish two strides up on him forty meters behind Danny. The two novices surrendered a lot of ground to the trio over the last four hundred meters.

"Way to crank guys," exclaimed Jimmy surprised, "you guys were tight."

"4:33, 4:34, 4:37, 4:47, and 4:50," Thorpe read off their times as they passed the finish line. "Great job guys! Way to go! We're going to make a point in this sport around central Ohio." He was nearly swaggering as he walked with his exhausted pack while they picked up their gear lying on the ground inside the track oval.

"Yea guys," exclaimed Katie finished logging in the times on her pad, "you did good. Coach, pay up now; I told you they would run a humdinger, didn't I?"

Thorpe grinned, as he seldom coming out of his serious cocoon had any appropriate response to Katie's jollying. However, Eli having recovered from the run had a pitch for her. "Pay her Coach, after all those red-headed dudes won't have two nickels to rub together. You know she's going to have to pay her way, and she may have to put gas in the dude's car."

Everybody bent over in laughter with that; especially Jimmy.

"Okay, that was pretty good," countered Katie, "you got me on that one but you know I'll be looking for an opening on you; keep your guard up."

"That's right Katie," laughed Jimmy and Roy echoing, "sat 'em up; you always going to get the last word, girl I believe that," issued Jimmy continuing his laughing.

Danny and Kasper were of a serious mood and were pleased with the run. Danny was not sure he had the endurance to hang with Kasper to the final meters where he could use his superior speed. Kasper was surprised. He did not think Danny and Eli had the staying power to stick with him inside the final lap. Eli thought he did well. Terry and Greg did not know what to feel. They had little idea as whether their performances were any good or not, since they had no history of races to compare with.

They group milled around in various states, walking in circles, sitting on the grass and just standing to get their breaths back. Katie disclosed the 'splits' of the run at 200 and 400 meter points. "The school record was shattered, you know. It was four-minutes and thirty-nine-point-two," she revealed.

"But the record has to be broken at an official track meet," said Kasper in the back seat.

"I'd say by the end of the season," Katie continued, "one of you guys should have it down in the low twenties. You think so coach?"

"If we can stay healthy, I don't see any reason why we can't get times down there," Thorpe said. Then with caution he added, "We don't want to peak-out now. We'll go for speed in the last few weeks and back-off on the mileage."

After cooling down, Danny and Katie climbed aboard Thorpe's old van. Jimmy was driving his rickety pick-up with Roy, Elli, Terry, and Greg as his passengers. In this carriage, the atmosphere was jovial. "Shoot dudes, with me turning over a sub-fifty for my leg, we should clean up in the relays....Now we're all going to get faster when it gets hot and we be on some fast turf."

"Yea, but coach is going to enter us in these Division 1 events," Greg cautioned.

"No sweat dudes. We got three under 4:40," Jimmy explained, "This time in the season, believe me we'll dominate!"

𝕏𝕛 𝕝𝕔 𝕕𝕙 𝕖 𝕙𝕛 𝕚 𝕝𝕨 𝕜𝕙 𝕏𝕒𝕒 𝕏𝕪 𝕙𝕙𝕒𝕪𝕙 𝕝𝕒

Kasper pushed the time trial behind him in his thoughts. Not pleased, he thought of the other hurdle he had to take grips of his studies. He had a couple ideas about the physics problem he left dangling the other night. He had gone on to other exercises and assignments.

Hours later, having received the compliments of his efforts from Dad and Mom Kasper lounged upon the sofa. He had a glass of cool-aid within his reach upon the right and a pile of crumpled papers, evidently newly studied, near at hand. Beside the couch was a little wooden stool. It was stacked with several books opened to some page, suspended in this manner for the purpose of reference and examination.

"You are engaged with physics again," said Greg. "Eli went over to the Luke's," he informed. "Would I be interrupting you...I would like to see how you tackle some of these problems, Kasper."

"Sure. Actually, it is very helpful to have someone to discuss with and explain the answers. I've been stuck on this one problem, but I have it now," Kasper said. He had a problem concerning finding the density of the earth and he described his difficulties to Greg.

"The key to the solution was surprisingly trivial but subtle." Kasper was almost excited to disclose his success. He explained, "Let me show you, brother. The key points that made the correct connections are of instructive interests."

Greg seated himself on the floor next to the couch. "I probably won't understand anything, but given I have a sense of humor go ahead give it a shot," Greg smiled, "I need to learn the clues and methods. When I get stuck, I'm stuck and can't seem to know any other approach to a problem, you know."

"Just experience, just experience, in doing a lot of problems; there's no short cut." Kasper assured his brother. "Now in this problem, you know the force is equal to mass time the gravity, Newton's second law. Set this equal to the Universal Gravitational Law…the mass of the objects cancels…we have…

$$g = GM_E/R_E^2$$

"Solve this relation for the mass of the earth, M_E, we get

$$M_E = g\, R_E^2/G$$

"Substituting for the constants g and G, and using the average radius of earth, R_E, then we get

"Where do you find those constants?" asked Greg.

"In the index or cover of any physics book," answered Kasper. He showed his brother this with the text he was using. Then he wrote

$$M_E = (9.8 m/s^2)\, (6.37 \times 10^6 \text{ m})\,^2/6.67 \times 10^{-11} \text{ N m}^2/Kg^2$$

$$M_E = 6.0 \times 10^{24} \text{ Kg}$$

"We use the volume of a sphere to calculate the volume of the earth, V_E, so

$$V_E = 4/3\, \pi\, R_E^3$$

$$= 4.19\, (6.37 \times 106m)\, 3$$

$$= 1.08 \times 1021 \text{ m3}$$

"Now, here's the key: density equals mass divided by volume

$$\rho = M_E/V_E$$

"Substitute our mass and volume into this and thus we have density equals

$$\rho = 5.5 \times 10^3 \text{ kg/m}^3$$

"This is the average density of the earth." Kasper looked at his brother with pride.

"How 'bout that," responded Greg. Kasper could detect his feeling of inadequacy.

"Hey, I've completed several other problems in that section; they are easier now that I understand the math tools and techniques in finding the solutions. Hey! Let's call it off for the evening," suggested a very pleased Kasper; with that, the two boys retired for the evening.

"Faith is the essence of things wished for, the evidence of which is not seen," exclaimed Pastor Morse, quoting from the bible at church service that morning. Kasper reflected on the quote as he and Danny ran silently along the narrow country road leading from the church. This was a backwoods way to home six miles away. The rest of the family went home in the more conventional manner by car. The two skipped over dead animals, avoided a snake, waved off bees buzzing about their heads; enjoying the breeze and occasional cloud cover that bought relief from the hot sun beaming on sweaty bodies. Diverting from the road, they took a path that cut through a grassy field. Here they treaded slowly careful not to roll their ankles and being injured.

Kasper did not press Greg to run with him and Eli was not interested. "I'm a middle distance runner; I don't need runs that long. It will hurt my speed," Eli explained adamantly.

"Got to have faith, Danny," Kasper continued an earlier conversation as they trekked down a slight hill. "You beat me the other day and you catch on quickly in school. Just keep working hard, the grades will come. You will make a college. We are just juniors. There is time to improve in everything."

"Yea, but," Danny responded, "people like me just don't go to college. Everybody in town…well all the dudes they laugh at these goals. They say I'm nuts I'm in dream world."

"Forget them. Losers always expect the 'hommies' to suffer their fate as well. Hey, what is this 'people like me' nonsense?" Kasper displayed an angry tone. "They're dummies, Danny. They are not going anywhere and they do not intend to try! Working at something is a waste of energy for those dudes."

The pace picked up as their muscles relaxed and the blood began to flow easily as the blood vessels widened. Breathing was even and relaxed while long and effortless strides carried the pair along tall weeds. Wiping sweat from their faces, the cousins talk continued.

"Yea Danny," Kasper had to close his thoughts of their discussion. "When you go in town to visit grand; stay away from those dudes."

"Haaa, haaa, haaa," was the sound of sucking deep breaths and exhaling; between the intakes caused by the expanding chests increasingly demanding larger gasps of air. While their circulatory system wagged war with the blood rushing through it, attempting to rid the invasion of lactic acid from the muscles. This made control signals from the brain more and more difficult to decipher. 'Move the legs…move the arms faster you say….lift the legs…oh no! We don't have enough oxygen to work any faster…need more oxygen…' Poor nervous system, it reaches a point where it just cannot respond to the brain because the owner of this body is demanding too much oxygen. With these physical issues held in abeyance, the boys slowed to a conversational gate.

"On the contrary, Danny, you can make big schools in track. Get down in the four- twenties by end of season. Next year who knows how fast you can get. My goal is four-twenty-three myself, and I don't have your natural ability."

"You're not the least timid in drawing your inferences, are you?" Danny said using words Kasper would use in his mostly formal way of talking.

"If we don't believe in ourselves is there anyone in this county who will give us credit for anything but mediocrity?" suggested Kasper.

The pair had to negotiate a small gully, climb a short hill, and stride downhill for about a quarter-mile until they intercepted a deer path. Following the path through light brush, they ran for a mile in tandem until reaching another dirt road.

Running, shoulder to shoulder, the duo chugged along interested in completing the run in a strong manner. This would be the last long run before they left for the relays in Indiana on Friday.

"Haaaa, haaa," their breathing sounded. Chests heaved with increasing regularity again. Eyes fixed on the horizon as fatigue grew. They had to increase concentration on their efforts directed to reach an abode where a sanctuary of rest for the remainder of this Sabbath day.

It was about ten minutes before the two regained view of a little cluster of trees hiding a row of small homes tucked in amongst them. A narrow road curved around the cluster. On the eastern side of this road were bushes and shrubs. Farther over was the lake. The Lakeport community, with all its natural beauty, lay mostly hidden around the big Crimsheads Lake amongst these small clumps of trees and scrubs. The boys gradually closed then melted into the first woods. There they slowed to a walk choosing not to race over the final meters.

"Good run, Danny," said Kasper.

"We were cranking pretty well," Danny replied.

They continued to a lawn table in the yard at the house where they proceeded to stretch Untangling and relaxing the taunt muscles they had so relentlessly punished to this weary finale.

"That was good, our last long run," Kasper spoke.

"Yep, go to speed the remainder of the week," echoed Danny.

"Yea, we should do four to five miles of interval work all the time from here out."

With a feeling of completeness, some form of hope was returning to Danny's continence. The pair walked around the small yard. No one appeared at home. They went inside. As the two showered and dried-off, a sudden seizure of merriment enveloped the pair.

"There are really some opportunities for the team, Danny," said Kasper. "I think we can beat most anybody," he said with a little smile.

"Yes, we may not be as fast individually but we've got balance. Yea, and Jimmy can run a sub-fifty four-hundred meters, no doubt. We should clean-up."

"So it seems."

"What about that physics test and those college entrance exams," Danny said breaking the glee.

"Yea, yea, I'll be getting at them this evening," responded Kasper. After pausing in thought for a minute, he said, "I must...well we must be successful in the exams or the running won't reap our goals."

"It seems like we've just taken a load upon ourselves," Danny replied seriously.

Kasper knew his cousin too well to disregard his words. He turned to him with caring, searching for the right words.

"What do you mean Danny?"

"Only, that there is so much to be done physically and mentally. We seem to jump from one frying pan to another. We've taken a tiger by the tail."

"Can we do anything else?"

"No, I guess not. Except just give up and take the easy no stress route...just hangout, like the dudes in town."

"So we just got to do it...do both the running and the books."

"We must believe in ourselves, Danny," pleaded Kasper. "If we don't then we won't put out the effort to accomplish anything worthwhile."

"I will do my best alright," Danny mused, "Sometimes I just wonder will it get me anywhere. That is, will anybody think my efforts are worth anything?"

"What do you mean? Danny this is your home, we are family. Everybody is supportive in our family no matter what we accomplish or not," Kasper said somewhat upset, "Your dad is so proud of what you've accomplished in school and track this year at Lakeport. Heck, I didn't really get my head together until this year, either."

"Perhaps, but I sure want to feel like I'm living up to someone's aspirations."

"Well, like Dad says," Kasper interrupted, "he just wants us to do for ourselves. He's there to get us the support, but we got to do the cranking."

"Okay, then let's get some grub," Danny said, breaking the subject. "And then, I need to look at some algebra. You think you have a few minutes, I'm stuck on a couple problems."

"No sweat," Kasper assured him.

After a snack, Kasper and Danny stashed themselves at a table. "How do you approach a problem like this one," Danny asked turning his notebook to a page scribbled math annotations. "This is a logarithm problem: 'Six to the power of x, equals one-hundred and fifty-two'. The base is six, how can you find x?" Danny looked at Kasper with desperation.

Kasper looked over the chapter and some examples. After about five minutes of mumbling and reflecting, short suggestions and reflections, he suggested a plan of attack.

"First, we should make a good guess as to our answer. Six squared is 36. Six to the third power is 216. So for some power of six to equal 152; our power has to be close to three, around 2.7 or 2.8," Kasper looked at Danny, "makes sense?"

"Agreed."

"Now for the details," Kasper began, "First, what is a logarithm? A logarithm is the power to which 10 must be raised to give a ratio like, $5/3 = 1.67$, for example. See here," Kasper, wrote: $10^x = 1.67$. "What is the power x?" Kasper proceeded to answer his own question. "We can find this by looking it up in a book of log tables or using a calculator. So $\log 1.67 = 0.22$, that is $x = 0.22$. We have to use this property. I can see this will do it for us."

"If you say so," Danny responded, still lost as to how Kasper's suggestions would find his solution.

"See here. Set 6 equal to the base ten to the power of k.

$6 = 10^k$ taking the log of both sides of the equation gives

$\log 6 = k$,   From the definition of logarithms, $\log 10^x = x$. So Danny, k is the power of 10 that gives you 6."

"Okay, I see," responded Danny.

Kasper continued with the problem: "Our problem says:

$6^x = 152$. Substituting for 6, we get

$(10^k)^x = 152$

Danny's eyes brightened, "Ah, I think I can finish it from there," he said. "Now take the log of both sides of the equation, yields

$\log 10^{kx} = \log 152$

"Utilizing the power-of-ten property to the left side, we arrive at

$kx = \log 152$

$x = \log 152/k = \log 152/\log 6$

$x = 2.80$

"Two-point-eighty," Danny beamed, "that's the answer, and our guess was real close. Thanks pal."

"I'm glad to help. However, this was a tough problem. Let's look at a few more problems at the end of the chapter," Kasper suggested. At that, the two buried themselves into the task once more submitting themselves totally to the challenge before them.

Lying on his back in his bed a few hours later, Kasper reminisced of the day's events, particularly the sermon at church. "Now, faith is the substance of things hoped for, the evidence of things not seen." Then he fell asleep, resting peacefully assured with himself.

𝖷 𝖷𝖷 𝖷𝖷𝖷 𝖷𝖷𝖷𝖷 𝖷𝖷𝖷𝖷𝖷 𝖷𝖷𝖷𝖷𝖷𝖷

Two days later the Lakeport track team assembled on the rickety wood bleachers of the football field that encircled a cinder, rock, and gravel six-lane running track.

"In the field events we'll enter the shot-put relay; George, Chuck, and Tony will participate," said Thorpe. "We can't field anything else. Coach Webster will field a high-jump trio. They should do pretty well."

He spoke of Caroline Webster, coach of the even smaller girl's team. "Now, we'll enter the four by sixteen hundred, the four by eight-hundred, and the distance medley. In the individual events; Jimmy will run the four hundred meters, and Kasper the thirty-two hundred meters."

"No sixteen-hundred meter relay?" Jimmy asked.

"No, because you guys would have had to run two races Friday just to qualify. But guys, there are teams from the big cities that'll go under 3:30 and won't make the finals."

"Shoot!" Interrupted Jimmy again, "We can be down there!"

"Listen Jimmy, the first three will be under 3:23." Thorpe submitted.

"Now, guys, another thing has come up. Sheila will be training with you most of the time now. She is quite a talent but has no one to run with. So she's going to be jumping in behind you guys particularly when we're running two-hundred meter repeats."

"Sounds good," exclaimed Jimmy with a smile, "she's cute. Now don't you guys be losing your concentration in the workouts?"

"Yea, she can run as fast as the Division 1 girls after training with us," Kasper added. "She'll be tough. We'll get her to run twenty two-hundreds…"

"Twenty!" Jimmy exclaimed with the others, interrupting, "Kasper, you trying to run her away?"

"I meant, at the last couple weeks of the season, she may be able to do twenty," Kasper tried to clarify.

"Handle her like yourselves, very carefully," Thorpe said, "Listen to your body, don't get injured and build slowly, okay?"

With the last discussions, the group dispersed. Jimmy and Danny were grinning, while Terry and Greg wondered-off with amazement, expectation, and decision chasing each other across their features. Thorpe stood watching as everyone left with an air of a conjecturer who had just performed a trick.

CHAPTER 3

▼

The athletic grounds of the Prince Edwards School lay in the valley surrounded by small hills that bordered three sides of the grounds. The fourth side was the entry to the stadium where a parking lot, now filled with a few dozen yellow school buses displaying an assortment of names on their sides exemplifying the many schools present at this event. They represented their school districts from all parts of Indiana and some from Ohio, Michigan, Illinois, and even Arkansas. The running track was eight-lanes with a red all-weather surface. Dozens of little colored figures scurried about, circling its grounds. Warming-up before their respective events, participants enjoyed displaying pride and team spirit by advertising the colors of the home schools while jogging around the track.

Girls in colorful uniforms with bouncing ponytails were swaying their lithe figures as they jogged, revealed a carnival nature of these events. Joggers were displaying their pride by waving to family members in the stands and sidelines. Giggling issued constantly from the small packs assembled within the grounds. This was the common scene at these track and field engagements. It was enough to get the adrenaline flow from spectators even before the realization of the races and field events waiting to perform. Participants had a contingent of aspirations ranging from 'just participation' to 'a college scholarship offering'.

It is in this setting, this time, and in this space, that the Lakeport boys and girls track team arrived with their own baggage of desires. Seldom had Lakeport ever made an expense of sending a track team so far away.

"Come along!" Cried Thorpe abruptly as the team filled inside the big oval ground. Except for Jimmy, none of the team had ever been to a meet of this scale. Most surprising for the team were the hundreds of spectators present; back home except some family members, few spectators attended track meets. The swiveling heads slowed their progression into the stadium.

"The art of track and field is serious business," Greg assessed as he moved up the stadium stairs.

"No doubt they know what they're doing on the track and field, too," commented Terry ominously gathering agreement from his teammates.

"One-hour forty minutes until the four mile relay," Thorpe reminded his entourage, "get yourself situated, then get warmed-up. I'll going to the check-in tent."

"And I'm going to try and find some place in the bleachers where I can see the finish line," announced Katie, concerned about recording the times of all the team. She could see that the early arrivals had already claimed the choice seats overlooking the finish area. However, away Katie went while the remainders of the team sort space on the opposite set of bleachers where many teams stashed themselves and few spectators abounded.

There was little time for adoration, little time for anticipation, little time for reconciliation about their soon coming event, and no time for procrastination. Anxiety, nervousness, and just plain fear played havoc on the brain's time mechanics until finally the relief when the pistol fired awakening the sight.

"Bang!" Quickly the field of sixteen runners bolted with batons in hand, around the first curve of the track in their staggered lanes. As the mob of runners entered the backstretch, they clustered together, a few figures pulled slightly ahead of pack. As they arrived on the straight completing the first lap, the figure of Danny emerged working to the outside of a lead group spread into the second lane.

"Move to the outside," Jimmy yelled. "Don't get trapped inside, dude."

"66!" Katie disclosed Danny's time as he entered lap two, "Fifth-place."

"He looks smooth," Thorpe observed.

Down the backstretch, Danny moved to fourth. The mob of runners was falling in tandem with no real gaps having developed. Little change occurred through the third lap. Coming toward the fourth lap Danny moved suddenly to third, then second. Only Katie and Thorpe were in the stands to see Danny accelerate, overhaul two runners and then pass his baton to Greg giving him a two-meter lead over the next team.

"4:30, on the button," Katie exclaimed, excited.

"Looked easy, I told him to run about ninety percent," added Thorpe.

One runner quickly overtook Greg, who wisely tucked in behind the kid. The roused spectators issued steady screams of names: "Come on Tommy!"... "Stay in there Bobby..."... "Come on move-up Chuck!"... "Stick with that guy Randy!"... "Haul 'em in now!" Then there was the chanting and high pitch screaming from girls on the perimeter of the track and bleachers. The cadence never ceased while the runners ran. Sound emanated with the pitch and tone of the immature. The young, unlike older college football, basketball, or baseball crowds applied howls that were softer, and demanded an attention as only a parent would to the alarm of their child cry in anguish.

"He's running his heart out," Thorpe said with trepidation watching the freshman pull up to the heels of struggling blue-green clad boy as they leaned into the turn 200 meters to the finish line.

"Go Greg!" Katie yelled watching him run wide passing the leader. "4:43...." She said as Greg crossed the finish of his four-lap leg and handed off to the third leg Eli, two meters ahead of the field. "He's only a freshman," Katie pointed out to befriended spectators seated next to and around her.

Eli chugged his first lap collecting distance between him and fifteen chasers, strung-out single file on the backstretch it was poetry in motion watching the boy move away from the trailing field of teams. The space grew to forty meters over the second team by the time he ended his effort. "4:33," Thorpe read his watch. "Now, Kasper should just float his run." Thorpe watched Kasper take off with his enormous lead while Katie's watch clicked for the timing.

"Our little school is tearing them up!" Katie exclaimed. Then just as quickly, she recoiled in embarrassment. She did not mean to demean the other participants. Head down a bit; without turning the head, her eyes checked her audience for any adverse gazing upon her person. Thorpe stared straight ahead pretending he heard no such outburst.

Meanwhile, Kasper was making the most of his lead. Following runners did not make a run at him. Some thought he would slow for them, being that the third runner on most teams is the slowest. Kasper cruised through the eight-hundred-meter in two-minutes fifteen seconds. Pursuers fell farther behind the wavy haired boy. Danny, yelling from the inside of the track, checked him. "Pull off the horses, just float it in now!" Kasper relaxed his second 800 meters and crossed the finish with a 4:31 in his effort. The following runner behind him received much applause for he had closed to within twenty meters of Kasper in his dash to finish.

"18:15.45," Katie recorded. Thorpe glanced at Katie and the fans about him. Receiving accolades, he nearly melted with pride. In a business tone, Thorpe spoke to Katie, while glaring through his binoculars at the field events inside the track, near the football goal post on his left. He could see the girl's high jump was underway. He could see the placard showing that the crossbar was at four-feet ten inches.

"Lacy and Nadine have cleared," Katie said. "Just, need to get Janet over the height," then she paused. "I think there are about five teams over already. These big schools they produce.

"The boys shot-put is about to start."

"When's our next event?"

"Sheila is entered in the girls open sixteen-hundred meters. It will be starting at 1:40 pm. Golly coach, looking at the roster of entries, there are two girls near five-ten and three under five-twenty!" Said Katie concerned.

"Sheila should PR today," Thorpe said. "The field will pull her under her best of 5:41."

"I'll go get some popcorn at the concessions," Katie announced as she stood up and proceeded to make her way through the crow packed in the bleachers.

Thorpe relaxed and took relish in his boys' recent victory. He could hardly believe his four milers had averaged about 4:34 each. "We'll be making a point back home," he thought. Again, he found himself reminiscing about the months earlier when he had engaged in a nasty encounter with an assistant coach at Marlborough, "That arrogant little Kasper Wise, implied favoritism on our part. We are glad he is gone from around here. The little handicap thinks we didn't give him a fair shot…the guy has no ability…thinks we owe him something because he's a minority!…head coach says that is what happens when you get too many of 'em on the squad…"

Thorpe sat back relishing his position. "It appears we have an opportunity here," he finished his thought. Then he observed Sheila walking with twenty-three other girls down the center of the track, led by officials to the start lines. Broken-up into four lines of six and assembled in staggered lanes, they readied for the start. Four staggered lanes held six runners Clad amongst the brown, blond, red-haired composite of young tykes ranging from tiny eighty-five pound pixies to tall thin girls with rangy legs. Sheila blended into the list as average in size and stature. Brunette, with a high bowed ponytail she was a sophomore who had never experienced such an accolade of runners.

"How is Sheila? Thorpe asked Katie, as he had not really talked to her that morning.

"Ready as Mary Queen of Scots for her beheading," quipped Katie, but she received no smile from Thorpe and continued in a serious note, "She has been talking about what she will run in a few weeks. She knows training with the guys will drop what ever time she runs in this meet."

"Indeed. That is very refreshing to know that she is confident of her training," Thorpe said feeling an urgency to see what she will run in this race. After which, he felt he could gage what Sheila is capable of running by season's end.

"Runners take your marks!" warned the starter. The arrays of competitors leaned forward, some off balance about to fall, nervously waiting for what seemed like minutes; the gun blasted sending the groups of girls speeding into the long left turn. There was jostling on the backstretch; a stumble, then another stumble near the front of the pack, fortunately no one falls. A diminutive pink clad girl with a page cut hairdo moved away from the pack.

"Must be a freshman," Thorpe observed, speaking to Katie at his side again. "They're fearless."

"75," Katie read staring at her stopwatch while logging the time on her pad.

The first lap pace strung-out the field of girls into a lead pack of six with the trailing runners running single file. Sheila was in the middle of the lead pack, appearing to be flowing with the group as a floating log moving down a river. The pack of girls were bouncing and bumping as well, until the field further thinned on approaching the end of the second lap. A girl with a red-spiked hairdo replaced the little pink dress girl. "2:34! Halfway…come on Sheila!" She crossed 800 meters in fifth. "2:41 Go! Sheila! Go!"

The two lead runners continued pulling away from everyone. Sheila appeared to lash onto a blue-green attired runner in third place. Behind her, a yellow and black outfitted runner completed the sandwich. Continuing through the penulti-mate lap, sudden acceleration from the red-spiked girl allowed her to pull away from the pink girl. Far back, Sheila appeared comfortable; however, the yel-low-black attired little girl scooted by her. Into the final stretch, three girls with fanning arms and legs were within a couple seconds of each other. Following a significant gap of distance, another two approached and finished then finally, Sheila. Tiring arms and legs flaring outwards in desperation, she was loosing con-trol with every stride now. Too tired to lean forward her chin rose higher as she leaned back and slowed almost walking across the finish, absolutely exhausted finishing in sixth place.

"5:28!" Katie exclaimed, not disappointed. Then she scrambled down the bleachers. She wanted to both congratulate and console Sheila who was already covering her face with tears.

Katie managed to hustle through the crowds gathered at the fence restraining them from the track. She caught up with Sheila at the end of the track near the one-hundred meter start area. There the officials gathered the runners before each event.

"Way to go, Sheila," Katie quipped, grabbing her and hugging her tightly from behind.

Then it hit, the tears, the boo-hoos. "Aaaa…I was so bad…" The tears flooded freely down Sheila's face like rain off a glass pane. "I couldn't hold onto those girls…" More floods of tears, running nose, and sniffing. Katie led her toward a clear spot on the grass area of the infield. There she added more consolations, emphasized the new school record and enlightened her as to the future.

"Your time's going to take a dive over the next weeks, Sheila," Katie consoled her. "You're going to train with the guys a lot from now on instead of by yourself. Consider this a dry run for the future, girl."

"Oh, I'll never run like these girls." Sheila rebutted. "What was the winners' time? Like five-twelve something? The first three…they're unreal…aaa…" Off she went again bellowing, tears flowing, nose running.

Such was a common seen with the young lass like Sheila. Throughout the day's events, such scenes duplicated themselves. It is a mistake to construe the girl's display of emotion as a criticism or as an adverse personal trait on the part of these young lasses; but merely a release of tension and pressure that boys would manifest in a less docile manner and a more anti-social manner. Neither are these observations an indication of some inferior motivation on the part of the female athlete. Quite the contrary, the girls' events had all the intensity of the boys' events, however with visible sentiment.

The display by the females showed the lack of animosity toward their competition. Girls, more so than the boys blamed themselves rather than others in competition, boys like to say, "Oh, I wasn't ready…They sneaked up on me…He cut me off…See how old that guy looks…If my feet wasn't hurting….." Now the girls would say… "I didn't try hard enough…I could have run faster…I shouldn't have stayed up late last night…I not really good at all…"

"Stop it Sheila," Katie insisted, interrupting the sobs. "I compliment you in your effort. This was an extraordinary field of runners. You held your own, but like I said your day has not arrived yet." The warmth of Katie's praise drove the despair gradually from the girl's mood.

"Oh, maybe I was expecting too much from myself," Sheila surmised. "You're right in what you said and it is really best for me to focus on the future. I hope training with the guys will help." With that, the girls packed up and sorted their way through the fence crowds heading to the stands.

Inside the oval in the midst of many clans of girls scattered about the infield, Lakeport girls sat stretching their legs. Waiting in anticipation of their turn these were the springbucks of track and field the high jumpers. Allowing no distraction from their own stretching, they fixed their eyes mostly upon the bouncing and shaking legs of the one figure about to spring into action. The girl was waiting for the officials to replace the crossbar upon the standards pegged at four-feet eleven inches. Concurrently, a blue-yellow clad girl, who knocked the crossbar down on her attempt was climbing off the jump pads and heading to her rest area. Her dejected mood revealed what must have been a last of the three attempts to clear the crossbar.

Not too soon after the bar replaced on the standards, Janet, the third of the Lakeport jumpers eyed the bar, bounced a few times on her toes, then stopped. Like a stature, not a muscle moved.

"Bang!" The start gun blasted for the benefit of a new race undertaking on the track. However, there was no effect on Janet's concentration. Of her own accord, she suddenly sprang forward. Long strides, eyes focused on the bar unwaveringly as she propelled herself toward the center of the space between the two standards supporting the crossbar. Swiftly...the last plant of her feet struck the hardest. The left arm reaching up from her side, guiding her body as the feet left the ground...the arc of her back increasing as her behind rose higher and higher...arm over...shoulder over...then the legs snapped up...her rear following....clearing the bar comfortably. She almost fell to the mat face first.

"Nice job," Nadine called out loudly as Lacy joined up with her making their way back to their rest spot. "That should cinch fifth place. If we were in a small school meet we would have won this thing," Nadine projected.

"Let's go find where everybody is," said Lacy; and the girls proceeded to gather their things to leave the infield. "We'll listen for the results...it'll be a while."

The four by 800 meters relay was nearing its start time. The officials were already leading the sixteen lead runners toward the start area. "Good luck guys," greeted Katie. The high jumpers, conjugated along the bordering fence of the track to watch the race. Katie rushed through the crowd to find a seat where she prepared her clipboard and readied her stopwatch, glowingly excited.

On the infield, the pole vault event was reaching its climax, anticipating an attempt at a record height. The bar was set while the relay race was about to start. As everyone's attention was on the starter, a low moan from the crowd suggested a pole-vaulter failed to clear a height. Without warning the blast of the starter gun followed by the rush around the first turn, sent runners down the backstretch into the second turn and into the stretch toward the first completed circuit. Only then did the image of Danny emerge. Spread out into the third lane, a pack of five floated into the second lap. Danny was in the second lane in fifth place, although only one-second behind the leaders pace. "57, 58…" a timer called out to the passing runners.

"Stay out-side, Danny," Thorpe warned from the fenced first turn. Armed with batons, the swift pack rounded through the turn. Feet were flying, arms pumping up and down, short people, tall lanky fellows some with long strides, some with quick relatively short strides. Longhaired fellows, short spiked colored hair donned a couple competitors. Others consisted of a skinhead kid, a black fellow with cornrows, and not to be out-done, a blond fellow with cornrows. All were feverishly striving for position.

The backstretch witnessed a flurry of these position changes. A few stumbles, then a quick movement to the outside by someone. Outside Danny's right shoulder, a skinhead, accelerated into the lead, coming into this group's final meters before another exchange of batons. Danny moved to lane three so he would have a clear run for the exchange with Terry. Run he did, pulling up to third place as he passed off to Terry.

"2:00!" Thorpe shouted, along with hundreds of other fans in the galley. The coach was ecstatic as Terry snatched the baton from Danny's outstretched arm and sprinted to tuck in right behind the two leaders. Hauling themselves around the turn with an intensity of speed and effort disregarding it seemed the nearly eight hundred meters of ground to be covered ahead. Closely pursued by three teams while another pack of three was in close pursuit, Terry went flat out once he snatched the baton from Danny. Already, the remainder of the field lost contact with the three lead teams.

Terry tucked in behind the two runners in front, who un-agreeably were pushing masses of air to the side relieving Terry of his effort a bit. With naturally good speed, Terry moved with confidence gave away no ground to the pair leading. "These guys are not quicker than me." Then he second-guessed his staying power. "The crucial point would be the last 200 meters," Terry predicted as he crossed into his last 400 meters and curved into the turn.

"Get 'em on the backstretch, Terry!" He heard from someone amongst the constant onslaught of shouting commands from the outside the fence. "Sounded like Jimmy," Terry thought on. "Shoot! I am hanging on for dear life to these dudes and he wants me passing 'em?"

Terry leaned toward the inside of the turn as they sped forward. His crippled left arm could not help him with the rotation so his right arm tended to rotate higher particularly on the left curving turns. His head compensated as well by leaning to the inside. Out of the turn, into the stretch, rounding into this his final turn Terry allowed himself to float into the second lane feeling the slowing pace of his lead. Moving wide he committed his last store of energy. Legs and his one arm went into over-drive, reaching higher and turning over more rapidly and passed the runner ahead pulling over to the inside lane he set his sights on the leader.

Under the deluge of screaming and shout commands from spectators and teammates Terry's momentum carried him pass the leader. The skinhead's wobbly legs and flaring arms were unable to support the commands from the brain anymore.

Five meters, seven meters, eight meters, Terry's lead increased steadily until he leaned toward Kasper's outstretched arm. With the snatch complete, Kasper set off in the lead with all the turn over rate his legs could muster. The second and third runner behind quickly latched onto his heels. Tense and uncomfortable with such a fast clip as the 800 demanded, Kasper coaxed himself on. "Turn over, turn over…got to be quicker than the mile rate…keep turning." He tried to emulate the 200-meter repeats in training. "This feels like about a 30 second 200 meter pace…"

The first 400 meters disappeared under his feet. Both sides of the track seemed to close around Kasper. The unceasing commotion demanded pace, forcing these subjects of its attention to run senselessly. Pacing plans, prior expectations now relinquished in subjection of this gripping spirit. "300 to go," he thought without caring the least of the impeding efforts about to take place behind. Kasper had no reserves to withhold for his finale. His turn over was maxed-out. "If someone wants me, I'm for the plucking!" Unbeknown to him, however, the trailing runners slipped farther and farther behind. He negotiated his final turn and as the curve straightened Kasper's legs lifted higher while attempting to rotate faster.

"Do it, Kasper, do it!" exclaimed Thorpe from the stands watching Kasper's last strides and his hand-off to Elli. "Way to go Kasper. 2:02!" Beside and behind Thorpe the supportive glee from the girls of Lakeport echoed in resonance.

"Terry ran 2:03!" Katie revealed excitedly.

"Eli should be hitting about 1:58." Thorpe added glancing at his stopwatch. The digits flickering increasing in a maddening rate it seemed to him.

Accelerating, Eli's pursuers where attempting to reach their relief some thirty meters in arrears. "Storm it dude," a voice echoed amongst the many others. Eli was moving faster than the previous legs. "Pop it, babe! Pop it!" said another. He was rounding his second curve, lifting, rotating arms and legs synchronously. "They ain't doing nothing! They ain't doing nothing!" said other voices. The screaming crowd increased steadily as the group Eli towed closed the space that separated them from him. A bandy legged, black socked, corn rowed runner pulled within five meters of Eli's heels.

"Here come the thoroughbreds." Thorpe thought. "Now we're going to see what Division 1 tastes like."

"Bang!" Last lap barked the gun. Racing across the curve Eli straightens his posture and tried to relax without dropping pace.

"Float now, and then accelerate all the way in from the top of the curve." Eli planned. With that thought, he was suddenly surprised as a figure strode in his right periphery. A figure with legs and arms rotating higher than his own effort passed Eli and pulled over to the curb lane. "Crap!" Eli thought, leaning into his stride attempting to latch on. Nonetheless, another figure caught his periphery taking to his outside again. Eli's run to victory now turned into a 'desperation effort' to survive.

"Hang with 'em, Eli!" demanded a voice his way. The cornrow headed runner strode down the final stretch with only a small lessoning in his rhythm. Eli had to go into his final efforts, which were not enough to keep a blue-white clad aggressor from pulling tandem to his shoulder.

Thorpe, Katie, and the girls witnessed the onslaught on their feet as everyone else in the stands. The leader floated across the finish ten meters up, with arms raised, and a cocky attitude. Eli started leaning his final strides to the finish, while his cohort on his shoulder tiring horrendously slowed allowing Eli to hold onto second place.

"8:02.2," Katie stated in a so-so manner. "That guy who won must have run about 1:55 or something." She added. All the unspoken instincts, the vague suspensions suddenly took shape and centered upon Katie's pad. In that impassive inert paper, Thorpe seemed to see something superb – a realization of near infinite potential. With a smile he thought – 'state champs here.' He dared to think.

"I scratched Jimmy from the 400 meter run," Thorpe announced to Katie as he took a seat. He had left the bleacher area in the interim where the girls' 4 by 800 meters and the 4 by 200 meter relays were completed. He returned nearly an hour later with the new assignments. "I want him fresh for the distance medley."

Once more, the agonizing cry from the crowds bought their attention to the infield. A competitor in the open competition of the high jump had brushed the crossbar down at an attempt at six feet nine inches. "Aaaa…" they moaned. The rancor continued as they focused on the other end of the field. The pole vault presented an attempt at a height of fifteen-feet four inches. A pole-vaulter readied himself at the top of the run-up. His attics only increased the tension as he fidgeted with his pole. Raising the end of the pole and then lowering it. He appeared to stare at the crossbar some twenty meters away. He rocked back and forth with his pole positioned. Then, he attacked. The pole's far end lifted off the ramp and the jumper with high knee lift started his sprint down the approach ramp. Faster, faster, then the arms rose above his head with the pole he planted its end into the pit. One knee raised, feet came off the ground. The athlete rode his implement as momentum carried its end to the vertical where skill in mechanics took over the timing of his turning, straightening, clear the bar, arc the stomach, push off the pole…success!

"Yea…!" exclaimed the crowd as bedlam broke-out throughout the stadium. "New record…!" The announcer stated over the intercom.

As these events proceeded, Kasper stretched-out next to a fence near the hundred-meter start area. There other competitors stretched, bounced on their toes and just congregated with other competitors waiting for their event. The peculiar batter of half-jokes and horseplay remained an option for a few, however most sat mute contemplating their fate. Waiting in abeyance for them at the far end of the track, Kasper, Eli, Danny, and Jimmy gathered for the distance medley relay.

"Hey everybody ready?" Thorpe asked his arms extending over the fence bordering his group. Danny the neared of the foursome shrugged his shoulders. "The officials are calling. Let's do it men. You've had two great efforts, busted the records for Division 2 in those events…now finish off your day!" Thorpe made his way to his position in the stands once more. He looked forward to going home after this race. "Kasper won't be tired from the earlier races. That is where the mileage strength comes in. He'll run the best sixteen-hundred in spite of his earlier races."

"Coach Thorpe," greeted a voice belonging to a more mature voice than his own. It was Coach Paul Rudolf, of Southeast College, checking out the talent. "What you doing over here in Indiana? Sort of far from the stable aren't you Matt."

"Hey! How you doing coach?" Thorpe responded, "I just want to give my kids some exposure to the big leagues."

"What kind of athletes you got Matt?"

"Well, I know you didn't notice but we won the four by 1600 meters. We averaged 4:34. Got two guys that should get down to the middle to low four-twenties in the 1600 meters," quipped Thorpe proudly.

"Wow!" Rudolf said impressed. "That was your team?"

"Those were my boys. Three of that team ran the four by eight-hundred in 8:02.And we are entered in the distance medley coming up."

"What!" Rudolf's eyes widened, "Sounds like I better keep poking around, by the way any college material in the lineup?"

"You bet my friend." Thorpe proudly commenced to describe Kasper and Danny. It was evident that Thorpe had come upon the subject on which he needed to disclose to someone. He told many details about the boys. He gave account of Kasper's fortitude, self-motivation in his studies, and his quest for a physics scholarship. Rudolf listened attentively to everything throwing in a question from time to time.

"About your plans, you entered at the Cross Roads Invitational, Matt?" asked Rudolf. "I'd like to see your boys in their best event there."

"Ah! You know, I do not think they will allow us to show. It's all big schools there but I am hoping the performances here will let them know we can compete with anybody," mused Thorpe relaxed and confident.

"Very good, hey looks like they're about to line-up for the distance medley now. Look there's old Frank Stamps starting," Rudolf said watching the wobbling figure of a man leading the new group of competitors. "Old Stamps started me in many races in high school twenty years ago."

"He was middle aged then," added Thorpe, "he's ageless it seems."

"You know he's been starter at the college nationals, all the Ohio state high school championship meets, Olympic trials; he's a real icon in track and field officiating."

"The man totally loves the sport, "Thorpe said. "I can't believe he's here, however for any major track and field meet Stamps seems to be the man on the field with his starter-gun and holster."

"Yep he's totally serious, professional and he keeps the meet moving on time." Rudolf added.

"You can set your watch by his start time," Thorpe replied, "If the schedule says four-fifteen for a race he won't start a minute before or after."

"Only an act of God could interfere with his schedule," Rudolf smiled.

"Guns up!" somebody announced in the bleacher crowd.

With the crack of the pistol, another act in the theater of events opened. Its actors performing with all the attempts of carrying out the times they so much had planned and desired. However, unlike stage actors, innovation is crucial as competitors seldom perform, as you would have them.

Terry was carrying the baton on the first leg, eight-hundred meters. He came by the first loop in the middle of the pack. Rounding the curve the runners started stringing out. Down the backstretch into the final one-hundred meters, Terry emerged moving wide into the final meters. He waved the baton then extended his arm allowing Jimmy to grab the stick from him and quickly accelerate for his four-hundred meters. Now three runners were ahead by two or three strides. Jimmy made on attempt to suck in behind them; he just ran wide and rolled right by them before the end of the turn. The boy then moved over to lane one, now three strides ahead and pulling away from five close contenders.

"Float Jimmy, relax," said Thorpe.

"Hope he's not going out too fast," Rudolf warned, "he'll pay in the stretch."

"Look at that guy sweep 'em up!" Someone in the multitude commented eyeing Jimmy's movements on the track.

Jimmy curved into the second turn, long strides leaning into the inside rail. Sweeping strides, powerful push-offs contrasted with the distance runners more relaxed efforts. The quarter-milers or four-hundred men, the proper metric description, are generally the tallest, strongest, and most powerful runners to take to the track. Jimmy demonstrated that power as they rolled into the stretch to the next hand-off.

"Go to the arms Jimmy! Go to your arms!" Thorpe yelled watching him rotated into the stretch. Behind two pursuers were closing the gap ever so slightly on Jimmy. Eighty meters, seventy meters, sixty meters. The trailing runner ceased progress toward Jimmy's back. He was three meters up on them as he passed-off to Kasper.

"I got him in 48.2!"

"Yep! That's about what I got too!"

"Fantastic!" Thorpe had to add. Then his attention turned back to the track. The noise from the throngs of spectators reached its highest pitch as Kasper took off for his 1200-meter leg in the lead.

"Got to go out like in the 800 then just start a long strong float the last 600 meters," Kasper thought.

A growing roar came from the crowd. Kasper knew it could only mean one thing: someone was making a big move in the arena. Cutting the gap on someone from behind usually would bring on such an accolade. "Most likely, someone is moving on me," he concluded.

Indeed, by 200 meters the three teams that had snapped at Jimmy's heel; now had closed to zero meters behind Kasper's rear. Coming toward the 400 point, two runners overtook him. Now Kasper locked on to the two. A third runner, clad in yellow, stalked from just behind him. Moving uneventfully through the second lap then rounding into the third lap then he was in the stretch again.

"Aaa…," Thorpe moaned as Kasper re-passed one boy then a second, back into the lead. "He's popping. He's running his heart out…2:09 at 800…Go Kasper…give Danny some pad."

Katie, Thorpe, Rudolf threw accolades at every stride Kasper rolled-off. The stadium crowd gradually started standing and would continue until all the runners finished. The field stretched 200 meters behind as Kasper, fifteen meters up on the second team, rotated his arms and legs toward Danny.

"Ata, boy," Thorpe praised glancing at his stopwatch. He watched the digits change and noted as Kasper passed-off to Danny. The digits read 6:06. "Kasper ran about three minutes-sixteen seconds, not bad."

"Gosh! Everybody's chasing me," Danny thought as he secured the baton sprinting the first meters. "Okay, take it easy now. Get into your mile rhythm now." He cautioned himself. Now the screams were high-pitched with emotion and quite partisan. The runners were strung-out enough such that it was clear who was chasing whom. Fans bellowed-out the team mascots but mostly the unending screams said, "Come on Joey! Tim…Jack! Bobby!…" The participants could hear all the common names and some names not so common, while they were scurrying the last meters of the race. Danny thought, "I didn't hear my name." At the 400 meters, Danny was ten meters ahead. At 800 meters, five meters ahead.

"Bang!" barked the pistol. One lap remaining in the race.

At 1200 meters, two runners followed too close at his heels not a meter behind. Satisfied they settled behind him pleased with their accomplishment. Without looking, Danny was conscience as only a runner can tell. Stalkers kept pace with him waiting to rush pass nearing the finish. Stoically, he held his pace. It was quick, 3:21 through 1200 meters.

"I'll hold this…hopefully they won't pass. If they do, I'll try to hang on and see if I have anything down the stretch," Danny thought. It was as if his pursuers could here Danny thinking, because the follower in close third accelerated as they entered the final backstretch. He went pass Danny to the extent of startling him. The boy lengthens his lead. Danny recovered, increased his effort, while the third runner behind the two started fading off the pace, falling behind with every stride.

Into the final turn, Danny began accelerating. Now the lead runner owed dearly to the 'Saint of Fatigue' for the large energy debit withdrawn earlier. Payback time was as stressful as any financial crisis experienced, but pay you must. Thus, the leader began to fade rapidly the cost of passing Danny so swiftly earlier.

"Reel him in Danny" Katie screamed with teammates in unison. Now, the whole galley was on their feet and bedlam erupted. Coming out of the turn Danny had made up all space on the kid in front. He swung for room to pass. Into the stretch, shoulder to shoulder, thirty meters to finish. Then with the crowd screaming, Danny started lifting higher in arms and legs and made his pass. He pulled away steadily, crossed the finish baton raised four seconds ahead of the fast fading second runner.

"10:38!" Thorpe said staring at his stopwatch.

"Awesome!" Rudolf praised. "About 4:32, I got."

"That was outstanding."

Runners were still finishing, in all states of exhaustion. The Lakeport team could be seen hugging and high-fives to each other. Smiling faces beaming as the infield finish area filled with runners and team members gathered around their compatriots struggling to re-gather composure from their exhausted physical states. Congratulations, consoling, and a job well done, irrelevant to the order of finish, dressed these fellows.

Thorpe almost in tears just wanted to go home. He just shook at the talent he had witnessed on this day, because of the dire predictions heaped upon him for most of the year from colleagues.

"Now, we just fine tune for the grand finale in June."

᛭᛫ᚱ᛫ᚾ᛫ᚼ᛫ᚱ᛫ᚾᚼ᛫ᚼ᛫ᚾᚼ᛫ᚼ᛫ᚾᛘᚼ᛫ᚳ᛫ᚳᚾᛘᚼᚼᛘᚾᚼᚾᚼᚾ

The Lakeport Review, the local paper for the rural areas, gave Coach Thorpe and the track team nearly a full-page spread. Interviewing, commenting, and the editor's comment made the pride of the community. Never before, had this small community successfully competed with big schools of any sport.

At the school, the two winning trophies and the second place trophy won by the team took a place at the cafeteria entrance for all to see. The team, all of them, high jumpers, shot putters, the girls; all were given as much of a celebrity status as was ever experienced at the small school. Except for Jimmy, the runners were cautiously coy about their exploits.

In the observation of the school staff, many begged for an equal performance in the class subjects from the athletes. As for college, they were dubious even of Kasper, who they knew wanted to attend an 'Ivory league' school. Although Kasper described as focused, hard-worker, and determined. No one from this school district had ever accomplished such lofty goals as admittance to such a college.

No one was necessary to forward these sentiments. Kasper, as he was well aware of this 'outstretch' he had set for himself. Unaffected, he focused working the immediate days following the 'meet', on the academics. Rather than study his school physics text, he studied physics problems, described as 'typical' of what he may expect at testing, according to the brochure of the 'Physic Scholarship Test'.

On the occasion, of this evening, Greg and Eli had the privilege of accompanying Thorpe to Columbus, with the intent of ordering new uniforms for the track squads. The fading colors and tattered state of old uniforms and running togs was not to be the covers for such an esteemed club as Lakeport. Thorpe spent little time and effort in convincing Principle Stromberg to this matter. He sustained the funds by passing this plight to the Sports Fan Club, which obtained more than substantial contributions from the Lakeport community businesses. Taverns, boat sales businesses, and private contributions padded the 'slush accounts' for the local school's sports programs. With all the delight of a 'child at a toy store,' Thorpe set-off to town with his helpers for this buying spree.

This left Kasper and Danny in the privacy of the kitchen, where they were set at the task of deciphering another physics problem.

"Okay it says," Kasper started to read the problem, "A car moving at 60 meters per second coast to a stop. The equation of motion for this vehicle is…" Kasper rote down:

$$v = v_0 e^{-kt}$$

Kasper continued. "Where v is the velocity at time t, v_0 is the initial velocity, and k is a constant. At t = 20 seconds the car's velocity is 30 meters per second. (a) Find the constant k, (b) what is the velocity at t = 60 seconds?, (c) Show that the acceleration is proportional to the velocity."

"What area of physics is this problem in?" Danny asked

"Oh, linear dynamics," Kasper replied, "let's use some intuitive guessing. The car is moving at 60 m/s. Look, the speed is halved in 20 seconds. In another 20 seconds, 40 seconds, it' halved again…down to fifteen meters per second. Finally, by 60 seconds speed would be reduced a further half. So when t = 60 seconds the speed should be seven and a halve meters per second, right?"

"You don't hear me arguing, do you?" Danny queried further. "But, how do you show this algebraically?"

"Substitute the initial conditions into the equation of motion," Kasper explained, "so v = 30, v_0 = 60, and t = 20". Kasper began writing out the steps for the solution. "The problem reduces to," he wrote-out:

$$30 = 60 \, e^{-20k}$$

"So, divide both sides by 60.

$$0.5 = e^{-20k}.$$

"And taking the natural log of both sides

$$\ln 0.5 = \ln e^{-20k}$$

$$-0.693 = -20k$$

"Solving for k

$$k = 0.0347 \, s^{-1}$$

"Huh, that was sweet," Danny, said impressed. Then his large oval eyes brightened. "Aha, I see its easy now, to part b. Just substitute the k value and t = 60 seconds, with v_0 = 60 meters per second."

$$v = 60 \, e^{-60 \, (0.0347)}$$

"Now, Danny, since we don't have *e* on our calculator, use *e* = 2.71. So:

$$v = 60 \, (2.71)^{-2.082})$$

$$v = 60(0.125) = 7.5 \, m/s$$

"Right on, what you guessed, 7.5 meters per second!"

"But, for part c, I don't have any idea how we're to even start it." Danny looked perplexed.

Kasper turned his attention to the question and thought for a couple minutes. "Yea, how do you get from the velocity equation of motion to acceleration?" Kasper went into think mode again. Danny watched pleased that a problem that was difficult to him was agreeably perplexing for Kasper.

"Crap!" Kasper said, about the closest he would come to the vulgar. He continued staring at the problem then said. "Let's start with the definition or acceleration and use calculus. Now, acceleration is the differential of velocity with respect to time. So let us write:

$$v = v_0 e^{-kt}$$

"Then since

$$a = dv/dt$$

"Taking the derivative of velocity, v gives

$$dv/dt = -kt \, (v_o e^{-kt})$$

"The argument within the parentheses is v, velocity.

"Thus, with substitution

$$a = -kt \, v$$

"Hence we proved that acceleration is proportional to velocity.

$$a \approx v$$

"If a person didn't know any calculus, there's no way they could have answered part c. Kasper, you're a genius."

"Ah, I just get lucky sometime."

With that, they were off to writing an essay on the perils of 'Don Quixote'.

CHAPTER 4

▼

By the following week, the team had participated in two dual meets treated as mere workout sessions. Their times were not note worthy as Kasper and crew completed full workouts without rest between these encounters. Now, the team was participating at the Painesville Relays, in Painesville, a community as much a 'hick' town as Lakeport. However, Painesville High did have a decent track and field facility. Eight other little schools were to attend this affair. The attendants, mostly family members of the participants, deluged participants with praises, adorations and encouragement unmatched at any social event of any kind. Only a local carnival mimicked this occasion.

"The weather is forecasted to be lousy, the competition is soft, and we have the Marlborough Invitational next Thursday," Thorpe reminded his team gathered in the school gym. "Painesville is a nice meet and a great community. We want everyone to participate, but we cannot suffer any injuries. Jimmy, no blasting starts. You distance men, float 'em out, 'bout eighty-five percent effort. "At Marlborough we have Bill Riese of Logansport, he's run 4:27, and Jack Matela has a 2:01 in the 800, for Galamoor. These people can go faster. You guys will need a personal best there."

Thorpe's plans were gradually revealing themselves. These convenient thoughts suggested aspirations in agreement with the idealism Kasper would credit to himself. He carried these thoughts as he and the others suited up for practice, after leaving the gym. All matters were serious ahead, but for now, they had a tough workout waiting.

Leaving the school grounds, the troop of runners including Sheila headed north to the camping grounds area of the park around the lake. They trudged slowly along the curving access roads. Winding amongst the trees and foliage, they headed back to the school at this point having covered about three miles. After stretching for several minutes, they were sufficiently warmed-up for the real onslaught of work. On this rare occasion, they gathered about the humble track around the football field.

"Okay, lady and gentlemen!" Thorpe called out to the clan of runners in various stages of stretching, lacing their shoes, and waiting for their orders. "What I want is 200's. Eli, Terry, you are 800, 400 men. So hold 29 seconds on the run. Walk 200 and repeat. I need twelve repetitions. Then we need to run ten 100 meter straights at moderate effort with high arm knee lift, okay?" The boys acknowledged meekly. "Kasper, Danny; I'm looking for 32 seconds for twenty, walk between. Sheila, you follow behind them. Lets' shoot for 35 seconds a piece for twelve, okay," Sheila appeared perplexed. "In the following weeks we'll increase the repetitions and lower the times. Keep your rest periods short stay focused, the rest interval is just as important as the run. If a muscle is strained, pull over and stretch for a while. Speed kills so this is where you get hurt, usually."

This day was warm and breezy, as the fleet of runners tackled the workout. Kasper was pleased. "Such training sessions as this will get the times down," said he.

"Yea, if we can survive," commented Eli, forcing a smile.

"Let's get on with it," urged Danny, "we'll see what goes in a couple weeks."

Sheila, Terry, and Greg moved silently behind the trio, willing to be obedient to the task. Sheila hung on closer than want anyone would think as the runs started Katie had to coax her to back off, as she was running under 35 second splits. It was Katie, who called out to the times to the runners and filled her logs. Thorpe was the critic correcting their running posture and commanding compliance with the rest periods, after which he then directed his attention to Jimmy's training. Caroline Webster directed her attention to the high jumpers and shot putters. No one was training for the pole vault on the team. However, Caroline did have two middle school girls, gymnast's, who spent a lot of time with her learning to handle the pole. She was confident these girls would develop into a talent for the school in the future for this new event for girls in high school track and field. These activities slowed to a halt after an hour-an-a-half, completing the training session. Thorpe briefed them:

"Ok, good work today. Ah, the target times were slow for some of you but you must stay right on your target time. Sheila, you did great. However, you must stay at 35 seconds per 200 meters, for now. We will be increasing your repetitions. So they will be getting hard. We want to build strength. Running lots of 35's in practice a few times a week. See it will be easy later in a race to average 37 to 38 for the 1600 meters run. A morning run a few times a week is okay. Thorpe pranced in-place, big grin on his robust face and waving his note pad showing his excitement with her potential.

"That's about a five minute pace," Greg stated.

"Yea, Sheila," Eli interrupted, "and you'll be training faster than that before State."

"Now, don't be surprised if you get sore tonight," Thorpe warned, "You're body is not used to this speed. So rub yourself down, with some muscle rub real good before you hit the sack. You all have a good evening, now."

"More the same tomorrow, coach?" asked Kasper.

"Similar, people," replied Thorpe, "similar."

Within the confines of a small yard surrounded by mostly untrimmed rose bushes and shrubbery. Kasper retreated with his cousin and brothers to the back yard of the Wises's home, where they gathered at a picnic table to relax, eat and 'shoot the breeze'. Jayce Wise joined the boys hoping to get more in touch with the goings on with the whole program of events involving his 'boys'. A man of short stout stature with a robust face and wavy thinning hair he listening to their conversation intently. He could not help reflecting back to his son's leg disfigurement. Now, crediting running for his Kasper's health as well as his ambition for academics; Mr. Wise never tired of discussions related to the aspirations that posed in their wake. Equally, he was leery of all events that appeared to benefit his three sons and their cousin. In the last year it was like coaches, teachers, and sport events had evolved to take over the boys' lives and direct them to places he and his wife had no hint of where they would end. The feeling of inadequacy prevailed upon his thoughts. He witnessed the progression of Kasper as being nothing less than astonishing. Such was the state of mind of Jayce as he listened to his boy's conversations.

Endeavoring to hit upon some theory, which would reconcile his lack of knowledge of the sport, Jayce hoped hear those words, which would reveal the starting point of the enormous progression that his boys had realized. He made little progress toward this understanding, however. Pursuing discussion, Wise questioned the group.

"Those guys running four-ten and there about," Jayce queried, "they're tall aren't they? You don't think we're shooting too high for your age do you?"

"Dad, the Kenyans are seldom taller than 5' 9" of so," Kasper said. "The best ten-thousand meter men average about 5'6".... The greatest distance runner ever, is from Ethiopia, and a member of one of the oldest Christian church communities in Africa. Dad, he's 5'3"."

"Yea," Eli added, "Gebrasalaisse has run a 3:49 mile!"

"That's right," Danny, said, "size is not our problem, but some dudes are more mature than others."

"Amen to that." Kasper added.

"For high school kids, it's a factor," Greg said, "Some guys can be just under twenty years old, before graduating. Shoot! I'll still be seventeen when I graduate,"

The senior Wise was secretly bothered again at the thoughts of the commitments facing the boys and the seriousness with which they set for themselves. Equally, he recognized the possibility of college education; nevertheless, a scholarship for track for his little skinny boys seemed beyond the realm of possibility. Not knowledgeable about track performances he could only trust the feedback from his sons, and coach Thorpe, whom in private other people in the community described him as a dreamer.

"Be cautious in any speculation from him," they would say. "He's a swell person, but 'knock on wood' about any thing he says." Yes, student loans, partial grant funding would be available, but what about the academics? No one in his family or in Kasper's mother family had ever attended college. Jayce, a truck driver stationed at a large facility just a few miles from Lakeport; not intimidated by the gravity of the ambition of his boys and nephew, he was just unsure as to how he should go about it.

"You boys sound very knowledgeable." Jayce said finally. Then he stood-up and departed, feeling no more at the grips of things than before this discussion. Nevertheless, he was impressed that they knew so much about the sport and its history. "They seem to know the path they have laid before them," he thought in finale.

It was the Thursday before the Painesville track meet. The boys had just retired to bed. There came a knock to the Wise residence door about the hour when one would normally give the first yawn and glance at the clock. Jayce Wise sat up in the old recliner, while his wife Beth laid her magazine down in her lap and made a face of disappointment.

"A road call," said Beth, "you have to go out now?" Jayce groaned, for he was more weary than normal from a long day. He stepped to the door peeped through the window curtails, and opened the door. A middle-aged woman entered.

"You will excuse my calling so late," she began; suddenly losing her self-control she ran forward threw her arms about Beth's neck and sobbed upon her shoulder. "Oh, I'm in such trouble!" she cried; "I do hope you all could help me with my predicament."

"Why," Beth replied, "Helga, we would certainly help you in anyway, if we can. You startled me, ma'am the way you came in all hysterical."

"I didn't know what to do so I came straight to you."

In Lakeport, such was the way folks in grief acted they were not impeded with inhibitions of false pride in these parts of Ohio. A large portion of this populace has the cultural values and the heritage of the South. Their manner or speaking and were likewise rural and candid in presentation, while their candor was sincere and admirable.

"My Uncle is visiting from Germany. He is the oldest of my father's brothers. Last week he fell, hit his head and suffered a bad concussion," Helga explained.

"How is he now?"

"Oh, much better; but he can't read. His eyesight is all fuzzy, he says," Helga hesitated briefly. "What happened is he's gotten letters from his grand kids from Germany, but he can't read them. I left the country as a little girl after the war with my parents. I totally forgot the language."

"Well, you came to the right place," Beth interrupted. "All my boys can speak and read German. My boys stayed with my parents a lot. When he went TDY to other places in Europe, we would leave the kids with them, so I could go with Jayce. So the boys attended Germans schools up until we left there two years ago."

"Oh, everybody knows all that about you all. Good gracious! I did not want to impose upon you. Uncle Johannes, however, has been frantic, hostile, and just plain difficult the last several days since he received a letter from his great granddaughters and no one could read them for him. So now he rants and raves that we can't read his letters."

"We'll have Kasper drop by after school tomorrow," Jayce said. "They have a track meet Saturday, so there will be no practice after school."

"Oh, that would be great," Helga, exclaimed. "I would have bought the letter with me but he wouldn't let me have them."

"Understand." Jayce said hoping she would leave quickly now. "Don't worry they'll be right over after school, maybe around three o'clock."

"Thank you so much for being so kind." said Helga, "Your boys are so nice and Kasper. Our grandson talks to uncle about Kasper all the time. Uncle will get along with him just fine."

Jayce had to drift away from the pair. "I can't wait for these eternal partings to end." He thought, as he departed quietly to his room leaving his wife to suffer the final woes of a drawn out departure he suspected was developing with Mrs. Sweigert.

Friday evolved to be a full day for Kasper with responsibilities abounding from several events. Homework was due, assignments taken, physics problems turned in. After which, gathering and checking gear for the Painesville meet and finally, a date with Uncle Sweigert after classes. First for Kasper, however was his physics. He had to solve one problem during his free period at school. He wanted to relax at home in the evening and get to bed early. Often, if Kasper attempted a problem in the evenings and found some difficulty he would worry about the problem as he lay in bed. Rather than such an occurrence to happen he chose to work on the problem in school where he could get help from Thorpe or Mr. Billington the Pre-calculus teacher at Lakeport.

"How fast must a twenty meter projectile be moving if its length is observed to be ten meters in the laboratory frame of reference?" Kasper read the problem to himself, sitting in the far corner of the small library of the school. "This is a relativity problem. I must use the Lorentz transformation equation for length. He wrote down:

$$L' = \gamma (L - vt)$$

"Since there is no change in time, I set t = 0, then

$$L' = \gamma L$$

Now $\gamma = 1/\sqrt{1 - \beta^2}$

"Now, substitute, 20 meters for rest frame L', and 10 meter in the laboratory frame, L

$$20 = 10/\sqrt{1 - \beta^2}$$

$$\sqrt{1 - \beta^2} = 10/20$$

"Squaring both sides,

$$1 - \beta^2 = 0.25$$

$$\beta^2 = 0.75$$

"Beta equals velocity divided by the speed of light,

$$\beta = v/c,$$

"So we have $v^2/c^2 = 0.75$. Take the square root of both sides.

$$v/c = 0.866$$

"While we know the constant c, equals: $c = 3 \times 10^8$ meters per second.

"Finally then,

$$v = (0.866) \ (3 \times 108 \ m/s)$$

$$v = 2.6 \times 108 \ m/s.$$

"Ah, the twenty meter projectile would have to be approaching the observer at 2.60×10^8 meters per second, for it to appear as only 10 meters long, Wow! That was satisfying," he thought.

Kasper pleased tucked his books under his arm and departed the library. The task of meeting with Uncle Sweigert would be up to him alone. Eli the playful fellow preferred to catch a movie with Jimmy and the young Greg had his own class work to complete. He was off with a clan of freshmen friends. Thus, Kasper set off on foot toward the Sweigert residence a few blocks from school.

Kasper passed a little cottage, moved through heavy foliage of shaped bushes that bordered the Sweigert's home. At his arrival, Helga Sweigert greeted him and led the boy to the living room.

"What a pleasure Kasper to see you," Helga exclaimed, as he was lead inside her home. Uncle lay stretched upon the sofa while Bill paced the room. Kasper thought he appeared nervous.

"Glad to see you, dude," greeted Bill with a mischievous grin, ushering Kasper toward the couch.

Uncle raised himself a bit from his position and offered his hand. He was a man in his seventies, with thin grey hair, six-feet tall, bone skinny, and imposing, with a massive heavy featured face. It was not difficult to imagine him in his prime as atypical of a black uniformed German officer of the Third Reich. Dressed in an expensive looking silk bathrobe and grey silk trousers with shinny slippers completing his attire; he appeared over dressed for this modest home and setting.

"Glad to meet you young man," he said in a heavy German accent. "Excuse me but I'm not feeling my best. I've taken pain pill and aspirin so I feel druggy."

"Nett Sie zu tieffen, mein Herr (Nice to meet you, Sir)," said Kasper, grasping the old man's hand.

"Froh Sie, ebenso zu treffen, junger Mann (Glad to meet you as well, young man)," Uncle answered with a broad grin. "Oh, es ist so gut Deutsch sprechen zu hören Es geht mir schon besser (Oh, it is good to hear German spoken again. My spirits are better already)," He shook Kasper's arm vigorously.

"Es ist mein Vergnügen (It is my pleasure)," Kasper responded, "Meine Brüder und ich sprechen Deutsch mit einander (My brothers and I speak German amongst ourselves)."

Helga and Bill just looked on admirably pleased that the two seemed so cordial with each other rattling German between them.

"Ich werde English sprechen damit wir nie manden beleidigen (I'll speak English so we won't offend anyone)," suggested the uncle.

"Lassen Sie uns Deutsch sprechen dann können wir uns über sie unterhalten (Let's speak German. That way we can talk about them)," said Kasper winking an eye at the man, smiling. Uncle Sweigert chuckled.

"Why don't we leave so you and Kasper can look over the letters and have a pleasant visit?" Helga suggested taking a reluctant Bill by the arm.

"Ah, Grandma I want to listen too," said Bill anxious resisting Beth's coaxing.

"You and Uncle Johannes can visit later, come on Bill." With that, Bill and Beth departed from the room.

"Here is the last letter I received from my great granddaughters," said Johannes, "they are little darlings. The oldest is just learning to write. I enjoy reading their little notes." The man handed a letter to Kasper. Kasper then read out-loud in German:

'Großvater,Wir vermissen Dich sehr. Wir wollen, daß Du bald nach Hause kommst. Vati hat Mutter eine hübsche lampe als Geschenk gekauft als sie aus dem kranken haus kam (entlassen warde). Ist America schön? Hast Du Cowboys gesehen? Beeile Dich nach Hause zu kommen. Wir wollen Dich sehen.

Alles Liebe,
Grechen, Heidi, Gerlinda'

"Grandfather, we miss you very much. Will you be coming home soon? Daddy brought a new lamp for mother when she was sick. Is America nice? Have you seen any cowboys? Hurry back home, we want to see you.

Love,
Grechen, Heidi, Gerlinda"

Johannes explained that his young great granddaughters sent him letters all the time. He continued to explain that his wife in Germany was not in good health and she was deaf and incoherent mostly. He said he would be returning in a couple months. Then after a slight pause, it seemed he warranted some time as to know how he wanted to express his thought.

In German Johannes continued. "Glücklicherweise kann ich besondere Materien sachen mit Ihnen auf Deutsch diskutieren (besprechen), da diese privat gehalten warden müssen. Ich glaube, Sie stimmen mir in dieser Gelaegenheit bei (It is fortunate I can discuss a particular matter with you in German, as this requires the up most privacy. I trust I can secure your agreement for these matters)?"

"Meine Lippen sind verschlossen, mein Herr (My lips are sealed, sir)," Kasper assured him."Nichts das zwischen uns vorgeht, wird irgend jemanden offenvart warden (Nothing transpired between us, will be revealed to anyone). Ich kann sehe, daß Sie nicht gut geschlafen haben da Sie sich um (über) diese Sachen (Materien) Sorgen machen(I can see that you have not slept comfortably worrying about these matters)," Kasper said in his easy, genial manner. "Kann ich fragen, wie ich Ihnen helfen kann (May I ask how I can help you?)?"

"Die Briefe von meinen Enkelinnen haben immer eine geschlossene nachricht an Bill dabei (Those letters from my granddaughters, well they've always accompanied with a sealed note addressed to Bill)." Yohannes looked very serious. "Bei Gott, ich hoffe ich täusche mich, aber etwas geht nicht an zwischen Bill und meinem äHesten Enkelkind Wilhen, der Bill diese Nachrichten schickt, in den

Briefen der Madchen (I hope to God I'm wrong, but something not good is going on between Bill and Wilhelm my oldest grandchild, who is sending Bill these notes with the girls letters)."

Johannes spoke with much emotion. He seemed painful in making these disclosures. "It's a very delicate thing," said he continued in English. "One does not like to speak of one's domestic affairs to strangers. It is dreadful to discuss the conduct of a relative with you whom I have never seen before. It is horrible to have to do it. But I've got to the end of my wits and so I must get to the bottom of this matter."

Kasper detected a reserved man with a dash of pride in his nature more likely to hide his wounds than to expose them. Then suddenly he slapped his hands on his knees like one who throws reserve to the winds, he began.

"Die Tatsachen sind diese (folgende), Kasper (The facts are these, Kasper)," Yohannes motioned his head toward those in the kitchen, "Bill hatte ein Drogenproblem (Bill has a drug problem). Deswegen lebt er mit Helga, seiner Großmutter(That is why he is living with Helga his grandmother). Sein Vater was wirklich nie in seinem Leben und seine Mutter hatte Probleme wie jede junge Mutter (His dad really has not been in his life and his mother had problems like any young mother). Sie könnte ihn nicht richtig pflegen Sie konnte sich nicht richtig um Ihn kümmern(She could not care for him properly). Deshalb lebte er beinahe sein ganzes Leben mit Helga (So, he's been living with Helga off and on most of his life)."

After looking towards the kitchen, Johannes whispered in English. "Last year, just after Bill arrived here, I came over with grandson Wilhelm who had been a problem at home as well, affiliating with 'Skin heads'. You heard of them?"

"Oh yes; they're neo-Nazis."

"Indeed! Kasper I suspect Bill's receiving information and materials from Wilhelm, and its not cordial greetings. The nature of this is a mystery."

"Why haven't you just read one of the notes to determine the nature of their business?"

"Indeed, I did just so but they're cagey. Wilhelm sends the notes in English. I do not read English too well. But, I gathered enough to tell me Wilhelm sends materials to a post office box in town."

"So no one knows what he's receiving there?" asked Kasper.

"Beth doles on the boy. She says he is in no trouble at school. She's happy he's with her," revealed the man.

"How do you figure I may help this situation?"

"First, if you can read the letters for me; just give Bill his enclosed envelope for now, but could you keep an eye on him in school and around. Bill goes out every night, and on the weekends, he is gone all day. If he is into some mischief, I would like to find out about it. It would upset me, if it is found out that these unscrupulous activities leads, from my Wilhelm."

"Verstehen Sie (understand). Ich kenne jemanden, der ist so etwas wie ein Lager Leiter (I know someone, who's like the leader on campus). Er kennt alle Tätigkeiten der kinder (He is privy to all the happening the kids are into). Falls irgendwelche interessante Aktivitäten aufkommen, wird er Bescheid wissen (If there is any activities of any interest he will be in on it)."

. Kasper was speaking of Jimmy Luke, of course. "Jimmy's the leader of all the toughs around here and he knows most of the scoundrels in and about Columbus as well." He thought.

"Thanks son," replied the man in English, "You can imagine young Kasper as a guest here how uncomfortable I am at these dismal affairs. But I feel better already," then rolling his eyes toward the pair in the kitchen, "I assure you Helga will feel better as I will display a pleasing decor."

"I am equally pleased Sir that I gained confidence with you. Certainly, if there us some adverse activity with Bill it is best for Mrs. Sweigert and all of us to confront the matter." With this reassurance, the pair shook hands smiling at each other.

Helga and Bill could sense the conversation was winding down so they eased their way toward the pair.

"Did ya'll have a nice visit?" Helga asked.

"Oh yes, everything's fine," said Kasper. "I am so pleased to have met your uncle such a fine German gentleman."

"You have a jewel of a young man here, Helga," Johannes said, "speaks perfect German."

Bill stood back silent and meek in his demeanor.

"Well, I've got a track meet tomorrow so I need to get home; I need to get a good rest tonight."

"Give your mom and dad my regards," Helga said, "and you take care now."

Kasper made final greeting. My regards," Johannes said while giving Kasper an envelope as he exited the door. "Prüfen Sie Dinge aus mich jetzt (Check things out for me, now)," Johannes called to him.

"A day's work ended," Kasper, thought striding across to the road home. "Ha! So ole Bill may be up to no good." Then he wondered what the note could disclose. "Why didn't we look at this before, maybe he just wanted to make sure I come back again?" He opened the envelope and saw notes all right; bank notes, three twenty-dollar bills.

It really isn't much, as for as housing developments compared to the suburbs of Franklin county: an ordinary set of small homes as old as his parents, Kasper guessed as the school bus loaded with the track team made its way along a rickety road to the Painesville High School to participate in the Painesville Invitational. "But I like places like this. For I could get some good runs out here," Whenever Kasper traveled anywhere, he always saw himself running along the countryside. "Nice woods will keep it cool along the trails." The woods tucked into the crescent bend of a slow, greenish river. There are houses across the river, and a wastewater treatment facility that stank. The bus left the 270 outer-belt on Route 23. Lined with motels, gas stations with convenience stores and a smorgasbord of fast-food franchises; Kasper knew these businesses catered to the many expensive housing developments intersperse behind them. "Typical suburbanite people; they like lots of asphalt, pavement, and concrete," he blurted to Eli sitting next to him, "don't care for plants and trees; but they will grow a lawn to brag about, I suppose."

"You won't be seeing any distance stars from around here, huh brother," Eli understood what his brother would be thinking as he gazed the landscape from the bus window. "The concrete be heating your feet and the sun be burning you black; how can you get any mileage under those conditions?" The boys laughed in mockery. Kasper thought people where bland and unimaginative who sort group refuge and patronized clusters of everything. He was one who would run to the opposite spectrum of socialization, seeking isolation and singular desires.

They turned east leaving the Interstate and had traveled for some time. Now these woods largely insulated from all that they had recently jested. Plots of farmlands, heavy patches of grass lands served to comprise a wide moat between the refuge-woods and the concrete and steel of mid-America, making man made things disappear, leaving Kasper alone with thoughts and the affection of this good land. Finally, the small homes appeared a small trailer park, then more small homes. Such was it as the school bus pulled into the small campus of the school.

Painesville's weather was as bleak as forecasted. Cloudy, a wet slushy track, windy, and a team more concerned about the Marlborough meet the following Thursday. Coach Thorpe had hoped the team would run mostly individual events to sharpen their skills for Marlborough. The weather precluded this possibility however. Thus, Thorpe withdrew Jimmy from the hurdles and the hundred meters. He waited with inquietude along the bordering fence for the imminent start of the boys 1600 meter run.

Although Thorpe preferred the woods, he liked the fields, too. Fields, he thought brings breadth to the surroundings, a depth of vision not available in the midst of trees. Fields were all around the school and track grounds. When standing on an upper deck of the bleachers, he could watch the giant thunderheads advance angrily from the west, survey the reddening sky and lean back to gaze over all.

"Bang!" It occurred exactly as scheduled. Thorpe snapped his stopwatch. Kasper and Danny moved from the start of the run slowly. On the backstretch, two runners led the pair and three others followed closely. "Too slow," thought the coach, "Someone could step on their heels or they could trip." The observation was uneasy for him.

"71, 72..." Yelled a timer as the succession of runner cruised through the first lap ducking into a gusting head wind. Another official standing clear of the runner's path held a large card with the number 3 on it, denoting the remaining laps to finish.

"That's slow enough," exclaimed Katie as she logged the splits sitting midway the length of the track in the bleachers. She saw three runners close to the pair while the remaining field could not keep up with this pace and surrendered ground behind the three leaders. Lacy and Nadine finished with the competition in the high jump sat with Katie urging the boys to more action.

"Danny, Kasper! Pick it up guys!"

The wind tugged at Kasper's curly hair as he awkwardly moved to the lead. Danny's awkward style seemed more exaggerated with this pedestrian pace. Both seemed to be bothered with the gusts of wind.

"2:23...2:24..." Katie read as the second lap was completed.

"Ok, let's see who's got the horses," suggested an impatient Thorpe.

"Float dudes, float easy," called Jimmy.

"Come on Davy!" yelled another fan to a runner in the trailing pack. Davy did not seem the least bit interested in attempting to catch the lead group ahead. A serious scowl on his face he was struggling as it was.

"Pauli! You doing good boy! Hang in there Pauli!"

The trio approached lap three. "3:31, 3:32…" The timer read, as Kasper and Danny were clear from any interference of the others.

"Come on," Coach Thorpe yelled, "Let's see you guys run now! 3:31! Sixty-eight seconds for lap three, now let's see how they can press down on the last lap!"

"Danny will win," Katie, commented to the girls from the stands, "Kasper doesn't have his leg speed, but it's an excellent exercise for him. He needs the experience of running the second half faster than the first half."

Observers could see the tandem pair change their cadence as they toured the turn, rolled into the backstretch and again with more and quicker rotation.

"Pump! Kasper pump!" said Jimmy moving in quest of a closer trackside view.

"Oh, there goes Danny!" Katie said. Indeed Danny rushed by Kasper then pulled over in front of him, but stopped accelerating allowing Kasper to remain only one stride back. Bucking the wind, they rolled onto the final turn.

"Stick with him, Kasper!" Katie yelled standing with everyone else in the bleachers. "The last 200 was about 31 seconds."

Into the straightaway Kasper moved to the outside and pulled even with Danny. Shoulder to shoulder 80 meters, 70 meters…30 meters Kasper slipped a stride behind Danny. Two strides, then three strides Danny was behind at the finish.

"4:32.3, 4:33.8," Thorpe said turning to the trio of girls. "They ran about 62 to 63 the last lap."

"And about 2:10 for the last 800," added Katie, "not too shabby!"

"That was a great effort," said an elated Nadine.

The remaining runners raced to the finish and were barely able to gather themselves off the track before the officials usurped the girls to the start of their 1600 race. A few minutes behind schedule, the officials would have to recover that time so they waited. Thus, an anxious colorful group stood poised for what seemed like many minutes before they were racing around the track.

Sheila Adams took control from the start, after the blast of the gun sent them scampering. A slow group for her was this field of runners. Accordingly, the audience of spectators watched almost quietly as she sped ahead of the others.

Seventy-four seconds was the time for lap one. The second 800 meters passed in 2:32, and 3:50 at 1200 meters. Sheila was forty meters ahead. However, the girl looked wearing as she began slowing over the final 400 meters. Her head dropped to her chest and the arms failed to rotate, but rather pumped up and down weakly.

"Come on Sheila," Katie called out detecting her friends' exhausting state.

"She's tiring," Thorpe said. "She didn't look rested on the bus ride. What we are seeing here is the results of the workouts with the boys. Her body has taken a beaten the last couple of weeks. So we're experiencing retrogression." Thorpe explained watching Sheila struggled over the final meters.

"5:23," Katie disclosed as Sheila nearly collapsed at the finish line. Katie leaned toward Lacy and Nadine checking to see that Thorpe was not paying attention to them. "She may be in retrogression, but I know she was over Julie Troy's house late last night partying. That didn't do her any good."

"Maybe, this is a good experience. Maybe she will focus on her race for next week and not be partying around," suggested Lacy.

"She still won this race easily," said Katie, "but next week there are two girls who have run 5:13 and 5:15. She better not fall apart on the last lap, because those girls won't."

Thorpe made no comment of the race. "I'm headed down by the track again. You girls gather Sheila up if you may," was his instruction as he departed.

Sometime later Jimmy Luke made a travesty in the 400 meters. He moved out quickly, not explosively then fell into a sweeping fluid gate on the backstretch. Thorpe timed him in 25.2 seconds at 200 from his vantage point. He was impressed as Jimmy relaxed on the last 100 meters and crossed at 50.5 seconds. Roy Jerome followed in 52.7.

Inside the oval, Kasper, Danny, Eli, and Terry gathered around Jimmy and Roy after their race just as the other competitors where receiving 'a job well done' as well.

"Looked easy Jimmy; when the weather gets warm you ought to buzz down in the 48s and Roy you should be bouncing off 50 flat," said Eli in a 'matter of fact' deliverance.

"We going to be dangerous in the 1600 relay man," said Roy. "I think we can whip any of the big schools."

"Shoot dudes, it wasn't bad. But I felt tight on the stretch, had to go to my arms to maintain," admitted Jimmy with a rare concern of his effort.

"Well see you guys," Eli interrupted, "we got to go check-in tent for the 800."

"Do it dudes," Jimmy forwarded, trying to be upbeat.

"Hammer 'em boys," added Roy.

"Just don't get hurt." Jimmy warned, "At the start everybody's going to come off the turn flying even if they can run only 2:20. So watch out cuzz," said he to Terry.

"Yea, they'll knock you down, and cut you off. Be careful, dudes." Roy added. With that, everybody exchanged high-fives with each and departed. Another area of the campus held some persons in relaxation before the next event.

Greg lay stretched out next to Nadine, Sheila, and Danny, who had just joined his seclusion. "I am running in the 3200 meters," Greg told the group during some conversation, "That's what I'll be running at Marlborough."

"Why don't Kasper run it? He's runs distance more than anyone," asked Danny.

"Coach, wants him to run a lot of shorter races for now, to get some speed in his legs," answered Greg.

"You will have and easy going. Nobody has been under 10:40." Sheila said.

"Hey, they are about to start the 800," Sheila warned.

The crew got up and lined themselves around the track perimeter to view the race. At the bark of the start-gun, participates went into a full sprint not unlike the shorter races. These 800-meter races required the runners to remain in their staggered lanes for 300 meters of the 400-meter oval. A turn, the backstretch, second turn, there they broke from their lanes and surged toward the two inside lanes. Positioning was crucial and the athletes were desperate at these moments.

"Look at that," Thorpe yelled, "Eli went right to the inside lane...wrong move!" Wrong, because three runners pulled in front of him. Then two others passed him, one of whom was Terry, trapped.

"61, 62, 63...," announced a timer.

"He's got to drop back and move to the outside of them." Thorpe suggested.

Terry, however, moving in the second lane throughout the turn, entered the backstretch with a slight lead. Eli maneuvering tucked behind in trail with his teammate. Terry continued down the stretch increasing the lead over the field of runners, only Eli close.

"Don't pass on the turn, follow Terry!" yelled Thorpe.

Entering the final turn the two pummeled with instruction from the sidelines, from the support crowd of Greg, Sheila, Jimmy, and Danny, increased pace. "One, two...you guys...go!"

"Let's see some speed in the stretch..." Jimmy ordered.

Around the turn, Eli moved to Terry's shoulder. Into the final 100 meters there acceleration started. Both gritted their teeth, but Eli pulled swiftly away from his mate until they crossed the finish.

"2:03, 2:05. Not too shabby!"

"Eli must have run about 60 or 61 seconds that second lap," Katie explained.

"Man the third guy must have been about 2:10," said a spectator, "your guys were the class of this field."

"Yea, but we'll be running Division one, next couple meets. Things will get terse for us then," answered Katie writing notes and times on her clipboard. She could no more careful than if she was logging figures in a business account.

Jimmy was supposed to run the 200 meters. However, Thorpe did not want him blasting off in this relatively cool, damp weather, and had him scratched. "Too risky for sprinters," thought he, so after scratching Jimmy from the event, then found Greg readying for his race. "You're going to have to strike out on your own pace. Lets shoot for ten minutes so be about 72, 73, the first lap and get into your rhythm." Thorpe then departed the bleachers to find his 1600 relay foursome and proceeded back to the stands. He would watch this race from the bleachers.

While waiting for Greg's race, Jimmy and Kasper were sitting and stretching on the grass, continuing an earlier conversation they had engaged in that morning. Kasper had queried Jimmy and reflected his concerns of this Bill Sweigert situation. Bill attended classes at the career center with Jimmy. Therefore, Jimmy knew him well. Kasper's confidence with Jimmy was a correct one as Jimmy relayed in his vociferous, insensitive, fun making manner, about what was going on.

"The dudes' weird," Jimmy revealed. "He claims he is in the import-export business with a friend in Germany, selling souvenir items like collector spoons, glassware, plates, with German art on it. You know, stuff you buy in little gift shops at truck stops along an interstate."

"He ever show you any items, he sells?

"Sure have!" Retorted Jimmy, "One time he showed us a small wooden case with a set of little fancy spoons. Looked expensive to me but I wouldn't know about stuff like that. It could be like cheap cosmetic jewelry," admitted the boy.

"So, he does get stuff from someone?"

"Yep, other kids said he's shown them things too."

'Where does he sell this stuff?"

"Well, he always claims he has got buyers in the city and up in Cleveland and other big cities. People around here won't pay his price so he doesn't sell much around here."

"What about Nazi stuff?"

"Ah, I haven't heard or seen any evidence of anything like that."

"Well," Suggested Kasper, "some people would presume such since he's getting stuff from Germany. Is he a gang member?"

"Naw, he's too much of a gick! Man, I am glad you told me this. Everybody wondered where he got all this crap from…so he has somebody in Germany sending him this stuff, wow! He must think he's big time."

Jimmy laughed. "Yea old Bill thinks he's a big man about town."

"Why haven't I heard anything in school?"

"Like I said," Jimmy interrupted, "the kids around here don't have money for that stuff and like I said, he goes to the Cleveland area for his dealing…that is where he is going on the weekends…his contacts are there as well. Some of them have shops that he supplies with his merchandise."

"Blam!" Jimmy and Kasper were startled. Alex's 3200-meter run was off with the blast. Kasper and Jimmy got up to observe from the fence facing the middle of the backstretch.

Greg moved to the lead on the backstretch where he heard commands from Kasper, Jimmy, and other team members. "Come on Greg, dominate!"

Indeed Greg complied, as this was a 'weak' field. As his brother disappeared around the second turn, Kasper took up where they had left off in their conversation.

"Jimmy I wouldn't expect for you to know this, but in Germany it's against the law to be dissimulating Nazis paraphernalia."

"Don't they have freedom of speech and all, like us?" Jimmy answered looking surprised.

"Not for Nazis material, they don't. And since he's using the mail the FBI would get involved, this is some serious stuff Jimmy."

"Far out!" exclaimed the boy, "but, like I said. I haven't heard anything dealing with that sort of stuff unless he's hiding that aspect of the business."

"Well, his Great granduncle who has been visiting over here from Germany for some time. I was called over to meet with him; he thinks Bill is dealing in some unscrupulous activities," said Kasper disturbed the more he thinks of the affair, "Mrs. Sweigert is fine people. She took Bill in from his slothful mom, how dare he bring in such an egregious behavior into her home."

"She doesn't need to be dealing with his nonsense," Jimmy answered, "That's for sure."

"Looking good Greg," Kasper said directing his attention to his young brother as he passed the pack behind comfortably. "Keep your rotation long and smooth."

"Yea, way too go, Greg," Jimmy added.

"Well, what we need to do is put a crimp in his escapades. Lets think about this a while and decide how to best handle this."

"Agreed"

Their attention turned to Greg and the race.

"4:53," announced Katie as Greg passed 1600 meters. The second place runner appeared sixty meters behind. The fifth lap is where the adrenaline wore off. The sixth lap he pressed. The seventh lap he gradually tried to increase his tempo. The final lap Greg thoughts were inspirational as he sped along. "...Indeed we count them blessed who endure...He is compassionate and merciful...tiring rapidly, Greg's thoughts demanded an unrelenting pace. He was running harder as if he was running neck and neck with someone. "Push, push, don't let up." He was actually getting delirious. Finally, the finish line was in focus.

"All the way in Greg!"

"You can break ten, dude...power it in now!"

His arms flaring, legs wobbly he crossed his threshold.

"10:04!"

"Way to go! He's just a freshman!" Katie disclosed to nearby spectators.

Greg exhausted stepped to the inside grass area bent over bracing himself on his knees with his arms. Greg panted and panted, "That was the hardest thing I ever did in my life!" said he to himself.

CHAPTER 5

▼

Late Sunday it was. Kasper Wise listened to 'Brahms Violin Concerto,' as he dressed for a long run through the park and around the lake. He mimicked being the conductor for several minutes, arms waving as if he held a baton directing an orchestra. Very well practiced at this he thought of himself as being 'pretty good'. As Brahms entered the final movement Kasper's heartbeat increases, his breathing intensified. He kept pace with the emotions of the music and allowed himself to wind down with it.

After the finale, he was ready for his training run with Brahms music captured in his mind like a CD repeating itself. He strode swiftly from the house, then across a grassy meadow. Dandelions were everywhere, other weeds blossomed as well; all made a beautiful sight, however, these seeding brought out bees, butter-flies, wasps, and all species of bug it seemed that wanted to buzz the boy's head or fly into his eyes. He swatted at them and continued his way. Intercepting a small bike path, Kasper continued along this trail, which circulated Crimshead Lake. It would take him several miles to return to this point. Brahms was in a slow move-ment now, so Kasper slowed and floated effortlessly. Thursday, he had something to prove to himself, and he wanted to punch a hole into the skeptic's views of his ability. The coaches at Marlborough and other big schools think they know who the stars are around this county…we're going to put an end to the 'trash talking' when we're done…got to PR big though…finally I've got to get in the four-twenties…"

Kasper left the path and ran across a pick-nick area weaving through the tables and grills. Not conscience of the people in these areas, he drove himself to the rhythm of the beat in his head. Running alone had no comparison that could match its serenity, he felt. Withdrawn to himself, he allowed his imagination to roam freely.

In Kasper's mind, he was onto a couple Kenyans. Riding their rears, he was. They tried to run away from him, but Kasper would have none of that. He kept pace with the pair. In reality, he had to cross a park area less than two miles out from home. Brahms concerto was subsiding, as was Kasper's energy reserves. Now he just had a desire to finish. The Kenyans were gone. The violin in his mind was playing vigorously. Kasper desperately held his turn over rate. Less than a quarter mile from his finish area, a table at the park edge his mind held steady the high momentum of the Brahms concerto movement. Then the music finale and Kasper leaned back and allowed him to slow until he stopped exactly at the table. Drenched in perspiration, chest heaving in and out, he climbed the table, sat on the top with his feet on the long wooden seats.

In Kasper's fatigued mind, he thought of how difficult running was. He thought of the physics scholarship then his family's lack of financial means. He wondered about his increasing interest in girls but because of his selective burdens, he could not get off the ground with any romantic notions. With these thoughts, Kasper allowed himself the privilege of walking the short distance to his home. He was glad he had run alone and that no one was at home on his return.

"I will use these pursuits and trials to learn to withstand tenaciously the pressures until it is removed at that appointed instance in the future." The he finalized his thoughts.

"Arbeit, wenn es mich nicht tötet wird es mich besser machen (Work, if it does not kill me it shall make me better)!"

Kasper had a hard run yesterday." Thorpe announced. "Now I don't know what the rest of you did, but I shall tell you today will be hard…we rest Tuesday and Wednesday." After that introduction, he sent Jimmy and Ray off to practice starts for the 100 meters and hurdles, equally instructive in reminding them of the 200-meter curve running Jimmy needed to work on.

Katie was set up to log the times of Sheila and the distance runners. They were to complete twenty 400s at 70 seconds, jog 400 meters between; then walk 400 meters and complete eight 200s at 32 seconds. Sheila was to stay at 76 and 35 seconds for her runs. She was restricted to just ten and five repeats respectively.

Eli did not like the 400-meter workout at all. He felt repeat 400s were too strenuous and would hurt his speed. "We ought to be doing just 200's," he said to Terry in a low voice as the runners made their way to the track after calisthenics and stretching.

"Let's get on with it troops," Thorpe called out, "last workout!"

They spread-out as they approached the start then lunched forward. Katie snapped the stopwatch as they crossed the start line and streamed around the first turn.

For the next hour and a half an observer would hear a steady, consistent, barking of times, "69, 70…73…too fast Sheila!…" A pause would occur, then again…"69, 70…75, 76…" This went on throughout the session. "Eight to go…Rotate, faster, bring the arms up more, pump…watch the lanes…head down…keep your head level and steady…arms should come up to eye level…" Jimmy and both girls and boys sprinters were receiving their orders.

Shouts, orders, and suggestions changed somewhat as the session progressed. One could hear: "…30, 31, 32, 34, 35, okay Sheila…a little fast guys." After a short time lapse, "looking good…31, 32, 36…good job!…Three more to go!"

Struggling, panting, and heavy exhales began ceasing at the conclusion of these series of runs until it was almost too quite. The figures gathered amongst themselves. There was hardly a whisper except among the coaches. With the workouts coming to completion, the athletes began gathering in the bleachers along with some who had been in the weight room. They grouped to satisfy Thorpe who had to issue his concerns and aspirations for the coming Marlborough track and field meet.

Once everyone had gathered on the bleachers some still sweating, some wiping themselves with towels, others stretching, a few bandaging legs and feet. Thorpe proceeded with his presentation.

Kasper detected a concern on his coaches' face. "Mehr Stürme lauern immer nur über hinaus den Horizont mit Thorpe (More storms are always lurking just beyond the horizon with Thorpe)," he thought.

"I'm pleased with the output I witnessed this afternoon. People were focused and concentrating. Runners were making the splits. However, you have to maintain this preparation level the next couple of days. Otherwise, you loose that mental edge and you shall fall off your expectations you have set for yourself. Do not allow your personal trials to fog what you have set for yourself Thursday. The mediocre allows any and everything to interfere with the tasks before them. People you must realize that everyone has some obstacle that maybe blocking the visions you want to realize whether it is in sports or the everyday world. Realize kids that every trial becomes a test of your faith. If you respond wrongly, your burdens shall muddle everything leaving you with the feeling that you must carryout some desperate action to recover. Team, you should never allow yourself to become desperate. You endanger yourself and maybe others when your emotions are out of control and you are mistake prone. So let us continue to be meticulous in our preparation, unwavering in faith, stoic in our determination, dismissed!"

"Next problem," Kasper gasped. This physics test was his most challenging ever. The first three problems were rigorous, but he was sure he got the correct answers. No one else accompanied Kasper doing the exam he was the only student taking physics for college credit at the small school. Kasper read to himself:

"For a simple harmonic oscillator with a mass of 1.5 kilogram, and the length of the arm is 1 meter. While its amplitude of the swing, A, is 10 centimeters. Calculate its (a) frequency of vibration, (b) find the restoring force constant, (c) find the energy of the oscillations, and (d) calculate the quantum number.

"First, I know the period, T, of a harmonic oscillator is: The square root of, the length of the pendulum, L, divided by the force of gravity g, times 2 pie, π." Thus, he began to write:

$$T = 2\pi\sqrt{L/g}$$

"Now L =1.0m, and g = 9.8m/s^2 then with substitution....I get." With a calculator Kasper arrived at

$$T = 0.64 \text{ seconds}$$

"The frequency ν is the reciprocal of the period, T.

$$\nu = 1/T = 1/0.64s = 1.56/s = 1.56 \text{ Hertz}$$

"The force constant, C in terms of the classical oscillation frequency is

$$\nu = 1/2\pi\sqrt{C/m}$$

Kasper had to look this relationship up in his notes.

"After plugging in frequency, and solving for C, I get...

$$1.56/s = 1/2\pi\sqrt{C/m}$$

$$9.80/s = \sqrt{C/m}$$

"Square both sides,

$$96/s^2 = C/m$$

"And m = 1.5 kg, solving for C, I get,

$$C = 144 \text{ kg}/s^2$$

"For the force constant," Kasper had to spend some moments flipping pages in his notes to find the energy relationship for the simple oscillator. "Ah! It is, directly related, to half the amplitude squared with force constant….

$$E = 1/2 \ C \ A^2 \text{...ok, A is given and I've figured out C, so...}$$ He worked out,

$$E = 1/2 \ (144) \ (0.1)$$

$$E = 0.72 \text{ joules}$$

"0.72 joules is the energy of the swings, now the quantum number n, I can find from the quantum number relationship with atomic energy levels in an atom. That is:

$$E_n = (n + 1) \ h\nu$$

"I just found the energy; and Planck's constant, h, I know. I figured the frequency, ν already, so

$$0.72 = (n+1)6.64\text{x}10^{-34} \ (1.56)$$

$$n + 1 = 0.72 \ / \ 10.36\text{x}10^{-34}$$

"Simplifying and solving for n, gives

$$n = 7 \text{ x } 10^{32}$$

"n, equals approximately 7 x 10^{32}…this discreteness in the energy levels can not be detectable in this macroscopic device." Kasper concluded. "So for large objects we ignore the quantum nature of matter. Only at the microscopic level is the quantum number significant." He was not surprised at these results.

Kasper checked the time he had about forty-five minutes before school is out. "Last problem," he read: 'What is the speed of an electron which has a total energy of 1 million electron volts, 1 Mev?'

"This is easy," thought Kasper. Then he proceeded, to write:

"The total energy, E of a relativistic particle is given as: $E = \gamma m_o c^2$

"Solving for gamma, γ and then looking up the rest mass of an electron, m_o, in a table of constants. He then substituted for the given energy, $E = 1$ Mev = 1×10^6 eV, we get

$\gamma = E/m_o c^2$

$\gamma = 1 \times 10^6 eV/(9/11 \times 10^{-31})(3 \times 10^8)^2$

$\gamma = 1 \times 10^6 eV/82 \times 10^{-15} J$

"Got to convert electron volts to joules, since γ is unit less

$1 \times 10^6 ev$ (1.6×10^{-19} joules/1ev) = 1.6×10^{-13} joules

$\gamma = 1.6 \times 10^{-13} J/82 \times 10^{-15} J$

$\gamma = 1.95$

"Finally, since gamma, γ by definition is

$\gamma = 1/\sqrt{1 - vv/cc}$

"I can substitute for, γ and solve for v^2/c^2....I arrive at...
"After squaring both sides

$\gamma^2 = 1/(1 - v^2/c^2)$

$3.80 = 1/(1 - v^2/c^2)$

$3.80 - 3.80 v^2/c^2 = 1$

$-3.80 v^2/c^2 = -2.80$

"Dividing by -3.80 we get,

$v^2/c^2 = 0.737$

"And v equals

$v = 0.86c$."

"So the velocity of the electron is eighty-six percent of the speed of light or $0.86(3 \times 10^8$ m/s) = 2.58×10^8 meters per second." He felt good. "My answers were reasonable and I showed the calculations."

Kasper gathered his material dropped his test in the receiving bin and started for home. "But first I better drop by the Sweigert's and let Herr Johannes know what I've found out about Bill." He thought. "I don't want anybody bugging me about anything till Thursday night at least."

"Marlborough," exclaimed Kasper as the bus pulled into the large parking lot, after the short drive from Lakeport to this campus, "this is where I saw my first track meet. Coach Larsons had me helping at the long jump pit."

"His reputation is that of a real mean football coach," reminded Danny, "you like him?"

"Yea, he actually, made me go out for wrestling. That's how I started running. We had to run around the gym during the winter, lap after lap," reminisced the boy in a fond deliverance.

"I was at the middle school," responded an unimpressed Eli as the team streamed off the bus, "everything was pretty boring there, but now let's go beat up on 'em." Then Eli departed with his gear unconcerned with any history. Kasper held some animosity for the place, as this was an environment where one fell in line with one's proper social ethnic clan. The expectation was required as much from the kids themselves. Lunchtime made the groupings all apparent. Just scan the cafeteria once; and without any doubts, the labels assigned would be appropriate and quite accurate. He would like to make a point that all the social jostling is unnecessary and more so it was unproductive toward an education environment.

"Wait until they see our little mixed group, whoop-up on them," predicted Kasper.

"Last call for the 110 meter high hurdles," Blared the announcer over the stadium intercom. Jimmy Luke was flexing, stretching, a very serious countenance scouring his face at the start line. In the bleachers sat the Principal of Lakeport high, Mr. Stromberg, sitting next to Katie with his wife. Next to her was Thorpe's wife, Glenda. The Luke boy was paying no attention to the crowded stadium complex. Occasionally he would stare down the track. Then from the start blocks, he would suddenly blast out and complete three hurdles and pull-up quickly. Then he would return to his start block. After three such warm-up runs, Jimmy placed himself in his blocks and readied for the starters beckoning. Other participants were simulating their runs as well, but all ignored each other, as the ten obstacles in each of their lanes demanded the focus of their attention.

"The milers should be warming up now as well, shouldn't they?" asked Principal Stromberg.

"Yes Sir," answered Katie. "After the hurdles there's the 100 meter dash then the 1600 meter girls and 1600 meter boys."

"I've seen the team doing some wicked workouts," Mr. Stromberg revealed. "I don't expect anyone to handle Jimmy but how are the distance people are stacked-up?"

"This is so exciting," said Patricia Stromberg, the wife.

"They're going to be awesome you'll see. And Sheila is going to drop some time off her best 1600 meters today as well."

"I do not doubt it," commented Patricia, "she training with the boys and all."

"Guns up!" warned Glenda as not everyone had been paying attention for the race about to start and before anyone could hardly prepare.

"Bang!" Jimmy had the first leg over a hurdle then his head dipping only so slightly as his left leg was reaching over the next hurdle. With this cadence, he quickly added distance between himself and the seven other to his left and right.

"Beautiful rhythm, Jimmy!" admired Mr. Stromberg.

At the eighth hurdle, the second closest was just climbing the seventh hurdle.

"Jimmy's clicking!" exclaimed Katie.

However, approaching number nine Jimmy was moving too close so he chopped his stride slightly, clipped the top of hurdle nine, as he was unable to clear its top. This positioned him off balance a bit and off stride as he posed for number ten, which he struck with his lead leg knocking him further off balance and almost out of his lane. Straightening, Jimmy closed out the remaining meters to the finish.

"14.25." Katie announced.

"He got a little wobbly the last two," said Mr. Stromberg smiling nevertheless. The others were not yet over number ten when Jimmy finished.

"More like, he dodged a bullet," quipped Katie closing her pad.

"Yea, he'll get under 14 by tournament time, considering the hits he took on that run," said a knowledgeable fan sitting nearby.

Jimmy strutted among the line officials and the other athletes. His body language emulated some coyness. He knew he blew a great time because of the last two hurdles.

"He certainly dominates division three," remarked Mr. Stromberg. "Division one will fair no better with Jimmy," said Glenda Thorpe in a matter of fact manner. She took out a video camera. "I should have taped that race. Now, if you will have the goodness to open that bag over there for me Katie so I can load the film in this thing. I'll tape the girls and boys mile races. I'm ready for them now."

At this moment, Beth and Jayce Wise were climbing up the aisle of the stands heading toward the contingence of Lakeport supporters.

"Mr. Wise." Glenda Thorpe called out motioning an arm directing them their way. "Over here." She motioned again.

"Let me introduce you," Mrs. Thorpe said, "Mr. and Mrs. Stromberg, Mr. and Mrs. Wise."

"Glad to see you, squeeze in. This place is packing in real fast," said Principal Stromberg.

The pair took seats on the narrow bleachers armed with a pair of binoculars and a camera, Jayce and Beth sat themselves amongst the group.

"I was scared we would miss the mile," Beth remarked.

"We're ok; looks like half the county's here," Jayce said, scanning the bleachers.

"I never been to a track meet this crowded before." He commented again.

"What's going on here is more than just a track meet. They have activities like at football homecomings," disclosed Patricia Stromberg. "Past graduates are invited. They have a queen selected and a court from each school participating today." She paused, "and there are activities for the small kids as well in the Civic Center and Lewis Park."

While this dialog was going on, the girls' hurdles was completed and the boys and girls' 100 meters were under way. Principal Stromberg and Patricia left to greet other school principles and spouses. The gathering hummed with conversations. People enjoyed their reunion as much as any activity. Warm with a bit of breeze, nearly everyone dressed in shorts and light colorful clothing for the events. Every who was somebody was there and it would seem, they had to be there, or else. Their absence observed; people would talk about them:

"Yea, Thomshack's safe...if Bates was going to try for the school board, she ought to be feeling things out...she don't have the energy for the job...she can't even get out here!...We got an eight o'clock tee off time George, don't be sand bagging me now...Sally Truex going to Holly Cross, we reserved the Wolf House for the graduation party...Closed that deal, yea having the closing Saturday...they in a bad situation won't see them until things blow over...rumors are his contract will not be renewed...but he doesn't care I got good information that he's into that development deal in Lancaster..."

"Hey, is that Jimmy?" Patricia asked, back from her social excursions with her husband.

"Yep, that's him."

"He's running the 100, too?"

"Our team is small," answered Katie. "Everybody has to double up particularly our distance guys. Jimmy can enter four running events in competition such as we have here. He can run the 110 hurdles, the 400, 200, and the four by 400."

"The 110 hurdles and the 400 meters are Jimmy's thing," submitted Jayce Wise. "He's the man in the 400 and he'll cap off the meet with his leg of the relay."

"Yea, but the biggest thing about Jimmy is keeping him out of trouble and keeping his grades up," said Principal Stromberg. "It helps that he's focused about driving tanks in the army, but more effective is his being around your boys Mr. Wise, who are so serious and has high goals in academics."

The Wises gleamed proudly with the comment.

"I think Jimmy's going to be responsible this year," interrupted Glenda, "he's excited about the school winning the state meet since he has help from the distance crew. Last year we had no distance runners at all."

"Well on the books, no one should come close to us, but the tough part of the season is before us." Principal Stromberg added.

"Guns up!" Someone warned.

"Blam!"

Jimmy in lane four moved out like a shot from a cannon. His powerful legs reached to the outside of his lane, but eventually moved to the center as he straighten-up from the crouch position. Arms pumping at 20 meters he was two strides ahead of the field. At 50 meters, he was still pressing and accelerating, at 60 meters acceleration his ceased and he just floated, relaxed.

Tommy Sikes, of Lubbuck, a division one school was two strides in arrears of Jimmy. Hank Sizemore was in lane two a further stride behind. However, it was Mr. Football Ohio, Thad Brownel, of Roseville, who was closing. Slow out of the blocks, he cut to three strides then two, but had no more room to close. Brownel was one-half stride away when Jimmy stopped the watches.

"10.9!" Katie exclaimed, unmoved, "he just held that guy off."

"At division one state level they'll go 10.8 and under." Jayce reminded them. "And that's automatic timing."

"Is there much a difference?" asked Principal Stromberg.

"About two tenths of a second difference," explained Jayce, "In hand timing, timers start their stopwatch with the smoke of the gun. In auto-timing, the timing starts when the pistol fires. The watches are connected electrically to the gun."

"So hand-timing is at best about two-tenths faster than auto-timing. Is that right?"

"Yes sir. So Jimmy's 10.9 would be about 11.1 with auto-timing."

"Last call for the girls 1600 meters run," blasted the stadium intercom.

"It's been hard for Sheila running with the guys," Katie disclosed, "but the first benefits we may see today."

On the opposite side of the stadium and near the bordering fence of the track, Coach Thorpe stood stopwatch in hand waiting for Sheila's race. He would scream orders to her as she passed by. Inside the track, activity was still buzzing about the 100 meters. Mr. Football was upset. "My hamstring is not fully healed…I didn't know about this Jimmy dude…otherwise, I would have been ready for him…I had to go easy out of the blocks…" He went on with excuses and started in with some 'trash talking' about next time he get hold of Jimmy. Indeed the big schools, thought of this gathering was just a tune-up meet before their serious schedule. They were unsuspecting of small school penetrating and snatching away points from their events.

Weather was good. Temperature was in the upper sixties, slight wind only.

A great day for the distance runners, although sprinters preferred warmer weather still lessening the chance of pulling or straining a muscle. Kasper and Danny were warming-up for the 1600 meters. They usually started jogging one hour before race time. After the jog, stretching would follow a few calisthenics and more stretching.

Kasper was not confident of his speed in a fast finish. He felt threatened not only from Danny but to a couple others as well. He began to doubt his hard work would bare him above his competitors. Then as quickly, Kasper recessed himself. "What am I thinking about? I will attack boldly. Maybe this tactic will cause consternation. It may even rattle Danny. I must hold on and be confident and steadfast to this end."

"The girls are about to start," someone said.

"Bang!"

From their seats, people could see a wall of runners on the near horizon sweeping around the far turn of the track. Only a few bobbing heads could be seen from Kasper's vantage point because of the infield crowd of pole-vaulters, high jumpers, and officials moving about. As they entered the second turn, he could see the unobstructed view of the pack.

"Sheila's fourth." Danny observed.

The pack of over twenty girls passed next to the boys warming up next to the 100- start area. Up in the stands Katie had a clear view of the runners as they approached the completion of the first lap.

"72, 73, 74…" Katie read-off the times, "74 for Sheila." The girl slipped past the front galley, more fluid and light of foot then ever seen of her before, such that it defied the quick pace.

"Is that fast?" asked Zoe, Katie's little sister plopped beside her and sucking a large popsicle. Zoe, ten years old, blondish, skinny, and chatty; she donned a cap like her sister while insisting on helping log in the times and taking water to the team members where needed.

"She's going pretty fast, sis," said the little girl.

Strolling with confidence Sheila made as if she was following her troop of fellows at workouts. "These girls behind me can't be tougher than the guys….I heard about 74 when I passed the 400…felt more like 77or 79." She tried to relax.

"Come on Trudy," said someone on the sidelines of the backstretch. Trudy was game. She pulled right up behind Sheila. A short girl in dark red and blue uniform built more like a gymnast, Trudy had all the toughness of any aggressive tumbler.

"Where's any supporters…" Sheila thought a bit rattled. Everyone was supposed to fall back but not this girl Trudy. She was stalking Sheila's heels. As Sheila and Trudy moved through the second turn, the crowd buzzed with supportive cries.

"Float it Sheila," she heard from the group Kasper and Danny amongst them at the end of the turn.

"This is so hard not letting up from the pace," Sheila said resigned to hold her rhythm.

She moved into lap three, after hearing 2:35 at the 800 meters. With Trudy, almost striking her heels with her toes so close was she was to Sheila.

"I better slow, I am not going to run myself in and have her milk off me," thought Sheila. "I'll keep slowing and see what she does. If she follows I'll wait till the last fifty meters, then turn on my speed…the speed and strength I gained by running with the guys."

Her tactic she hoped would enable a victory to evolve in this race. She cared the less about the time.

Up in the stands the slacking pace was apparent. "Sheila's losing confidence. She should keep pressing. Why is she slowing with that little blond tagging on?"

Katie timed 3:55 at the gun lap. All the boys watched with anticipation as the runners filed into that last 400 meters, "Sheila will turn it on at the turn here," said Kasper.

"She'd better," commented Danny.

On the final backstretch Trudy decided Sheila was a lost cause for a finish that would give her the record time she sort in this race. Therefore, the girl accelerated past Sheila. With the rapid turn over of her short legs and quick arm rotation, Sheila lost three meters before responding.

"Got to close, before the turn," said she. It was then she felt another body pulling up to her from behind.

"Pass her! You can do it Wendy!" yelled someone.

"Stick with her Pam!" yelled another voice.

Now realizing two new figures had pulled up behind her, Sheila's emotions flared in spite of her fatigued state.

"All that running with the guys and now everybody's trying to pass me."

Sheila pulled up behind Trudy with a Pam and a Wendy in tow. As they ran the final turn, the gathering of 1600 meters boy runners started screaming for their respective team female counterparts to make their final move to the finish.

"Come on Sheila," Kasper and Danny yelled in unison, "where is that kick?"

Streaming into the final straight Sheila allowed the turn's centripetal force to fling her to lane two. The girls had their backs to the galley of boys now. However, Katie could see Sheila lift. The arms rotated up to her eyes, the knees reached to her waistline. At sixty meters out from the finish, Sheila was even with the lithe girl. Then with every stride, she pulled forward on her rival. Pam and Wendy running shoulder-to-shoulder were unable to accelerate with the duo ahead.

Kasper and Danny could only see the backs of the girls from their vantage point so could not tell whether Sheila was in the lead or not. However, Katie observed about four meters of space between Trudy and Sheila as they crossed the finish.

"Wow! That a girl!" Katie screamed barely audible in the frenzy of fans equally vocalizing their feeling.

"Did she break a record?" asked Zoe. The crowd was now clapping and applauding the competitors as they streamed to the finish and strode exhausted to the infield. Some of the girls required assistance. A couple stumbled as they came to a halt.

"5:12.2," Katie said, "Yes Zoe, she broke the record."

"She can go faster," commented Principal Stromberg, "She got serious that last half lap."

"Katie looked like a gazelle on the stretch," Jayce says smiling.

"Oh, she did not look any such thing," said Beth with a sour face looking at her husband, feeling sorry for the strenuous effort the girl had to make over the last meters.

While the bleacher crowd and sidelines buzzed with activity, the officials brought the band of 1600-meter boys to the start area. The cycle of anticipation, excitement, and anxiety took grip of the galley of people and team members readying themselves for another rise and fall of their already battered emotions.

Jayce looked down upon his son and nephew as they took their positions in the staggered lanes. Confident of their training and preparation nevertheless his upbeat outward demeanor was a façade for his fearful, nakedness. He almost wished he had announced no predictions toward any of these outcomes. Such was his fear he was reflective and thought of a biblical passage:

'Let everyman be swift to hear, slow to speak, slow to wrath...'

Jayce rubbed his eyes and took deep breaths to relax waiting for the start. He did not wait long.

"Bam!" The pack of bobbing heads struck off into the first turn with an aggression that made one feels as if this is the start of a much shorter race.

"Hey I see Coach Thorpe over there...see him about midway on the fence," said Katie.

"Yea I see him," answered Principal Stromberg.

"Come on Kasper, Danny," Beth Wise called out.

"They're all filing out behind him," said Glenda Thorpe as she peered through the sights of the video camera.

"Kasper and Danny are so small," observed Patricia Stromberg concerned.

"This is going to be the fastest first lap for Kasper, I think," said Katie glancing at her stopwatch and set her sights on the race.

"Run the race fast! Kasper! Danny!" yelled little Zoe shooting her arms over her head.

"61, 62, 63...63...for Kasper and Danny," Katie called out times.

"But three other guys are following right on their heels," said Jayce.

On the backstretch, Kasper looked relaxed, never before had he paced out and continued to maintain the effort into the second lap.

"This is going to be a PR for both."

Coach Thorpe was leaning over the top of the fence and shouting toward his boys as they sped by him. Kasper, Danny still unrelenting in pace. The followers let loose of the invisible twin holding them to Danny's back.

"They're flying," said Jayce, "they're going for a big one."

"2:10, 2:11, 2:12…"

"Concentrate you guys, work this third lap."

A gap of five meters separated Danny from a Logansville runner and a kid from Fremont.

"Kasper had better keep it up. Those two guys behind have beaten 4:30."

Behind these four, the next competitor was some ten meters back and slipping farther behind. The stadium audience was busy with their common attics of bellowing directions, orders, and encouragements while a few competitors received scolding.

"Hey isn't that the kid who used to go here?" Someone was asking.

"Yea, that's the Kasper kid," answered another voice.

Then some conversation issued that was inaudible to the ears of Lakeport supporters because the noise level increased as Kasper started into the final lap.

"3:19, 3:20…"

"Great split," said Katie. Everyone else remained silent having questioning how the pair would be able to handle this last lap.

As they completed the turn, Kasper's arms started reaching higher and he moved ever so slightly away from Danny. The two following had no change of tempo.

"Kasper's trying," Katie, exclaimed, "but Danny always out kicks him!"

"They're going into the final turn. Kasper is still holding out," said Jayce hoping his son would beat his cousin Danny for a change.

"Look at that move!"

"The guy in second is closing!"

Everybody in the bleachers was standing, yelling, calling out names of their favorites. Clapping started increasing as the final meters.

"I don't think he's going to catch 'em."

"Good Job!"

"Alright, one, two, for Lakeport," announced Beth clapping with the others.

As the runners flowed across the finish, slowly, the crowd ceased the applause and they sat down once again.

"I got it all," exclaimed Glenda Thorpe checking her video camera.

"What was the time, Katie?"

"4:23, 4:24," said the girl.

"Yea! That's what I got…4:23.3." Jayce reaffirmed.

"Kasper held him off this time," added Katie.

"What happened of he went out real fast. Danny didn't have that turnover over those final meters because of the fast pace," explained Jayce.

"They're both fine athletes and scholars," Principal Stromberg interjected, "they both have a great future ahead of them."

Beth Wise smiled delighted. "That was so exciting my little Kasper beating all those good guys."

Zoe chuckled heartily. "They left everybody way behind," said she. "I want Mr. Thorpe to be my coach when I get in high school…Sheila won the girls race too!"

Down on the field Thorpe collared his victors. "That was some brave running boys. That's how you just man-handle an affair when you have too."

"Kasper got me today," said Danny, "dude you set a mean pace."

"I was running scared. I didn't want to end up fourth," said the winner.

"Precisely the correct tactic to use," said Thorpe.

"Ok, now go and get Eli and Terry pumped up. I know you don't have to pump Jimmy up." He patted the pair on the back and then headed toward the Lakeport contingence in the stands.

"Well, would you ever believe that," Coach Wiley Smith of Marlborough said to his assistant coach Andy Bell surmising the 1600 meters from their vantage in the stands, "we'll never hear the last of our ole boy Thorpe now."

"That Kasper last fall he couldn't break five-minutes," said Bell.

"But, look what Thorpe's doing," said Wiley. "He's over training those boys. They won't be around long, mark my word. I've been coaching for thirty-five years, every once in while some coach comes along demanding eighty, ninety miles a week of his boys. Thorpe's doing will tear them apart. They will be plagued with injuries and emotionally ripped apart. When they find they are not steadily improving…Yea, he is going to break records, which will make him look good. But the kids, even if they make college somewhere they'll be fortunate to improve, if at all."

"Yea, all that mileage then in college the mileage will increase," added Bell.

"That Kasper does not have much natural ability. If he did he would be running 4:10 from the work he's doing."

"You know he's had those guys over here on our track doing hours of quarters and stuff."

"I guess we can give 'em credit for hard work. I understand they train like slaves."

"That's a bad word you used coach, slave," warned Bell grinning.

"Opps," he said, "gotta watch, that's politically incorrect, alright."

They both had a hearty chuckle. "I think we're seeing these guys at their peaks right now," continued Wiley. "Ole Jimmy Luke is running his behind off. Now he's got as much talent as any hillbilly ever had," another hearty laugh.

"But, they won't keep him eligible or out of trouble for long."

"Ain't that the truth! He needs to run that fast to stay in front of the authorities!" Chuckle, chuckle, continued the two.

"Speaking of the devil," interrupted Bell, "here come the 400 meter runners and the famous Luke boy, now."

With a gasp some onlookers riled at the sight of the muscular, Thad Brownel, Mr. Football Ohio as he nears the starting lanes. As he paused, he shacks his legs more as to display his might than to relax. His wide shoulders and stance enveloped the entire lane. Imposing a demeanor suggesting why anyone would bother to make the starting line with such as him aboard.

"Come on Jimmy!" some coaxing from the crowd. Mr. Football's eyes rolled toward the bleachers as to say, 'How dare you'.

Indeed Jimmy Luke pranced backward and forward in his lane, not the least nervous, but a show of confidence. He seemed to be enjoying himself. This was not Thorpe's idea of a good time. Thorpe wanted a victory over this cocky fellow. It would give him the attention and prestige as a track coach, that otherwise would be long coming. After eight years as assistant at Marlborough, Wiley Smith demoted Thorpe, reassigning him to coach the junior varsity upon the arrival of former 800 meters star and alumni, Andy Bell.

Thorpe short, paunchy, with big eyeglasses was a second string footballer at his small high school at a country school in the southeast hills of Ohio. He never clicked as one of the boys among the coaches at Marlborough. The reason he got a job there was the 'quest for inclusiveness' of some sort of fellow as Thorpe. Marlborough relished their reputation as being some kind, of a 'snobbish' institution. It required only a short time there for Thorpe to realize this condescendence permeating from most staff.

"Runners set!" commanded the announcer on the public address system. Everyone interested zeroed-out their stopwatches as others aimed cameras and video cameras in the direction of the 'principles' on the track and the field spread out before them.

"Bam!"

Mr. Football wasted no effort in bending himself in a fit around the start turn. Ungainly, but powerfully he stepped high in his cadence and curved his body to the left to get to the backstretch where he would be more comfortable. To the contrast, Jimmy appeared comfortable, smooth, and turning over rapidly in his effort. Thus, he negotiated the curved distance with his main rival and settled into the backstretch having lost no ground to his main rival. From his trailing stagger start, Mr. Football took aim of Jimmy who was to his outside. He closed all the stagger distance by the end of the straight. Into the turn, Thad continued to add meters between he and Jimmy.

"Come on Jimmy!" Jayce called out, "…Jimmy runs a mean turn! Look how he's slowing in the turn…See Jimmy, he's still rotating…no let-up…haaa, huh…they're coming out of the turn." The stadium was in bedlam, now.

"Jimmy' back a little," said the principal barely audible.

"Now we see who's got the arms," announced Jayce smiling broadly, "…Jimmy's pumping high look at Thad's legs flaring out…Who's got the arms?" People screamed toward the pair.

"Jimmy's pulling ahead," said Katie.

"Go! Jimmy, go!" screamed Zoe her arms pumping up and down trying to peer through the thong of adults masking her view of the finish.

"Do it, dude!" Do it!" Jayce signed off as Jimmy crossed the finish four strides up on Sir Brownel.

"48.2!" announced Katie, "school record!" Zoe grabbed and hugged her sister. All the men and women settled into conversation about the recent scene. Everyone disclosed his or her interpretation of the action.

On the infield Sally Tomshack, sportswriter of the Lakeport Lake News interviewed Jimmy surrounded by competitors, coaches, and officials.

"So what'd you think, about beating Mr. Football Ohio? Your plans worked out just right, huh?"

"Plans?" Jimmy looked at Sally perplexed. "I ain't ever planned anything in my life, I 'm not that clever! Sure I figured a win," Jimmy added with arrogance, "didn't see why I shouldn't win. This ain't no football game and he wasn't carrying a pigskin…I wasn't impressed the least."

"You sure got a lot of confidence. Brownel looked shocked," replied Sally.

"Well, I know he wished he was playing football for this occasion."

Sally laughed as Jimmy strolled off. "Jimmy' doesn't recognize any short comings others may think he has. He's fearless," said she to herself.

It took some while for the stadium's fans to reduce to its equilibrium hum of activity after the discussion of the recent event. As the 300 hurdles, boys and girls got underway many took the opportunity during this long event to refresh and anticipate the remaining events.

By the time the girls 800 meters run was completed the mood of the track meet had changed to a more festive mood. A queen of these festivities and her court lovely young women representing each school participating were presented before the crowd. Several alumni of this event received honors some as far back as twenty years. A few record holders showed up. One was the mile record holder: 4:19 set back in 1972. Kasper was impressed with the two-mile record of 9:24 set that same year by another athlete.

Then there was the call for the boys 800 meters by the public address system. Eli and Terry lined up nervously in the staggered lanes. They were in the middle lanes. The pair had the second and third best times entering the event. The Lakeport duo approached each other and exchanged high-fives.

"We got to do it, dude."

"One, two," Terry said, "we can do it."

Earlier performances of Jimmy and Kasper had the pair hipped-up although with some additional anxiety. They both were surprised that Kasper and Danny went out as fast as they did in the 1600 meters. "This track is fast and we rested for this meet. We're probably faster than we think we are," Terry had said, "Hopefully we'll surprise our selves."

At the firing of the pistol, Eli went out aggressively. Staying in the staggered lanes, Terry keyed off his right through the first 300 meters. As they entered the straight and broke the staggers Eli crossed from his lane four toward lane one. Terry already to the inside surged to the lead in lane two and pulled over to the curb lane.

Eli pulled next to Terry on his right shoulder. That is how the race entered lap two.

"57!"

"Bam!"

Terry determined to finish close to his mate pushed the pace entering the turn thereby holding Eli in lane two through the curving distance. Using a bit more energy in the outer lane, Eli relaxed and slipped back a stride from Terry as they left the turn for the straight. Already three meters up on the pack of runners trailing, Terry relaxed only slightly, "Got to save something for Eli when he makes his move."

"If they finish hard both should break two-minutes," said Katie. Principal Stromberg watched intently as the women videotaped and snapped pictures of the event.

"He's going to step down on it in the stretch," said Jayce, "and Terry will stick with him."

Just before the start of the turn, Eli forced himself pass Terry then pulled over to the curb as the turn began. Terry maintained his rotation. Rounding into straight toward the finish Terry floated to the outside to lane two then started his lift. Shoulder to shoulder the pair aimed for the finish.

"They hit about 1:29 at 600 meters. They're moving," exclaimed Katie. "They should be under 2:00!"

"Haul it in boys!" demanded Jayce.

Sixty meters, fifty meters, then a surge and increased lift of the legs from Eli. This propelled him away from Terry whose head went down as he tried to rotate faster but the legs could not follow. Space grew and grew until crossing finish.

"1:58.76; 2:00.44!" Katie announced watching Zoe log the times on the clipboard.

"What an effort for Terry," said Patricia after laying her camera aside and joining in with the clapping and celebrations amongst the fans.

"I'd say he did. His missing arm has to affect his balance; he's just a great kid." Principal Stromberg reminded everyone.

"I am so happy for him, too," said Beth, "Eli had to muster all he had. Both of them are going to be hard for anyone else to beat."

"Terry doesn't need anybody's sympathy he's a tough fellow. Better athlete than most and he just proved it," explained Jayce Wise.

"He's a Luke; they're all just tough people."

"You don't have to remind me," Principal Stromberg said, "I've lived in this community all my life and the Luke's has always been of interest one way or another."

Patricia chuckled. "You can say that again. However, Jimmy is straightening out. He wants to drive tanks in the Army."

"Way to go son!" interrupted Jayce calling out and waving to Eli on the infield. Eli and Terry walked back to gather their sweats and gear. Satisfaction beamed from both.

"Oh Man! I missed breaking two minutes," said Terry to coach Thorpe on the far side of the field after he found the pair resting in the bleachers.

"You'll get it on your next outing. Both of you boys ran like you know what you were doing," said Thorpe. "Colleges will start inquiring now, but you want to stay focused and stay healthy."

"Like I've been telling him," said Eli, "Terry made the race. He went right out and held a solid gate. I never ran a race like that before. It was hard."

"He certainly did. Now boys rest up and rub down. The four by 400 meters is going to be a race. Mr. Football will be anchoring so we got to stay in contact so Jimmy can take care of business."

With those instructions, Thorpe departed looking for Jimmy. He would scratch Jimmy from the 200 meters, so the team could concentrate on a big effort for the relay race.

"Last call for the boys' 200 meter dash," announced the public address system. In the stands, Katie and Zoe had just returned after meeting with the small girls' squad on the other side of the stadium.

"Nadine got third in the high jump." Disclosed Katie to the Lakeport contingency, "and Lacy was sixth in the long jump."

"Our little school is making a fantastic effort today," said Patricia cheerfully. Everyone agreed while impatiently waiting for the 200.

"I don't see Jimmy," said Beth peering through her binoculars. She scanned the far turn where the 200 would start. She observed runners adjusting their starting blocks and making short runs. Thad Brownel's imposing figure stood out from the others.

"He's not running," said Katie, "I saw coach we're saving him for the relay."

With that announcement, the fans now relaxed and sort some refreshments and readjustment of their gentile countenances before the final display of racing.

"We just have Greg in the 3200 meter run and the relay left," Katie revealed to her sister. "Then this long affair will be over,"

Thad dominated the 200 meters. His fans and followers of his game raved at his talents: 'He'll be playing on Sunday one day!' Lakeport fans mostly ignored the event and directed their attention to the awards won and leveled praise and shared experiences amongst themselves.

Avoidably is a principal element of distancing one from tragedy and Coach Thorpe's fear of injuries, although understandable perhaps in light of the team's small number, allowed his avid use of the resort. The coach would scratch at the least provocation leaving no or little warning to his athlete and with disregard of any state of readiness that one may have. This burdened the team and was the cause of some friction particularly with Jimmy who would take issue of his decision. Published fast times of other athletes sent Thorpe into petulant despair.

For much of this track season Lakeport possessed the best times in the running events accomplished with only, eight varsity class boys. This superiority could wane, if injuries occur as times from other teams increasingly improved throughout the region. Thorpe had no misgiving, the early hard training had given his team a jump on performances but the best performances were still to be seen from the historically 'track powers' around the state.

"Guns up!" Jayce warned. "Come on Greg!" With the crack of the pistol a surge around the turn and immediately the entire field of runners, some twenty-four of them meshed into one huge pack as they toured the backstretch. Warned of this early impediment, Greg maintained a far quicker than race pace throughout the stretch. He thereby approached the second turn in fourth place in the second lane.

"He's just a freshman," said Principal Stromberg, "anything he does here is good for such a young man."

"I'll say," agreed Glenda throwing a smile Beth's way.

"Stay to the outside Greg," warned his father staring at the race below, fearing he would be trapped if he hugged the curb lane. Beebe Stuart from Plymouth volunteered for the task of lead. Rail thin, pale, skinhead and at six-feet-one, he was always the tallest in these long races. Beebe also, knew he was one of the slowest finishers. This placed a demand upon himself to forge to the lead of races attempting to slow the ability to rotate for the fast finishers near race end.

Four hundred meters passed underneath their feet. Greg did not hear the time he was trying to adjust his pace. "That guy is not settling down he's still cranking...that's too fast." Greg ran a half stride off the right shoulder of senior Theo Mann, of Elmo. "This guy has gone 9:50...I'll let him pull me along." Greg allowed Theo to slip ahead some more so that he could fall in trail behind him.

"Stay relaxed, just go for a little ride," Greg recognized his older brother commands.

"You will break ten today!" That sounded like coach the boy thought.

His breathing finally settled to a rhythm, his legs automatically flowed forward and swept back in a pattern almost. The arms were going just for a ride for now.

Beebe could be scene every time they rounded the turns. "He's about thirty meters up on us now."

"3:39!"

Finally, Greg noticed the time. "Ah, well under ten pace." He thought then as if queued, Theo made a surge and moved ahead of him. Greg did not respond. "I better stay here." Theo saw the race was slipping away with Beebe so he demanded pace to get back into a race for first.

"Looking good Gregory!"

He was falling farther and farther back from Beebe but he really could care less. "I 'am just a freshman." He reasoned.

"Come on Greg!" said a voice.

"That sounded like Sheila." Greg thought.

"Beebe passed the 1600 meters in 4:47," said Katie, "Greg was 4:55."

"Greg is running all alone," Zoe said. "Two guys are way up front and everybody else is way behind."

Thorpe watched the boy moved majestically over the red surfaced track. Greg was moving flawlessly, he could not ask any more from the boy. "Good job Greg," he called, "got a great time going." In the stands, Jaycee rocked himself nervously watching the boy pass into another lap. Beth sat anxious, biting her nails. "He's just floating, good job," Jaycee said, speaking to his wife but not taking his eyes off the runners chasing his son. He did not really want the boy to go after the two leaders. "He's doing just fine," said he as the race entered the final lap. There were no other moves from the principals to the finish. Beebe won holding off a fast closing Theo. Then Greg floated in sixty meters back.

As usual, the finishers bunched up quickly as they crossed the finish line and staggered about the immediate area in sort of stages of fatigue. "Do you know my time?" Greg asked an official while he as wandered still exhausted.

"You were 9:57 good job young man," said the official wondering near the finish.

"Thank you, Sir."

Greg continued toward his rest spot watching the girls getting their escort to the start of their race. "I can't believe I did it," said he. He remembered to look toward the stands and wave to his parents and fans, but no way could he actually focus that far and see them. However, he knew that were waving to him and they would be very pleased. Now he wanted to get himself some snacks and a drink and rest until the relay started. Other competitors, including Beebe offered a handshake as the all move lazily toward the rest area. The boy enjoyed this camaraderie, losing time and sight of the girls' race, as Danny and Kasper caught up with him and pummeled him with high-fives.

"You were floating dude," exclaimed Danny.

"Yea you looked smooth, steady," said Kasper, "that was smart not to hang on to those two dudes. You ran your own race. They would have hurt you, if you had tried to latch on to their pace." This trio were in continual discussion of racing when the start gun blasted, catching them by surprise. The girls' 3200 meters race was history and the four by 400 relay was starting.

Roy jumped out of the blocks and accelerated swiftly into the turn. With difficulty he searched for all the speed, he could muster. For Roy, at one hundred eighty pounds had to fight to stay in the turning lane where centripetal force was trying to throw him outside of his boundary.

"Float that stretch, Roy!" yelled Jayce from the stands. Observation revealed a shift from the choppy strides on the curve to a long ground grabbing motion as Roy covered the backstretch. Nevertheless, in lane three to the inside of Roy an athlete from Roseville closed the stagger. Short and bandy legged this fellow realized an easier effort to make his pace on the curving surface. Rolling into the second turn the boy continued pulling out from Roy.

"Come on Roy, give us something to work with," Jayce screamed unheard as everyone in the stands nearly were standing, cheering on their favorites.

Relief for the second 400 meters leg of the race was lining up with the lanes of their respective teams. Eli bounced in his space made stretching motions then placed himself ready to receive the baton from Roy. The Roseville kid was first into the straight. A Foyerstown runner in lane five overtook Roy for second after which the other five lanes filled with tiring finishers. Roy's large statue was now demanding too much energy for him to maintain the effort he wanted in these final meters. He wobbled side to side of his lane arms rotating weakly as fatigue gripped his efforts but he leaned and extended his right arm out hoping Eli could grab it before he would fall forward to the ground. Grab it he did. Eli snatched the baton and in two strides, he veered to the curb lane nearly at full speed pursuing the two runners leading into the third turn of the race.

"Roll into it baby, roll into it!"

"Go Eli!" Beth cried holding her face with her hands appearing fearful observing reckless intensity of the runners.

"This is usually the most tense, exciting race in a track meet," Principal Stromberg says.

"Ohaa!" The stadium crowd moaned as two runners in the middle of the pack, tangled legs and down they went. With a strong stride to the outside, a following pair avoided the spill.

Ten meters up from the spill, Eli overtook the second runner and took aim of the leader as they met the turn of the track.

"Reel him in Eli!" said Kasper, Danny, and Greg in unisons from the trackside. "Go to your arms, Eli!"

Roseville's Tyron Supe started fighting to stay with the turn such was his fatigue.

"He's tying up now!" Jayce said. "He borrowed from the 'bear' early on, now its pay back time! Come on Eli! You can get 'em now!"

Equally poignant comments emanated throughout the galley of spectators as runners streamed to their impatient relief waving the arms insisting that one 'should hurry up'.

"51.2! I got!" said Katie as Eli handed to Terry, one stride up on Tyron at the hand-off. Terry ran to the curb, his right arm pumping vigorously to make up for his missing left appendage. Cocking his head to his left and leaning into the curb he hugged the turn until it straightened.

"Roseville's coming back on him," observed Jayce.

"I bet that guy won't hold up," said Principal Stromberg. Everyone watched quietly as the three teams following smoothly through the lap. This group seemed more relaxed than the earlier tours of the track. That is until the exchange stretch.

"Don't let them pass you before the turn.

"Terry!" warned Jayce, "hold him off!"

Roseville passed Terry mid-turn. Wide in lane two coming out of the turn, Roseville aimed for his relief. Terry was not finished he had his last effort and applied it gradually.

Katie could see an opportunity in lane one. "He's coming from the inside!" A dangerous move; and just as Katie thought, the Roseville runner suddenly moved over to the curb lane cutting Terry off. Terry chopped his stride to avoid hitting heels and then stutter stepped trying to accelerate in lane two. Barry Cruz, of Roseville was wide legged as his arms flagged with little control. Desperation issued from the runner as Terry collared him fifty meters out and moved beyond him with every stride.

"There it is, there it is!" Jayce yelled pumping his right arm up and down.

"Alright young man fine job," Principal Stromberg reacted more subdued.

Beth clapped as with Glenda Thorpe while Patricia swept the view with the video camera in silence. Jimmy and Mr. Football with the other six runners lined up fanning their arms, beckoning their pals to give them the baton. Jimmy rocked from one leg to the other in a crouch ready to spring forward.

"This is going to be a meet record," Principal Stromberg said confidently.

"No doubt Jimmy's going to sizzle, this leg," responded Katie.

"47, and a little change!" added Jayce his face beaming with excitement.

Jimmy snatched the baton from Terry. In two rapid strides, he was in full run leaning into the big turn. Thad was a full second and a half behind.

"Power it Jimmy," came a call from the curbside from Coach Thorpe who had situated himself to observe the exchange zone. "Float that backstretch!"

Like a cheetah, like a hawk diving on prey. Thad started closing at a rate that placed himself on Jimmy's heels midway on the straight.

"That's a mistake," said Jayce.

"Yea, making up that distance that quick," agreed Principal Stromberg, "he'll pay on the final stretch."

"Gota pay the 'bear' his dues," chuckled, Jayce.

Pay back indeed was forthright into the final turn one could see Jimmy relatively small statue compared to the tall figure dogging his heels. The large figure, however, did not rotate arms and legs as quickly as the small one. As the pair straightened toward the galley, the big figure wobbled to lane two as if to pass, however the small figure undaunted moved away from its rival unabated.

"Told you he would tie up!" exclaimed Jayce.

"Go to your arms Jimmy! Pump the arms!" The boy crashed through the finish flaring his arms with elation. The buzzing jubilation of the crowd reached its peak and slowly waned as people packed up to leave for school and home.

With Jimmy's closing, so closed the meet and so retired the 'burden' on Thorpe's spirit. His boys had untied a knot in his continence that left him speechless.

"I hardly know where I go from here?" He thought to himself. Success he expected but these performances were unprecedented. "The kids ran beyond the goals I had for the season." He finalized perplexed.

CHAPTER 6

▼

It is a dismal story that has become all too familiar to Kasper haven been labeled an egghead, of a sort. A uniquely Kaspervian profession, that folds all the skills and passions of a social worker athlete and scholar into a single eclectic vocation. That is why his present mission not to make contact with the Sweigert's. Rather Kasper wanted to gather information on the extent of Bill's activities. Information Kasper will use to bolster his efforts to protect the Sweigert's as well as this community. Any adverse publishing toward the village would only add to its apparent backwardness and thus contribute to divert any interest of any higher institution toward his call.

As Kasper and Jimmy queried confidently concerning details of Bill's businesses they got vague, contradictory tales, third-or-fourth-handed accounts of sightings of Bill with drugs, strangers purposively from as far away as Detroit and New York, visited with Bill at The Clubbed Feet bar and restaurant in Wheelersburg.

"What I have found out that I did not know before was that Bill has a post office box number. He picks up packages you know his souvenir stuff and then he sends many small packages out. The ole German drops letter off there and picks up mail like every week He doesn't appear to do much with Bill's business." Jimmy informed Kasper as they sat at Fisher's Boathouse, a tidy little store with restaurant on a bank of Crimshead Lake.

"For the most part," Jimmy continued, "he mails the money to the same German address."

"Profits from the business, probably," answered Kasper.

"No doubt," responded Jimmy.

"But, at school and around, it doesn't appear he's selling and drugs or passing any material around," said Jimmy looking puzzled.

"It sounds innocent enough so far, but what bothers me," charged Kasper his forehead wrinkled while he pondered confused, "from what you have told me and from what I've gathered is that Bill doesn't seemed to me he's receiving that much stuff but he sure appear to make a lot of deliveries to Germany."

"The dude's got to be selling something, just not around here but in the cities when he goes off the weekends."

Kasper shook his head. The matter he thought was more complicated than he realized.

"I have a suggestion," said Kasper after completing a thought. "We're not going to get anywhere until we find out who is on the receiving end of the mail in Germany."

"You're right if we can follow the money trail we can get to the bottom of all this," said Jimmy.

"Let me go over to the Sweigert's and see if we can get any information about whose receiving all this money. "I should have thought of this earlier."

"There! There!" said Jimmy soothingly patting Kasper upon the shoulder. "It was too bad to spring it on you like this but you can handle this and I will tell you, this sounds exciting to me."

"A touch of the dramatic won't dampen our spirit, hey Jimmy!" Kasper rose from his chair.

"I better pay Johannes a visit."

For an instant, there was hesitation in Kasper's face. Then some new strong thought caused it to set like a mask.

"Yea, I am going over there right now. Let me get back with you later buddy."

"You better dude!"

Kasper took his cap and shrugged his shoulders. "I'll see you," he said and left the place.

Within the hour, Kasper stood before Johannes as they walked slowly in the yard of the Sweigert home. "Ich hatte gehofft, das diese Materie nicht erschwert würde (I had hoped that this matter would not be complicated)," said Johannes after Kasper suggested him contacting someone in Germany who he trusted to inform him of his concern.

"Wir wissen das noch nicht. Es kann eine banale Angelegenheit sein (We do not know that yet. It may be a trivial affair)." Kasper answered in his gentlest voice, "Ich hoffe dies macht Ihnen keine unnötigen Schwierigkeit nicht aber einmal wenn wir wissen von Wilhem's kontakten, diese Affowen werden aufgedeckt werden (I hope this doesn't cause you any unnecessary trouble, but once we know of Wilhelm's contacts these affairs should become apparent, Sir)."

"Dies ist, was ich machen werde (This is what I will do)," explained Johannes, "Wilhelm empfängt diese Geldquittungen. Ich kenne jemanden, der erfahren, kann wo er das Geld deponiezt und für was er es benutzt (Wilhelm is receiving these money receipts. I know someone who can find out where he deposits the money or what he uses it for)."

"Ja Herr, wenn wir das Reiseziel des Gelde erfahren, werden wir wissen welche Ahtion, wenn überhaupt zu unternehmen (Yes Sir, when we find out the money's destination we'll know what action, if any is to be taken)," said Kasper.

"Sehr gut! Wir werden damit noch fertig warden (Very good! We'll be done with this, yet)!"

"Kasper," announced Beth Wise as she stood at a window looking toward the street, "here comes some strange looking fellow."

The boy who had been watching a World War II documentary on a cable network rose lazily from his chair and stood with hands in the pockets of his shorts looking over his mother's shoulder. It was a bright, crisp April Sunday afternoon and Kasper, Danny, Greg, and even Eli had already completed a long run, after church services. Kasper was in blissful relaxation before his mother's interruption. The grey pavement broken, cracked with missing sections was slippery from the day's earlier rains. Beth was concerned with the stranger's progress toward their home.

He was young black man of late twenties, tall, skinny, and imposing with heavy rimmed eyeglasses on a thin face. His gaze roamed about as if lost and confused even though he continued toward the residence. His attire was not that of a businessperson, as he appeared quite casual. As he got closer, Beth could see a backpack donned a shoulder.

"Oh, yes. He must be the fellow from the Physics Society, I told you about," answered Kasper. Now his face appeared awaken from the earlier display of indifference and fatigue.

A few moments later, the stranger was in the living room displaying an upbeat, friendly, cordial nature. This manner of the man, set all at ease after proper greetings and introductions.

"I parked just down the street. I think it was at a picnic grounds. I didn't know which of these houses was yours, so I just walked down the little road looking for this address," said David Bernard as he identified himself. A member of the American Society of Black Physicists, David a PhD worked for the US Air force in the Dayton area. Notre Dame had forwarded Kasper's name to the Society as a person of interest. Beth left them, while Kasper pulled a chair to the little table next to David's right peering at the texts that David had retrieved from his backpack and placed on the table.

"My mission is one of encouragement and support for you," said David.

"I am pleased, Sir," acknowledged the boy, "I never knew there were enough black Americans with college degrees in physics to form relay, let along a physics society." Kasper relayed not attempting any sarcasm.

"Understand most people are surprised just as you," commented David unfazed. "Well we're here and I want to leave with you several texts that are excellent and will enable you to compete with the suburban and private schools."

"Ah thanks," signed Kasper.

"This book," David flipped the pages of one book, "has physics problems that require calculus and it has excellent examples in the utilization of calculus in physics."

"Wow! Just what I need as much calculus as I can get."

"And let me know if I can help. Please call me if you are stuck on a problem. Understand now, you need to do all your work in physics with these texts. The problems in this book in particular are like the exam you will be taking in June."

As for Kasper's observation, he was in awe, of this David. Here was a young black man, a PhD in Physics. Kasper found him ominous. The man's speech was fast, erratic somewhat changing subjects from the village, to physics, then to Kasper's running. Then, just as quick, he would be in the subject of mathematics and calculus again. "A complex mind for the complex," thought Kasper.

"These set of problems, covers the subject matters of the exam," David explained, showing some pages of a notebook spread out on the table. "Now, my showing you these is quite proper as these sets of material are available on request in the instruction documents for a cost, however. Through the Society I am able to pass these to you free of charge."

"Here is a tray of sandwiches and drinks," interrupted Beth depositing a tray on the table pushing aside material.

"Ah, yew," David said as he turned hungrily on the simple fare provided.

Kasper snacked with him and thinking, "This amiable, nonconformist looking fellow is a physicist!"

The boy further observed worn down shoes with nearly a hole in the soles baggy trousers topped with his ever-present sympathetic smile and general look of peering and benevolent curiosity were captivating.

"Tell me, do I hear an accent, German?" asked David suddenly.

"Yes, you do," answered Kasper not caught off guard, "born and went to most of my schooling there."

"Yep, there are several German speaking scientists at the labs where I work. You people got the good schooling and the cultural background for such things. Well I must be going," David, says quickly rising from his seat.

"Your interest in helping me has been humbling," remarked Kasper as his quest paused preparing to leave.

"And Mr. David you're so well suited. Your interest in my son is admirable beyond my words," said Beth appearing amongst them again.

David took a step backwards cocked his head to one side and gazed at the pair until they felt quite bashful. Then suddenly, he plunged forward wrung Beth's hand, and then Kasper's and congratulated them warmly on the pair looking alike.

"You are certainly a mother son pair," said he, "Well, good day, Casper Wise, and let me congratulate you once more on the important endeavor you have so seriously taken upon yourself." With that, David unaware he mispronounced Kasper's name, secured his book bag and departed with his ever-present smile.

"I would have taken offense at his staring and almost too nice attitude," said Beth, after he left in the direction of his car, "but with his eccentric nature. I know he wasn't being offensive."

"Well, he's a typical physics egghead. Sort of cookie, but I bet he is that way with everyone. Like you say, the word for him is eccentric!" Then Kasper looked at all the material left on the table. "Looks like I am in the physics program for sure. No turning back got a lot of work to do."

Conversely, the boy wondered about himself. He considered whether he was too normal. Kasper did not think of himself as eccentric, so maybe he could not be like David. Maybe being weird is a necessity for being genuinely smart. Kasper suddenly brushed off these thoughts. There were many kids at school who thought he was weird enough, he concluded.

"Finally, we've got some radiation soaking on our bodies," Danny said, as the troop of he, Sheila, Kasper, Greg, Eli and Terry ran down the dusty bike path circumventing most of Crimshead Lake. Being forced to run single file most of the journey since much of the distance would suddenly shrink to a mere footpath with tree and bush branches fanning at the intruders most of the way. Fanning insects away, striding the occasional ditches this long sojourn a welcome relief from twenty laps of tense interval runs with short rests barely allowing recovery between runs. This five-mile run was relaxed, as the group conversed freely jogging along slowly.

"You would like the heat," gasped Terry trudging behind next to Sheila.

"I'd rather be sweating than cold anytime."

"'bout two miles to go," said Kasper. Kasper was not enjoying this run with the group, as he preferred to run in solitude. In particular, he did not care for the conversing about various affairs or anxieties. Solitary long runs, is when he allowed his imagination to wonder. There was no Brahms reverting in his mind as well as no Kenyans to be conquered. Instead, trite conversation and irritations like sore calves and rubbing shoes took the space in his mind.

They fanned out as they departed the heavy foliage of the woods and after cresting a small hill. A clearing lead the way to a sparsely traveled road, which allowed a quickening pace. However, the pace remained slow as they trudged along passing an occasional walker and overtaken by several bikers moving quite swiftly. Sheila, in the middle of the pack was comfortable with the pace so she moved up front.

It was nearly four o'clock when they finally passed through the beautiful flowerbeds, and over the broad gleaming lakebed, found themselves at the park's picnic areas. As they arrived, they stated-out a couple tables and stretched. They continued small talk and filled their stomachs with well water, cold and fresh as a gushing spring.

"There he is!" shouted Sheila in a frightful voice, "There's the weirdo I told you about!" The boys followed her sight and focused about sixty meters away, they saw a lean, ferret-like man, furtive and sly-looking gazing their way. The man discovered that the group had sighted him. He quickly sorts refuge behind nearby trees thick with new, fresh, and thick leaves.

"Come on!" Eli ordered, "We need to let this guy know we're on to him."

Quickly they set off in the direction of the stalker. Sheila encountered this figure, three times over the last several weeks while she was out on her morning runs. These incidents occurred, as Sheila had desired an increase in her mileage by running before school started. This was convenient, since the girl lived on the perimeter of the park. The Adams had a home complete with a boat deck right on the bank of Crimshead Lake. The park area was Sheila's back yard.

The faster sprint runners Eli and Terry were first to round the bend of trees that had blocked the view of the escaping subject.

"No sign of him!" exclaimed Terry as they looked around.

"Look there's a car pulling away over there!" yelled Sheila, "That may be the pervert!"

"Everybody! Get a make on that vehicle!" Kasper yelled as they all arrived and spread out looking in the direction of the culprit.

"Hey that road winds around, but it comes out at Sigmore Road and Johnson Path," said Terry.

"Come on then," said Kasper, "let's cut across this field. We may be able to make the intersection and get the license plate."

With no hesitation, six runners accelerated into near sprints across a short, grassed meadow. There they found a curving bike path and raced toward their destination. Indeed as they approached, the vehicle of interest was just about at the intersection.

"There he comes!" Danny called-out.

The culprit spotted the entourage making to the corner. "He's taking off!" The car accelerated and made the intersection. It went through the stop sign spinning tires in the process. As the car turned, the boys could read the license.

"Ah...23!" announced Eli.

"I saw the numbers, 428 or 423?" said Terry, questioning himself. "I think..."

Everyone caught up and stopped along the side of the road watching the car speed away.

"At least he knows we're on to him," said Danny taking deep breaths in his attempt to recover from the sprint.

"I won't run out here again," said Sheila sounding and looking afraid, "We didn't get all the plate."

"I think we've got enough, Sheila," said Kasper, "We know what the car looks like and we have partial license plate. We'll tell Sheriff Palooka and give him this information. He may know who the guy is, right off."

"We'll keep looking out for you in the meantime," Greg added.

"Don't run by yourself girl," said Eli.

"Yea Sheila, we'll come by and you run with us," agreed Kasper.

The troop then dispersed to their homes after agreeing to keep a look out for the stalker, and also inquire around the community and see if anyone can identify the creep. Crucial, however the boys warned Sheila not run alone. A discomforting event loomed among these young people, but with almost excitement and with a pride that they were protecting their Sheila from harm.

"Where are the innocence, glee, and absence of malice we kids should be experiencing?" thought Kasper as he jogged the short distance home with Danny and brothers. "It looks like something is always upon us, always something we've got to be dealing with."

Gloom and dome had to take a back seat immediately as Kasper needed to complete several problems in physics then he was supposed to call on Johannes, who wanted to talk to him concerning their common matter. After which he planned to watch a movie on TV and then relax for Saturday's conference track championships at Honerstown.

"Here's the deal, you and I go through a physics problem, then I will help you tackle one of your problems," said Kasper explaining to cousin, Danny.

"Deal."

Danny watched as Kasper, turned the pages of a neat looking binder. He stared as he watched his companion peruse his material in a most serious manner. Danny detected the pride in the undertaking the boy had. Although by no means did Kasper appear arrogant with his endeavor. He seems to relish the challenge before him. "Kasper's like that," Danny thought, "taking on tasks as if he's an expert and so will eventually overcome the matter no matter how imposing the obstacles maybe."

"Ok, let's get started," he read, 'A comet orbits the Sun in an elliptical path. The distance at perihelion is **d**, and the distance at aphelion is **3d**. First, show that the angular momentum of the comet is a constant. Next, determine the ratio of the comet's velocities at perihelion to that at aphelion.'

"We have to involve Kepler's Laws," suggested Danny feeling useful. He remembered the discussion in class concerning planet orbits.

"Exactly, so let's look them up in the text," said Kasper flipping pages. "Okay, here we are. Here's want we want."

The pair studied the description of Kepler's laws wrote out examples, recognizing mathematical techniques used and started writing toward a solution.

"Let's see the second law says the area swept out per unit time by a radius from the Sun to the comet is constant.

"Now Danny a wedge of area maybe described as: One half times radius squared times the differential change in angle,

$$dA = \frac{1}{2} r^2 d\theta$$

"This expression, changing in time maybe written, using the calculus:

$dA/dt = \frac{1}{2} r^2 \, d\theta/dt$, here an angle changing with time, $d\theta/dt$ is what we call, angular velocity, omega, ω; so we have

$$dA/dt = \frac{1}{2} r^2 \omega.$$

"We must understand Danny that the magnitude of the angular momentum, L of the comet, about the Sun is equal to the mass times the velocity times the radius distance from the Sun. That is:

$$L = mvr$$

"Furthermore velocity is angular velocity times radius, so $v = \omega r$.

"Thus, $L = mr^2 \omega$. Now, rearrange this so we have

$$r^2 \omega = L/m$$

"Then if we substitute this expression into changing area with time, we get:

$$dA/dt = L/2m$$

"What does the second law say?" Kasper asked.

"It says the area wept out in a given time is constant," Danny answered confidently.

"That's right, so dA/dt = constant and also, $L/2m$ = constant, that is L = constant, since the number 2 and m, mass, do not change with time, makes sense?"

"Yep."

"Now, for part b, and look Danny, since angular momentum is constant we can set the angular momentum at the perihelion equal to the angular momentum at the aphelion." Kasper looked at his cousin with a broad smile indicating confidence. "So the product of mass, velocity, and distance of rotation; then

$$L_{pe} = L_{ap}$$
$$mv_{pe}d = mv_{ap}3d$$
$$v_{pe}/v_{ap} = 3$$

"That's what we want; the ratio of velocities of perihelion to aphelion is three," observed Danny.

"Yep, the comet is moving three times as fast at its closest distance to the sun than at its farthest distance from the sun," Kasper pointed out.

"So the velocity ratio is identical to the distance ratio," Danny observed.

"That's right."

"Then if the distance ratio was one to five, then the velocity at the aphelion would be five times the velocity at the perihelion," reasoned Danny.

"Precisely, now, let's look at one of your problems Danny," said Kasper closing his book while leaning over looking at a book Danny had opened.

"Here's an extra credit problem in Pre-calculus. Teach says it's a physics problem with calculus." Danny read:

"Calculate the moment of inertia, **I**, of a hollow cylinder of length L with inner and outer radii of R_1, and R_2 and a total mass, M.'

"Terry, me, and Craig Ort worked and worked on this one, but we can't get it right," said Danny, "the answer is, $I = 1/2M (R_1 + R_2)$. We got some close answers, but not this."

"This demands strength of calculus," suggested Kasper seeing the difficult digression necessary to complete the problem.

"That's for sure and we're missing it."

"Let's take it step by step," said Kasper, then he started writing:
'The definition of rotational inertia, I, is

$$I = \int r^2 \, dm$$

A chunk of mass, dm is the product of density and volume, we write

$$dm = \rho dV$$

"Lets write dV, a section of volume, in terms of radius, circumference, $2\pi r$, times a differential section, dr, times the length of the cylinder, so $dV = 2\pi r(dr)L$

"Put everything together, and remove the constants from the integral, we get

$$I = 2\pi\rho L \int r^3 dr$$

"Now, we must integrate between the radii, R_1 and R_2; the inner and outer radii, he wrote:

"We got that; but now here comes the hard part!" exclaimed Danny.

"Ok, let's see now…" Kasper completed the integration and wrote:

$$I = 2\pi\rho L \tfrac{1}{4} \, |^{R2}_{R1}(r^4) = \tfrac{1}{2} \pi\rho L \, (R^4_2 - R^4_1)$$

"Now, we must rewrite the density in terms of the dimensions of the object."

"Density is mass divided by volume, $\rho = M/V$. The volume Danny, of this hollow cylinder is the product of pie, radius squared, and length of the cylinder. That is

$$V = \pi R^2 L$$

"So for this object

$$V = \pi (R^2_2 - R^2_1) \, L$$

"Why, the minus, Kasper?"

"Because, it's hollow between the radii in the cylinder," said he.

"Oh, I see now."

"Let's put it together…substitute for ρ into the moment of inertia expression, I. We get

$$I = \tfrac{1}{2} \pi L \, M \, (R^4_2 - R^4_1)/\pi \, (R^2_2 - R^2_1) \, L$$

"Its all algebra now, pal." Kasper said. After a few minutes of working, Danny sort help.

"I still don't see how to reduce this mess." Kasper looked over Danny's shoulder.

"You have a difference of squares in the numerator, now look at your denominator," suggested Kasper. Some passing minutes, with algebra and simplification then Danny wrote:

$$I = 1/2M \, (R^2_2 + R^2_1)$$

"Success! That was hard. I never would have gotten that integration."

"It was tricky, but I've had to compute moments of inertia before. Experience goes a long way," disclosed Kasper. "Now, let me give you another problem relating to that type. Then I want you to find a problem in my book for me, deal?"

"Go ahead, shoot for it," agreed Danny.

"If a disk was rotating at 120 revolutions per minute what would its kinetic energy in joules be if the disk has a mass of 40 kg with an inner radius of 100 cm and outer radius of 150 cm?" Danny wrote down the description as Kasper described. He proceeded:

"The kinetic energy of a disk is described as,

$$KE = \tfrac{1}{2} I \, \omega^2$$

"We must convert the radii from centimeters to meters, for consistent units, where the rotational inertia is

$$I = \tfrac{1}{2}\,(40)(1.5^2 + 1.0^2)$$

$$= 65 \text{ kg-m}^2$$

"Now we plug in the 120 for ω," added Danny.

"Watch it," Kasper warned, "the units for 120 is revolutions per minute. You cannot substitute such units in your equation. The units for your answer would be nonsense."

"Yea the units, has to be in radians," Danny said hesitantly, confused. "I don't know how to do that." He started looking through his text.

"Wait I'll show you to save time," Kasper interrupted. Kasper started writing

$$120 \text{ rev/min} \times 2\pi \text{ rad/1 rev} \times 1 \text{ min/60s}$$

"This is the conversion factors that will give you radians per second. Simplify, after canceling units, we get

$$\omega = 4\pi \text{ rad/s} = 13 \text{ rad/s}$$

"I see," said Danny, "now, I can substitute for KE:

$$KE = \tfrac{1}{2}\,(65)(13)^2$$

$$= 5,577 \text{ kg-m}^2 /s^2$$

$$= 5,577 \text{ joules}$$

"The disk of the dimensions given would be generating 5,577 joules of kinetic energy," surmised Kasper, "That's a lot. Now find a problem for me. Then let us go over to the Sweigert's, you can come with me, can't you?"

"Sure," answered Danny. "Ok, let me see now," said he flipping pages of a text.

Kasper sprang out of his chair and crossed toward the kitchen. "Let me check out what's on the tube tonight," he suggested. "Call me when you get something so we can cut out of here."

Danny continued his scanning of texts for a short while, studying. Then he began writing out what he wanted to present to Kasper. He found a solved example. He pursued to change the given data. When done he looked at his hatching proudly and readied for his running mate to solve the problem.

"Oh, come on I have one for you," Danny called toward the living room suavely. "We're dealing with similar concepts, but I made up this problem. Let us sit down and complete this together. I've got to learn how to 'brute force' these problems like you do."

Kasper arrived promptly, listened to cousins' description writing down the details. He then moved to a chair collapsed in it he stammered impatient thinking he would not be journeying to the Sweigert's for a while. The boys sat huddled up next to each other with their heads sank near their breasts. They were utterly determined. The problem they thought did not read hard. The flash indeed came suddenly for Kasper. He stuck his feet up on the corner of a footstool and leaning on the corner of a footstool and leaning back with his hands folded behind his head and began talking more to himself, as it seemed, rather than to Danny.

"So we have a ten meter tall, 500 kg telephone pole, with a 0.5 meter diameter fall over from its upright position. With what velocity will the top of the pole hit the ground?" Kasper leaned forward and started writing. While Danny's eyes assisted with every scribe of Kasper's hand. Wrote he did, explaining:

"From conservation of energy we can set torque of the pole falling equal to the kinetic energy of the falling pole. Torque is center of mass multiplied times force. For kinetic energy of the pole because of its shape we use a pole's rotational inertia." He then:

torque = kinetic energy

"That is

$$r \, F = \frac{1}{2} \, I \, \omega^2$$

"The pole is uniform, so set the center of mass at its center. The length is ten meters so r = 5 meters is the center of mass. Since, force is mass times the gravitational constant…and the moment of inertia for the pole is what?"

Kasper turned to a section of a text that tabled moments of inertia for various shapes.

"Here we are," said Danny, "for a pole rotational inertia, I; it is one-third, times mass, times length squared." He wrote down:

$$5(mg) = \frac{1}{2} \, (1/3 \, m \, L^2) \, \omega^2$$

$$5 \, (9.8) = 1/6 \, (10)^2 \, \omega^2$$

$$100 \, \omega^2 = 294$$

"Thus, we have after using a calculator, to get the square root of omega

$$\omega = 1.71 \text{ radians per second}$$

"Finally, linear velocity equals length of pole, 10 meters, times angular velocity.

$$v = r\omega = (10)(1.74)$$

So

$$v = 17.4 \text{ m/s}$$

"Make sure when you do any of these problems to carry your correct units as a check that you're completing the problem correctly," Kasper warned. "So the top of the pole hits the ground at seventeen meters per second," said Kasper, summarizing.

"What is that in miles per hour?" pleaded Danny being that the meter units was meaningless to his miles per hour culture.

"Well, let's convert.... There are 3600 seconds in an hour, and an English mile is 1609 meters, so...," he wrote:

$$(17.4 \text{m/s} \times 3600 \text{s}/1 \text{ hr}) \times (1 \text{ mile}/1609 \text{m}) = 39 \text{ miles/hour}.$$

"Wow!

"Yep. Well let's wrap things up here and get going before it gets too late," suggested Kasper. Quickly they shut texts and notebooks, shoved papers between pages and prepared to leave.

꒳ꞎ꒳꒳ꞎ꒳ꞎ꒳ꞎ꒳ꞎ꒳ꞎ꒳ꞎ

They walked slowly up the winding narrow streets. Kasper always enjoyed the close kit homes, small and surrounded by bushes and shrubs as high as the boy's shoulders. No, fancy two story homes here, most are thirty years and older and raised three generations of families. Older residents with the present generation took up part of their space by inheriting from their parents. It was difficult to realize that these little old homes would fetch as much as the large new housing developments because of their lakefront or near lake location.

"Let me see," said Kasper standing at a corner and glancing at a line of docks with boats bordering Crimshead Lake; farther his line of sight caught a restaurant near a boat sales yard, "I should like all life as this tranquil, warm, natural. Could any place ever be as such….I love this place Danny, I really do."

Danny wondered why this sudden mood of reflection on the part of his cousin. This sentimentality in this fellow was infrequent. Kasper preferred to show his stoicism the practicality of things and events not the 'romantic'. Not a confrontational person he was really stretching his character with this Sweigert affair. The swing of his nature took Kasper from extreme languor to devouring energy necessary for his athletic feats. Danny knew all too well that Kasper was never as formidable as when he had been amid his tackling math and physics problems. Then the chase mood would suddenly come upon him and that brilliant reasoning power would give rise to shear competitiveness. Danny glanced askance at him, as a fellow whose knowledge and expression of his faith left him unchallenged as a competitor in all aspects of confrontation, be it physical or intellectual.

"Come on, let's get on with it."

Danny tried to puzzle out this affair, but gave it up in despair and set the matter aside hoping this evening should bring an explanation.

It was quarter past eight when they made it to the Sweigert's home. As they approached, the boys saw two men standing out front the home. One of whom Kasper recognized as Johannes. While the other man was, a tall, thin, serious-faced man too well dressed to be a native of the Lakeport community.

"Ha! Here comes, the fine fellow," said Johannes in slow broken English.

"Kasper, young Danny, this is Mr. Patrick a detective with Columbus. After a short pause, "Kasper Mr. Patrick made contact with me last week his office has been keeping tabs on Bill for sometime. I told him about you and your friends' effort to find out about what's going on."

"You, young men just keep up your observations," said the man after shaking hands with the pair.

"We're going to continue watching and keeping track of Bill and his cohorts. So keep cool, do not get too close. We do not want him to find out that he is under surveillance. Now, you must not tell anyone about this meeting with me. You can just say you met with Mr. Sweigert, here. Don't even tell your folks," rattled off this fellow in a somewhat overwrought manner.

Kasper thought to himself. "He's being somewhat over-dramatic. It appears he thinks we are some British sleuth." Kasper did not see the necessity for this involvement.

After a few minutes of small conversation, 'Sir' Patrick left their presence to answer the phone in his car parked a few yards away, Johannes called the boys to his attention. "Now, I have some interesting information, about what's going on in Germany with these activities. I didn't divulge this to Mr. Patrick."

"Great!" said Kasper as Danny listened silently.

"Wilhelm takes the money he receives and exchanges it for Deutch marks. Now they get three times as much to money! You see Kasper. He then gives all this money to family. Things are much harder in Germany these days. The unemployment rate there is five times what you Americans have here." Johannes wrinkled brow depicted a serious concern. "Können Sie verstehen, daß das nicht Sie, Jungen kann (You can understand that can't you, boy)?"

"Ja können Herr, ich sicher das verstehen (Yes Sir, I certainly understand)."

"Good." Johannes said, looking at Danny apologetically, continuing in English. "Now, about all this Nazi stuff; nothing is being spread around the locals, according to Detective Patrick, so there is no problem there, aye?"

"None," said Kasper moving away to avoid further conversation. "Let me know if you need my assist with anything. Have a good day now." He quickly, turned from Johannes. "Let's go Danny." They shook hands with Patrick, who was making his way to Johannes, exchanged greeting and departed.

Danny complied silent still and somewhat perplexed. He knew Kasper was irritated. Something was not right in this convening with Johannes, but he wanted to get his mind back to the track meet for now and that's were their conversation took them as they strode home. He figured Kasper would disclose his concerns at some more appropriate time.

"I am angry with the weather this day. I am angry about the lousy track we run on today. I am angry with the pervert glaring after Sheila. I am angry with Bill Sweigert. However, mostly, I am angry because I am not smart and have to struggle to find the answer for problems in my studies. And I am angry because I am not fast and have to train too hard," Kasper moaned to himself. Mid-Lakes Conference was underway, at Honerstown's Churchill Stadium located southeast of Lakeport in the rolling hills of southeastern Ohio. Coal country where there was no coaling anymore, hill country but no mansions looked down from these hills. This was nearly Appalachia. Heavy wooded and thick brush populated with too many deer. Besides the captivating scenery, avoiding squashing your tires on road kills was a sport when driving the curving steep paths.

The tasks before Kasper Wise posed ominous. He was in his reflective mood waiting for the 3200-meter run. With the state championship just a few weeks ahead the interfering adverse events and obligations drew into his emotional reserves leaving this young man burdened and contemplative.

Lying on his back on a grassy spot his hands folded behind his head Kasper's eyes scanned the horizon. It was unusually quite inside the stadium. Then, upon the quite, there suddenly broke a tremendous clangor of sounds. A roar came from the distance. Kasper sat up. He was transfixed, a terrific medley of screaming issued from the bleacher area. Unmistakably, he was able to focus and see bobbing heads of hurdlers bending over the final hurdles and the breaking crash sound of contact with the little structures as feet struck them.

His mind pulled back from scrambling. He conceived that Jimmy had won by a huge margin. He listened for a time from the public address. Then he got up and jogged closer to the bordering track fence. The girls 1600 meters would be readying after the hurdle races. Today he would observe he would run the 3200 meters only. A strained leg muscle had demanded this precaution.

"Sounded like Jimmy broke fourteen," said Greg coming from somewhere to Kasper's side.

"Probably the track is not the greatest, but he's got a good wind pushing him and he's hand timed so he should be under," said Kasper.

From their positions, they watched the final efforts of the high jumpers. The bar was a six feet-four inches. They watched Scan Hitte as he bounded toward the crossbar in a curving approach long stride, then the final plant, the spring now his back bending backwards bottom shooting up then his bottom moved higher than his head as it passed over the bar with the legs tucked below. Suddenly, like an explosion they come up and over the bar.

"That always amazes me," said Kasper.

"What?"

"The high jumpers, I can not understand how they can get their behinds higher than their heads. It doesn't seem natural."

"Why don't you figure out the physics of the jump? Figure out the power required in the spring to get a mass over the bar."

"Yea, I guess, I will do that sometime." He said grinning sociably.

The pair climbed the bleachers opposite the start area. There they sprawled out luxuriously to observe the races and relaxed.

Kasper put away this melancholy with the speed in which he gained the thoughts.

"As falling droplets make their complex designs of a snow flake all different, but all somewhat alike. Shall adventures come into order? Something demands meaning to the meaningless, order to disorder, and time for the timeless."

The boy said without warning. "Never despair brother, that's the forever victim thinking."

"Yep," Greg agreed pleased to hear his brother's change of mood.

With a violent blast of the start gun attention focused toward the oval track. Sheila raced around the turn.

"Sheila's got it easy today," said Greg, "I don't think anybody else in the conference can beat five-forty."

"She's not going to push it either not on this slow track. Jimmy had the wind to his back and he only went fourteen flat," Kasper forecasted.

The conversation of these fellows dwelled along the lines of how historic a win would be for the school. "Lakeport had not won a conference title in eighteen years," Greg reminded the group.

"And no one from this school has ever been recruited by a Division I college for track," said Kasper.

"I hope he haven't laid his own trap, by dedicating himself too rashly and later having to consider his vows," thought Greg worried of the tinkling display of stress his brother revealed. "A little college would be fine with me. I prefer the small town, country setting, anytime over the big schools but brother wants something else."

"Ladies and gentlemen," interrupted the public address system, "we have a new conference record and one of the top marks in Ohio from Mike Agar of Yankee City; with a throw of sixty-two feet-four inches!"

Roars came from the crowds with clapping and the increased hum of conversations of the feat. They then turned their attention to Sheila's run. Into the third lap carrying a twenty-meter lead she looked graceful and relaxed. "Sheila's just out for a workout," suggested Greg, "she completed a full hard training session Thursday."

Seeing that Sheila was in control, Kasper had to comment about the shot-put record. "Agar doesn't have to worry about recruitment. That's Division I class all the way." He hoped his brother did not detect his envy.

Up in the bleachers Coach Thorpe was in awe as well. "Agar, the kid is only about two-hundred pounds. Most guys throwing that far are two-hundred forty and heavier. However, Agar has tremendous speed in the ring," said he to Katie admirably.

Katie said nothing as she focused on Sheila racing toward the finish a hundred meters ahead of the second runner.

"5:25," announced Katie, "walk in the park."

"Now, for Danny and Eli," said Thorpe preparing his pad for the timing.

"Eli is running the 1600?" queried the girl.

"Yea, we need the points and he needs to run this distance and run the 800 with Terry." Thorpe announced.

Thorpe explained they were doubling up in events since they had such few efforts in the field events. Thorpe left the stands and walked along the track fence, excusing pressing through standing spectators watching the events. He engaged himself with his own internal debate. He could persuade himself from dwelling upon the insecurities he faced with these kids. Thorpe informed of Sheila's stalking incidents and the rumors about major drug dealings in the community. Things seemed to be escalating. Then there was Kasper desire to attend an Ivy League school, but as of today, he had a strained leg muscle. "If all this stuff blows up my program here will fizzle and me with it."

"Bang!" The race was underway. Thorpe only wanted to win the championship. No record attempts. Too risky he figured. Thorpe was primed for the following week – the Districts. "Come on Eli stay on Danny's rear!" Thorpe shouted after coming to conscience of the race underway.

In the bleachers Kasper and Greg turned quick eyes upon the field. They discerned forms begin to swell in masses out of the turn speeding toward the straight.

"They're surrounded," exclaimed Greg.

"Come on guys," whined Kasper impatient.

"Look how slow they're going."

"It's going to be a sprint the last lap. Eli is running the 800 and Danny's running the 3200 with us," said Kasper to his brother, "so they are trying to get through this with minimum effort."

They watched the precession for two more mechanically run laps. Both arms and leg rotation synchronized as the two moved from the followers. Unsurprising to the knowledgeable attending crowd, in paired matches as this an aggressive move would occur in the last circuit and the excitement with it. True this is as the boys changed their tempo approaching the backstretch. From the stands, everybody saw the deliberate move by Danny attempting a long sprint from three hundred meters out. Danny displayed the zeal of a sprinter in his purpose to keep Eli in his rear. Finding himself in unabated screams from the bordering fence and the bleachers, the boy focused straight ahead concentrating on his rotation. "This feels like about a 65. Yet, Eli's still right on my rear...Got to go all out in the stretch."

A furious run by the two on the final turn caused core uproar in the bleachers. Fans were making maniacal motions with their arms urging the runners toward the finish. In the infield, some scrambled toward the finish area for better view. They could see the taller figure moving to the outside of the shorter figure when they entered the last stretch to the finish. Steadily the smaller figure lost ground to the taller figure approaching the last meters. Not by much was the margin as they passed the finish and with almost a shock, the noise abated.

As the boys warily moved to the infield they heard someone callout: "4:34! They covered the last 400 meters in about 60 seconds!"

The slim Eli made it to the line a stride before Danny. "You're stronger than I thought," said Danny grinning, not the least upset. He was pleased that he could run so fast over the final circuit and that he would not be running against Eli again at this distance.

"And neither did I," responded Eli his face aflame with excitement. "We were cranking dude, we were cranking!"

The crowd, the athletes, the officials reassembled themselves for the next act from Churchill stadium. Intermission to the next event of interest for Lakeport and the other teams as well allowed a sorting of emotional preparation as well as assembly of tactics for coaches. Frequently over this tumult, jovial jokes burst from amongst alumni at these events throughout the crowd. Notwithstanding, the participants of the day had little consciousness other than the tiring trials they had to confront.

Girls and boys 4 X 100 meter relay events concurred ushering in an intensity of commotion crammed into just some seconds. Dropped batons, failed exchanges, poor exchanges all contributed to a level of barrage unrivaled in other events. Tears flowed from the young women while expletives unleashed for some young men. Mostly the athletes themselves were the source of any defilement on their person. Such is the nature of self-driven motivation of teenagers who alternates between aggressive defiance and petulant despair.

"Last call for the men's 400 meters," announced the public address system. It was a welcomed call. Little Lakeport had scored no points in the interim of events since the 1600 races.

"There's Roy and Jimmy," pointed out Katie positioned with her stopwatches hanging around her neck and clipboard balanced on her knees.

"Come on guys and proclaim your victory!" Declared little Zoe gleefully.

People around grinned at her innocent, but brash zeal.

"She's the cutest team supporter I've seen," said a woman nearby smiling amiably.

At the crack of the gun, Jimmy set off in an almost too casual effort. Nevertheless, this effort was enough to make up the staggers on the runners to his right, including Roy. He was taking no chance of getting hurt on this raunchy day. So they watched as Jimmy with Roy in tow account for a one-three finish and sixteen points for Lakeport. The time splits of these performances were inconsequential considering the slow track and lack of interest, because of the impending districts where a failure to finish in the top four results in a requirement to 'stay home' the remained of the year.

Some more time, more settling, another scene was set for the stage. "No one hurt so far," thought Thorpe, walking through the crowds coiling around the perimeter of the track with his clipboard of entries and results with a dangling stopwatch about his neck. Turning his attention to the 800 girls as Sheila closed toward its climax. She had raced ahead of the field for 500 meters then accelerated herself away, exercising her newfound power and confidence. She had cruised through her first 400 meters poking slow 77 seconds, from there she raced 600 meters 1:52, then it her just took 33 seconds to reach the white line. "Ata girl! 2:25! That was a classy effort. You showed me some grit girl," said Thorpe with a rare display of arrogance and then headed off to some other part of the grounds.

"Sheila can double in the Districts," said Katie observing in the stands.

"Her main event comes first so it should be no problem," said Glenda next to her.

"Here comes, the guys," announced Zoe watching the gathering for the boys 800 meters.

"Come on Terry," yelled Katie, "He's fresh; he should try to beat Eli who ran the 1600 meters earlier." As they listened to some preparatory conversations, the officials sorted the competitors into the stagers and lanes. Continuous distracting clamors from the crowd came from all directions at an event as this one. So many of the people inside the track ground were surprised when the gun sounded sending off the two-lap race.

Within the gleam of colors reflecting from the sun, runners of various sizes with motions identified as smooth, awkward, and erratic; they covered three-hundred meters, at the end of the second turn and there the pack broke their staggers and sort a space near lane one or two. Leading the bobbing heads, Terry in lane two led as they crossed 400 meters.

"58, 59, 60," called an official as the tightly packed runner streamed pass, entering the final lap. Danny was in second three strides back. Terry with his head leaned to the inside of the track in his characteristic manner and his right arm rotating closer to his chest than most continued this pace into the second and final lap.

"Keep it up baby," said a matured woman's voice. Katie looked in the direction of the call and recognized Sophie Luke standing, anxious, shaking at the sight of her, sometimes called 'handicapped' grandson make pace in a foot race encompassing the best athletes in the conference. She was proud beyond description. Standing, she did not care if she blocked the view of many behind her in the stands.

"You run boy, you run Terry!" said the woman, sounding very 'country'.

"Ah, he's gone. Only Eli can beat 'em!" said a bearded gentleman, Sophie's husband Jack Luke sitting next to the standing woman. He pushed the beak of his cap back. He awkwardly made further predictions. "Jest as I thought," he added, presently. "Look at 'em fall back, Terry's going to wait and sprint at the end like they do in practice running sprints on the dirt road on their country home.

With the remaining pack ten meters behind Terry and Eli on the backstretch, the pace slowed. Danny struggled. The fast pace he required to stay with Terry was taking its toll; he had expended a great amount of his energy at the finish of the 1600 meters. Terry knew that all too well; his mate must be tiring and that is why he made a final acceleration as they started straightening from the curve. His friend would be making his bid otherwise.

"Ata boy!" screamed Sophie, she could see Terry's increase in arm swing as he bounded toward the finish. "You kin do it boy! You kin do it!"

The surge caught Eli by surprise. Usually Terry waned in the final meters. Now he leaned his into the finale. Eli moved into lane two for a clear run. To no avail, he could not wear away the two strides Terry padded between the pair.

"2:00.8," said Katie staring at her watch amid scream, "2:01.2 for Eli."

The Luke relatives cried out hysterically. "I told yeh he would sprint at the end."

"Yes-yes- I tell yeh – that was so exciting Jack!"

She could not speak easily because of the gulping in her throat.

"Gawd! He was running!"

The two leaders clasped each other on the field and congratulated other rivals as they strode slowly toward their places of rest. Terry had been, twisted into an expression of agony; now a smile cut across his face walking with his friend.

"I still didn't break two," he explained to Eli.

"If this had been a fast track and a warmer day, we both would have been under two minutes," answered Eli. Silence set between them as they strode the remaining meters to retrieve their gear.

"Good job guys," greeted Greg as Terry and Eli approached. Kasper smiled and greeted the pair with his weak handshake, remaining seated on the ground occasionally stretching his stiff leg.

"Great run boy," they heard a voice behind them.

The group looked around to see Coach Thorpe arriving laden with clipboard and stopwatches, his forehead sweating, his voice scratchy and nervous.

"How's ya' leg Kasper?"

"Just stiff, I'm alright."

"Ok, Jimmy and Ray should get fourteen or sixteen points in the 200 meters," said Thorpe again. "Eli I'm pulling you and out of the relay. Terry you're on with Tom." Then the man who never stopped his walk continued to some other area of the complex. Evidently, he had to warn Jimmy and Ray of his change of agenda. The boys looked after him pondering the stress of his hype.

"He's more nervous than all of us," commented Greg after Thorpe departed.

"Well, our little team can win state if we don't get busted-up with injuries," said Kasper.

On the track Jimmy dominated from the crack of the pistol; even with a float he closed in 22.24 for the 200 meters with Ray following in third place, unable to outrun Yancy Bolt, from Minister City. This set the stage for the trio of 3200 meters runners to compete this day and bring victory for this occasion.

With the completion of the girl's 200 meters race, there was no delay in arrival of the twenty boys for the next event. Quick assortment of the competitors and a roar from the start pistol sent the group off to their eight-lap tour of the track. There were no great times sort for this event, just a one, two finish, as Danny was to run a leg of the 4 X 400 relay instead of Tommy Black, another unexpected change by Thorpe.

"Tom's complaining about his hip," explained Katie retuning from her own excursion around the track grounds. "Danny can run about 55 seconds for 400 meters. He won't lose any ground to anyone here."

The 3200 meters boys strung out quickly; already, the Lakeport boys were dictating the pace. While this race unraveled, another affair was in the making from relatively isolated corner of the far side bleachers. Terry was at conversation with his mom whose appearance surprised the young man. He was touched emotionally since she seldom attended any of his activities.

"Oh, son I just don't have the words to express my pride," Sondra Luke said her voice whimpering. A pale red head, sporting a long braided ponytail reached to the waist of the stoutly built woman.

"See mom, I won't break," said Terry quickly.

This response headed off his mother's self-apparent quilt. Sondra was responsible for the accident where her son lost his arm. In the interim years, she applied the extremes sometimes over protecting, but in recent years, she rarely visited her mother or her son. The sight of her son amongst other youngsters was exacting; suggesting her quilt for his deformity in the most explicit way. Thus, she withdrew from all but a few of her son's affairs.

"Mom says, you and your friend are 'bout the best around here," said Sonya, distressed, but attempting to console herself. "You beat all those guys. I want to see all your races when I can from now on," she finished, her face still flushed.

"Cheer up, mom, there are a lot of tough dudes in coming races but I absolutely love the competition. I love the fight for ground. It's great mom!"

"Yes, indeed. I see you really do," said she looking perplexed, "Well I will not take an unpleasant remembrance with me. What I saw you accomplish in that race will prop me up for a long time, Terry."

"Hope to see you next weekend."

"That is my intention."

The visit ended. Terry strode to his gathering of 400-meter runners for the relay, just in time to see Kasper rushing off the final turn to the finish the 3200 meters, Greg was a football field length behind in second place.

"9:49 and 10:07, that secured the team championships," said Katie tallying the team score on her pad, "The relay will be just gravy."

"Then can we go," asked Zoe tired now, after a long afternoon, "we been winning everything mostly."

"Yes we can go."

"Come on boys," yelled Sophie with Jack in cadence. The pair thoroughly enjoyed these affairs having never attended a major track gathering before this day. However, from the constant conversations they made with the bleacher crowd; one would have identified these people as old track vagabonds. What the Lukes enjoyed more than talking about the boys, was to discover some recognized surname as being someone they knew all about. "Is that the 'Morels'…from Cobalt County? Shoot I know them well…They had the biggest whisky still in the county…They and my Uncle Leroy made a ton of money running whisky from the back counties all the way to Cincinnati, Memphis." The Lukes kept the nearby listeners tickled and laughing with these barrage of tales right up until the event was announced as starting, the four by 400 meters.

"Come on Lakeport!" Sophie called toward the forming line-up of runners. Then the start, they witnessed Roy big as he is hurling himself over 400 meters of oval, and making the first pass of the baton to Danny. Skinny Danny appeared half the size of the powerfully built Roy. Thinned legged Danny completed his run with more meters between himself and the boy chasing. With that done Terry, accepted a twenty-meter lead, and then capitalized by finding another five meters to the lead as he rotated his awkward style with even more flare around the track. This pad of nearly thirty meters passed to Jimmy, who cranked off a very fast finish to suit the delight of the screaming fans, nevertheless and thus closed the Mid Lakers Conference track meet.

CHAPTER 7

▼

"Hello Casper. How you doing?" asked the voice of David on the phone. Kasper and family had only been home from the conference meet and hour barely.

"Oh just fine, what's up?"

"Like, I said to your dad. I have a meeting with a physics colleague at Notre Dame tomorrow. I would be pleased if you and Danny could come along. We'll have a great time."

"Oh, wow! Yes, we'd like to go."

"Great! However, I need to pick you people up this evening. It is about a five-hour drive. So we could get there about midnight. We have a room all set for us on campus." David explained they would return Monday morning. Jayce Wise had advised him that he would inform the school of their absence.

"Can we take our running togs?" asked Kasper, "so we can get some running in?"

"Certainly," answered David, "We can also check out the campus and then talk some physics. My friend is an associate physics professor. We'll have a great stay."

"Sounds great, we'll start getting ready. See you soon."

"I'll be there in a couple hours," said David, "by the way can you guys drive?"

"Oh yes. I have my license."

"Great, see you."

He stared at empty space. "I can't believe it. I'm going to be at Notre Dame, before the nights out."

"So you guys are going?" asked Beth.

"In a couple hours the eccentric Mr. David will be here."

Jayce was already with Danny and Beth getting a couple duffle bags and suit-case for the pair. Almost frantic, they gathered material they wanted to take plus running gear and pitched them into a heavy duffle bag. "I'll get as many prob-lems as I can complete, need to make good use of David as much as I can."

Kasper was glad he did not have to ask his father for any money. Johannes had passed him another envelope of several bills at their last meeting. At the time, this transaction bothered him along with other concerns, but not anymore. Besides, his dad said David would cover any expenses through the Society.

There were moments of waiting while in solitude the young Kasper had thoughts how this trip could had come to realization. He remembered how he held no aspirations but thought his dad or someone would point out what he should pursue in life. He remembered how he envied, then hated kids who could run, and participate in physical activities. He remembered how he felt that all those 'jocks' were 'stupid'. Now, the pages of life had flipped on him. Would he test out 'stupid'? Would he crumble when he matched up with 'real' gifted ath-letes? Could he meet the challenges before him? Possibly, he thought was life teasing Kasper Wise. Would he fail under the onslaught?

Then Jayce cried, "He's here!"

There was rustling and muttering among all. Eli and Greg displayed as much excitement as their departing compatriots.

"Bring back some mementos for us," asked Eli as the boys walked toward the waiting car with gear and bags under their arms. David greeted the family from his car side opening the truck and doors for his passengers.

The young men in their contemplation was smitten with astonishment as they transverse the state of Ohio and into Indiana. There were too much space and more small towns than one would imagine. Kasper loved to travel, as these expe-riences rekindled in him a deep primordial feeling, perhaps the same feeling an ancient hunter would have, an emotion that he first experienced as a boy pulled in a wagon by his dad, as he was crippled and could not cover such an excursion on his own. After the family would complete some trip about the German coun-tryside, a tenuous, melancholy gripped Kasper. It was as if the journey's end marked a stopping point, which to complete later.

Danny took much pleasure in the drive equally, as the boy had never been more than a couple hours drive from home in his life. A often describe, most peo-ple in the ghetto 'ain't never been anywhere, but down the street'. Thus, Danny struggle against the rapidly setting sun, enjoying the images of the countryside under the waning sun light. To no avail, however, the darkness descended and the remaining awe came from the steady deluge of interesting experiences of

David as a boy. Driving, talking sometimes aimlessly, sometimes descriptively of events leading then to conclusions that Kasper and Danny found discerning. Such was the complex mind of such a fellow they thought.

The trip seemed shorter than the four plus hours it took for the drive. Dark, the area was unlike a well-lit big city area. Surprisingly, the boys found it as dark almost as the Crimshead lake area. It was no delay in parking, unloading, getting their rooms, and making their bed. Plans for the morning were set "Let's run around those lakes," Kasper suggested studying a campus map, "that'll give us some good mileage."

"That's a favorite jogging area and it's beautiful," added David. "The campus is really not huge like most of the Big Ten schools."

"So let's swing around the campus and circuit the lakes," suggested Danny.

"Sounds good," said an excited Kasper. He was excited and awe struck that he was on such an historic campus. "It's like we are now a part of the history of these grounds just because we're here." Kasper had said to Danny, while gazing out the window at the grounds. Contrarily, Danny he felt more like a fleeting wind blowing threw these premises.

"Huh, this is beyond me I am afraid," commented Danny, "I 'm just a visitor, there will be nothing of me left here when I leave. Now you cousin have that capability of mating yourself to such an institution as this. You've got the vocabulary and the preppy mannerism when you need it."

Kasper did not pursue the line of thought Danny had proposed. Nevertheless, he shoved it off as idle talk. "Shoot, I would have to adjust here too," he thought falling to sleep looking forward to an exciting run early in the morning around the campus.

It was a quarter past seven, mild, cloudless morning with a light wind switching directions. A pair of lightly clad boys jogged silently alone a walk path. Not a sole was in their view. It was as if its inhabitants had abandoned the town.

"It's just what I like little traffic, few people, lots of flat space," commented Kasper to Danny. He felt great and shivered with excitement as he planned make this run long, and finish as fast as he could muster.

They had studied a campus map and planned to tour its entirety. Leaving Cavanaugh Hall lodging they stretched, and then jogged the short distance to the Basilica of the Sacred Heart, turned south crossing open space crisscrossed with sidewalks and manicured grass space filling between the concrete walk paths.

"Look for Holy Cross Drive on the right," said Kasper, "It borders the golf course and will take us to the lakes."

After adjusting to a comfortable pace, Danny questioned. "I wonder how fast the milers are at this place."

"Oh, probably under 4:10," guessed Kasper.

"What you think they would want to recruit a runner for here?"

"You probably got to run under 4:20, with great SAT and ACT scores. Most every athlete graduate in four years here; Notre Dame is not a 'jock mill.'"

Kasper's knees wanted to buckle at what he just said. "Is that me? Can I qualify?" He thought. "I must be crazy. People who come here are debonair, wealthy, always been smart, and they have always been around fine fixtures.

This was like Kasper. In an instant, he would leave a confident: 'I can do everything' mood to a melancholy: 'I don't know what will become of me!'

Danny strode shoulder to shoulder with his cousin. His continence was in the 'present' only. "How's the leg?"

"It's as great as this experience is!" Kasper answered. There was no demand on his part to secure these environs for his own. Danny would not project himself ahead as his Kasper so liberally explored.

"There's our turn," said Kasper. Thinking made the trot seem short. They caught sight of the golf course on their left. Now this road started curving to the right.

He was alone in his mind and so retreated to his own visions and relaxed in the run with no gage for the time it would take them to complete the route. However, he did not care either.

"There is no superman," said Kasper after a silence. "There are just those who work and those who don't."

"Yes, but some people are destroyed by their work." Answered Danny surprising Kasper since Danny seldom had anything to say following Kasper's assessments.

"That's true."

"You know its how we get through this that counts. It is biblical. We must trust that ultimately all things will prosper for those who stay the path, no matter what."

"Difficulty is of little importance, it is the struggle that matters," Kasper continued. "How we fight the fight before us. It's the effort emanating that's what we glory."

"Yep."

"So, let's create some more difficulty so our faith may be emanated and our heroic manners may be realized."

Danny turned and smiled toward his friend.

The pace quickened as the road descended as it turned them within sight of St. Mary's Lake. Leaving the road as it turned, they found a path that led them to a dirt and gravel trail circumventing the lake. Moving counter clockwise the path pitched up and down and curved with slight changes of directions. Green pillows of moss dotted the woods. Bent grasses hint at the passing of unseen rain or winds earlier. Spires of dropping trees, branches hanging down to their face as they pair trudged through heavy foliage on this unfamiliar tour. Kasper wished he could capture these elusive images to take home, however, he knew he could not even describe such scenes in words.

The boys jogged cautiously not knowing where twenty meters ahead would lead them to the right, left, smooth footing, or rough footing?

"Hey, there's Columbia Hall," said Danny, "this is where we cross over to St. Joseph's Lake."

"That figures," thought Kasper, "leaving St. Mary for St. Joseph. Sounds just like my spiritual dilemma, jumping from one realization to another."

They both took long and slow breaths, as careful as their stride. Gravity pulled them down a crest and then they took up another path around the lake.

"Kasper, your trying to understand and control everything," said Danny after an interlude of winding slowly again on another curving path. "Thy will be done, Kasper. We are running and do not know what is ahead, do we? But we're not frantic are we?"

Now Kasper turned toward his cousin. Kasper had seldom witnessed Danny make such an insight. "Your point is well taken."

Then he turned to his friend, smiled while gasping for breath.

"Let's get back on path," said he, then more winding and climbing with meandering through narrow dirt and grass paths requiring a slackening of pace. They met an occasional jogger mostly females carrying a smile and some greeting with each encounter.

"These ladies look somewhat different than girls at home jogging," observed Danny.

"These are women," emphasized Kasper, "these are not little skinny teeny boppers in high school."

"Yea, they fill-out everything, that's for sure."

The two fellows completed most of the circumference of the lake then exited near the Moreau Seminary building and turned east after arriving at Douglas road. Now they were moving like runners not joggers again. The pair of youths sped toward a perimeter road that would circumvent the eastern campus and take them to the Notre Dame running track. As they progressed, thoughts of the impressions and the envying from classmates, replaced the theme of conversation.

"Of course they'll say." Suggested Kasper, "You guys will only be there as visitors, fat chance of anything else."

"Probably," agreed Danny uninterested.

"Kasper had a conviction that he must ready for the missiles of ridicule that waits for them for making this trip. He had no strength to invent a tale of why he was here. He would be a soft target.

"Maybe, we shouldn't say too much about this trip, thought he, "this is a non-recruitment visit anyway." He passed his thought to Danny.

"I wouldn't say anything to any body, really." Danny thought Kasper was over reacting. "Most kids wouldn't pay this any mind," he thought.

He made vague plans to circle to entire campus but these was changed by the voices of exhaustion from his body as he realized the pair was moving down this smooth road at a full run. Experience and knowledge of his body told him a hard run to the track area was about as far as they could maintain at this pace. Passing Wilson Commons they swing unsteadily toward down Leahy Drive.

"Just a couple minutes out, now," Kasper said. Suddenly out of nowhere came a monstrous figure of a dog's leaping toward them barking with its tongue hanging from his mouth. "Hey! Hey!"

They were dismayed a second. Kasper hated dogs. They have teeth he would say: "They bite. They are too protective or too friendly when you do not want them around." The two came to a halt, closed together for protection while this dog barked and snarled before them.

"The best way to stop an attack is to stop and stare them down," said Danny, "if you keep running they'll maul you for sure if they're intention is to attack."

"Why is there a loose dog out here anyway?"

They walked slowly but the dog followed walking and barking threateningly.

"Dover! Dover!" called a chubby man coming from amongst some housing. "Get back here, boy! Don't worry he won't bite…get back here Dover!"

The dog turned toward his master then he turned back to the boys and continuing barking and slobbering all the while. Collaring the dog the man grabbed Dover and wrestled with him. Grinning at the pair as to say his Dover is just a playful. Nothing serious, his dog is harmless.

Kasper and Danny stepped off and resumed their run, upset he snarled himself, "They always say that. People with their stupid dogs they can't control; allowing them to roam around harassing people; them they call to animal like it's a person and of course the dumb animal doesn't pay them any mind."

"They won't bite," exclaimed Danny mockingly.

"Yep, they always saw that; meanwhile the dog is fuming at the mouth wanting a piece of you," said an angry Kasper as they increased the pace of the run.

"The track should be right up there let's haul it in now," suggested Kasper.

It took only a minute before they slowed at the sight of the red surfaced track enclosed by a spiked fence. With little scrutinizing they found an opened gate that allowed their entry. The panting and agonies of the last few minutes they quenched from their memory.

"Ah man, this is neat," uttered Danny.

Standing on the track the friends shoulder to shoulder was thoughtfully staring across the grounds. From this sight Kasper's expression was at that moment very meek.

Danny regarding him with sidelong glances felt impelled to speak. "Oh, wish we had a track like this," he said.

His friend turned his head in some surprise. "Why would you ever dream such a thought?"

"Well, we're going to state," said Danny, "if it is like this one we'll knock off four or five seconds in the 1600."

"At least."

He resolved not to deal any negative thoughts. It was sufficient that they would have the opportunity to compete on a track this fast if they made state and remained healthy so one could realize a fast time.

"Let's christen this track!"

"Yea, we need to run at least a mile for a christening, well four laps."

Danny did not know where Kasper came up with this, 'christening' of a track but he was in good humor so the duo proceeded into a conversational jog. Four laps later task completed, they choose to cool off by stretching on the infield and just relaxing.

Then an event occurred something to log in the minds of these boys as an unexpected anomaly. Some middle-aged man had observed the boys and thought they were opportune for introduction. The man was touring the track in a jog, grey haired as was his white attire shoes. Wearily he trotted pass them throwing a friendly greeting and smile their way.

"Probably a professor in some department we couldn't pronounce," said Danny, after some observation.

"Shucks! Looks weird so he is most likely a physics teacher remarked his pal.

"Ha, ha," laughed Danny then Kasper joined in.

From there the conversation centered about an easy jog back to Cavanaugh Hall, a hot shower, and that big breakfast at the Morris Inn. During this moment of leisure they were engaged in, suddenly a voice from behind beckoned. Turning, the old jogger was next to them. They too, had become the subject of speculation.

"Hello young men, welcome to our great university," greeted the man grinning sociably. He sprawled out on the ground next to the boys. "Hope you don't mind my imposing upon you."

The visitor disclosed his identity. He was not in physics, not with the University, but a quest as they. Courting closer to Danny's ebony figure, pale as one could be, the man captured them with a diatribe about how he invites young people from many campuses to explore their spirituality with others.

"We have a group that meets at private homes. I would like to invite you young men to come and explore your spirituality and also hear from others, like yourselves."

The boys were quite attentive, intrigued by such a person as this fellow making conversation and showing such keen interest in young boys as themselves. Truthfully, they thought him odd, but interesting. The two absorbed little of what was said, finding his character the object of their curiosity. They listened distantly as the man continued.

"Sharing these higher powers amongst our fellow being...I have Doctorate in Psychology and Masters in Religious Studies...I taught at several universities and am proficient in Oratory...I'm retired now..."

"So you get people together," interrupted Kasper exploring "and everyone talks of the 'higher powers' and what it means to everyone." Looking at his cousin, he sort for Danny's agreeing gaze.

"Precisely!" said he loudly. "We explore the philosophies and technique of all the religions. We learn to expand our thoughts beyond the horizon merely what one can see, and sort out the why of our existence and the true meaning of life."

"Exploration of opinions of all sorts of beliefs," added Danny questioning.

"Yes, precisely," repeated the man. His eyes and mouth widening delighted of agreeing successful talk with, his fine catch of youngsters. "Then we have a date do we?" There was now a pause. Kasper and Danny communicated with just another eye contact. They both thought this was improper for a stranger to ask minors to attend some gathering that may infringe upon the morals and religious values of a family.

"Nope!" replied Danny not excepting this offensive intrusion.

"Not a chance," Kasper persisted. "I don't need to hear of such things. I already know what I believe in and why I exist. Now I can use my brain cells the rest of my life for creativity." Both boys fixed an unflinching gaze at the man. It was sufficient. The man got up slowly his demeanor changed; eyes scanning the horizon did he need to say something, or what he had heard was it adequate?

"I've never heard of one defending a view with such a proposition," said the fellow finally, "Understand my dear friends, that in institutes of higher learning you will find challenging outlooks that will galvanize your wisdom as to other views."

"That won't happen," countered Kasper. "People who know me say I'm a close minded sort of fellow. I seldom listen to other points of view and don't care what others think."

"I'm his cousin," added Danny, "I'm like that too, but take no offense sir. We are friendly fellows and we do not argue much, we just don't pay other's people's opinions any mind when it comes to all the sorts of beliefs going around."

The man caught off guard with the rebuttal he received from the youngsters. Although, he bristled with a show of resentment as he departed, attempting to maintain his dignity, he suddenly turned and said condescendingly, "You'll learn as you expand your spiritual horizon."

It took a few seconds for the pair to fully absorb and respond to this intrusive behavior. Then both burst into laughter, "That was interesting," said Kasper with a commonplace smile, after then chuckling ended. "That dude's a 'space cadet' if there ever was one."

"As old as he is he's still going around trying to find his spirituality. He'll never find it." Kasper needed to finish what the man started. "It never ceases to amaze me, how people such as he probably believes the universe has been in existence for billions of years while mankind has been in existence for only an extremely short time comparably speaking; nevertheless, they think mankind can figure out everything about our existence if we think hard enough."

"Preposterous!" suggested Danny using Kasper's vocabulary, "Pure arrogance."

"How can something created suggest its own realization? Can a puppet figure out how and where the strings come from that controls his every move? Can a flea figure out why it needs to be on the body of its host? Can a cartoon character figure out whose hand drew its depiction on paper?"

"Yea, how can something created understand its creator?"

"Exactly, it's like a person building a toy robot then the robot tries to put the person which created it together."

Kasper had listened with an air of impotent condescendence spoke now in firm and undaunted tones. "I don't care of his credentials he's an example of one who has a lot of knowledge but being vastly short in wisdom. There's a light-year of difference between the two concepts," said Kasper severely, "that man is shooting darts in the dark and I'll have none of his nonsense."

Danny made an agreeing gesture. "Let's get to the good eats," he said. They got up with an air of being content with themselves.

The boys developed a tranquil philosophy for these moments of irritation. "Oh well," Kasper, rejoined, "He must think we don't have any values worth cherishing and indeed we would be receptive to his enlightenment."

Kasper spoke soothingly to his pal as they jogged.

"Well, we both did good repelling a vicious man eating dog and a dude that probably tell us eventually that Jesus was really an alien!" Kasper laughed.

"Better watch, this is what happens to you when you go to college," declared Danny stoutly with sudden exasperation. "That dude probably believes in more gods than the ancient Greeks." They laughed.

"Hey did you notice," said Kasper, "he looked like an ancient Greek." Chuckled they did for a while. Conversation ceased as they had come to hurrying up toward this destination. The runners encountered more trafficking of people and vehicles as they wound around the football stadium. Pausing they sort an entrance, but were unsuccessful. Continuing north winding by a museum of art and a science building, they approached the dorm slowing to a walk so they could warm-down.

Again, as the two sprawled out and stretched their figures on the grass next to the dorm catching observations of more domestic figures moving about with texts and some with laundry bags. "Must be going or coming home," the boys thought. "Future leaders in business and government, these people are."

"These kids come from the best of everything to be here," said Kasper with some envy.

"Yea and they will get the best of everything, too," emphasized Danny pointedly, but without malice just dispassionate observation. "Now don't put yourself down. I am sure every kid here, do not come from rich families. Some are like you just real smart, got scholarships and other aid."

"I suppose," acknowledged Kasper. The boys shelved away adverse thoughts. They were very happy and their hearts swelled with grateful affection for the 'eccentric' David who provided this opportunity.

𐤙 𐤚 𐤛𐤜𐤝 𐤜𐤞𐤜𐤟 𐤠𐤡𐤢𐤣 𐤤𐤥 𐤦

David was taken aback by the energy and excitement his guests retained. The boys had finished such a vigorous sum of exercising, so early on this morning; yet they appeared refreshed and anxious for the day. However, he had no interest in the details of the boy's morning agenda.

Kasper was pleased that David quickly made conversation of plans for the remaining hours of this day. He particularly, did not want to mention the encounter with the 'spiritualist'. He feared David might have some affinity for some of the stranger's belief of 'many higher powers'.

It was a long breakfast at the Morris Inn; fine chinaware, elegant crystal and attentive professional service. The boys joined by David's colleague, Mark Purcell an associate professor with the Physics department.

Pancakes, bacon, sausage, eggs, hash browns, Danny, and Kasper had never seen so many courses on a table. Consumption eliminated most of the food. Conversation clarified plans that they would spend the remaining morning and afternoon touring the labs of the Physics department, then take some time looking at some physic problems to help Kasper's upcoming examination.

Mr. Purcell received the young men with usual courtesy. He was sharp-featured, thoughtful face, and his curling hair prematurely tinged with gray, while his dress was comfortably causal.

"Your name is very familiar to me, Kasper Wise," said he, smiling. "After, David informed me you and Danny were runners it donned on me who you were."

Kasper was caught flabbergasted.

"Your coach sent our department a letter, expressing your athletic ability and interest in studying physics at UND," continued Mark. "He expressed your tenacity in preparing for the Physics Subject Examination."

"Yes Sir," replied Kasper re-gathering his composure, "and I have been fortunate enough that David has steered me toward the materials that will help me for the exam."

"He's got good study material," interrupted David, "I have a text in Physics with Calculus, by Samuels and Jobs."

"That's a great text. Their problems are quite instructional, as well as creative, "continued Mark. "We'll look at some problems in these materials after the tour."

"Young Danny," reminded David, "he wants to pursue medicine or Dentistry did you say?"

"I'm not sure, yet," responded Danny.

"Outstanding young men you have here David. We'll set our sights on the Biology and Health Science building as well on our tour."

Several hours passed while the youths were mesmerized in objects and subjects only experienced through picture books and videotapes prior to this day. They were overwhelmed with the histories of the buildings and personages that help create these college departments. At lunch while the two were along briefly, they expressed the tour experience.

"They talk to us like we're important people," stated Danny. "The people we met, so cordial and all."

"People who's successful and like what they are doing generally they like other people and know how to treat others. Besides, we are important."

"Until we get home, then we are just dudes"

Laughing with each other suggested comfort. The defensiveness experienced early that day waned from their present state of mind. This bless was interrupted, only as David and Mark arrived to escort them to a classroom in one of the spacious physics labs.

"Gut wir dürfen sehen, wie dumm wir sind (Well, we get to see how dumb we are)," thought Kasper as the men departed the cafeteria.

Moving toward pedagogical session Kasper reflected that his sense of belonging had gripped him once more. The last time he had such felling was while he had been at Marlborough High school Old and traditional, a former student from Marlborough became governor; others were now ranking officers in the military, a few were millionaire business people. They were aloof toward influx of the minorities and country people at the school. At Notre Dame, the people were just opposite, but that offered him no comfort. It was the institutions, its majesty, history, and something more than the collection of buildings – its soul. A group of fancy buildings at a city center has no such eminence and emits no soul, just its big and gaudy tapestries blinding out nature's features and clarifying the smell of fast foods and floor polish. This ominous sense in this place burdened Kasper.

This introspection was consistent with Kasper's own gripe of his personal belief system. He was very much conscience of what he felt was important, what was sacred to his being. Once committed to something, the task remaining is that of preserving and protecting. Outside influences had a minimal affect on him and he was prepared to parry any attack on his passions, just as he had handled the 'space cadet' that morning.

"Shoot, I can make it if I was here," Kasper thought feeling gung ho, "Most kids here are just fulfilling what's laid out for them. If you're creative you'll stand out." The boy knew his strength was his relentlessness with 'brute force' he could apply to matters.

"Let's look at a problem that requires some fundamental physics where it cannot be solved simply with the calculus," Mark proposed breaking the philosophical mood as the visitors sat before him facing a large long blackboard in this large classroom empty except for this small group.

"You can find this problem in the Frank text," David interrupted, "section 3.4."

"A small woman of mass 50 kg jumps from an airplane. She reaches a terminal velocity of 50 meters per second. Determine the time it takes the woman to reach 75 percent of her terminal velocity." Mark looked at the pair and observed eyes saying 'how do you start this?'

"What's fundamental here? We have a falling object and it eventually reaches a constant speed in free fall."

"There must be a force against gravity to prevent her from falling with increasing speed," Kasper offered bravely.

"Excellent! Now, this force must be related to velocity right?" Mark received agreement from the two. "If you're falling at a low speed air resistance is low. As you get faster the retarding force gets larger right?"

"How can you express that mathematically?" Asked David; looking at the boys askance.

"You can say resistance is directly related to speed," said Kasper.

"Yes, so we can write:

$$R \approx -bv$$

"Where 'b' is proportionality constant that depends on the units of the problem."

"In the vertical direction the retarding force is opposite the direction of fall, hence the minus sign, okay?" He received nods from the boys.

"Ok, we're talking about force, mass, falling object. Any suggestions as to what laws of motion we should be using?"

"Newton's second law?"

"That's correct Casper, good," said David. "Newton's second law is a powerful tool, in an enormous family of problems in physics and engineering."

Mark turned to the blackboard and wrote

$$F = ma$$

"Now the vertical components of force must be equal and opposite weight at terminal velocity."

$$mg + R = ma$$

"Then the weight of the falling woman and the resistive force of the atmosphere must equal her mass times her acceleration as she falls. Substituting we get

$$mg - bv = m \, dv/dt$$

"Since, acceleration is the change in velocity over the change in time

$$a = dv/dt$$

"Rearrange $\quad m \, dv/dt = mg - bv$ divide both sides by the mass, m

$$dv/dt = g - bv_t/m$$

"This is a differential equation. How are we going to solve this for velocity, v?"

"Can't use arithmetic that's for sure?" shot back Danny smiling and so did everyone else.

"Good observation," commented David, "So, Sir Isaac Newton faced many physics problems so he had to invent, what?"

"Calculus, to deal with events that changed with time," said David.

"Thus, to accomplish such, let us first separate the variables, t and v on opposite sides of the equation," Mark continued, "We have

$$dv/dt = (mg\text{-}bv)/m$$

"Rearrange

$$dv/(mg - bv) = dt/m$$

"Then let's take the integral of both sides and use the natural log to get

$$\int dv/(mg\text{-}bv) = \int dt/m$$

"Since $\int df/f = \ln(f/f_0)$, a property of logs where f_0 is a constant of resulting from the integration.

"Let

$$f = mg - bv$$

"Take the differential of this, we get

$$df = - b \, dv$$

"Solve for dv

$$dv = - df/b$$

"Then substitute, f and dv into the integrals

$$- 1/b \int df/(mg - bv) = 1/m \int dt$$

$$\int df/(mg - bv) = - bt/m$$

"And applying the log property

$$\ln (mg - bv)/f_0 = - bt/m$$

"Solve for v as a function of t by taking the exponential of both sides and using log properties

$$(mg - bv) = f_0 \, e^{-bt/m}$$

"Now, we solve this expression for velocity, v." Mark wrote out the algebra steps and arrived at

$$v(t) = mg/b - f_0 \, e^{-bt/m}/b$$

"But we still can't solve for v, because we don't know what the constants, f_0 and b are."

"Have any ideas?"

Kasper and Danny sat silent, staring at the script on the blackboard.

"For such a problem as this we must use the initial conditions to find the constants. So at t = 0, beginning of her jump, v = 0, then the equation above simplifies to

$$0 = mg/b - f_0/b$$

"Thus $f_0 = mg$

"Plug this into v(t), we get the final equation

$$v(t) = mg/b \, (1 - e^{-bt/m})$$

"Now to find b, at the beginning of the jump b = 0, so we must find what it is at terminal velocity."

"So in the differential equation, dv/dt = 0, at terminal velocity, v_t = 50 m/s as given, so

$$dv/dt = g - bv_t/m$$

"becomes

$$0 = g - bv_t/m$$

"Solving for b, we get

$$b = mg/vt = (50) \, (9.8)/50$$

$$b = 9.8 \text{ kg/s}$$

"Ok, now substitute b = mg/v_t into the velocity equation." Mark simplified to

$$v = v_t \, (1 - e^{-bt/m})$$

"So $e^{-bt/m} = 1 - v/v_t$

"Take the natural log of both sides

$$\ln e^{-bt/m} = \ln \, (1 - v/v_t)$$

$$bt/m = \ln \, (1 - v/v_t)$$

"Solving this for time, t

$$t = - \, (m/b) \ln \, (1 - v/v_t)$$

"Ok, since we need to find the time of fall for seventy-five percent of terminal, set b = 9.8, m = 50, and v = 0.75 v_t into the equation." Mark made the substitutions, then after some algebra and using a calculator to compute the natural log, he wrote

$$t = - \, (5.10) \ln 0.25$$

$$t = 7.07 \text{ seconds}$$

"So it takes seven point seven seconds for the falling woman to reach 75% of her terminal velocity; that is 0.75 times 50 meters per second, equals 38 meters per second.

Kasper looked at his notes, copied from the board. He had not understood all the algebra particularly on the use the natural logs and exponentials.

"Any questions?" asked Mark.

"Yes," said Kasper who asked for clarification. Mark was pleased to review with him and Danny the basics of concepts of the problems.

"You can expect to have at least one falling body problem," said David. "I would study this problem and make up some examples like it."

A bit of time passed as Mark flipped through his binder, finally he turned to his audience. He was impressed with how Kasper seemed anxious and nervous that he did not grasp the essentials of the problem. Other visitors had shown either a total ellipse as to what transpired or they tried to brush the problem off as something to tackle later at their convenience.

"What kind of problems may I expect covering relativity?" asked Kasper.

"Yes, I am looking at one now," answered Mark not surprised. "Here is another typical problem requiring calculus. It's a derivative."

"Don't expect but a few plug and chug problems," remarked David.

"Yea, any peasant can just memorize a formula and plug in the numbers," continued Mark. "We're looking for the ability for a student who can use math and physics fundamentals to put a solution together. David, could you go over problem fourteen-point-twenty with them, while I check to see if those east coast people have arrived yet?"

"No problem," answered David jumping up from his seat then scanning the pages of a text. Mark took his leave, after excusing himself. David finished his tour of the section pushed his glasses back firmly to his face and turned to the blackboard. He moved down from the already occupied section and started:

'The problem asks for us to show that

$$k = \int F \, ds = mc^2 - m_0c^2$$

"That is, kinetic energy represents the difference between the total energy of a particle moving at near the speed of light and the rest energy when we take the integral of force, F, applied to the particle, from a velocity, u = 0 to u = u."

David checked on the boys, it appeared they had just heard some Chinese dialog reckoning their response of his question.

"The classical expression of Newton's second law is that the net force on a body is equal to the rate of change of the body's momentum. If a body moves at speeds near the speed of light allowances is made for the fact that, the mass of a body varies with velocity. That is

$$m = m_0/\sqrt{1 - uu/cc}$$

"Familiar?"

"Yes," said Kasper

Danny nodded, "yea, we just did a few problems last week, using the mass, time, and length dilations."

"Good, so keep that in your head for now, we will be back to it. Now we have

$$F = ma = m\, du/dt = d/dt\,(mu)$$

$$= dp/dt$$

"Since $p = mu$ = momemtum,

"The kinetic energy, k, of a body is equal to the work done by an external force in increasing the speed of the body from zero to some value 'u'. Since work is force times distance, we can write

$$k = \int F \cdot dx$$

"Then after substituting

$$k = \int d/dt\,(mu)\, dx = \int d\,(mu)\, dx/dt$$

"Know how to complete the derivative?" David looked at the two.

"Yea," said Kasper.

"Come on up to the board," David ordered. Kasper proceeded and found a clear portion of the board.

"You take the derivative of u, hold m constant; now add the derivative of m while holding u constant." He scribbled as he spoke.

$$d(mu) = mdu + udm$$

"Good job," exclaimed David, "you see that Danny?"

"Yes sir."

"Now, speed is the change in distance by the change in time. "Right guys?" He looked over his shoulder for nods, which he received. "So we may write under the integral." Since, $u = dx/dt$

$$k = \int (mdu + udm)u$$

$$= \int mudu + u^2 dm$$

"Stop there now let's look at something else so we can simplify that expression, okay?" We know,

$$m = m_0/\sqrt{1 - uu/cc}$$

"When we square both sides we get
$$m^2 = m_0{}^2/(1 - u^2/c^2)$$

"Rearrange this to
$$m^2(1-u^2)/c^2 = m_0{}^2$$
$$m^2(c^2 - u^2)/c^2 = m_0{}^2$$
$$m^2c^2 - m^2c^2 = m_0{}^2c^2$$

"Now, since mass, m can be changing and speed, u, is increasing if we take the differential of the expression we may see something useful. Kasper, you should be able to do this, give it a try."

"Okay, here we go," volunteered Kasper meekly as Danny offered only a perplexed stare.

The boy went before the board and thought out-loud. "I'll take the derivative of the first with respect to m, multiplying the constant c^2. For the second term, we must take the derivative of m just as before; but now I have to add the derivative of u, and multiply m^2. Then distribute the minus sign for these two terms." He wrote on the board

"We arrive at,

$$2mdmc^2 - 2mdmu^2 - 2udum^2 = 2m_0dm_0c^2$$

"Great job!" said David. "Alright, let me ask you something. Is your rest mass, m_0, changing or is it a constant?" David looked at both boys. "What do we mean by rest mass, Danny?"

Danny was surprised a question directed his way. "Ah, I think it means the mass is not moving," answered the boy. Kasper nodded in approval.

"That's right, m changes but m_0 does not. The expression for changing rest mass, dm_0, has to equal zero."

"Thus the right side of the equation equals zero," interjected Kasper.

"There you go!"

David walked over to the board. "Let me show you something. Rearrange and see what we have." He wrote

$$2mc^2dm = m^2 2udu + u^2 2mdm$$

"Divide by 2m, we have then

$$c^2dm = mudu + u^2dm$$

"Hey, guys this expression is the same as the integral expression in k. You see!" revealed David pointing to the blackboard script. "So that means, we may write

$$k = \int_0^u (mudu + u^2dm) = \int_{mo}^m c^2dm$$

"Integrating from rest mass to some future moving mass, we have our expression, we're looking for." He wrote

$$k = \int_{mo}^m c^2dm = c^2m|_{mo}^m = c^2(m - m_0)$$
$$k = mc^2 - m_0c^2$$

"So we accomplished our problem. Kinetic energy represents the difference between the total energy, mc^2, of a moving particle and the rest mass energy, m_0c^2."

"I have an ominous task before me," commented Kasper dimly, with a humble smile.

Danny smiled slightly as well and thought to himself, "I am fortunate not to be pursuing physics as a major."

"Just review over and over these problems we're going over. These methods are used time and time again in solutions," said David reassuringly. "Ok, Kasper did you find any particular questions or problems when you looked over the packet?"

"Yes, I have one," said Kasper turning pages in his notebook.

"Here's one. It says, 'Know the properties of the Photon and prove such properties.'

"That's a good one," answered David his eyes flashing surprise, "and it's a must know for you. Okay, here we go. The photon or light we see through experiments can be shown to behave like a wave or as particles."

"We can do an experiment that says, it's a wave, and then we can do other experiments to show it's a particle," revealed Kasper confidently.

"Exactly!" agreed David. "If light is a particle then it must have characteristics such as energy and it must possess mass and momentum."

David was back at the board erasing everything. "Let's consider the mass of a photon. We know relativistic mass is…" He wrote

$$m = m_0/\sqrt{1 - vv/cc}$$

"But, the photon is a particle of light which moves of course at the speed of light, "So…

$$v^2 = c^2 \text{ and } m = m_0/0 = \text{undefined}$$

"Anything divided by zero is undefined. You can't have zero in the denominator in mathematics." Turning to the pair, "How can you get out of this dilemma? Danny, what must you assume, if this occurred?"

"What ever you have in the numerator has to equal zero, if you did the problem correctly."

"Excellent!" David saw Kasper nodding in agreement. "We must define the rest mass, m_0, as equaling zero…" Writing

"For the photon $m_0 = 0$

"Clever deduction," murmured Kasper taking aback at this insight.

"Also, we know the photon always exit moving at the speed of light, so again it has no rest mass. Now Einstein's equation…" Writing

$$E = mc^2$$

"Says, that energy maybe exchanged for mass and mass maybe exchanged for energy, so let's write

$$m = E/c^2$$

"Energy, E is equal to Planck's constant times the frequency of a wave, right? So rearranging

$$m = hv/c^2$$

"Now, we're ready to solve problems. A typical problem is, "If a photon of reddish light has a wavelength of 720 nanometers, what mass would this particle of light possess?"

"Wave frequency is inversely related to wavelength, λ so

$$v = c/\lambda = 3.0 \times 10^8/720 \times 10^{-9} = 4.2 \times 10^{14} \text{ Hz}$$

"So substituting into the mass, energy equation above, we arrive at

$$m = (6.63 \times 10^{-34}) (4.2 \times 10^{14})/(3.0 \times 10^8)^2$$

"Tell me what you get, guys."

After moments of algebra, Kasper and Danny finished. "We get a mass of,

Kasper went to the board and wrote

$$m = 3.1 \times 10^{-36} \text{ kg}$$

"This is a very small mass," added David, "For prospective, compare this to the mass of an electron which is

$$m = 9.1 \times 10^{-31} \text{ kg}$$

"See, a photon is about five orders of magnitude smaller."
"What was the energy, again?" asked Danny.
"Oh yea, we didn't find it directly, suggestions?"
"We had E = hv," Kasper, reminded himself.
"That's right. So, if we have the frequency of the red light, we may use E = hv,

$$E = hv = (6.63 \times 10^{-34}) (4.2 \times 10^{14})$$

$$E = 27.6 \times 10^{-20} \text{ joules}$$

"We prefer to express energy in terms of units of electron volts, eV. So let us convert joules to electron volts. One electron volt is equal to 1.6×10^{-19} joules...

$$E = (27.6 \times 10^{-20} \text{ J}) \times (1 \text{ eV}/1.6 \times 10^{-19} \text{ J})$$

$$= 1.7 \text{ eV}$$

"About, one point seven electron volts of energy," said Kasper.
"Good job. Now, what momentum does the photon have?"
"Momentum is relativistic mass times velocity," volunteered Danny. David wrote

$$p = mc = m_o \, c/\sqrt{1 - vv/cc}$$

"That's true, relativistic mass times the speed of light," agreed David. "But, I want to introduce momentum as related to total energy and rest energy. This formula will be much more convenient for problem solving those various concepts.

So, let's do a derivation first," David started writing on the black board. "Let's take the square difference between total and rest energy. Here we go." Writing again:

$$E = mc^2 \text{ and } E_0 = m_0 c^2$$

"Square both and take the difference.

We get $E^2 - E_0^2 = m^2 c^4 - m_0^2 c^4$

"Where $m = m_0 \gamma$

"Now γ is

$$\gamma = 1/\sqrt{1 - vv/cc}$$

"So we write $E^2 - E_0^2 = \gamma^2 m_0^2 c^4 - m_0^2 c^4$, after substituting for m,

$$= m_0^2 c^4 (\gamma^2 - 1)$$
$$= m_0^2 c^4 (1/1 - v^2/c^2 - 1) = (m_0^2 c^4 - 1 + v^2 c^2)/1/1 - v^2/c^2$$

"Get a common denominator, then this simplifies to

$$E^2 - E_0^2 = m_0^2 c^4 (v^2/c^2)/1 - v^2/c^2 = m_0 v^2 c^2 \gamma^2$$

"Here's a trick, since $m^2 = m_0^2 \gamma^2$

$$m_0^2 = m^2/\gamma^2 \text{ substitute}$$

"Then

$$E^2 - E_0^2 = m^2 v^2 c^2$$

"Since

$$p = mv$$
$$E^2 - E_0^2 = p^2 c^2$$

"And by rearranging and setting $E_0^2 = m_0^2 c^4$

$$E^2 = p^2 c^2 + m_0^2 c^4$$

"Finished, this is the often published relation between total energy, momentum, and rest energy." David surmised.

"I've seen that in texts, but nobody ever derived it," said Kasper.

"When you get to graduate school you will have to derive all physics equations," David said. "We don't just plug and chug. You are given a problem you then formulate, maybe derive, approximate with expansions, and then make your conclusions with some numerical values." David waited briefly for effect.

"Okay, we're not done. From here we can solve for momentum, pc, and get

$$p^2c^2 = E^2 - m_o^2c^4$$

"And we know the rest energy equals zero, because the photon has zero rest mass thus

$$p^2c^2 = E^2$$

"Further simplify by dividing by c squared and taking the square root, we have then

$$p = E/c \text{ or } p = hv/c$$

"In terms of wavelength

$$p = h/\lambda$$

"Is the momentum of a photon?"

"Man, that was a lot of work to show that relationship," said Danny.

"But, like you said these formulas are used a lot in problems asked," replied Kasper.

"Yes, like this example. If a light has a wavelength of 300 nanometers, what is its momentum? We have

$$P = h/\lambda = 6.63 \times 10^{-34}/300 \times 10^{-9}$$

$$= 0.0221 \times 10^{-25}$$

$$= 2.21 \times 10^{-27} \text{ kg m/s}$$

"So, what we have realized here is that the photon is a particle, but its properties of mass, energy, and momentum are described in terms of frequency or wavelength which is wave phenomena."

"That was revealing," stated Kasper.

"Revealing, aha," David chuckled, "okay, why don't we break here? Guys, what would you like to do now?" "Can we go to the bookstore and browse?" asked Danny.

"Yea, I'd like to get over there and pick up a few things," agreed Kasper.

"Great idea, let me see what Mark found out about our expectant guests and then I'll find you guys, okay?"

No more words needed. There was a clatter of closing books, a rush for the stairs and then quick footfalls from the room.

It was nearly eight o'clock when the trio returned from their excursion. Fatigued, excited, pressured and anxious. All these entwined on Kasper's emotions, as he lay in bed. Danny lay unconscious in the twin bed next to him. They had watched TV until their eyes resisted watching any more of the figures acting before them.

As he closed his eyes, he more so than not, reflected on the substances of the day. What he found unique in his experiences was the orderliness, systematic natural means by which those problems resolved themselves, after some simple fundamentals of nature and a bit of expanding from there. "Delicately suggestive, but nothing overtly complex," he thought. "The math you become familiar with and use it as a tool." He surmised an approach of thinking that would enable him to reap success toward his endeavor. Kasper slipped into some adverse thoughts, however. The man the pair met at the track that morning, he reminisced further, the affairs concerning Johannes; something was not right with him, he needed to speak to Jimmy further about this.

Kasper finally fell away from controlled consciences with his most fearful challenge – getting an outstanding performance that would make him worthy of a track program such as the one at Notre Dame. As usual, he ultimately purged his anxieties when he bedded and slept peacefully; he had to be ready to run and afterwards apply his newfound knowledge to those physics problems he had to withstand from David and Mark.

"Consistency, consistency, gentlemen," said Thorpe. "And lady" he added as Sheila was with the group. "Let's lay down two sets of ten 200's. I want my 800 runners at 28 seconds, distance men 31 seconds. Sheila, keep 'em at 35 seconds for ten first ten. Then we walk 400 and again repeat for the distance people. Eli and Terry, I want eighty percent on the straights, walk the curves, do six laps, okay?"

"Yes sir."

"Katie will be calling out the lead times. Keep the pack tight." Thorpe said. "It's going to be tough workouts today and tomorrow. Wednesday we will have a light effort. So let's hit it!"

Moving toward the start the pack sprang into the first lap. As Thorpe turned his attention to Jimmy and Roy, Caroline Webster was working with the girls. This old over worn cindered track grounds buzzed in activity on this warm sunny afternoon. There was little talking among the working pack. Only an occasional warning: "Spread out, watch your legs…" Contemplative activity in thought was at a serious height nonetheless while the relentless pounding took place. Most vision their being in a race where they stubbornly maintained pace positions. These fellows thought of the competition as forces that threatened to distract his future. Here was the opportunity to prove their stubbornness.

"28.3…30.8" announced Katie as the two groups finished, "33 Sheila! Too fast!"

Kasper's thoughts lead to predictions: "31…maybe I can average 33. That's a 4:20 mile…maybe 9:20's for 3200 meters." He had a tough hall before him. Thorpe had entered him in both the 1600 and 3200 meter runs in the Districts.

"28.3!…30 flat!…35.2 Sheila!" Katie called loudly.

Sheila. Kasper thought about her. She had not seen any sign of the stalker, but she told him the anxiety had increased at home since her mother appeared to have become more upset about the stranger than she. She said she is sorry she ever disclosed the incident to her family.

"29.2! 31.5!…35 flat!"

He thought of why he was worrying about the Sweigert affair, more going on there than one would guess. "I don't need my name to come up in the papers about some mess." The walk between his runs seemed like only seconds. All were reaching deep into their lungs with each breath as they prepared for the next sprint. A hand would drop as they sprang into the run. Katie would snap her watch and Thorpe might find their attention: "keep your strides long!" He would call out. "Stick with Danny…pull up on his shoulder…yea that's it…float across…"

"28.1…31.5…36 Sheila!"

"I think my work is good…but am I doing what I should?"

Yes, do what I can to help Mrs. Sweigert and Sheila. If you want something good to happen to you, then you must strive to help others…This is what I must do." Thought Kasper tired and getting more contemplative as his fatigue wore on.

"Walk and stretch, before the next set people!" Thorpe called out. They moved to the outside of the track silent, thoughtful as to now they would get through the second set. Each run was getting more difficult as lactic acid built up in the muscles.

"Hey guys," Thorpe directed his call to Eli and Terry.

"Jimmy and Roy will complete four 200's at 24 seconds. They'll start behind you and pass, okay?"

"Getting into the hurts zone now huh dudes?" said the ever-gregarious Jimmy, breaking everybody's solitude. "Ya'll working guys, way to go Sheila, you hanging tough. We ought to do some serious damage this Saturday." Then the boy strode next to Kasper, "Got a thing I want to pass on to you 'bout our business. We need a couple minutes after workout okay?"

"Yea, Jimmy," responded a pleased Kasper, "I need to get with you on that, too."

Terry, Eli, and Sheila peeled from their own group to prepare for the stretch runs. At a faint mark on the track, Kasper with Danny on his outside pumped his arms and legs into acceleration then slowly sought his gate for a 31 second 200 meters. Around the curve starting into the final 100 meters was when Jimmy and Roy. This pair started a couple seconds behind but floated past Kasper and crew to get to the 200 no later than 24 seconds.

"24.4!" Katie called out then quickly, "30 flat for Danny and Kasper crossing together." Thorpe was standing near this time.

"A kid from Moulendorf went 4:19 then he rolled the 3200 off in 9:25," then the man turned for another session of activities that required his attention. Kasper was tired so Thorpe calling out such a performance by someone irritated him. "Was ein tackless weg der Handhabung uns, während wir au hier Leiden sind. (What a tactless way of handling us, while we're out here suffering)," he thought.

"They're our division aren't they?" queried Danny.

"I am afraid so," answered Kasper disconsolate.

"I heard that," It was Jimmy commenting. "You dudes gotta pop. You guys gotta suck in a little closer to me and Roy, rotate faster dudes." Jimmy in his mannerism seemed somewhere between advisory support to just plain jollying. Kasper often thought Jimmy delighted in seeing him stressed-out. Indeed Jimmy thought Kasper too serious about matters as well as too predictive.

"The dude needs to loosen up," Jimmy said to Roy after finishing the series of 200's.

"Kasper's not really a jock type," clarified Roy, "he's not spontaneous about thing. Everything has order in his mind."

"Well my man had better get ready for the disorderly. At Regional and State he is going to run with an aggressive, got 'em get 'em bunch of people." Jimmy warned.

"Yep, the time they go in with means nothing people will drop a lot of time off by States," agreed Roy.

"And, Kasper is going to be surprised. Now, Danny he won't rattle as much as Kasper he'll go with the flow."

"Yea, Kasper will try to stick to a plan." The two shook their heads in agreement and departed for the showers. Out on the dusty track Kasper and Danny finished the series of runs and stretched after the session panting with exhaustion.

"Why does everything have to be stressed out around here?" questioned a pensive Kasper.

Danny chuckled ignoring his cousin's seriousness. "Well, we need such circumstances to make us run faster so we are sure to make it big time. All things work together for good, you know."

"I guess you should look at it that way," responded a reflective Kasper, checking himself, "Danny, for us there is no such thing as chance. Providence brings us into circumstances that we cannot foresee at all. Sometimes we are brought into places and among people and into conditions in order that we take a particular path, therefore let us not think it strange concerning the circumstances we find ourselves in."

"Hey guys," interrupted Katie walking toward the two, "You guys averaged 31.4 and 31.6," said she looking at her clipboard and continued pass the pair.

Kasper's mind went back to a poignant line. "Durch Versuche wird Ein Ganzes gemacht warden (Through trials one shall be made whole)." He longed for some solitude by which he sought the quiet possession of himself, but there was unavoidable business in abeyance. "I'll meet with Jimmy in a while and see what's going on with Sheila. Early tomorrow I want to float off an easy six miler and think," he planned Kasper begged the opportunity to relieve some of the burden felt for this while. So solitude was required to cultivate and adjudicate the self and resist the lure of recent circumstances.

On his short trip, in the evening, Kasper walked across the small park that leads from his housing complex to the small eatery, Fisher's Boathouse, that over looks the big lake. There was no one at any park tables, but several people where at the task of launching their boats from trailers positioned on the banks so the boats may slip into the waters. Many boats where speeding through the lake from all directions; a couple boats pulled water skiers donning life jackets. There were a few people fishing alone the banks of the lake, seemingly enjoying the peace more than any urgency to catch anything.

"You guys are running good young man." A man called after Kasper. He turned to see a man reclined in a chair under the shade of a tree; he recognized the man who was often walking the paths of the park as he and the guys were running in the area all these months. He waved to the man, for he had no idea the man's name. He continued his way reaching the short steps of the business and entered. No sign of Jimmy, then a heavy bark haired middle-aged woman greeted him. "You looking for Jimmy Luke?" she asked while directing him to a corner near the back of the room filled with tables and small booths bordering the walls.

"What's up?" Jimmy asked leaning back in his seat as Kasper approached. Jimmy always asked, "what's up?' It was his form of greeting. The two took seats and ordered grilled hamburgers and drinks.

"First off, you remember that I remarked to you about the last meeting with Johannes," asked Kasper.

"Yep," answered Jimmy, "you said you didn't feel right about something said by the old dude."

"I'm beginning to think Jimmy," said Kasper, "that I made a mistake in my dealings with Johannes.

"You better," interrupted Jimmy, "Old as he is, the dudes has to be an ex Nazi. I bet he could do a mean goose step in his day," he jollied as Kasper displayed a long grin.

"Really, Kasper," Jimmy continued, "the ole dude has a friendly reputation with some of my ole scoundrel friends and homies you know."

"Is that so?"

"Tell me." Queried Jimmy, "What set you off on him?"

"First, he said the American money sent to Germany was exchanged for several times the amount for Dutch Marks. Now that's, nonsense. Actually the dollar is weak; you only get some percent on each dollar."

"He thinks you're stupid, huh?" Jimmy assessed with no timidity.

"Definitely." Says Kasper appreciating the agreement, "the old man goes on telling me about Bill's helping his grandson, Wilhelm, take care of his family with all Dutch Marks he gets with these dollars. This is so farfetched it strikes me as a fairy tale or a poorly devised lie."

"He's a lot of bull and he thinks you're stupid," Jimmy leaned over toward Kasper to emphasize the point. "I tell 'ya, the dude told my homies he's an ex storm trooper, SS. He's super bad I tell you."

"Sounds like you been on to him for a while."

"Yep, you're the innocent type, but you're smart. I figured you would be on to him soon enough Kasper." Jimmy chuckled and wriggled in his seat, as was his habit when in high spirits. "I wonder what Sheriff Palooka thinks of all this."

"If Johannes told this cock and bull story to them they wouldn't believe it either. They'd know something is not right with him," surmised Kasper. "That's a flaw of the criminal mine they think they're smarter than everyone in their dealing. They don't appreciate their own stupidity."

Jimmy nodded, "but Mrs. Sweigert, she's not aware of these conniving. I feel sorry for her and ole Bill. He's probably just making a few bucks from the ole man."

"Yea, Johannes gives me money liberally every time we meet."

"You kidding," Jimmy looked surprised.

"Wow! The dudes a crook, I tell 'ya. Ole Johannes was a serious Nazi I bet."

"I am going to pass our thoughts to the Sheriff at least to see if he's on to Johannes as well."

"Good idea. I want to come with you," reassured Jimmy, "Its best they know we ain't into any of Johannes's crap or what ever he's doing."

"That would suit me very well," said Kasper, "By the way have you gotten any feedback on the stalker bothering Sheila."

"Well, that's who I am worried about," Jimmy volunteered. "When I last tried to ask her about it she brushed me off sort of like it was no big thing."

"That's interesting because Jill Story and Barb Hick are a couple of her chums, said Sheila's mother is real upset more so than Sheila. They said Sheila's mom said she would call the sheriff. Well, the next day her mom told her the stalker wouldn't bother her anymore." Kasper revealed to Jimmy.

"How would she know that, for sure?" Jimmy questioned.

"Maybe moms knew who the stalker was?"

The dark haired waitress interrupted the conversation with the sandwiches ordered. While Kasper tore into his voraciously washing his mouthful down with a long draught of pop. Jimmy took little time to devour his meal as well.

"Were we hungry, or what?" Jimmy remarked as they finished and sat back relaxed.

"Starving, I didn't have an appetite at lunch worrying about all this mess."

"Shoot! I am hungry all the time," said Jimmy. "This was a bad burger it hit the spot for me."

"Well this conversation has certainly cleared a few gaps for me," Kasper revealed with a sign of relief.

Jimmy shrugged his shoulders with a glance of resignation.

"Don't be worrying about any of this stuff. You want to go to a big college and I want to drive tanks in the army. We got to worry about ourselves dude."

It was destined, however, that Kasper came to some terms of these affairs. It was not his character to allow things evolve on there own devices or conclusions. The discussed affairs had obtruded themselves upon Kasper in such a way that it was impossible to ignore them.

The fellows enjoyed the remains of the evening on the subject of their running and anticipation of performances. Kasper was impressed that Jimmy had some multi-dimensional aspects with more insight into affairs than he would have credited him for; as this one on one meeting suggested Jimmy held prudence not revealed with a group.

The leader of the pack the top of the food chain such was the identity Jimmy placed in the social structures amongst young culture. Medium in height, rounded headed, his hair was red-brownish, usually very short. Brown eyed with a short nose, he is the archetype of the dominant male as described by anthropologists. Jimmy was not the 'victim type'. It was his nature to seek and lead the 'unsure' and dominate with nurturing.

Kasper posed to be a most unusual fellow for Jimmy. Kasper could be both submissive but also he was inspirational. His ability to remain focused on his tasks and the high goals he begged of impressed the whimsical Jimmy. However, most impressive to Jimmy was Kasper's non-regional mind. He did not think nor spoke like a local. In Kasper, Jimmy experienced an outsider's mentality. A country boy who had hardly ever been anywhere, Jimmy believed Kasper's presence was an education and experience beneficial to his socialization to the sophisticated. Kasper could fit in with any of the 'knuckle head' groups unlike himself who looked like 'the country'.

"Well let's get out of here," surmised Kasper, "I am going to push a hard run in the morning. You already have some class one performances, but not me as of yet."

"Just go with the flow Kasper. Don't plan your races too much," cautioned Jimmy. "Improvise and be ready for anybody, then you'll be more relaxed and your times will drop dude."

CHAPTER 8

▼

It was in the early hours of the night and the equinoctial gales had set in with exceptional violence. Most of the remaining night the wind had screamed and the rain had beaten against the windows. Even under the cover of framed wood, one would be forced to question the routine of carnal existence and recognize the presence of those great elemental forces which shriek at mankind remaining untamed however our efforts. As the night grew and the storm strengthened the wind cried like cats in heat. Kasper Wise slept on undisturbed. Soothing he would describe the rain and wind howling. Sleep was deep as he tucked under his covers in the fetal position.

Finally, the weather would retreat or better said moves toward the virgin ground toward the east; allowing the low rays of the sun to penetrate within his abode. Then slowly Kasper would rouse, stretch between his disarrayed covers and then eyes opened he would lie on his back for a while then climb out of the bed. Danny on this morning would pursue his lead, rousing with more resistance. He really did not want to leave the bed. Greg did not have to leave his bliss. Thorpe told him not to run the mornings anymore this season. He was to run on the four by 800 meters relay only. Greg needed speed for his 800 meter run not over distance runs. Many 200-meter runs waited for him in the afternoon workouts this week.

"Why," said Danny glancing up from his seat on the edge of the bed at his companion, "it's clear out now."

"But, it rained a lot," answered Kasper, "We'll have to avoid puddles and streams of running water."

Anyone with less commitment would note consider moving from bed at such an early hour after such weather. However, this pair of youths assured themselves that this assault against the morning elements would lighten any resistance to that future performance when these familiar elements may flare upon them. A hardened, fearless, regimen they thought would protect them from the anxiety that appeared upon their minds like so many obstacles. Yet in his studies, Kasper remained fearful and nervous of the simplest physics test. It bothered him that such feeling were absent when facing an English exam or a biology test. He mounted little emotions for an algebra examination. At the results of any of these subjects, though they be less than his expectations, they harbored little response other than an, 'oh well'. So, why the nervous stomach, sweaty arm pits at the approach of a physics exam? Why these symptoms whenever he even thinks of the regional and state meets? Being honest with himself, he remembered that these anxieties occurred whenever he had to extend all his efforts holding back nothing.

"I don't like that extending myself early in anything," Kasper thought as he and Danny worked there way up a short incline still running slowly. "You have got to have something in reserve so you can deal with someone surging from behind and catching you off guard. That's true in races as well as in life in general."

As they ran, eyes watchfully focused on the ground before them. Little puddles to avoid, slippery grass, and muddy dirt paths traversed. A cool mist licked their face as they trudged through the heavy humid air. The woods were calm as the boys ran through somber bogs, while the air still smelled of dawn. Perhaps because this area is not overtly beautiful _ no bike paths, no keep lawns, no magnificent towering trees _ it remains untrammeled. The wet ground inundated with mushrooms and other fungus grew everywhere it seemed to the boys.

"Ah, haaa…Ah, haaa," Breaths were slow and reached far within the lunges. This early energy carried them effortlessly along a narrow road that led deep into the park woods surrounding Crimshead Lake. "Is my infatuation with running or is it the nature that surrounds the run?" Kasper was not sure. It was a ritual as much as an exercise; In the run dwell all the essence of his connection to eternal time. Eternity is just filled with pauses between repeats of identical events, 'there is nothing new under the sun, nothing' says the adage.

Silent they were, moving in a swift cadence. Both imagined their pace would challenge any Ethiopian or Kenyan. Perspiration flowed freely and profoundly because of the heavy humid condition. They began to work their way from the woods to free themselves of some of the clammy air. The fresh odor of pines and slimy earthworms was profuse. Their nostrils sucked in all these fragrances. Finally, at some clearing they slowed panting from the efforts of these bursts of speed. Mostly the pair jogged rhythmically as deep breaths retreated to soft relaxed efforts.

Tidbits of dialogue occurred in short jerky sentences: "Say, what's with this Johannes?....Sheila's doing alright...I am understanding physics a lot better..." Gradually the runners closed to home area. The pace naturally quickened. The run was back in charge seemingly taking control of the body and mind. This is where the body allows itself to flow along with the pack when in a race.

The sunrays spread, and one by one, the horizon disclosed more view. The boys perceived that the time had come for the long final assault of effort. Kasper was about to be measured. As he perceived this, it occurred to him that not too long in the past he thought only the stupid engages in any exercise with such intensity. It was as if his free will was hijack. He felt dragged by the merciless competitiveness. For the once he was front and center, off to the slaughter.

The two had to stride down a slight bank then skipped over a little stream and found solid footing once more. On level ground and only some minutes from home, some spontaneous reflection occurred to Kasper. "I know I can and will handle all this because there is another side of these eminent circumstances that will prevail." Swiftly the boys moved stride for stride not a foot separating them. Scrambling across a slight grassy bank, this led to a straight shot for home. The distance fell away; five-hundred meters, four-hundred meters, three-hundred, two-hundred...fifty meters from home, both gave up. There would be no slacking between this morning, "Better head right back and hit the showers we went a bit longer than normal," said Kasper, after they had slowed to a walk. Both felt at their strongest, neither felt intimidated by the other. The boys thought themselves as being on task.

"We got to do what we got to do," said Danny.

"It's alright Kasper," Sheila pleaded, "you do not have too worry about that anymore." They were in the school library and Kasper had listened but he thought she was more like suggesting that he stay out of her business. Kasper choose not to press her further on the subject. Instead, he reverted to the challenge they all were facing at Districts. Sheila expressed her dismay with the sudden appearance of a junior transfer from California. Lacy Cox; the girl was sixth at 4:52 at their state championships.

"She's hovering around five minutes already this year," said Sheila, "did you know her freshman sister is only a dozen seconds or so behind her?"

"Nah, I did not hear about any sister."

"Shoot, division three is going to have the fastest 1600 meters race in the girl's races, I bet."

"Looks like it," said Kasper then parlayed, "but you're no slouch girl. Just keep on our rears and keep healthy. Next week coach is going to back off on the workouts so we will, be rested for the Regional. You cannot control what others can do but you can place demands on yourself. Just think Sheila how surprised people are going to be when they match with you this year."

A quick blush passed over her fresh young face as Kasper proposed with a questioning glace at her.

"What's Thorpe got us doing today?" said she.

"Four-hundred meter runs I think."

From there, the conversation wound down to some concerns with strained muscles and the remedies appropriately applied. "Wenn sie nicht hervordritt wegen der Verfolgungs affaire, wesde ich mir keine Sorgen darüber machen (If she's not forthwith about this stalking affair, I'm not going to worry about it)" Thought the boy as the couple split. Kasper had an English grammar test the next school period and Sheila had Chemistry before track practice.

"Lassen Sie uns jetzt sehen, ob ich ein B auf dieser Prüfung erhalten kann. Englisch grammatik stinkt!(Now let me see if I can get a B on this test. English grammar sucks!)."

Kasper briefly reminisced on the conversation he had with Mark at Notre Dame. Kasper and he had a talk outside the physics building in the parking lot while waiting for David and Danny to appear before their departure. "I notice you still have quite a German accent, at times. I would have thought you would have lost it in the several years you've been over here." Mark had inquisitively asked.

"Most people would have certainly done so," replied Kasper, "but, I wouldn't consider such, you see I didn't want to lose my accent," Kasper had replied with no supportive comment.

Mark looked at him then another observation. "I gather you're very strong believer in your 'faith' as well." He queried here because of Kasper's numerous inquiries concerning the protestant church groups present on the campus.

"Certainly, I see no use in beliefs held spuriously. Such associations are dishonest to oneself as well as just a wasteful trait for others who may query you about the status of your beliefs."

"Huh," Mark had said after some long seconds of silence. "No offence meant but if I may say Shakespeare would describe you Kasper Wise as 'a strange and elusive fellow.'"

"No offense taken," Kasper had replied not perturbed the least at the inference. A smile likewise had showed that the comment had pleased him.

Amish men donning straw hats and women in bonnets driving the roads in buggies are a common sight of these culturally rich farmlands of central Ohio. Carefully laid out plots dotted with large barns and rows of chicken coops told of the history of these lands and the people who populated it. Here however, at the expansive Walnut Plaines High School athletic grounds and track that the first leg to greatness began for the aspirants of Lakeport and dozens of other schools interested in the arts of track and field activities. The treeless parking lot filled with yellow school buses; between them colorful youthful figures filed between them with long poles and carrying other equipment necessary for the event, they choose. Mature figures followed the young ones everywhere and even tiny figures dotted the sights, some clinging to the bigger figures.

Preliminaries for the District II Track and Field Championships started an early 9:00am Friday with the 4 x 800 meter relays, boy's and girl's finals. There were no other finals, as the distance races had no Friday qualifying rounds. Kasper and Danny were just observers on this day. While Coach Thorpe had a dilemma even before the first starter pistol fired. For this competition Danny, Kasper, and Greg could easily go 1-2-3 in the 3200 meters. However, Ohio rules for the track and fields tournaments allow the first four finishers to advance to the next level. Of the four only two qualifiers from the same school could advance. The third and fourth would have to represent another or other schools. Thorpe wanted Greg's participation, as did everyone on the team. Thus, Greg would take Kasper's place on the 4 x 800 meter relay.

So the young fourteen year old paced nervously amongst the crowd of waiting boys waiting for the race. He knew he was no classic 800-meter runner his natural speed or correctly described, his lack of speed propose that he was a distance prospect not a middle distance runner. However, Greg assessed that he should make a credible effort today. The toughies he would have next Friday.

"Danny, Terry, und Eli können zwei Minuten pausen (Danny, Terry, and Eli can break two minutes)," he reasoned to himself, "so das wir noch den Staat gewinnen (so we should still win at State)."

"Be cool brother you're alright," reassured Eli seeing his nervousness, "we'll take care of business."

"Just get it to me," added Terry slapping Greg on the shoulder.

"Don't over tack yourself that first 400," Danny consoled his brother.

"I am okay," Greg responded feeling his mates were a bit too fearful of his participation.

In the stands, Jayce and Jack talked mostly of the crowd. Neither had ever been present at a track event where such a large stadium was at capacity with fans.

"There area couple dozen schools here at least," stated Jack pulling his beard as he scanned the stadium, "I've never seen so many school colors, banners, and uniforms in one place before."

"Me neither," agreed Jayce, "this is like at a state fair."

"Yep, and we have a great day as well." The pair watched the boys being lead forward by meet officials, uniformed themselves in white shirts with red caps.

"I bet Greg's nervous," said Jack, "now he's got to sprint for 800 meters."

The men's conversation changed as the packed bleachers began to revel with people standing, clapping, and calling out to participants lining up in the lanes. Each with a baton in hand some waved back. Others ignored all accolades and appeared preoccupied with the task waiting for them. Danny was in the middle of the spread of sixteen teams.

Supporters for Lakeport were scattered mostly, unable to find other friends in the humongous crowd. Jayce and Jack could see Katie, Zoe, and a couple others girls sitting below them. They spotted Thorpe briefly; he was walking along the fence on the far side of the track.

The starter was on the stepladder the pistol raised above his head "Runners to your marks, "announced the public address system, "…get set!…"

"Blam!"

Danny struck out furiously. "He needs to get away from the pack!" Jayce suggested in spite of the surrounding bedlam of equally fervent fans.

The sweep of runners finished the backstretch. Straightening from the turn everyone wanted lane one, but the pack knew better so they settled to spread itself out to lane three. Danny was actually leading slightly from lane two as they passed 400 meters.

"57!" Jayce muttered concerned that the pace was too fast.

By 60 seconds, the entire group in the race had finished 400 meters. Sixteen runners with different combinations of colors, some short, tall, longhaired, shorthaired, skin-headed and one with a spiked Mohawk cut. It looked dangerous as they covered the turn as jostling and some bumping was occurring.

"Danny's moving out from them a bit now," said Jack a telling observation as contestants caught up in emotions that demanded they maintain close contact the first lap. Now those same fellows began falling back on the far stretch.

"I feel like relaxing finally," said Jayce.

This was the first and only final of the day. Every supporter who could find a space on the fence bordering the track urged each subject to maintain position or move out and pass someone.

"Stay in there Phil," yelled someone toward a runner in blue with a huge letter 'H' on his chest. "Stick with that guy ahead."

Danny on the second turn was fully ten meters ahead. "Good, Greg needs a lead! Most teams will have a fast runner on the second leg," suggested Jayce.

Greg was in the exchange zone his left arm up waving legs spread his weight on his right leg as he leaned ready to launch himself forward.

Danny closed on Greg extending his arm the last few meters. Greg started moving just before grabbing the baton and going into his run. Katie caught Danny's time, "1:58!" she stated.

"Go on Greg! Crank it!"

"Run fast Greg! Don't let them catch you Greg!" yelled Zoe jumping up and down.

"Well, that's what Greg wants too." Katie added. "I doubt if this next guy can make up twenty meters."

Thorpe had his spot on the second turn. More subdued than usual he just wanted Greg to get in without incident. "Ata boy, Greg," he urged as the boy passed in front of him, "just keep that rhythm right there son!"

As Greg raced by the front stands, Jayce urged him on, "Come on son...good job!"

"He looks smooth," observed Jack

"60 seconds!" Someone said amongst the nearby crowd.

Looking to his rear, Jayce decided Greg's pursuer had not closed any distance. "He should run about 2:04. The kid behind would have to run two flat to catch him," surmised the boy's father. Indeed not a competitor behind made any dent into Greg's lead. Greg sped on fluidly until 200 meters from his finish, but then he clearly began tightening up. However, he rallied in his last 100 meters to hand the baton over to Terry ten meters ahead of Rose Hill Park.

Terry pumped and leaned his head to the left as usual after he made the snatch from Greg. He took no mercy on the trailing teams, as he wanted a fast split for his own on this fine day on a fast track.

"Good grief! 56!" exclaimed Jayce surprised at Terry's split and his twenty meters ahead of Rose Hill Park.

"Go on boy," encouraged Jack a bit in awe of his grandson. "His sorry mother should be here to see this," said he out of nowhere. Now the boy slowed as he angled into the turn. He like others rushing out furiously at the start had a price to pay in terms of oxygen debt. Terry struggled his face grimaced as he rolled the head too much trying to keep his feet far out front of the body. Nothing was going for his followers fortunately.

"That was about 1:57," Jayce announced, "I was so tense with Greg's leg that I did not get a good start for Terry I fear."

"It had to be at least that, the way he was moving," says Jack.

Eli sprinted away with a forty-meter lead thanks to Terry. On the track the three finishers supported each other patted Greg down for his effort.

"I didn't know you could turn over like that boy," hailed Danny to Terry trying to catch his breath, "you took care of your territory in a fine fashion." They watched Eli finish his 400 fully fifty meters over Mays City's team who snatched second place from Rose Hill.

Entertainment could be what they were watching Eli's last 400. The distance ahead of the runner in second was sixty meters. By the end if the final turn, the lead grew to seventy meters. Then the boy could be seen easing up and just float across the finish.

"Eli has to run the 4 x 400 to end this day so he saved a bit of himself here," reminded Katie.

"You get a split on him?"

"7:57.47…not too shabby," announced Katie, "so Eli was about 1:58."

As quick, as this stage was set up admirably it disappeared in a shorter time. Hurdles were being set up and Jimmy was in the first qualifying race. Meanwhile, Thorpe had completed his tour of the field event preliminaries. Lakeport young sophomore girls failed to advance in the high jump as did the one shot putter participant.

"So it's going to be Jimmy, Roy, and my distance men," murmured Thorpe settled in the matter, setting down amongst the Lakeport group.

Likewise, Lakeport supporters relaxed as they watched Jimmy cruise to victory in his heat race, nearly a full hurdle ahead of the second competitor. The three behind would join him at the finals Saturday along with the four in the final qualifying heat about to start.

Next were the two heats of the qualifying 400-meter runs about an hour after the hurdles. During the interval, Kasper enjoyed the conversations in the galley covering topics encompassing: anticipation of performances with particular athletes, past races at this meet and difficulties present on this day. Others in the galley were not the least interested in any track dialogue of any sort and sat reading a book; they were only there for a son or daughter in participating this day. Finally the 400 meters, Jimmy's 49.6 seconds was just ahead of a surprising Matthew Sowell of Hazel Park, in 50.1 seconds. Thorpe withdrew Roy so he would be fresh for the 4 x 400 meters.

"With people like Sowell showing up," Thorpe pointed out, "then there are three other kids under 51. Roy's chances were slim. Then he has had his recurring leg problems. I just want one fast 400 meters out of him today."

Jimmy had no time to celebrate; he had the 200 meters qualifying rounds. The first four will run in the finals Saturday. Not entered and not interested Roy felt. Even he said his awkward style and bulk causes too much difficulty for him to run this race where one-half of the distance is on a curve.

"What!" exclaimed Principal Stromberg at this disclosure, "Roy I thought could have been in the top three, that hurts us a lot...So that's why I couldn't find you until after the 400 meters," questioned Stromberg, "I thought you seemed bothered by something other than this meet. Well, if the distance men perform up to their potential we should still out point anyone else comfortably."

"Northeastern Ohio with the sprint dominance and relays will be difficult," stated Thorpe, "You just can not tell what talent they will show up with. We must not forget there is always some sprinter who can long jump as well. That makes it even tougher."

"Well Jimmy will help counter any field event points with the 200 meters," suggested Jayce. With agreement, the entourage waited patiently for the qualifying heats for the 200 meters. Jimmy was in the first heat to his supports pleasure. Moreover, the boy responded by powering his way through the distance in a record time.

"21.84 seconds," said Katie. "That time is better than the winning time in last year's State."

"And he was just floating," observed Jayce, "Didn't break a sweat."

Immediately, Thorpe excused himself to gather his foursome for the final event of the afternoon.

"So you do not think we are stretching it; that is the idea of winning the State meet, and your boy Kasper going to an Ivy League school?" asked Principal Stromberg speaking to Jayce and Beth after Thorpe left.

"Kasper thinks both will be accomplished," answered Beth surprising her husband. "My boy has always carried a vision and I am supportive of all he dreams of. Kasper said to me one time that 'If I have only what I have experienced, I have little; if I have the inspiration of some high goals, I have more than I can experience'".

"Our reach must exceed our grasp," added Jayce.

"Well said," responded a Principal Stromberg impressed, not expecting such a lucid riposte.

As events closed, one could recognize those who were finished of this season; maybe for some here they would never be an audience for any crowd again. Never again will any crowd watch their person act on stage. Kasper felt he recognized the finalization on the faces of so many. He wanted to offer his sympathy, his consideration for their sportsmanship. He wondered want would propel them forward now that this chapter in their life was over. 'Beware of the danger of satisfaction' he wished to advise them all.

The day ended with the four by 400 meters foursome having just as easy a run as the four by 800 meters. Thorpe watched Jimmy's every stride scared, but the tough kid ran smooth. Roy ran a comfortable 51 seconds flat; Terry made 52 seconds and some change look easy, as Eli showed off with a 51, and Jimmy went 49 and just a bit.

With the Saturday meet starting at 10:00 am Kasper and crew performed no work or study at home that evening. They just filled up on spaghetti and melons, "Easy to digest," reasoned Kasper. The boys retired early. Kasper's only source of contemplation was that everyone but himself had run a race. They had unlocked the virgin wraps off and tasted the adrenaline for a while allowing them some measure of what they could do Saturday. "I will just have to brute force it." The boy thought.

Jimmy started Lakeport's day at the finals of the District II Championships. Seeded a second and a half faster than his nearest competitor, he was relaxed. He was not a nervous person; too unassuming, seldom serious, and when pressured, Jimmy would turn the affair to his favor with his own aggression. Others may strut about verbalize an aggressive, provocative demeanor to cover lack of confidence to prevent a further scrutiny of shortcoming. Not this fellow; Jimmy saw himself as 'the man', 'the beast of prey'. A predator on events, situations, and circumstances was Jimmy.

"Shoot! Got a breeze at my back, great track, gotta get my time down there with the 'brothers'…gotta go third-teen something…gotta do it right now!"

Jimmy thought. He was not planning either; he would accomplish his task by shear will power.

"Runners to your marks!" commanded the starter. The eight hurdlers went to their knees, backed up to the start blocks. It took a minute before the starter determined the group was ready. He wanted no movement or fletching. Completely frozen in time and space runner must be.

"Set!"

Butts rose and stopped in a brace…hold…hold…

"Bang! Someone moved just before the firing of the pistol…Blam! Another firing. Runners were two and three steps out of the blocks at the callback. Jimmy went on and jumped the first hurdle before slowing to return to his blocks.

"Shuts!" said Jimmy.

Another official saw the runner in lane two moving before the gunshot. 'Jumping the gun' in these events gained no sentimentality. Forgiveness was lacking for any who violated the frozen stance. The violator in lane two fingered by an official made no hesitation to lift his start blocks and quickly departed the area; embarrassment assisting in hastening the entry's exit from the track. The seven remaining competitors then stood at positions, reclaimed readiness, and once again obeyed orders to 'get set'. Some time…some time.

"Bang!"

Jimmy's first two strides were wide reaching to the right and left borderlines, as he straightened from the crouch quickly. It was an explosive start. Jimmy's left leg cleared number one hurdle as the boy started bending his body toward the track, searching with for contact. Trailing competitors were just positioning themselves to reach for their number one.

"Look at him go!" exclaimed Jack Luke.

"He's popping it baby!" Jayce said.

Jimmy planted the left foot, took a right, left, right and launching the body with uncanny control propelling across the implements. Attempting accelerate faster these obstacles started approaching faster and faster…time between hurdles shorter and shorter, until Jimmy couldn't get his feet off the track fast enough to clear the top of the hurdles.

"Aaa…"exclaimed, Sophie Luke. She watched Jimmy with the others strike hurdle number seven hard enough for him to flounder a bit. Erratic, off stride, he struck number eight, and then his leg hit the top solid. This pushed the pivoting hurdle to the horizontal. Rhythm destroyed, he chopped a step to regain his coordination so he could clear number ten, after which he leaned for the last ten meters to the finish line.

Up in the stands Jimmy was acting-up. He stomped his feet, changed his completion to reddish and just 'lost his cool'.

"Well he was too aggressive after hurdle number three," explained Jayce, "he's got to keep a steady rhythm between hurdles. He was trying to go faster and faster so he started coming up on the hurdles too quick."

"Yea, he couldn't get his legs over quick enough...ha, ha," Jack laughed softly

"Last call for the boy's 1600 meters run," blared the public address system of the Bedford high school stadium.

"Jimmy got us off to a good start," suggested Principal Stromberg sitting near the highest row of bleachers over looking the finish line. "Perhaps today is a beginning of a new chapter for our personages as well as for the school."

"Oh, let' not make so much of this," countered Patricia, "these kids are having fun. For many this will be their final sport event in their lives. The participants, who are graduating and will not advance to the regional, this is it for them."

"True, but then for others this is a step toward fame and college scholarships. For many, particularly from our community this is the only opportunity to get to college without amassing school debts from federal loans," added the Principal.

Before any more response from Mrs. Stromberg, the public address system, which was near their position, announced the top eight team finishers of the four by 800 meters relay completed Friday, "...and first was Lakeport...official time 7: 58.67..." Then began the announcing of the competitors and schools entered in the 1600 meters boys. Down below the Stromberg's Katie prepared her clipboard and watches. Next to her was sister, Zoe. Seated nearby were the Luke pair, Jack and Sophie, and Jayce and Beth Wise along with the majority Lakeport supporters.

"They called Kasper, Casper," said Zoe smiling while looking at big sister, "like the cartoon character." She giggled.

"Yea, but they'll get it right by the time he gets to the state championships," answered Katie.

The officials placed the twenty-four boys in the lane staggers. It was a careful thing they did. Competitors took warning that the toes were not to cross the panted lines; again, there was to be no movement.

"Where is Greg, ain't he running?" asked Zoe.

"Just Kasper and Danny, only two from a school may advance so Greg will run on the 3200 relay. Danny and Kasper will run the 3200 run as well. That way we can win the state meet."

On the track, the officials moved off from among the competitors. The starter scans them looking for something wrong.

"Okay, Zoe, be quite now," Katie warned, "get your watch ready. Start your watch with the smoke from the pistol like I explained to you, don't wait for the sound."

At this moment, Coach Thorpe took a position on the fence near the 200-meter mark. Ever anxious, he prayed for an uneventful contest.

"The Districts has everybody from the great to the slow, from the ambitious to those who just get a kick out of participating," Thorpe fearfully, "often times it's the slow ones that'll sprint like crazy the first lap, then just as quickly slow drastically forcing people to pass from all sides. That's when the accidents occur."

Thorpe reflected on some of these occurrences. He punished himself by deciding such adverse events would happen before him. This would ease the shock for a man so easily prone to settle with mishaps as what he should realize.

"Bang!"

The race was on. Bobbing heads rounded the turn. Into the stretch runners exited the staggered lanes then pealed toward the inside lane. Kasper and Danny refused this temptation, as they feared slowing runners would trap them.

"Stay to the outside, get away from the pack!" Thorpe yelled as his pair passed. Rounding the second curve then directed toward the start point completing 400 meters; Danny was in lane three nearly with Kasper trailing in tandem.

"60, 61, 62…" called someone as they slipped pass 400 meters.

"64!" Katie said for Danny and Kasper as the boys crossed in fifth and sixth place.

"Come on Kasper, Danny," called a voice in the middle of the packed stadium. Katie recognized Jayce Wise calling.

'They're just bidding time," said Greg sitting with his parents. "Those guys went out too fast." Beth sat stoic, quiet; she never felt assured of these events outcome when her boys were involved.

Danny continued progressing toward the lead pair. Kasper tucked behind him comfortably measured his every move.

"Gehe um diese Burschen herum Danny, so das wir zur Innenbahn können (Get around those guys Danny, so we can get to the inside lane)," Kasper thought.

He must have detected Kasper's every words, because Danny approaching the 600 meter mark right next to Thorpe's position, suddenly accelerated pass the pacers and claimed the inside lane as he rolled into the turn. Kasper lost three meters to Danny in this move before he could respond.

"Get on back on his behind!" commanded Jayce.

As Danny finished the turn, into the straightened lane Kasper flowed to within one stride of his right side.

"Ya'll popping, dudes!" that was Jimmy undoubtedly, "lay it down men!" said he from somewhere trackside.

"2:13, 2:14…," the new leaders passed 800 meters.

"Good float, looking relaxed," observed Jayce.

Thorpe had made his sigh of relief and was now making his way up the bleachers on the far side for a better view of the finish area. "Now, if they only do not fight each other to win." He had told them not to beat up on each other, "Just take first and second please."

On the backstretch, the pair ceased pressing the affair and floated. This easy pace was an unmerciful effort for the remaining field, which dropped back leaving Danny and Kasper to their own devices.

"3:21," said Katie as the two crossed 1200 meters.

"Eine sechzig sekunden Runde bedeutet eine vier einundzwanzig am Ende (A sixty second lap means a four-twenty-one at finish)," calculated Kasper his mind flickering in some desperation. The agreed plan was to float easy after they made the lead. Then sprint the last one hundred meters allowing a natural win between the pair. "Well, that means Danny will win…I can't turn over as fast as he….." He had pointed out to Thorpe, but the alternative would be to wear each other down. He would not do that, so such would it be.

"Good job," said Thorpe from his view watching as they filed toward the finish.

Danny relaxed even more as the pair entered the final turn fully sixty meters ahead of the runner in third place.

"Float it in guys," said Sheila as they passed her and the waiting girls for their 1600 meters race.

One stride behind, Kasper just continued at the steady tempo. They communicated instinctively and so agreed to place and effort.

"Four-twenty-nine!" exclaimed Katie, "No sweat!"

"They didn't even try hard," declared Zoe.

"They have to run the 3200 meters later."

Nearby, the Wise's were elated. "That's the first step completed," commented Jayce, "On to the regional meet."

"My little Kasper," said Beth, "I am so proud. Golly I was scared to death for him." Jayce's face beamed a smile of confidence and reassurance while gently stroking his wife's shoulder.

"Does Jimmy run next?" asked Sophie from the row of seats below.

"Yes ma'am," answered Jayce, "but that'll be a while."

"Sheila's running now ain't she?" questioned Jack. "Hey, there she is!"

The Again, the orderlies of the campus were bringing a large pack of girls to position them as majestically as were the boys. "Look how small some of those girls are. They look like grade school kids," observed Sophie.

"Yea, the distance girls trend to be tiny," agreed Jaycee.

"They look so cute with the pony tails and braid designs and all," said Beth.

"Don't they though," added Sophie, "they are cute as buttons."

From the stands, conversations buzzed concerning school records broken, advancement to the Regional, and congratulations to a job well done... "Parry finally broke five minutes today...Tony got the school record set twenty-two years ago!...Best race he ever had...and his last...4:45 and going to the regional! Nick is only a freshman!..." Such talk there was and much more, until some distraction interrupted.

"Blam!" as often happens there was no warning given by the PA system of the eminence of the start.

"Missed that one," said Jayce who had been in hipped dialogue with Jack as to his anticipated performance. "Why don't they have the courtesy of telling us the 'gun is up', start is about to occur," his face flushed with irritation.

Over to the right of the Luke's and the Wise's, Katie and Zoe had not missed the blast of the pistol.

"Come on Sheila run fast!" screamed Zoe. Then she peered at his sister and asked, discerningly. "Is she running anything else?"

"Yes, she'll run the 800 meters," said Katie, "Okay, let's watch this race."

The runners were approaching the far turn. Sheila had forged to the lead. The girls stretched apart from each other quicker than the boys had. Sheila looked smooth and relaxed as she passed in front of her fans, arms, and legs moving harmonious with her long ponytail flopping from one shoulder to the other.

"Looking good girl," said Danny from the outside fence.

"Alright good job, Sheila," added Kasper as the girl strode gracefully by hugging close to the curb.

The runners clad in every array of colors filled behind Sheila in pursuit. The bordering fence was paced with no gaps as fans leaned and stretched to throw their accolades, orders, and directions with great energy in all attempts to communicate to the subjects they had too much concern for. Danny and Kasper could not help scanning this most interesting people, enthusiasm had them pointing to make know their desires.

"Kasper," Danny nudged him, "look at that dude over there with that orange cap and gaunt face."

Kasper tried to follow Danny's pointing arm scanned the crowd but then finally settled on the figure Danny was directing his attention to.

"Yea, what about him," Kasper replied questioning.

"Look carefully," insisted Danny, "that's the man that's been following Sheila. We caught sight of him remember?"

"Hey, you're right," agreed Kasper recognizing the figure, "he's still wearing that same hat...yep! I agree, that's him all right! Glasses and cap and all, that's the creep no doubt!"

Both started at the man some thirty meter from them. The man's head turned with the passing runners toward the front as he tried to keep sight of Sheila. Neither discerned any sign of emotion upon the strangers face.

"Should go over and get closer?" asked Danny.

At first hunch, he thought he should get closer maybe even confront the man. Nevertheless, Kasper reminded himself of the brief conference with Sheila earlier and the actions displayed by her mother. "No, we should leave this alone." Sheila's mother says everything is under control. She probably was confronted by the authorities and she doesn't want Sheila upset about it, or worrying about the affair anymore," warned Kasper, blandly. "Just leave it be."

"But he's here, hanging around," continued Danny imperturbably. "It irks me!"

"In a public event like this it would be difficult to claim any sort of stalking," countered Kasper.

"Here she comes," said Danny as Sheila was rounding the turn near completing 800 meters.

"Way to go Sheila!"

"Got a fast time going Sheila, keep it up!"

Both boys redirected their attention to the stalker to check his reaction; such was the curiosity that surrounded the occasion. From their position, they could see that the stranger fixed his gaze on the Sheila. The man displayed no visible emotion although constant howling surrounded him.

The trailing runners moving singly far behind Sheila, "2:25," Katie called while recording on her clipboard.

"Go on girl," said Jack a smile barely detectable through his heavy beard.

"Her task is easy today; she's got no competition," announced Jayce, "but at regional there's these two California transfers she must face. The oldest one leads all classes in Ohio."

"Is that tight," responded Jack.

"Yea, she runs under five minutes."

Now seated within speaking distance was a nosey sort of fellow that made assortment of characters found at track meets. Liken to the football or basketball diehards, these sorts of people loved and followed track and field with an enthusiasm not out-matched by any of those most popular spectator sports. A track and field fan he was; knowledgeable of its histories, statistics and times for the mile run in particular. Outgoing, gregarious, these fellows affectionately know as 'track nuts', very well provided some continuity required for the evolving history of the sport.

Such an event as this would not have occurred with the presence of a most illustrious fellow named Roland May, who fitted the so described track fan described previously. Rail thin, in his forties, thick glasses riding his face, and dressed in baggy shorts with overly worn running shoes. Around his neck, a pair of binoculars, and at least two stopwatches dangled. He readily interjected his input to virgin conversations where such a person as he could tell his adroit knowledge was required concerning the art of the event or the primary personages noticed. So when Roland's ear caught something about the new miler on the local scene he pounced. "4:57 and 5:08 is the clocking those girls have run," informed the fan leaning over and making eye contact with Jayce sitting just below him. The man could tell these people were uninformed. Thus, he proceeded with some brief history of what is the norm and what times are fast and even revealed to his audience the records of all time for girls in this event. Of course, he had observed these subjects in races and could assess the girls' abilities as an informative.

"But your girl here has some talent here she comes," Roland donned his binoculars and followed Sheila passing the 1200 meters. "3:53!" Roland called out the time reading his stopwatch, "not too shabby, let's see what she can crank out on this last 400 meters," suggested this fellow peering through his binoculars.

Jayce, Beth, and the Luke's, thought Roland eccentric but friendly and informed. For the next seconds the group wished to keep their attention to Sheila now increasing her tempo around the final circuit of her effort.

"Way to go Sheila!" the Lakeport galley called out.

"She's got spunk," Roland interposed.

Down near the track, Kasper and Danny could not help not observing Sheila's observer as she made her last pass by them. The man continued following her with his gaze. Now, as Sheila closed toward the finish the man his back toward the boys suddenly turned and melted into the crowd outside the track fence.

"Wonder where he's going now?" asked Danny.

"Away from here, I hope," replied Kasper, "come on we got to relax and get ready for the 3200 meters," and at that comment Kasper with Danny following departed for a spot under the far bleachers where they could stretch out and rest.

In the Lakeport crowd unrepentantly satisfaction continued, "5:09 not bad," said Roland May agreed without the enthusiasm of the others.

"Ah, she can go further down than that," said Jayce.

"If I may give an opinion," remarked Sophie Luke to the track gentleman, "Sheila's my take for any race. She trains with the boys at our school and you have seen what they can do. It's going to be tough for her to let some girl run in front of her."

"Yes, the girls do that some time, but Madame your best bet should be placed on experience," said Roland. "Is she doing a lot of intervals? That is what they must be doing to get the fast times, you know."

"Oh yes, she does everything with them," added Sophie, "I've sat out by the track and watched her and my grandson train. My grandson has with most of his left arm missing." Then Sophie proceeded to tell the Roland Terry's life history with Jack clarifying some matters. This was conventional behavior for the Luke's and most people of small town and 'country' culture. Everyone knew nearly the entire history of neighbors in a community. If a major event occurred in the family every person know well enough to give conversation would be so informed. Likewise, for the listener as well they would diverge any happening of their own affairs particularly with the children.

However, this hit a nerve with Jayce when he moved to the community, he being a big city boy. He listened but found such open candor preposterous. "People ought to mind their own business," he would say. Jayce would add that they were a sincere people and the openness reminded one of an honesty and lack of vindictiveness experienced in the urban cultures.

From this state of affairs, more preparation buzzed around the stadium. The crowd dispersals would follow a surge of people coming in for particular events. The stadium sweltered with people, while Roland's excitement grew, begging him to move on to other fans and spectators continuing as assortment of track talk wherever he found an audience.

In the interim before the 400 meters, relay races revealed buddle handoffs, dropped batons, and missed passes. Anguish with despair issued forth in such experiences but not without the accompanying rewards of completion. The successful exchanges and the accompanied times affirmed the comradeship and hard work over the long season. The audience affirmed support for the participants regardless; a forgiven, non-hostility seldom rewarded to any experiencing struggle in the real world; a fundamental proof that these events are sport and not trials of life.

Readying for the 400 meters the Lakeport clan buzzed in anticipation. Jimmy was the most imposing athlete of the meet and confidence was not merely for victory, but for 'dominance'. Thorpe was not very communicative; self-conscience, and nervous, he just roamed about the arena conferring with his athletes and at times with officials. Little exchange was with other coaches. Past adverse and critical feedback from colleagues prevented any curiosity as to opinions they may utter toward his program.

"Old Roland is something else, isn't he?" said someone seated behind Jayce and crew. Jayce turned toward the speaker.

"Is that his name?" asked Jayce.

"Yes sir, if you follow track you will see him at almost all the tournament meets. He loves the sport and he loves to talk track with anyone he can get to listen," revealed a seat neighbor.

"Roland knows lots stats, too. He can tell you the times and splits of races years ago," stated another person nearby.

"You bet, but take my warning. I would not tell him any specifics about your team or their training. Ole Roland, see him over there," he pointed to a section of bleachers in the mist of a crowd. There was Roland even from a distance it was apparent he had found another audience. "Now, he'll be telling them everything you said about your girl,"

"Show nuff," muttered Jack, "he likes to talk about people does he? He's just like me," added Jack with a smile.

"Actually, he got on my nerves a bit," prayed in Sophie, "with all this talk about these California girls."

"They will be formidable but I don't see Sheila losing to them," said Jayce.

"Before the day is out he'll tell everyone your girl will be trying to beat these others and he'll be placing the odds," continued the neighbor fan.

With a few hurried words, the crowd had to turn its attention to the track and watched the 400-meter runners escorted down the track. This would be a quick sprint race. The crowd prepared by gradually standing from their seats for a better rallying point. This race calls for jumping, screaming, and flaring arms for expression.

"Ah, there's Jimmy!" Sophie cried pointing.

"Jimmy's about to run," Eli nudged Terry from his near sleep while they lay stretched out under the far bleachers.

"He doesn't need our help," replied an irritated Terry.

"Come on man," imposed Eli, "we've got to waken our bodies and get warmed up. Eli thought Terry was in somewhat of a melancholy mood. "Everybody it seems is dropping time like crazy. In the 800 dudes running 2:03 suddenly are at 1:58 at District," revealed Eli matter-of-factly. "We've got to go out quick so we can control the race."

"I suppose," came an unenthusiastic reply from Terry.

"Bang!" This noise signaled the start of the boys 400 meters.

"There they go," said Eli. The pair speeded up leaving their abode. "Maybe we can catch the finish." As they got around to the trackside peeping over heads bordering the fence they observed Jimmy alone up front and into the final 100-meter stretch.

"48.66 seconds!"

"That leads all classes, I believe," said Jayce as Jack and Sophie rolled their heads in delight.

Down on the track there was no time for celebration; Thorpe sorted out his boys. "There you guys are," interrupted Thorpe coming from behind them. "We need to get warmed up and stretch." Acknowledging Thorpe, they departed from the stadium area for a large flat grass area where participants were jogging and exercising. There they started into a jog. Eli wondered what preoccupied Terry's thoughts.

"I won't press him about it; he'll focus when the gun blast sends us off down the track. It works for me when something's on my mind," thought Eli touring the field slowly with the solemn Terry.

In the stadium bleachers, Lakeport loyalists discussed. "Unless someone is running faster at the other District sites, Jimmy's time should be the fastest in the state," replied Principal Stromberg who had just arrived, almost missing the race, "I noticed Roy didn't run."

"No, remember he didn't run the qualifying round Friday," said Katie, "coach wanted him fresh for the 1600 relay and there was little chance of him advancing to state in the 400."

"That is preposterous," said Principal Stromberg quite irritated, these young-sters are not here for business. These are lifetime experiences never repeated by most. The opportunity to be here and participate is unique. Roy qualified to be here, so unless injured he should compete. I may have a word with Thorpe about this." Many nearby people heard this exchange and absorbed its contents seri-ously, as many felt the Stromberg's point a fair consideration.

Out on the warm-up field Terry jogged with Eli for a mile. They then found an isolated spot and stretched every muscle they could feel. Terry knew this would have to be his fastest race yet. All his races were pressure efforts. This was his first year and he was trying to make it to 'states'. Last evening Terry had called his mom, he beat the odds in just getting hold of her. "Oh, that sounds excit-ing…Where's it going to be?…Oh…I wouldn't miss if for the world," his mom had said.

"Of course, I haven't seen any sign of her," Terry acknowledged. "She always does this saying one thing and never doing it. Saying she's going to see me or have me over, but never showing up."

Up in the stands, Sophie agreed. "Terry's mother claimed she was coming to see him run. She's so proud and all," said she addressing the Wise's and the Stromberg's.

"I know 'ya haven't been holing your breath on that promise," interrupted Jack. "I didn't pay her no mind; she's about as reliable as a gun shy dog at a hunt. "Short of expletives the man had nothing else to add on the subject of Sondra Luke.

The serious and sensitive tensions was fortunately broke at the eruption from the galley as Bedfort Fillmore's pole vault star, Niels Funk pushed himself over the standards at 14ft. 4in. Nearly the entire crowd was on their feet clapping.

"I always miss the jumps," said Stromberg barely audible.

"Yea, every time I watch the pole vault, they're always missing the jump," added Jayce, "then when you're not paying attention, that's when they clear the bar."

People chuckled, understanding and realizing the experience themselves. The afternoon continued to get warmer and the conversations had roamed in a desul-tory, spasmodic fashion from class to school discipline. Finally, after the long staging for the 300 meters hurdles' it was 800 meters time.

"There's Eli and Terry," said Beth, "Oh, I hate this, I am scared again."

"I hope they both make it," muttered Sophie.

On the track, Eli and Terry were toed the start line in their staggers. Once there, motions of stretching and bouncing up and down in place with some exchange of handshakes with competitors. Terry came to his friend's face and said. "Hope two-minutes come with a ticket to the Regional."

"You'll do it," affirmed Eli, pleased that Terry's mind was back on focus for the race. Then he approached his mate faced him and said, "We can't allow ourselves to get trapped by slow runners keep to the outside." The pair exchanged high-fives and stationed themselves waiting for the start.

One minute later, "Gentlemen to your marks!" the boys pressed toes to the colored line that bound them. A few swaddled nervously mouths moved – a last prayer.

"Okay boys-up!" commanded the starter observing too much movement.

They stood up some ran a few meters out; some like Eli, just stood and stared down the track irritated at the delay.

It is here that the level of noise gradually decreased in the crowd, as spectators like Beth were no less nervous than the competitors about to race. They had to wait again for another pause, then the orders and – Bang!

Around the first turn, down the straight, runners raced but remained in the array of staggered lanes. The second turn arrived. The colorful pack moving ever so quickly Were amazingly quite but some heads could be seen swiveling checking to the right, then to the left.

"Get your spot!" someone called out.

"Go to the inside!" yelled another as the runners streamed out of the turn. Now, allowed to leave the staggers most from the outside lanes, cut over toward the curb lanes immediately.

Terry was in lane three he looked slightly to his right where Eli had been. He was not there. Rotating his head more to the right, "there he is." This was surprising as Eli usually was ahead at 400 meters.

As they approached 400 meters, the two boys to Terry's left slowed allowing him to forge to the front, as runners to his right seemed eager to attach themselves to his rear and follow.

"Ahaaa…" exclaimed the crowd. Terry wondered what happened but he had to keep forging ahead. At the cut over Eli's heels were clipped, forcing his head to bend over. His arms went out from his body unbalanced. He pivoted out to lane five before catching himself and getting back in stride.

"Oh God!" Beth, exclaimed shutting her eyes, her face covered by the hands.

"Okay, okay…got back…he's okay!" deplored Jayce.

Terry was taking the turn as Eli and the trailing runners steadied and refocused.

"Eli's about seven, eight meters back!" Said Jayce scared of his position.

"With four guys between him and Terry, he's in trouble," implored Stromberg.

"Come on son start cranking, gotta be in the top four!" Jayce yelled as if he thought Eli could actually hear him.

Terry knowing there was some disturbance behind smartly forged the pace to get the advantage. The backstretch was ground for two near pursuers to close on Terry, as was Eli. Starting into the far turn Terry relaxed allowing the tall Mich Holbrook to attempt a pass to the outside. Terry responded with quickening arm and leg rotation. Eli was in fifth as the turn straightened.

"All the way Terry!" commanded Sophie.

"Come on Eli! You gotta put on the jets now!" Jayce yelled with anger now.

"Go to the arms! gotta pump!"

"Mich move kid! Move!"

"Tony! Tony! Come on Tony!"

The bleachers had only standing, screaming, commanding supporters, some actually jumping up and down at their seats. At this time and space of the event, physiology played out its hand. Weakened from the buildup of lactic acid lacing the muscles the legs and arms flared about nearly uncontrollable.

Eli kept his steady high rotation… "Vierter Ort!(Fourth place!)." He thought

He could see Terry between the second and third runners who had spread-out. He aimed his effort at this space and tried once more to accelerate.

Katie from her stance observed Terry out front by four or five meters. Eli closed and was able to weave from the inside of number three. Then the finish line and people crossed. Terry, Tony, Eli and Mich.

"1:59, flat!" Katie announced for Terry, "2:02.4, for Eli in third place,"

Amid the droning of the crowd, the Wises's had a sign of relief. "He's on his way to Regional."

"They both had made it," said Sophie relieved as well.

"But, Sondra didn't" muttered Jack angrily.

As everyone seated again, Sophie exclaimed, "I'll have it out with her when I see her."

"Why bother," said Jack, "this always happens. Her actions are nothing new."

"Well, let's get Sheila through this 800," interrupted Principal Stromberg, pleased to break the disheartening discussion.

"This will help her confidence to make the Regional in the 800 meters," suggested Jayce. The audience watching Terry and Eli saw the two, high-five each other. Then the Lakeport crowd applauded as the two walked on the infield. The boys recognized the attention and gave a wave in the galley's direction.

With only this short break the officials were bring forward the girl competitors for the 800 run. Coach Thorpe was certainly in a state of pitiable agitation watching the 800 meters. His heart he believed stopped at Eli's stumble. So great was his agitation, that he rushed to them and collared Eli and Terry with two outstretched hands.

"Thank God you made it!" directed to Eli. "I feared that you had given up."

"It was hard man! Why did all these people drop times on us?"

"Well, they want to go to Regional, too," added Thorpe still reigning in his emotions. "I hope this brings out the importance of vigilance while racing."

Meanwhile, most of the Lakeport gang left the bleachers and tried to push through the crowd for the fence facing the awards stand to take pictures and apply accolades upon their pair. Katie had a word for Eli particularly.

"Why you do that to me Eli? You dodged a bullet boy!" Katie exclaimed, talking to Jayce at her side, but directing her words toward the Eli strolling the infield with the finalists. Jayce laughed, taking in Katie's reprimand of his son.

"He certainly did that," agreed Jayce, "I just hope he's prepared for next week." Then he raised his camera to take pictures as the top eight finishers climbed the awards stand.

"Bang!" All the while, the girls' race formed and set off.

"The 800 girls!" said Thorpe who had joined the group, "Let's rally Sheila in everybody."

In the stands, Zoe stood on the bleacher amongst the other contingency of supporters anxious, rooting for her favorite subject Sheila; now touring down the backstretch. "Go Sheila! Go!" Katie scrambled up the bleacher stairs to get back to her seat.

Completing the second turn, the runners left their lanes staggers and everyone ran for possession of lane one. The sudden moves were dangerous moves. Moves too quick to avoid flying feet girls had to extend their arms to warn off contact with others. Unable to get to lane one, the pack spread out to lane three. Sheila was in the middle of the pack swallowed up by the fast first lap. She would soon discover that for girls the 800-meter run was the most consistently competitive of the girl's events. The reason for this is unclear. The paradox is that the girls do not run the 400 meters at a performance level commensurate with the boy's performances over the distance; and at 1600 meters competitiveness spreads out more so than with the boys. The 800 meters is the girl's niche on the running track.

Now Sheila seeing the turn approach tried to slide away from the inside of this group and free herself. Zoe screamed madly for this unfortunate plight.

"Come on Sheila!" said the little girl, "you can do it!"

"They are fast!" said Katie, "got Sheila in 69 seconds, slow."

"Go Tiffiny!"

"Stick with 'em Laurie!"

"You gotta get up to fourth Sally!"

On the far side of the track, people had advice as well.

"Stay with that girl! Don't let go!"

Slowly the pack streamed out in tandem, no one in lane two anymore. Sheila was in fifth place, but two girls were close on her heels and one to her outside. Sheila looked quickly to her right. "I am fifth and these girls wanting to pass in the straight," she thought.

"Can't wait until the straight," Katie advised observing Sheila's plight.

In the final turn, Sheila demanded pace allowing herself to drift to lane two and pull even with number four. The turn began to straighten for them.

"Ah, haaa…"fast breaths all around now. Sheila's tempo got her to third then second.

"One-hundred meters to go…haaa, ahaa…"

"Win Sheila win!" shouted Zoe jumping up and down.

She was in lane two focusing 90, 80, 70 meters to go. "No use looking people on my right trying to move on me."

Sheila over-hauled the leader on the curb lane fifty meters from the finish. Quick reflection, Sheila saw her boys up in front of her. "I got to close like in practice. I only have girls chasing me…drop 'em," thought she dipping her head to get more drive from her legs.

"2:16.6!" exclaimed Katie drowned out by the crowd in total bedlam as Sheila and the pack crossed the finish line.

"Not too shabby!" said Principal Stromberg amongst the smiles and glee surrounding him in the stands.

"Hey! That girl's good," said a voice. Katie and Zoe looked up over their left shoulder and there was the track and field extremist Roland May. "She'll have to get down to about 2:12 though. At state the winning time is always around and under 2:12 or so," he added in his matter of fact manner. "2:16 will get you fifth maybe."

"He's weird," said Zoe in a whisper to her big sister. Katie just smiled.

On the track Sheila bent over held onto her knees as she felt she was about to throw-up. Wondering about the grass infield with the other fatigued girls, she gasps for breath. "I made it hard on myself getting trapped the having to run hard at the finish," said she to herself.

"She had a negative split, "announced Katie writing on her clipboard.

"What that means?" asked Zoe.

"It means she ran the second lap faster than the first lap."

"Is that good?"

"Well, it means, she can run a faster time Zoe. It means she was not completely spent in the effort."

Zoe glanced reproachfully in the direction of the ole track fan. "Sheila can beat anybody!" said she.

"The last three events, we have Jimmy, Danny and Kasper, then the relay," said Katie breaking to another thought. "Lots of points, this is where we win the meet."

"Jimmy!" called Thorpe as he appeared out of know where as usual. Jimmy was on the curve where the 200 meters race starts. Already he was going through his routine before start. On the track, he was bracing in the start blocks feeling for that final comfort that satisfied his sprang position. "Like I said be conservative in this start nobody here is competitive so take it easy. To himself however, Jimmy needed to test his start. "Shoot, I don't want to wait until state to try my best," he reasoned. In spite of Thorpe, Jimmy decided the start waiting for him would be one of his quickest.

"See you at the finish Jimmy," someone called. Jimmy looked over the near fence to see the familiar faces of Kasper and Danny. They were walking toward the gathering of athletes for the 3200 meters run.

"One-two guys," Jimmy responded watching the pair continues their way. "Those dudes got to run eight laps, glad I am not them," he thought.

At this same time, high jump qualifier Lacy was congratulating Sheila when Thorpe appeared carrying a grin from ear to ear.

"Good job! Young lady," said he patting the top of her head while she sat on the ground.

"Thanks coach," she said sadly "sorry about getting boxed in. You told me they would go out fast, but I was still surprised by the fast pace."

"That's, okay. You gained some experience. You got out and did what you had to do to win," remarked a pleased a pleased Thorpe. "You regained composure better than Eli."

"Great run, Sheila," said Danny approaching.

"Way to go," added Kasper.

As the group continued heaping congratulation on Sheila, Kasper could not help but scan the fenced onlookers for the stalker. Then his fears came to, he spotted the man. The stalker had his back to Kasper and appeared to be being scolded it appeared by a woman. From the distance, one could see a woman shaking a fist in the stalker's face. Such was the commotion that Kasper could see some people close by staring at the pair. This ended as Kasper could see the woman turn and departed from the man, who likewise took his leave, thus both melted into the surrounding crowd.

Suddenly the pistol fired and everyone turned to see runners racing the curve; the 200 meters was underway.

"Great start Jimmy," Jayce said in the stands watching. "He's made up the stagger already on the two outside lanes!"

All there were was flying feet and bodies leaning into the curve. From those on the fence of the turn all they could see was speeding backs. They stared at the line of runners moving away from them.

"Jimmy got it easy," said Danny seeing Jimmy pull up and slow before the others.

"Man his start was a flyer wonder did he break 22 seconds?" asked Kasper.

Up in the bleaches Katie was logging in the time sheet of results. "21.8," said she, "PR for Jimmy and a school and meet record."

"Mr. Football would be impressed," commented Jayce smiling. His feeling was more serious than this display, some envy evolved. If only his boys could present a performance of the caliber of Jimmy's. Why they would have college calls from all around the country. "I've got three boys every one of them want and deserve to go to college, but I don't have a clear one cent to give them," Jayce was nearly feeling sorry for himself in this contemplation.

The Wise's perception of events is a constant reality for them. However, they have new conception that lives for the future, not temporal events of this day. That evolves from the faith of their boys, a faith allowing the growth toward the goal set before them.

"You think Kasper will reach the times he wants this year?" asked Beth. She too had been thinking the thoughts of her husband.

"The boys are going to make it, but maybe not on their time schedule."

"It's just that they have changed so much this year. The priorities, old plans are different. I worry if they are putting too much pressure on themselves."

"Yea, I know I feel that way sometimes, too. Now look we see them getting better all the time. Look at their accomplishment today fore instance. It's not over until it's over, Beth," surmised Jayce.

With the girl's 200 meters completed, the 3200 meters boys were forming. "Here they come," said Sophie, "Kasper and Danny again."

"One-two, and eighteen points," added Jack tugging at his beard.

"Come on guys, lets hit it," said Jayce feeling here was another step toward relief of these dynamics of trauma on his emotions. "I am telling you Beth, I could use a cold one when we get home."

𝑋𝐴𝑀 𝐴𝑀 𝑅𝐴𝑀𝐴𝑅𝑌𝐴 𝐴𝑋 𝐴𝑅𝐴 𝐴𝑅𝑌𝐴𝑌 𝐴 𝑋𝐴𝑀

Once again, the track filled with short, skinny, wiry fellows for most A few were tall and gaunt and all looked fit and anxious. Nervousness oozed from them as they constantly moved and stretched. Kasper and Danny relaxed and loose from the 1600 meters race appeared more at ease than their fellow competitors did.

They bunched up across from the main bleacher area before the start lines. Led to the staggered lines, both Kasper and Danny remembered Eli and Sheila's encounters. The two agreed to move out quickly and away from the pack. Getting knocked down by someone a minute slower than you would be a sad fate; it would be like all the work was just in a dream and a nightmare at that. Many a nights, Kasper had dreamed of arriving at the start too late and forced off the track by the officials. In other nightmares scenes he had removed his sweat pants only to find he had no shorts underneath, only his nakedness.

"We better blast out from this group," warned Kasper, "look how eager some of these fellows are."

"Yea, they're run over you, so let's watch it."

Kasper had to think of what he is to do in this race. He did not fight Danny in the 1600; but if he ran the same way here, he would be second again. Then at Regional and at State he would suffer the same fate. "Bin ich, um zweitens von hier aus zu stellen? (Am I to place second from here out?)," he thought.

"Runners to your marks!" Orders came from the public address system.

"Bang!" the starter pistol echoed in the stadium issued from a red caped man, on top of a ladder, on the infield near the start line.

Spread-out on the turn for the start, in seconds the runners finished the bend then they cut to the inside on the straight; attempting to get as close to the curb as possible. This catapulting effect from the turn squeezed the pack and gave vent to hoarse and frantic cheers from all around them.

The multicolored whirl of runners pulled so near to each other that it seemed there would be a close and frightful scuffle. Yells of warnings, directed scathing calls continued following the runners ever movements.

Facing the end of 400 meters Kasper was in lane two slowly catching three figures ahead and filling lane one. Danny was to Kasper's right and a stride back.

"65, 66…" were calls heard passing 400 meters.

"Diese Burschen haben noch micht mal zehn Minuten gebraucht…rennen verrückt (Those guys haven't even broken ten minutes…running crazy)," he thought breathing erratically still not relaxed into the race.

"Stay to the outside," Kasper planned, "float around them on the turn." Quickly, the space between him and the leaders dwindled until he pulled even at the end of the turn.

Then Kasper centered his gaze upon the end of the backstretch propelling forward. As he pulled away to take the lead, Danny in his head rolling style followed and settled at Kasper's right and back slightly.

Jayce watched his oldest son hugging the turn. He sensed a resolution that Kasper would press this race.

"We're out from 'em, now," thought the leader relaxed now, "Settle in, gage my stride…there it is…right here…this is good this should hurt Danny…take the speed from his legs…"

"2:18," announced Katie as the boys passed the 800 meters.

"Come on Kasper!" yelled Zoe, "I want Kasper to win. Danny's won already," said she from under her beak cap, with pigtails protruding to the middle of her back. Bravely, two figures clung onto Danny's rear struggling as they were. Reviewing the followers revealed retarded feet as invisible ghouls fastened greedily upon limbs. They began give up space to the leaders.

From the crowd, howling cheers slowed as the fans perceived favorite athletes were slowing pursuit. Watching, they enjoyed the two leaders with smooth, effortless, non-slacking rotations. Comparing to the pursuers it was apparent these boys were another caliber of athlete than their favorites. The galley clapped in admiration of a job well done as the pair passed them at every lap.

There was no change of pace for the pair. "4:42," at four laps, 5:52 at five laps completed.

"Ungefähr 72 für die letzten zwei Runden(About 72, for the last two laps)," Kasper thought feeling more stressed now. Breathing was smooth but long and deep. His face grimaced his teeth showed, chest heaved up and down. "Danny ist genau an meinen Fersen…geht nirgends hin (Danny's right on my heels…not going anywhere)."

The crowd got a bit noisier, the Lakeport pair was half lap ahead of the next trailing runner and they were holding a relentless turn over. Scenes as such this thrilled the crowd they joined in with the effort of these titans.

As he perceived the fact, it occurred to Kasper that he had the center stage of this theater he enlisted all his focus in his effort. The outer fence of the track had no space breaks as spectators leaned almost over the top of the jagged fence top.

Kasper could hear the comments in broken sentences.

"They gonna kick…second guy looks good…he's tiring…" And Kasper could hear recognizable shrills from Lakeport girls. "Run guys, break the record!"

"7:07, 7:08…"

Danny pulled even to Kasper's shoulder. The boy had lost his concentration and slowed. Danny wanted the record as well.

"Seven hundred meters to go! (Sieben hundert Meter, mehr!)," thought an anxious Kasper, "Muß jetzt handeln (Got to make my move now)." His breaths deepened, tired feet applied more ankle rotation and forged ahead. Danny slid back behind Kasper and followed in tandem. In the stands, Beth put her hand up to her mouth and started hyperventilating. Jayce fidgeted with a watch.

"Well," he gulped, "he's got to see where he's at before State." His light complexion had blood flushed into his cheeks with his nervousness.

"8:21!" announced someone, "Final lap."

Jayce remained silent for a time. At last he spoke. "Move out!"

Finishing the turn, all could see Kasper dip his head faintly and lengthened his stride. Danny's head moved viciously arms pumped higher as he too demanded pace of himself.

Someone cried, "There they go!"

Kasper rotated as fast as he dared. In the stands Jayce was thinking, "long strides…long strides…strong arm pump hold until the stretch then fan your arms as hard as you can."

Danny grimace his teeth. The stadium was rising to its highest clamor. Into the final turn was the pair. Daylight developed between them rounding unto the final 100-meter stretch. Many were silent trying to reconcile this performance with their own experience, but could not, the boys they watch runs nearly a minute slower then this lead pair.

"Faster rotation…shorten stride…gota get the feet on the ground faster…arms…go to the arms!"

"Kasper's pulling away…he's going to win," said Zoe her little voice not heard by anyone amid the bedlam of the crowd all around her.

Danny crossed the finish two seconds later arms flopping wildly and exhausted.

"Good," said Beth, "he needed a win." She could not hold back her satisfaction.

Jayce smiled agreeing, but now a feeling of guilt as to his desperate wanting a victory for his son over his nephew. "Way to go guys," he screamed toward the bent over boys on the infield. Jayce would rally his unbridled support for both and he wanted everyone to see his bolstering.

Gathering around the finish spent runners gasped for air and drink. Some sprawled on the ground while others like Danny bent over and braced themselves on their knees.

"O Lord!" groaned Kasper, "that was too hard." He wondered if his desperate pitch to win offended his companion.

Danny waved his hand reassuringly. "Oh, that was a wicked finish. That final lap must have been our fastest. What were the times?"

Kasper glancing at his companion could see by the shadow of a smile that he was making light of the affair. "9:27.31, guys," said a timer nearby.

"Just think we have to duplicate this performance next week," said Danny as they strolled toward the rest area with many of the other tired compatriots.

"The important thing is the times," reflected Kasper, "we're down there now."

"And after, running the 1600," agreed Danny. Kasper wondered if Thorpe wanted them to double at Regional again. "Man, just think what we could run if fresh?" Neither said anything as they walked from the infield. "I know we didn't go all-out in the 1600 either," Danny said suddenly, "Shoot! If I knew I didn't have to run again, I would have pushed a faster pace all the way."

"Yea, but coach want us the packing up the points for the team," added Kasper; then thinking in agreement with his cousin.

"Great job guys!" said Thorpe approaching the pair, "Get some stretching in and stay loose."

The boys stashed themselves on the ground. With only the girls 3200 meters run and the four by 400 meter relays remaining many of the crowd began to leave. The pair observed parents and colorful subjects mingling together increasingly as some prepared to exit the campus. Exhortations, commands, imprecations were conferred in an assortments of manners. Respondents reacted with tears, smiles, hung heads as many will never wear a uniform of any sport, ever again.

Lakeport fans lay fixed except for standing to stretch the legs. The girl's 3200 run proceed while Jimmy and boys were warming up for the relay.

"He's got to finish strong on his leg of the 4x 1600," said Jayce, "There are a couple teams that may stay with us the first three legs."

"The quartet could float the relay to an easy victory." Rebuked Thorpe in a fit of confidence, "And no injuries today!" He felt sublime. Enough elation, Thorpe left to find a place near on the track fence to observe the race and bark his commands toward his boys. Escorted down the track for lane assignments the group of thirty-two entries moved deliberately behind the track officials guarding them from four sides as if they were a prison chain gang. Slightly behind schedule, no time was lost before the pistol blast sent the first leg of eight runners speeding around the track in staggered lanes.

"Nice and smooth, Roy," Katie said watching him move in lane four. Roy ran in his powerful gate and came out of the turn two with a slight lead. A hand-off to Eli, sent him off for lane one. As Eli raced into the turn, there was no space between he and three teams trailing such was the closeness of the race.

"Look how quickly they caught up to Eli!" exclaimed Principal Stromberg.

"Where is all this speed coming from?" asked Jack looking perplexed.

"They won't last," said Jayce, "they're running on adrenaline."

At three hundred meters, the line of runners behind Eli began to stretch-out. The turn provided a good view of runners form and this is at the point where the 'bear' takes his toll on the body.

"Move Jake!"

"Struck with 'em Pat!"

"Take 'em on the stretch!"

Orders bellowed from all sides of the track. People on the rails of the stands leaned as far as they could to get their instruction to the ears of the tiring sprinters.

"Get it to him! Get it to him!" yelled Jayce to Eli.

Five meters out Eli reached ahead of his legs with his right hand extending toward Terry. Terry bounced side to side in his exchange zone then as Eli extended his arm; he started moving down track until he grabbed the baton from Eli, as both were still moving quite fast.

"Good exchange," declared Jayce.

"I'd say," agreed Sophie.

"Yea!" Jack yelled.

At Terry's snatch, he was two seconds up on Bate City's blue clad runners. With his head rolling in his unique manner, he spent himself into the turn at such a speed that it appeared he had difficulty hugging close to the tightening turn.

"Terry's fanning!"

"Chug it baby!"

It was evident Bate City's runner would not be making up any distance on Terry. By mid backstretch, Terry was pulling himself out of range of all competitors. Everyone seen was standing in the bleachers.

"Blow it out Terry!"

Terry rotated with all he had. From both the inside of the track and outside all the common command's exclamations pelted the runners. He was at one hundred percent and holding. Adrenaline Terry knew would get him to 300 meters, from there to finish its brute force.

Jimmy waited rocking in his place as Terry closed in toward him. The noise surged from the stands.

"Look of that lead," muttered Jack.

"He must have forty meters on them," added Jayce.

Then Jimmy grabbed the baton within three strides he was at full speed and so was the clamor of the crowd.

"52!" said Katie, "for Terry's leg."

"47 and some change!" suggested Jayce predicting Jimmy's time with a broad smile. Then they watched the rapid, long stretching run progress. Jimmy, not a big runner by 400-meter standards, had a fast turnover and a powerful arm rotation. One only had to compare him with trailing runners.

"Power it Jimmy!" Jayce urged him on wanting a fast time on this split as the nearest competitor was some sixty meters back when Jimmy raced into the final turn.

"He's breaking all records around," predicted Principal Stromberg.

"Bring it in Jimmy!" yelled Jack

And bring it in he did. Powerful and steady, Jimmy finished the turn and straightened into the last meters.

"Go to your arms Jimmy!" commanded Jayce and Jimmy reacted. His strong motions closed to 50, 40…20 meters.

"Alright…Alright!…All the way!"

Jimmy sailed passed the finish line then slowed quickly to a stop. The crowd remained pitched high, as they had to bring in their favorites still out on the stretch.

"3:21.2!" Katie announced proudly under the constant yelling around her.

"Is that good?" asked Zoe barely audible.

"I got 47.3!" said Jayce elated, "didn't I tell you...47 and change!" he chuckled.

"Yes you did at that," agreed Principal Stromberg.

"I ain't ever seen anybody run like that in my life," exclaimed Jack stroking his beard.

"Jimmy's something else!" added Sophie shaking her head side to side.

"Jimmy's a natural," said the ever quite Beth, "many guys train hard, but they'll never run that fast." She felt at ease complementing someone, now that her boys where out of hazard's way.

CHAPTER 9

▼

Kasper swirled his arms with the symphony. He was the maestro of the Boston Symphony orchestra and he was leading them into the last movement of Beethoven's Fifth Symphony. Standing before his small window, his stereo radio tuned to this classical music station. He swallowed with emotion as he swayed with the increasing and decreasing rhythms unabashed. His home was vacant except for himself. He loved these moments alone. After church services, Kasper, Danny, and brothers completed a brisk five-mile run, and then everyone attended to their own separate affairs. By mid afternoon, all had departed for their various activities. Kasper deepen his seeding within his mind, a necessary activity of his, thus he pivoted aside the external influences and sways. Worshiping satisfied the spiritual natures, but the carnal deviousness required taming equally. "The spirit is willing, but the body required self-control," he believed, paralleling biblical thought. He enveloped himself with Brahms, Beethoven, and Mendelsshon. They helped direct his thoughts inward, and reinforced his self-satisfaction with himself.

"Da, da, daaa…da, da, daaa…," mimicked he, "data, da, da, da…data. Da .."

He loved it when the symphony movement dropped to the low and quite beats, then rising steadily to another level and smoothing out to a harmony, serene and tranquil. Then he was finished as the movement finished. Kasper dispatched for the bathroom, washed his armpits, and dressed into a light shirt and shorts. He had intensions to address mainly those involving the Johannes affair. Solicited by phone the day before, Kasper was to meet with a Detective, Seth Wallace, at the Chadded Ballot where there would be some discussion as to recent matters that had evolved from the Johannes affair.

It took a peaceful while for Kasper to walk the distance to the small, cozy place on a perimeter road bordering Crimshead Lake. However, he enjoyed the trek. Upon his arrival and entrance, his eyes searched the booths and quickly fixed on a pale, toper-faced man rising up from behind a table. He appeared to be about fifty, but his haggard expression and unhealthy hue suggested he was aged beyond his years. The man knew this was the arrival of his subject and motioned Kasper his way in a polite way.

"Glad to see you young man," he greeted, "Seth Wallace here."

"Thank you Sir," answered Kasper, "I am delighted to meet with you sir." They entered some light conversation initially after some orders of refreshments. Detective Wallace manner was nervous and shy more so than Kasper. The man's shy decorum along with his frail, long fingers suggested to Kasper, that he had been in a position of administrator or something for the balance of his career. He could not imagine this man being quarrelsome and combative about anything. Additionally his forthright manner completed this consistent personage.

"I suspect Kasper what has been disturbing to you is that; I detected from our phone conversation that you felt something beyond what was said was going on when you met with Johannes and some private detective he had with him?"

"I certainly did," answered Kasper.

"First, I want to tell you is that, there has been arrest of several county people; but it's not about drugs and Nazi materials," the man paused then continued as Kasper sat mute, "Master Kasper, this was about Middle East business."

"Far out!" exclaimed Kasper.

"In this care we have established a very serious case against a group around the county whose been selling some small amount of drugs and some racist material. However, that activity is only a front. They receive large amounts of money from people with terrorist connections in this country. The money mailed overseas is then distributed to these surreptitious groups throughout Europe." Detailed Detective Wallace.

"Why do they need Bill?"

"As people of Middle East origins, they would be suspect if they transferred money abroad themselves."

"So the drugs and Nazi material is to divert attention away from anything connected to terrorism."

"Exactly, even if he's picked up for small amounts of drugs, no one would suspect he's mailing out large amounts of money through Johannes."

"Johannes! Huh!" said Kasper emotionless, his suspicions confirmed about the old man.

"Johannes mail packages to his great granddaughters purposively, but its large sums of money which makes its way to the bad guys." Wallace says.

"Man, this is heavy stuff!"

"So Bill is in the middle of this," asked a sadden Kasper thinking of Mrs. Sweigert.

"Well, it is possible," suggested Detective Wallace, "Bill could only know of the Nazi material, but may be unaware that Johannes under the pretense of obtaining material for him is involved with terrorist."

"Bill is not a bright fellow according to a friend who knows about everything going at school, he's deriving some self-importance from in the county for his escapades and dealings," Kasper continued to explain, "He says he's in the import export business supplying and selling German souvenir stuff, but sells a little dope and Nazi crap on the side."

"I must confess however, that the case looks exceedingly grave against the young man and it is very possible that he knows the extent of all this business."

"Ole Johannes recruited him obviously," surmised Kasper, "there is nothing more deceptive than some old father figure leading a gullible kid like Bill into some scheme."

"We haven't moved against Bill or Johannes yet, we want to see what actions they take and watch 'em a bit longer," explained the Detective. "The people arrested are just small fry we just want to see who gets nervous and maybe discover the full extent of these operations in Ohio."

"What about the contacts in Germany?"

"Authorities there have rounder up some businesses that sere fronts for the money laundering. Wilhelm was receiving a tidy cut for distributing the money."

"Well, better let you get back home," said Detective Wallace, "I am pleaded we got to talk. I wanted to get the news to you so you'll know what's going down."

"Thanks for disclosing these events to me," said Kasper.

"I have been worried a bit. Mrs. Sweigert is a nice lady she should not have all this mess about her."

Detective Wallace shrugged his shoulders, "I hope we have not been too quick in forming conclusions," said he. "Oh yes, you told me Johannes had some man with him claiming to be an investigator, detective whatever? He was probably just one of his henchmen."

"Gee, sounds like Johannes is a real crook. Could I call you and inquire of these matters?" asked Kasper.

"Certainly," answered Wallace, "so until we meet again or we talk. You take care, now."

Both hurried from the Inn as if they had urgent business to attend. Any third person would have presumed their meeting had been an impulsive occasion for those two.

It was late in the afternoon before Kasper returned home. He arrived to a tidy home for the family was preparing for evening church service. He thought of these adverse affairs nipping at his life. "Need to get energized for the eternal and withdraw from these temporal, physical, and carnal diversions of my existence." The boy suggested to himself feeling invigorated and refreshed.

He was pumped-up, with the prospect of his regeneration. For the following days, tough training sessions, class assignment deadlines, along with the usual physics assignments straddled his schedule. David would be over for dinner the Monday coming and they would have a physics problems session afterwards. Then Saturday he had the Regional Track Championships. "Nächste Woche wird alle von meinen Kräften erfordern (Next week will require all my powers)," he reflected.

Monday was as miserable as Sunday evening was pleasing to the boys. It rained all the school hours but all were pleased. "If it rains early in the week the odds are the Saturday will be nice," they figured. At one O'clock, Kasper was at study hall, which was a corner in the gym at this little school when Jimmy arrived. The pair isolated themselves as far as they could; then Kasper revealed to Jimmy his knowledge about Johannes as recently disclosed by Detective Wallace.

"I knew it! I knew it!" Jimmy exclaimed loudly such that others looked their way, "I knew that old dudes a Nazi! I told you he could goosestep a mean beat in his day," Jimmy could only smother his chuckles.

"Not all Germans were Nazi most were just soldiers in the Wehr macht…"

"Come on dude, Johannes is storm trooper. I could see it the first time I met the dude. Bill was driving the ole man around the lake. They came by 'Dougle's Garage', Bill wanted to show off his 'real German', I guess."

"So Bill and his two-digit IQ, thought he would make out to be a big shot amongst the camouflage crowd, huh," Kasper remarked.

"Ha, ha…" laughed Jimmy, "you got it dude!" he explained. "Johannes was wearing a grin of pride like he was in uniform or something. There was no doubt he enjoyed the attention."

"What an imbecile. He has no self-esteem at all to be looking for this type of attention," said Kasper gravely, "but he wears that 'Cheshire cat' grin like a badge. Whenever I see Bill, he nods and grins like he on to something, I do not know about. He gives me the creeps."

"The dude reminds me of that cartoon character 'Alfred Newman'. Curly red-headed, buck teeth with that ever present grin."

"Yea, I know the character you're talking about; yep I agree. That's who Bill looks and acts like," said Kasper in exasperation.

"You sound like you want to slug the dude, but you don't pay him any mind. Let 'em go on. You said they gonna pick him up soon, anyway. Let's just be cool about it."

"You're right, it's just disgusting the whole affair; so let's focus on the Regional, for now."

"Ata boy! Let's push this crap aside and worry about popping off some good runs."

"He could have told me about this early encounter, before now," thought Kasper, as the two departed for the locker room and track practice.

"Haaa…," Kasper sounded his exhales and followed Danny closely, but as the curve lessened he allowed the turn force to move himself to the second lane and abreast Danny's right. Stride for stride they covered the last meters.

"29, 30…32 Greg!" announced Katie as the trio crossed 200 meters, "34 Sheila! Good running!"

Walking bristly with chests rising and falling attempting to replenish the depleted oxygen, Kasper tired. "forth-teen down, six to go," he muttered rolling his head and rotating his arms attempting to relax his muscles.

Eli and Terry were half lap behind clipping off their own 200's at 28 seconds. Kasper turned back to Sheila walking slightly behind.

"Great job! I can tell its easier now for you to keep pace than when you started."

"You do?" said she surprised, "I don't feel it. This is real hard but I just got one to go."

"Yep, last one. You know Wednesday is the last workout. Then all of us will have two days rest. You'll pop off a good one, Saturday."

"Hopefully," smiled she, "and the weather's suppose to be great too."

"Lets do it gang," said Kasper as they approached the start point. The four-some spread out and started a slow jog. Danny to the inside raised an arm. As they crossed the start, he dropped the arm and off they were into a full run. At the other end of the field, Katie had started her stopwatch at the arm drop.

Kasper had been possessed of much fear in bringing up the affairs with the Sweigert's or the incident of the 'pervert' at the Districts with Thorpe or his parents. He understood how easily questionings could make holes in his feelings. Then they would never stop asking him about the subjects. Lately, everyone of his interest had thoughts on the upcoming Regional meet and the team's preparations. Kasper relished preparation; it was then that he would feel he is controlling events, so he was upbeat as he walked with his mates after finishing a 200 meters run.

"At least they won't be tantalizing me with persistent curiosity about what's going on," he thought pleased. However, the fellow felt apprehensive that his brothers and cousin would ask him to relate his visit with Detective Wallace. He had only briefly mentioned to his family that evening with the detective.

"Four to go," Greg said, interrupting Kasper's thought. Thus, Kasper, Danny, and Greg stated the jog into the next 200 meters. Sheila had departed and Thorpe arrived

"Looking good guy," greeted Thorpe, "got a great workout going." Thorpe sounded upbeat unlike his more normal serious tone displaying anxiety as to the future.

The coach felt immensely superior to his coaching critics, but he inclined to condescension. He adopted toward them an air of patronizing humor, neverthe-less when caught in audience with other coaches.

"Jimmy performed like a world class professional," commented coach Bell to Thorpe while they lunched in the teachers' lounge the previous day Marlborough competed at another District meet. The Lakes Side Review gave a detailed story and results of both District meets. Bell was bewildered with the performances recorded by Lakeport. None of the coaching stalls in the county would have guessed the short times required for the distance transverse by Thorpe's contingency.

"I told you my distance guys are partial to the Kenyans guess they let it go to their heads...ha, ha."

Although Thorpe met them with cutting coyness, most recoiled to avoid eye contact as a prideful Thorpe rebuke them by his 'boys performances'. Under the umbrella of its flourishing growth, he stood with self-confidence since nothing could impair the records his team established. He did not shrink from an encounter with his adversaries and allowed no thought of his own to keep him from an attitude of a coach 'guru'.

Indeed, when Thorpe remembered his fortunes of the weekend and looked at them from a distance he began to see something fine there. He had license to be pompous and master-coach like. His pointing agonies of the past he put out of his mind. In the present Thorpe foresaw to himself that it was only losers and faithless who suffered with circumstance.

"Why to wrap it up guys," said Thorpe watching his exhausted runners retired to the infield. Katie came to his side and some discussion issued.

"You've improved about two seconds for the 200's, great job! How you feel?"

"I am looking forward to Wednesday," said Danny, Kasper and Greg reaffirmed. Then Terry and Eli arrived equally exhausted.

"Two more workouts like this?" asked Eli.

"Two more and you can beat anybody, right?" Thorpe said wearing a broad smile still bubbling in humor.

"Come on guys. You have got to be harder on yourself at the start, or you will get swallowed up in the pack again, Eli," reminded Katie with biting glee.

In the present, humor was not appropriate to the boys. "Okay, I got behind these slowdowns; they won't be slowing next week; I just need to get there in one piece," mocked Eli in reply. Terry saw no point to complaining so made no reply. For him his grind was to stick with Eli, he saw no aspirations beyond that. Greg accepted his role as a novice and remained mute.

"I am just a freshman," he thought and took relish that, "anything I do will be fine. I am way ahead of most first year runners."

Kasper did not give a great deal of thought to these sparing. At this time, he was thinking of studies he needed to complete tonight. These physics problems were between his reality and his dreams for now. The Regional meet must be pushed aside for these evenings and wait its turn. He had been studying every night, physics mostly, rewriting example problems, and memorizing essential concepts. David would offer fresh exercises undoubtedly Kasper assessed.

"I've got to be able to recognize the fundamental concepts and categorize the problem; then work confidently with the math tools toward the solution," he thought while he was scrubbing in the showers.

"How has all gone with you, Master Casper?" David asked after the boys arrived home from practice. He chatted in the living room with his dad while Beth was preparing dinner. They cordially shook hands while offering small greetings.

"Your father has updated me as to your latest exploits of your fine running," said David.

"Running, it's as hard and exploitive on one's piece of mind as physics," answered Kasper staying serious.

The foursome tidied up and comforted themselves while Jayce pursued David by every which manner to access his son's possibilities of success with the physics scholarship and any support his 'society' could possible contribute.

"I have great confidence in Kasper's possibilities of doing well on the exam and so does Mark," reassured David. "We both have been surprised by the number of prospects we've seen that can not even start a problem without a formula to stare at."

"So you feel that Kasper is on the right track in his approach to studying?" quizzed Jayce.

"Quite so, he just needs to look at as many problems as possible," David says.

"I am delighted to hear that. Beth and I are most impressed with you and your guidance David," Jayce offered sincerely.

"It's my pleasure to be able to help in any way or means that I can."

With such positive prospect offered, Jayce's appetite ripened so he carried the conversation toward the direction of food.

The dinner was as revealing as much as it was fulfilling. David told of his upbringing in Mississippi, his school; his dad was a janitor at an Air Force base, which bought him to be interested in aircraft so he began paying close attention to math and science in school. David said he started college as a math major, but after a required course in physics, he switched his major to the study. Everyone remained transfixed listening to him.

"I love finding how math can be applied to real physical phenomena. The test you'll be taking Kasper expects you applicants to be capable of solving problems using fundamental calculus," David surmised.

"Not too much formulas, to remember?" Greg asked

"No, because everybody can plug in data in equations and crank out the answer," David emphasized, "applicants at this level can memorize anything."

During the discussion, Eli took the opportunity to suggest how the art of persuasion and study of people's interactions applied to him.

"I am thinking of foreign service as a career," revealed Eli.

"This shows how people differ so much," said Kasper, "Now, I think trying to persuade people studying their interactions and ideals are much more complicated than mathematics. Science and math has laws and rules you can observe or simulate, because they are constant, unchanging. People's ideas are fluid; they change without warning, without explanation."

More conversation branched to the merits of rural verses city life. Yankee and southern life styles, then big universities and small colleges took up conversation.

Finally, the subject of running came up, with Beth proposing: "Well, this coming weekend is most important for the boys David," said she, "won't you come up and join us and we'll all attend the events?"

"I can't this weekend," replied David, "but I would like to see the state meet in two weeks"

"Hey, that's a deal," said Jayce. The boys joined in with agreement. "Now Beth we better let them get on with this physics math business."

Only minutes later David had a captive audience before him. "One class of problems that you'll experience is problems that arise in situations in which two rates of change are related to each other in some way. If we have knowledge of one of these rates we can attempt to deduce the other," said David as the small group leaned toward the small chalkboard he had propped in a chair. "We use the technique of 'implicit differentiation'."

Kasper and Danny were taking notes. Greg was listening carefully; however, Eli's mind was already drifting, so he excused himself to join his Dad to watch a football game on TV.

"Let's look at an example to illustrate a related-rate problem" David started reading: "We have a ten meter ladder leaning against a wall with its base two meters from the bottom of the wall." David sketched this depiction. "If the ladder starts to slip at time, t = 0 and its base slides outward at one meters per second. After three seconds, how fast is the top of the ladder moving?"

"Okay Kasper, how may we express this using calculus language?"

Kasper with little hesitation said: "Well the ladder is sliding at one meter per second so the change in distance with time can be written as

$$dx/dt = 1.0 \text{ m/s}$$

"Good. Now let us find the rate at which the ladder top is falling. Lets call height, y. Then we need to find, dy/dt the rate of height change with time. Now, how are the variable x and y related?" David continued sketching more detail. "Now, look at this and think of the Pythagorean theory that says

$$x^2 + y^2 = 10^2 = 100$$

"Our x and y distances squared is equal the ladder's length squared. However, x and y are not a function of time. We call this a static relation First, if we differentiate implicitly with respect to time, we obtain

$$2x \, dx/dt + 2y \, dy/dt = 0$$

"Solve this for the moving top, dy/dt

$$dy/dt = - x/y \, dx/dt$$

"What does that expression mean physically?" asked Kasper, "particularly the minus sign?"

"Good question, look," said David pointing to the script on the little blackboard, "dx/dt means the base is increasing to the right. The minus sign tells us correctly, that the height of the ladder is decreasing, falling," he turned to look at each boy, "makes sense?"

They all looked with agreement.

"Question, guys is the rate of decrease constant?"

"Yes," volunteered Greg eagerly, "because dx/dt = 1 m/s always according to the stated problem."

"Right, anyone disagree with that?" David asked with a teasing smile that made everyone suspect the answer given should be challenged. "I give you a hint. When something free falls on Earth is the fall rate constant?"

"No," answered Kasper quickly. "Things in free fall accelerate."

"Precisely, so the ladder is sliding downward at an increasing speed like any falling object, because of the gravitational force, g. The foot of the ladder is slipping to the right at a steady one meter per second."

"So after three seconds, what is the speed of the top of the ladder?" asked David. "How are we to solve this problem?"

Kasper saw an opening. "Well the foot of the ladder three seconds later would be five meters from the wall. We have a right triangle relationship. This allows us to use the Pythagorean Theorem to find the height, y."

"All right, exclaimed David, "you are on to it now."

The boy rearranged

$$y^2 = 10^2 - x^2$$

Since, x = 5

$$y^2 = 10^2 - 5^2$$

Using his calculator, he got the height of

y = 8.7 meters

"Substituting into the differential equation for x and y, we arrive at

dy/dt = - (5/8.7) (1.0 m/s) = -0.57 m/s

"So, the top is falling a bit over a half meter a second after three seconds," concluded Kasper. David scanned his audience, "Good job, Kasper that's correct any questions?

"Now, let's look at another type you must understand absolutely. That is finding decay rate and half-life problems."

"Got to use logs now," asked Danny wanting to contribute to the discussion. "We have been doing those in calculus already."

"Great! And these are popular on these tests," said David. "Here we go:

"Radioactive material decays at a rate proportional to the amount initially present. If 100 grams of a material is observed, decays to 75 grams after 25 years, find the half-life of the substance." David cleaned the board and started writing.

dM/dt = kM

"We proved this a few weeks back. You must know that the solution for this equation is of the exponential form

$M = Moe^{-kt}$ where time, t = 25 years

"k is our rate constant we must find for this material. So substituting our initial conditions

$75 = 100e^{-k25}$

"Simplifying and taking the natural log of both sides, we get

$\ln(75/100) = \ln e^{-k25}$

-0.288 = -k25

"Solving for k,

k = 0.0115

"Now to find the half-life, substitute 100 grams for initial amount and use half that amount, 50 grams for the final amount. We have then

$$50= 100e^{-0.0115t}$$

Danny looked confused and motioned with his hand, for interruption. "How did you get the k25, from the step before it?"

"That's from our log relations; remember ln x is defined as that number y for which

$$x = e^y$$

"That is, y is the power to which the base e must be raised to produce x, and if

$$\ln x = y$$

Substituting for x, we get

$$\ln e^y = y$$

'We must know this rule it's a powerful simplifying tool. Thus, for our problem

$$\ln e^{k25} = k25$$

"Huh, I am glad you asked that Danny," said Kasper, "I really didn't know the derivation for that, but now I really understand."

"I thought it was just magic, myself so I didn't pay it any mind," said Greg smiling.

"Man, you gotta know everything," Danny said with an emphasizing tone.

"Ok, let's finish this problem now. Take the natural log of both sides and apply what we just learned,

$$\ln (50/100) = \ln e^{-0.0115t}$$

$$-0.693 = -0.0115t$$

$$t = 60.3 \text{ years}$$

"Every 60.3 years, half of this material will decay to something else." David leaned back in his chair "Know the steps in this problem in your sleep," he warned. "Now, did you guys find some particular problems you would like to look at?"

"Yes," said Kasper quickly, "problem 18, page 8 in the packet. I think you've got to take in integral of the function."

"Let me see," David looked at the booklet handed to him. "Okay…A microscopic slide with dimensions, he started writing

-3 ≤ x ≤ 3 and -2 ≤ y ≤ 2 measured in centimeters."

"A slide has bacteria with a density of four-hundred per square centimeter at its center; but that density falls off with increasing distance from the center according to

$$f(x,y) = 400 - 12x^2 - 12y^2$$

This describes the bacteria per square centimeter. Find the total number of bacteria on the slide.

"Okay, can anyone see a plan of attack?"

"I thought of taking the integral of $f(x,y)$, but I am confused. I don't see how the integral gives you total population, when the function is in density?"

"Excellent observation and question let me show you. If we have the population density, $f(x,y)$, in bacterium per square centimeter, at each point (x,y). If we look at the slide dimensions in terms of the x, y coordinates system. The population of the bacteria on the slide may be obtained by multiplying the density function, times area and taking the integrals over the coordinates, then

$$N = \int_x \int_y f(x,y)\, dA$$

"Because…look at the units.

$$\text{Density x area} = N/cm^2 \times cm^2 = N$$

"N, is just a number," said David.

"I see," said Kasper. Danny and Greg nodded.

"Proceeding…

$$N = \int_{-3}^{3} \int_{-2}^{2} (400 - 12x^2 - 12y^2)\, dy\, dx$$

"Looks nasty," commented Danny.

"Yes you're going from negative to positives," complained Kasper, "how can you have negative dimensions?"

"Ok…look at this…he drew

"Now you see," David pointed to the figure. "But, this figure reveals how we can simplify our calculation; by determining one quadrant and then multiplying it by four, since all the sectors are equal."

"Consequently, we get after integrating with respect to y,

$$N = 4\int_0^3 (400y - 12x^2y - 4y^3) \big|_0^2 \, dx$$

$$= 4 \int_0^3 (800 - 24x^2 - 32) \, dx$$

"Now, integrate with respect to x, we arrive at

$$= 4 (800x - 8x^3 - 32x) \big|^3_0$$

$$N = 4 (2400 - 216 - 96) = 4 (2088)$$

$$= 8,352$$

"So the slide has 8,352 bacteria on it."

"Do we use that method a lot in physics?" asked Kasper.

"Yes, the concept of integrating a density to obtain a whole number may be used for a lot of things. We may want to find the "charge density" on a condenser plate to compute the total electrical charge. Or, we may want to find the mass of a certain volume of space by taking a triple integral."

"Wow!" murmured Greg "so I am seeing how calculus is used in the real world."

"Hey, we've learned a lot in this little session, don't you think?" asked David looking tired. Kasper, Greg, and Danny looked relieved.

"Yea, I am invigorated now," revealed Kasper, "I think I can complete the other problems in the packet like these."

Everyone gathered note pads, papers, pamphlets, and books. It had been a fulfilling day, both physically tacking, and emotionally trying, and finally mentally challenging to close the evening.

It was windy, very windy such that it threw three boys off stride as they ran along the paths of Crimshead Park, often whipped by the branches of the foliage as they tread along narrow paths. They hurried to complete this run. The track was waiting for them and the twenty tours of the track, which would accompany the time the troupe, would spend with it. Eli, Terry, and Sheila required a shorter 'warm-up' run near the school territory, so they were not present on this out.

Beethoven's vigorous finale movement continually recoiled in Kasper's mind; it had claimed his background consciousness, since Kasper had fallen asleep under its influence Monday night. Now, he maintained a stiff relentless pace over these four miles.

"Aaaa, haaa,…," his breathing was strong and air gabbling. Danny stubbornly continued with him. They were less than a mile from the school when the pair impolitely began moving away from the young Greg, without any concern such was their focus.

The music rhythm instilled Kasper to press the pace. Danny wanted to improve his strength. Too often, he allowed Kasper to break from him in these long runs. "The first three miles were slow can't be losing ground now." Kasper would not let up, while Danny pumped a blistering sweat. Danny felt impotent as he followed struggling. He felt a tired anger toward Kasper for this, because he knew Kasper was deliberate in this tactic. Danny fought frantically for respite for his senses, as he fought for oxygen.

There was a blare of rage with a certain expression of intentness on both faces. This was a necessary struggle the pair knew would ensure survival of future combatants and these challenges would suffer no emotions of sentiments for them. Any withering of pace would be a signal of attack.

A kilometer to run, then only some meters to go, adds some small seconds then arrival. A trot to a walk and a small comment to tap the moment ended the run. Perspiration streamed down the boys faces. Kasper's curly waves now straight, had him pushing it aside away from his eyes. Danny wiped his eyes with his shirt. His mouth still parted open as he breathed heavily. Greg arrived, not as exhausted as the pair. His eyes caught their glances, but he did not care. He had run hard enough without beating himself up.

The three started walking to the falling tattered gate that marked the entrance to the grounds surrounding the narrow dirt-cinder track.

"Ok, let's stretch a bit," announced Thorpe calling from some meters away; decked out with clipboard and watches around his neck as usual. "Then let's do sixteen 200's at 32; walk 200 between, then walk 400 and complete two 400's at 65." He then turned without taking any comments from his subjects and departed for other training business.

"I am ready when you are!" called the familiar female voice of Katie. She was in the infield sitting on a movable stepladder.

"Okay, give up 15 minutes to cool off!" exclaimed Danny, somewhat irritated. They moved to a remote, grassy corner of the grounds and took the little break owed them. They watched the horizon of events around the track grounds.

The coaches at some tasks were bobbing back and forth around the track, calling out directions and encouragements. Baseball players, male and female, popped balls as others just played catch some seemed to be ever chasing fly balls. About the track, the high jumpers appeared to be always knocking the crossbar in their attempts. Sheila, Eli, and Terry were running the 100-meter straights, with Jimmy at the helm. Kasper had an observation: "Warum macht Leute, scheint wenn beschäftigt, an ihrem Vesten zu sein?(Why do people, when busy seem to be at their best?)"

"Well, we can't cheat death forever," said Danny. The boys moved out as adamant as any troops would depart for combat duty. They made the way to the worn track. Katie focused on the assembly coming her way. They relished her persuasive power, watching how the runners formed their new presence as if on a sacrificial offering was in deliverance.

"Why on earth do people watch this nonsense, Greg? Kasper stammered sitting before the TV watching some 'reality' program he and Greg munched on potato chips as they toured the cable channel programs.

"So it is," Greg agreed, "a little nonsense ever once and a while is entertaining."

Kasper proceeded to change the channels.

"Oh, stop there!" ordered Greg.

They stared for a few seconds. "This is the average Joe getting a crack at a beautiful girl," declared Greg.

Kasper looked disapprovingly, "Typical worship of mediocrity. It's easier to find a bunch of yo-hoes than creative people."

"Yea, this is just fantasy for yo-hoes who have nothing but fantasy to look forward to."

Panning the channels again, "This show used to be good. I liked it a lot," said Kasper looking stopping to a channel.

"ZP Pages," said Greg, "It had intrigue, drama, and scientific spoofs, but then they got into all that alien nonsense. It just got too much into all that stuff."

"Aliens were into everything. Aliens started life on earth, the pyramids, the Easter Islands statues; ancient building were directed by aliens," Kasper soured at every description.

"Notice, all these structures were built by brown skinned people, but the scientists say these people were not smart enough or had the mechanical means of doing any of this," disclosed Greg.

"Yea, where were the Germans and Englishmen to direct them," added Kasper.

"I tell you where they were," said Greg, "they were running around in small tribes. They were still in the hunting phase of civilization."

"You know the Chinese build the great wall thousands of miles long," revealed Kasper, "but I've never seen any of these science programs say aliens helped the Chinese to build this structure."

"Good point," the boys agreed.

"You have here is forced inferences," continued Kasper, "they don't have any choice but to believe in all that hogwash, since poignant critics have pointed out that evolution for instance cannot explain why the 'eye is identical in design in hundreds of species of animals. The eye purposively evolved at different epochs, different with totally different environments."

"But, the best proof that evolution does not fit the geological record," Greg proposed confidently, "that shows over a very short geological time thousands of different species have been found at the same geological period."

"See that's why," emphasized Kasper, "most paleontologists' figures life on Earth was introduced by extraterrestrial sources."

"Hey! Stop there!" interrupted Greg looking at a program that caught his attention while Kasper was flipping channels.

"You like 'The Hobbits'?" asked Kasper, "I do."

"Fantasy with lots of action," answered Greg. Thus, they found entertainment with short humanoids, orgs, and an assortment of creatures engaged in many escapades; all this, with visual effects and entrancing scenery. Kasper would place himself into the scenes. He was the heroic figure bringing the wicked to their ruinous defeat, thwarting their plans and revealing the truth that destroys the tyranny they espoused. Everything was tidy while the boys were enjoying some privacy. Little thought of the absence of Eli and Danny issued, for a household of four boys it brought no pains when a couple came missing for a while. This small tranquil was abruptly interrupted. The two heard the entrance of a couple voices, recognized as belonging to Eli and Danny. Voices of discussion of some distasteful subject undoubtedly, judging from the staccato exchange between the voices.

"Hey guys," greeted Greg, "what's up? You guys sound like you're on something."

Eli moved to a sit next to Kasper as Danny planted himself on the floor in front of the TV screen.

"Both of you look serious," said Kasper looking at two solemn faces.

Danny explained the afternoon events. After finishing their workout, he joined up with Jimmy, Terry, Eli, and Sheila. Jimmy was driving he was to drop Sheila off at her home, then they planned to help Jimmy with a term paper due;

plus Jimmy sort the help of his teammates with a final exam math worksheet. They would have a 'brain storm' session with their mate.

"Jimmy pulled into Sheila's driveway," Eli interrupted, "then everything happened," Sheila was walking into the house and Jimmy started backing out.

"Then police cars came from everywhere," imposed Danny. "First we thought; they came for us. I thought Jimmy probably had some dope or something in the truck."

"Yea, the first thing Jimmy said was: 'Ah, I knew I should have paid those parking tickets'," revealed Eli.

Kasper shook his head with despair, as to what tragedy he figured was about to be presented.

"What 's wrong?" I asked Sheriff Palooka.

"'Nothing with you boys relax,' he said."

Then Danny explained how three teams of police unloaded from vehicles and followed the sheriff. All of us got out of the truck anyway and we were standing around.

"That's when I notice another car parked next to the road. Standing next to the car, I recognized our 'stalker'. He was standing with a business dressed man."

Eli added. "They were looking like they were making sure everything was going as planned whatever planned was."

"It didn't take long before we heard all sorts of commotion inside," said Danny, "then the crying."

"I heard Sheila saying, "What! That can't be!...please!...please!'" added Eli.

"We wanted to go see what was happening...I have never felt so helpless; didn't know what to do," pleaded Kasper.

"Yea we did," Danny revealed, "they were coming for Sheila!"

"Coming for Sheila!" cried Kasper and Greg together.

"But it's not what you think. Sheila was adopted illegally."

"What?"

"Her family adopted her. Unknown to them, Sheila had been stolen from her real mother while she was shopping," Danny shook his head.

"Sheila was like a year and a half," added Eli, "Sheriff Palooka pulled me aside and told me that much. He said he could not say anymore. He advised me to check the papers next couple days, for the details."

"What happened next?" asked Kasper?

"Well Jimmy was highly upset as were we all, he said, "'this is like kidnapping her again!'"

"This crap sucks," swore Kasper, moved emotionally beyond his self. "Sheila must be devastated…So they took her away?"

"But, here this," Eli revealed, "there must have been some knowledge that this was going to happen; because Sheila came out followed by her Dad holding suitcases in both hands. Her mother had stuff in her arms and they were boxed."

"Sounds like they were forewarned alright," added Greg.

"And she appeared subdued to me," said Danny, "like, she was sad but knew it was coming." Everyone remained quite for some seconds as if to absorb what had transpired.

"I am going to bed," said Kasper breaking the silence and he left for his bed, the others fanned out for food, TV, or bed as well.

They waited and waited as the crowd of students buzzed with restlessness in folded chairs. Wednesday afternoon and Lakeport high had a guess speaker schedule in the gymnasium turned into an auditorium. During the wait, several clusters of students about the gym had subjects requiring resolution, or some opinion needing an ear to listen while they issued dialogue. True, the teachers waiting with them would surmise the chatter as trite nonsense mostly. However, there was much discussion concerning Sheila Adams. She was gone for good. She had to go live with her 'real' family in Hillsdale, a community bordering western Columbus.

Sheila's track and some classmates were distraught, confused; many felt vulnerable themselves. People forget that it is almost natural that every person at some time in their formidable years questioned whether the parents they live with are their 'real' mom and dad. Therefore, an experience that Sheila has realized just confirmed a justification for such insecurity about their pedigree. "Principal Stromberg made a task of touring the class rooms and speaking to those who displayed some emotion of the affair. He reminded them that Sheila called him at the school and left her home number so that her friends may call. "I talked to her parents and they agreed that her friends are welcomed to call Sheila at their home," said Principal Stromberg. Nonetheless, on this day Kasper was not consoled at all. He sat pouting as they waited, which just enhanced his already irritable state of emotion.

"Some kids come into this world do not have a chance because of the people always messing with them," Kasper said to Charles Hoyd sitting next to him after some discussion about the Sheila affair. "For some fate just overwhelms situations which at times one can never recover. They have messed up Sheila's running, taken her from the only home she has ever known…what a bummer!…but think about the anguish the natural parents went through all these years with their child stolen…" he thought.

Then Mrs. Socia arrived to the podium followed by Principal Stromberg and the quest. All of them took seats on the small stage. While Mrs. Socia made his introduction, Kasper observed the quest. Light complexion, shaved head, a dress coat that buttoned to the neck. This black man topped off his dress by hanging a large medallion around his neck.

"Sharp dresser," said some boy amongst them.

"Alle minoritie sind das gleiche über hier, erscheinend immer spat und über angelkleidet für den Anlaß (All minorities are the same over here, always showing up late and over dressed for the occasion.)," remarked Kasper disparagingly to himself irritated and not of a mood to hear any speech.

"And now boys and girls, Mr. Franklin Mims!" announced Mrs. Socia. Mims took to the podium and started his presentation. Introspect and anxious, Kasper only wished to get out of this place.

"Life can be rough boys and girls…." Mims started.

"Wissen Jastimme, Jastimme, Jastimme, ich daß Sie Schwarz Ihr ganzes Leben, Recht gewesen sind?(Yea, yea, yea, I know, you've been black all your life, right?)." he thought on, "Ich brauche einen harted Lauf heute(I need a hard run today)." Then Kasper leaned over to Charles and said, "Now I understand when people say, 'I need a stiff drink'."

The speaker was now rambling about how on can be determined and not fail at anything, if they just believe in oneself. "Nothing can stop a mind fixed on its target and driving forward…"

"Where's he been living all his life?" Kasper whispered mockingly leaning over to Charles. They sat back arms folded; many of the students were preoccupied as much as he and many continued talking about Sheila and did not even pretend to be listening to the speaker. "A little self-flagellation would fit the bill for me, now." He just wanted to leave and get to track practice.

Kasper closed his eyes and placed his elbows upon his knees with his hands clasped together. He impatiently listened.

"Let us open our minds to all options. Let us be ready to incorporate any needs that will enable us to accomplish, that sat before us…let us strive and be thankful for the diverse society that has empowered this country…let us except people as they are…"

"Yea, pedophiles, murderers, go on," snapped Kasper.

"…diverse lifestyles and cultures is what make this country great…we shouldn't judge others lifestyles…"

"What! Now he's one of those who don't believe in anything, but everything," jest Kasper turning to Charles.

"…except other beliefs as being as sincere as our own…"

"This guy's got all the worldly clichés and buzz words down pat."

Then it was over. The crowd applauded politely, even Charles. Not Kasper

"Enough of this nonsense!" he said, not caring if a polite person heard his last snipe.

The boy wasted no time getting to his locker and dressing into his running togs. There was little 'dress' as the day was warm and humid, so Kasper wore no shirt for this session. "I'll be sweating like a pig soon enough," he would say.

Danny joined up with Kasper equally naked waist-up. As the two entered the track grounds, Kasper sort out Thorpe. He wanted to express his distraught about Sheila having her life yanked apart and why where they continuing as if nothing horrific had occurred, or something to that affect. Thorpe's silhouette was absent from view.

"I didn't see him at the gym, either," said Danny. "He may be trying to get our new uniforms for Saturday. Yesterday he was ranting and raving about we were suppose to have had them at Districts, but the store could not get them to us."

"Hey, that's just like coach, he wouldn't be concerned with Sheila now that she's gone," added Kasper gloom and hurt in his tone "I spoke to him first thing this morning; he just shook his head and exclaimed his sorrow. He seemed as helpless as I was. Shoot I came to him for ideas as to how can we do anything to help Sheila; the dude looked like I needed to prop him up. Thorpe is not the type who knows how to make things happen."

Hanging their heads as they progressed to a patch of grass, they were to start stretching when interrupted by some commotion coming from the parking lot. The boys rose from their crouching position to focus the parking lot. They could see what they could only dream of: Sheila was running from Thorpe's car as several girls were rushing to word her from the track yelling with glee, as was she.

"It's Sheila!"

"Coach Thorpe got her over here."

They raced toward the group as every else around the track. For the next half hour, jubilations, inquiries with short explanations. Offerings with assurances well received; concern with no concern being necessary.

"I am going to finish the year out here," Sheila elaborated. "My real parents are nice. I will live with them, but they'll get me to school here and they will pick me up after practice." After Kasper got his hug, he stood mute with this realization. It was as if the correct event happened in a dream, now he waited to wake up.

After high fives and hugging most everyone, off the youngsters went to their various athletic tasks. Sheila, as usual teamed up with Eli and Terry to complete 200-meter runs.

"They say, they may buy a house near the lake," said Sheila after a few runs. Then she explained the coach's visit to the home. "Coach Thorpe, I never heard him do so much talking. He explained to them that I was a star runner on the team and that I was one of the best girl milers in the state."

"Naw, he didn't tell that lie!" it was Jimmy approaching having just arrived from the career center, "Hi girl glad to have you back. Thought I had to do some kidnapping of my own," Everybody laughed and Sheila gave Jimmy a big hug. Then another batch of queries flooded toward the girl.

"The paper said they are wealthy," questioned Terry between a run.

"Yea, they have a big house," she could not say more as they were about to start another run.

"Ok, for this 200 we need 29 seconds, 33 seconds for Sheila." Thorpe ordered. The trio set off and Kasper, Greg, and Danny followed completing a series of 300-meter runs.

"Go Sheila go! Go Sheila go!" They chanted just delighted the girl was out there with them.

"28.7! 32 flat! Sheila" screamed Katie from across the field.

"Aaaa, aaa…," the breaths were fast and reached deep into the lungs.

"We got a big boat," Sheila revealed proudly, "so it would be convenient to have a house out here," said she to Kasper who wandered close to her between his runs. He smiled as moved away to her run.

Kasper noticed Sheila said 'We got a big boat'. "She's certainly adjusting quickly," said he to Danny.

"See how happy she is," observed Danny, "looks like she's not going through any suffering, to me."

"She's definitely happy to be here, but she may still not be all that happy with things," cautioned Kasper.

Another 300 meters loomed before them. A few deep breaths, relaxing legs shakes and these two boys were running again. Greg relieved from the workout by Coach Thorpe, was in the showers.

"So the skinny guy with the cap," Eli queried, "who was he?"

"Oh, he is a private dick!" Sheila went on to explain. "He was scouting for my real family. They had to check a lot of things to make sure I was the girl they were looking for."

"How did they track you down?" asked Terry.

"The family doctor who delivered me suggested my footprints as a baby be cross checked throughout the area. He hoped that I had to be taken to some hospital for health reasons and maybe my prints be taken again for identification purposes. Well, that was done and they got a 'hit'," volunteered Sheila in a proud comportment.

"But they just got around to doing this years later," asked Kasper, "That's stupid police work."

"The police thought I most like would be taken far away from here, nobody thought to look locally," said Sheila defensively.

Interruption was again with then as it was time for a 100-meter stretch run. Conversation continued between heavy deep breaths, after the run.

"Yea, they found enough inconsistencies and with no record found of a pregnancy or birth for Mrs. Brown, they then went to court," continued Sheila voluntarily.

"Well, I am just glad you're back," disclosed Eli.

"Yes, and I am going to pray," added Kasper, back with the group again, "that your folks buy that property so you can go to school and run here next year."

Everyone agreed and the kids finished the workout and re-gathered on the bleachers. Now, the girls on the team surrounded Sheila and girl talk developed with all the giggles, playful taunts, and jollying long after Kasper and crew packed up and headed home.

"Had our last workout, Dad," said Kasper.

"So you guys will rest and stretch only until Friday?"

"Yea, one thirty Friday we run the four by 800 meter final."

"Well, you look ready to go now that things worked out with Sheila," reminded Jayce, "you were looking pretty down last night, son."

"That was something wasn't it?" replied Kasper, "Sheila said Thorpe told the Geyer's, that's Sheila's real last name, that the community here was great and she said he pleaded that they allow her to finish school here."

"That's good," relied Jayce, "they undoubtedly felt defensive and that everybody here would be against them. Coach should be given a lot of credit to gain their trust and friendship."

"It surprised me what coach did. I never figured him the type to wrestle with a situation like that and come out with a deal," pointed out Kasper. "Yea, that's the word I want. I didn't figure him for a dealer."

"But you know now something about the man you didn't figure for, don't you?" suggested Jayce. "And tell me, with what she's facing at the Regional is she ready considering all this mess she's been through this week?"

"Well, she's got little competition, but not us," stated Kasper changing his mood, "Bald East finished in 7:53, followed by Franksburg in 7:58."

"They'll probably go faster than that Saturday."

"I wouldn't bet against it," the boy reaffirmed. "And South Ridge's Ricky O'Neal went 4:28; in the 1600, at the Districts, in Gradsville, Jamie Dentist, cruised 3200 meters in 9:30."

"Things are heating up," replied Jayce, "you should expect that." He paused with Kasper's silence. "So what's up for tonight?"

"I want to concentrate on a few physics problems with Danny. He should be back in a minute."

"Sounds good, say good night to your mom, before you turn in."

"I will."

"Here's one Danny," Kasper stared at number thirty-four in the physics pamphlet. "It says: 'You should be expected to determine the energy released through the fission process of an element.'"

"That's a nuclear energy question," Danny explained.

"Yep!" Then Kasper turned to the appropriate section of the physics text David had given him.

"Okay, the example the here says: "The first nuclear explosion at "Trinity" was a plutonium bomb. If at critical mass, fission occurred with 1.0 kilogram of plutonium, how much energy would be released if each nucleus split releases 200 million electron volts?"

"Good problem," Danny commented, "I always wondered how they figured how much power an atomic bomb would yield."

Kasper read and studied the examples with Danny then he turned back to the booklet problem.

"So fundamentally we know that the mass of any quantity is equal to the mass of one atom times the total numbers of atoms in the quantity. He wrote on the pad between the pair:

$$m = m_A N$$

"So the number of atoms is N, and the atomic mass number, m_A for Plutonium is 244u. You can look this up in the index. Now we use the unified mass unit 1u = 1.66 x 10^{-27} kg as the conversion factor to get proper units, then we'll have the number of atoms." He wrote:

$$N = m/m_A = (1.0kg/244u) \times (1 \ u \ atom/1.66 \times 10^{-27}kg)$$

$$N = 2.47 \times 10^{24} \ atoms$$

"Now when you slit the nucleus of an atom, the energy released is 200 million electrons volts; so the total energy released is the number of atoms multiplied times the energy of each atom split which is

$$E = (200 \ Mev/atom) \times (2.47 \times 10^{24} \ atoms)$$

$$E = 4.94 \times 10^{26} \ MeV$$

"I want to convert MeV to tons of TNT, since that unit is more understandable to most people," said Kasper, "Now one million tons, a megaton, of TNT produces 2.6 x 10^{28} MeV of energy; you can get this figures from a physics reference book So set up a proportion will always work...

$$E/(4.94 \times 10^{26} \ MeV) = (1 \times 10^6 \ tons \ TNT)/(2.6 \times 10^{28} \ MeV)$$

"Solve for E

$$E = 1.9 \times 10^4 \ tons \ of \ TNT$$

$$E = 19,000 \ tons \ of \ TNT$$

"I saw on the History channel, a program about that first atomic bomb; they said Robert Oppenheimer missed this calculation by an order of ten. He thought the bomb would yield about 2,000 tons of TNT."

"Huh," responded Danny gruffly. Kasper thinks he should know who Robert Oppenheimer is. At this moment, Beth entered the room after a timid knock on the partially opened door.

"Excuse me boys for interrupting, but Kasper could you come talk with Mrs. Sweigert, she's here now." Beth moved closer to her son, "She's nervous and fidgety about her grandfather, granduncle, whatever he is; now she is sure he is up to no good. She wished he would go back to Germany," said the mother in a whisper. They left Danny alone.

A moment later, "Good evening Mrs. Sweigert," greeted Kasper extending his hand to a wrenchingly upset woman.

"Oh Kasper, I have been speaking to your mother for some days now, off and on concerning my Johannes. "I think he's got Bill in some strange activities."

Kasper shook his head as they took seats on the sofa.

"I understand your concern and unfortunately it is well founded. Jimmy Luke and I have been made aware of some not to nice things going on with Bill and it certainly appears uncle Johannes is his mentor, "said Kasper.

"I thought he had put away his old ideas," said she blushing with shame. "You know he was an SS officer in the war."

"I know all about the SS," Kasper interrupted, "you do not have to explain, Mrs. Sweigert."

"He's supposed to be leaving soon, isn't he Helga?" asked Beth.

"He can't leave soon enough for me. Actually, few in the family had any contact with Johannes except for my sister and me. I guess the older members know better of his character than we," acknowledged Helga. "Johannes acknowledges that he's doing business. He says its investments with imports. Kasper, what have you boys heard from your perspective about Bill's doings?"

"Well like you said, he's in business and maybe doing some drugs with Johannes behind everything." Kasper did not want to tell her of the Middle East connections and money laundering. She will learn soon enough when they arrest Johannes and every thing that breaks to the public.

"Sheriff Palooka is watching on to their activities and Bill's got to know it, since most of the kids around here have some knowledge of some of these activities. I do not understand why Bill continues dealing around," added Kasper.

"Oh my God," she exclaimed with painful concern, "Bill's in for it now!"

"Don't jump to conclusions," Beth warned, "you told me Bill said that Johannes can't get him into trouble, and that he's on top of any situation."

"Whatever that means," replied Helga.

Kasper cut a surprised glance at the woman.

"There were a gleam in his eyes and a suppressed excitement in his manner which convinced me, used as I was to his ways, that he thought he was ahead of these matters," disclosed Helga, "although I could not imagine how. Bill is not a conniving boy he's just not smart enough."

"Perhaps we're getting ahead of ourselves, Mrs. Sweigert," said Kasper, "with how things are going things should come to head very soon."

"I am just worried about Bill. That is all I care about."

Kasper was thinking, "Johannes, Bill, and all of their crew will be breaking up stones in prison soon enough. Mrs. Sweigert's wasting her emotions over the boy. The dude has no smarts; he dresses like a cartoon character, and carries a forever grin on his face. He seems psychotic to me."

"There's one other disclosure, I want to tell you about," the woman looked as it she was doing something wrong. "I spoke to Sheriff Palooka. He told me not to speak to anyone about this, but he said 'Bill will be alright', then he said, 'I know his every move.'"

"Sounds like he's saying what ever is going on between Bill and grandfather he's aware of it," said Kasper, then thought, "I bet ole Bill does not know this. Even if Mrs. Sweigert told him what Palooka said, people such as Bill think they're smarter than everyone around."

"Well, well, let us see how he gets on," said Helga imperturbably. "I am taking too much of your time this evening, let me get home now."

"You are always welcome," said Beth, "keep in touch about all the happenings."

"Things should come to a head in the next couple weeks," commented Kasper, "and Johannes will be glad to go back home in a hurry."

"My dear Beth, you have been so supportive. Kasper you are doing so well in your running and you are so smart. Even Bill said you are the smartest kid ever from around these parts. He says the big Ivy League schools are recruiting you."

"Huh, he said that did he?" The boy flushed surprised by this revelation.

From these perspectives, the meeting adjourned. Helga felt reassured she had an arm to lean on if things went bad and Beth and Kasper wished for some culmination soon of these affairs. Kasper returned to Danny and found him flipping pages of some notebook. "Back to the grind," said he. Kasper explained the jest of the conversation, though Danny could not help hearing the balance of the talk.

"Sounds like a mess alright," replied Danny.

"Well things are in motion now that will take care of itself," said Kasper solemnly, not wanting to talk about it any more.

"Kasper could we take a break from physics to look at an English assignment," asked Danny, "things are going good in physics, but our extra-credit assignment in Advanced English. How are we going to complete it by next week?"

"The secret code message," Kasper had dreaded the assignment, as he disliked English grammar. German has about 80,000 words in its vocabulary," he reminded Danny, "English has over 450, 000 words. It's quite, a formidable task Mrs. Bayrum has given us."

Danny and Kasper tucked to the narrow table the script of the assignment before them. Bent over in deep study, Kasper and Danny perused the brief note of the worksheet. The final code was a series of little human figures. Many of which were in a running form. There were two hints and three short coded passages to set some pattern for them.

"The two hints," Kasper read:

1. The subject of the code is concerning a student whose name is Freida who is having difficulty with a subject in a class.

2. The code addresses Freida's struggle to express herself on a subject in this class.

"The three coded messages are to help us find symbols that address words in the two hints given. They are:

1.

2.

3.

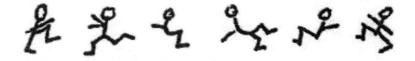

"Now the letter E is the most used letter in the alphabet, I know that," said Kasper, "I read it somewhere I forget. So let's find the symbol used most often and let's call this E." Then boys sorted through the symbols and found one that appeared eight times. "Now Danny lets assign E to the three passages that has that symbol."

"Hey, I know what to do now," interrupted Danny quickly, "the letter E is in the name Freida, which has six letters."

"And E is the third letter;" added Kasper, "so let's find a six letter combination in the three codes where the third letter is E. Let's hope that symbol above is for E."

"Yea, if that is right then we will know the symbols for Freida. The name Freida has to be in the coded messages somewhere."

"Yep," after some long minutes of examination, the boys found such a combination of six in each of the coded passages and they were delighted to find that the symbol they picked for E was correct.

"So for F, R, E, I, D, and A, we have the symbols

"But to what are the passages about?"

"Look at the hints again. They say Freida has difficulty in subject in class."

"The codes should have words like subject, difficulty, class?"

"But look here in the message," observed Danny, "the first to letters is 'if', according to the characters we got from 'FREIDA'."

"Enlightening!" exclaimed Kasper, "I did not see that. So let's place the letters above all the characters we know."

They completed this task and then looked at the spaces. "What's the best route now?" asked Danny, "start guessing words?"

"I think so, but let's look in the code for the word 'class'. It has two letters so we look for two identical characters. Then we should try to find a noun with 'if'"

It did not take them long to find such a combination at the end of each code. Thus, they had the symbols for 'class'.

"Now, if you? If we, If they?" suggested Danny.

"Well, the passage refers to Freida, so it shouldn't be 'if we'."

The boys guessed the three characters after 'if' was Y, O, and U. They filled the spaces for these letters. Looking at the hints, they decided to look for the word 'subject', since the word was in both hints. Indeed, they found repeated seven symbols in each of the codes. This gave them the symbols for the letters U, B, and T. After, filling theses in the coded message, they had:

If you - a n n o - e - - - e s s you – s e – f on a s u - - e - - - o - -

i - u n - i - you - a n F r e i d a.

"Look at the group, e - - - - ess," Kasper suggested.

"EXPRESS!"

"Yea, now we have the letters X, P, and R," exclaimed Danny.

"So 'If you blank express…'"

"YOURSELF, "If you can not express yourself on a…"

"SUBJECT," they said almost simultaneously.

"– O R -?"

"WORK IT!"

"UNTIL," finished Danny, "until you can!"

"The coded message is:

'If you cannot express yourself on a subject work it until you can.'

"Done." They looked at each other and smiled.

"Man it's nearly midnight," observed Danny, "let's sack it."

Cloudy with gusting wind, with rain threatening the day; the Mid-Ohio Regional track and field championships at the campus of DovScott High School were underway. Kasper and team left early, but Kasper studied the trip and took in little scenery.

Gloom and prospects of gloom lay heavy with many competitors for the events of this day; contrary opinion, however dwelled with the competitors that held high aspirations for a future beyond this day. Those unbeaten and competitors who were a close second at the district meet, attempted to parry avoided nursing the adverse or allow it to prejudice this day. Brute force if necessary, but one must go forward. "Mediocrity waits for the opportunity to stand back," Thorpe said to his crew once. "Losers and quitters have many paths to pick, however the successful look for the rare trek that moves them to their completion of the task. Once things get tough, use it as an opportunity to pull away from pack. Do that in everything in your life gentlemen."

Kasper believed there would be two types of beings in races today. Some would run scared - setting a furious pace hoping to finish top four; and those timid fellows who hope to latch on to the leaders and run beyond themselves to qualify for the state meet. He decided he press hard on his run in the relay. Pleased, he took delight that some competitors were complaining and showed their fears.

In the moments of waiting stretched along the bleachers over looking all the track activity, Kasper thought of the circus parade he saw back in Germany on a spring day such as this one. He remembered how he a small, thrill-full hobbling boy, prepared to follow a band along the narrow cobblestone road. With his mother, tugging him along Kasper remembered the stone streets, crowded houses, people leaning out their second story windows, the lines of expectant people cheering the parade. The boy particularly remembered an old fellow who used to sit real close to the marchers on the curb of the street and beamed a smile of awe as they strode by. Now, Kasper thinks that the ole man probably was imagining his hey day when he goose-stepped for the German army.

"Over here Coach!" Katie interrupted Kasper's thought calling for Thorpe. Sitting in the row behind him, she motioned Thorpe to their way. Kasper watched the Coach negotiate between gangs of people climbing the stairs and taking his place next to Katie. He was pleased he would not be disturbed and remained reflective. He turned his attention to the present. Kasper wondered what some of the old people around here were doing back in 'Jim Crow' days. "I wonder if that old man over there ever made some black person get off the side walk…what about that fellow over there?…wonder if he ever told some blacks to not drink in a water fountain in a park that was for whites?"

"Why," thought Kasper, "is it that everything has to evolve from some forced coercion from without. Why is it that some people have to learn from others? Ultimately, there must be some absolute right or absolute standard. In Genesis, why did God say Abel's work and offering was good, and that Cain's was not acceptable? Was Cain producing his best effort, and offering it to God? The bible depicts Cain as having an envious and jealous attitude of Abel. This tells us Cain knew his was not equal to Abel's, but was he doing the best for his ability? Why didn't God give him credit?" The boy answered his own question. "Cain's problem was that he set his own standard and ignored God's standard, unlike Abel. Abel's offering was excepted because he sought after God unlike Cain, who made his own standard from his intellect." Kasper thought to more refining detail, "Cain must have thought: 'God, you gave me free will did you not? So why can't I make my own offering as I see fit?"

Interrupted again, Kasper observed across the field a people infested football field. Emerging from this field Kasper was a foursome of persons. He recognized his mates approaching for the four by 800 meter relay. With a childish realization, Kasper was momentarily startled by a thought that perhaps they were just one among many foursomes that were as determined as they. There can only be one winner. It is going to come down to the best of individual abilities. Lakeport had no deserving preconceived placing in the scheme of things, the boy thought. "You can wish and try and work your heart out; but some times that won't get you across first, since you may not be 'the right.'"

Kasper was backtracking, "It's simplistic to think that because I've worked my best, therefore I should win my encounters. I am so disheartened with losses. Is it wrong to hate to lose?" he wondered. Then he got one glance at the foe-swarming field in front of him and instantly ceased to debate the question of the right of passage to victory. The various colors and designs affected him like a soldier's first glance of an enemy's flag displays—he threw his doubts and philosophical profiling away. Directly predatorily, emotions sent Kasper to join his trio for last preparations for the victory they sort.

Kasper's last concern was for himself; forgetting the menacing future he became a member, he became a part. He diminished as the crew evolved in importance. This foursome was threatened; this team, his community was in a crisis. He welded into a common pack mentality dominated by one desire—win. Just because he would be an observer for this race, Kasper was not relaxed. He wadded through all the emotions and tenseness of one readying to run.

The foursome was like a firework that once ignited proceeds unabated to circumstances until its blazing vitality fizzles; this and gleefulness reassured Kasper's confidence of victory. The stadium grounds filled with dozens of small color clad groups. A plentitude of name-calling for assistance, determining the 'where about' of someone, continued to emanate around the campus. Coaches in groups talked of the present season and past seasons and performances. Discussions of injuries and retirements took a prominence in topics while some revealed they were looking forward new assignments. It was a mysterious fraternity born of the adrenaline and hype of competition.

As his four by 800 crew gathered for the start, Thorpe was at a task. He was like a sculptor who has made many forms and was still creating another while at display. There was furious haste in his movements. He, in his thoughts, was careering off in other places just as the sculptor who as he works whistles and hums gleefully putting-off possible distasteful results. As the Regional meet began all his prior confidence waned. Although he ran the races in his mind, these dreams were never conclusive; they just remained an enigma of blurred images and outcomes.

Presently Thorpe began to feel the effects of the concluding competition of the immense Regional track championships—a final elimination toward the penultimate challenge, the State Championships at the Ohio State University in Columbus. A tantalizing roar filled Thorpe's ears. Some conclusion of a qualifying round had ended, whence forth a nervous urgency claimed him. He developed an acute exasperation of a pestered beast. Thorpe wanted to get on with the affair. Thorpe's impatience brewed from his habit of running races in his mind. This just threw fuel on an already blazing temperament and intentness on all these events.

In the stands, many of the fans were equally gearing in emotions. Mothers and dads hummed low toned noises with their mouths and subdued cheers, some prayers went as an undercurrent of sounds around the stadium. At last, an assembly of colors parted from the coral gathered bordering the track. They followed several officials to the start positions on the first curve. Each of the staggered lines held four teams. The lead runners engaged themselves in the usual attics of stretching, jogging in place, or just staring at the turn. Lakeport's fleet of supporters had a full day ahead. Starting with Jimmy and ending with him in the four by 400 meter relay.

Coaches and some parents were bobbing back and forth roaring directions and encouragements; amongst a constant deluge of announcements and warnings from the public address system; so when the starter pistol blasted half the populace of the stadium were surprised. The staff of runners pounded furiously away from their positions and into the curve. Bobbled emotions were unfastened. Careful pacing abandoned as they forgot about previous performances and set off on not losing ground with the boy running in their reach. The blur of colors and forms stacked upon themselves on the backstretch. Blurred together and shifting then growing larger to the viewer waiting down track. A sentence with variations went up and down the sidelines and in the bleachers.

"Get up there! Stay with the pack!" The onlookers ignored the people next to them who maybe routing for the runner next to their own subject.

"55, 56, 57…" Katie announced to Zoe, "57, for Danny." She watched him speed by in second place in lane two. "Good he's in position to take the lead."

"Come on Paul…come on Jack!…Looking good Pat…" calls ejected toward the runners. Such commands came from all around the track spanning the alphabet in names. The pitch of the exclamations increasing with time as the competitors ran.

"Good pace…hold it…relax," Danny thought moving on the one-hundred meters, "I am going under two minutes…ahaa, ahaa," he breathed rhythmically,…this guy is going to drop in the turn…" He moved into his final turn and slowly rotated quicker and quicker.

"Fan it in Danny! Power those arms," Thorpe yelled from his trackside position on the turn leading to the next handoff. He watched intently the final meters as Danny moved ahead of second place Wilkeville his arm extended as he sort desperately for Greg to snatch his burden from him.

Katie called out the time. "1:57!" Then followed Greg with piercing critical eyes, "Sprint Greg, sprint…" She said, understanding that this long distance runner would find it difficult to start fast enough for the 800 meters. Greg would be overtaken from behind she figured by fleeter starters.

"Ata boy, Rotate Greg!" encouraged Jayce.

"He's moving, okay," commented Jack, "I've never seen Greg moving this fast before." Jayce and Jack had made the trip alone to see the only final of the day.

"Ease back now…ahaaa…ahaa…" Greg was thinking himself through his run, "this is ninety percent of my speed…ahaa…," he breathed, but more rapidly than when running the 3200 meters. He felt like he was hyperventilating.

Wilkesville's runner pulled up to Greg in spite of his effort with Toberstown in tow. The remainder of the field floundered behind, too far for contention. As they finished the turn, Wilkesville's Randy Saad launched an attack and quickly passed Greg. Toberstown's Lonnie Harris hesitated then passed Greg as they crossed 400 meters.

"2:57!" announced Katie. "Come on Greg! They are going too fast! They'll come back!"

Jayce sat nervous rocking slowly, "If he can hang in there Terry will make up any space lost." Jack said nothing as they watched the progression tour the backstretch. Then there were a big fellow in orange catching up to Greg throughout the far turn, while the first two runners barrowed ahead still distancing themselves from Greg.

"They got about thirty meters on us," observed Jayce muttering and feeling scared now.

As they strode into the final meters, Wilkesville and Toberstown slugged it out for the third hand-off. Greg pumped his arms high trying to hurry up to Terry, who bounced in place ready for the spring into action. Coach Thorpe had warned him that most likely he would have to make up territory today.

"4:02!" Jayce said looking at his watch while the boy passed off, "I think his leg was about 2: 05, that's great for Greg." Terry was gone with the baton. The crowd's pitch heightened as some began to whoop frenziedly. Many stood silent trying to contemplate the last race of the season for the team realizing only the top four places would race anymore this season.

"Get on with it boy!" Jack yelled as the young man held on to the two running in front as if he held them by an invisible rope taught around Randy Saad's waist.

Up in the bleachers Katie was ecstatic. "We're setting an all time record. Terry and Eli are going to be way under two minutes."

Characteristic head rolling held the attention of on-lookers impressed by the one-armed boy speeding away from pursuers.

"Strong finish, Terry," called Thorpe softly so confident and proud he felt.

Terry raced as if the had been stalked and had to escape. He thought that a fast run here would prop confidence for a fast run in the open race.

"He's beginning to pull them back," said Jack Luke, "Come on boy!"

Jayce started clapping. "Let's get back on 'em Terry," he said. Terry was moving by in front of them. "57!" He's cooking!" commented Jayce.

Toberstown started loosening from Wilkeville, slipping into Terry's grasp. He was only a stride behind as the three entered the turn. As the turn straighten so did Terry. He straightened up his posture and passed Lonnie Harris. Then took aim for Randy Saad. Catching Randy as he entered his final 200 meters the galley hollered and screamed praising the shear bravery displayed by the 'handicapped' red head.

"Haul around 'em Terry!" yelled Jack.

"Watch it," warned Jayce, "watch it Terry. They're going to try and come back on you."

The turn straightened and so did Harris and Saad straight for Terry. Nearly everyone was standing, stomping, screaming, and hoping.

"Hold on!"

"It's okay!"

"Got him!" yelled somebody nearby.

"5:58!" Katie called. "They're on record pace!"

"Okay Eli, get it done son!" ordered Jayce as the boy snatched the baton a few strides behind Wilkesville and a strike ahead of Toberstown. Eli knew this would be his fastest run ever. Down the backstretch, he flowed magnificently. Long strides and flowing arm movements; he experienced the joy of one who at last finds a satisfaction in which his display of competence is observed.

"You popping off a good one Babe!" Jimmy Luke called out toward Eli. He continued his dash the trailing two runners however, did not fall behind. The pursuers latched onto him as if it was there salvation.

"56," Jayce read his stopwatch as his boy sped across the start point.

From the perimeter of the track, the sound of cheering and commands emanated with increasing intensity as the teams toured the final lap.

"One more time," Eli thought, "only one more time...I am not going to run much faster than next week, if at all."

"We're breaking the record!" Eli thought he heard Thorpe, "7:56, set nine years before." He remembered. With one long pickup as he entered the final straight, Eli gave all he had into his run. Behind the Toberstown, man was making a big effort on Eli. The boy wanted to get on Eli before the straight.

Katie's finger held anxiously on the stop button as Eli got closer and closer to the finish. The galley was clapping vigorously now toasting the competitiveness of the teams

"Hey, green and yellow is coming on him," Jayce warned

However, the boy stopped progressing as Eli stepped higher and rotated vigorously. Eli crossed with a forward lean.

"7: 54.7!" Lakeport supporters were elated beyond words. Thunderous applause suggestive of unnumbered support, but much of the elation was toward other teams streaming across the finish line.

On the end field Danny, Greg, and Terry surrounded Eli. They felt the thrill of victory bubbling from within. Hugs and high-fives accommodated his yet tired stance.

"State Champs!" they screamed. Kasper, Sheila, Roy, and Jimmy surrounded the foursome, as they left the field for the rest area.

As Kasper gazed around at the squad, he felt a flash of astonishment at their accomplishment. Kasper looked at all the various uniforms, the athletes some tall, some, short, many thin. Others looked like wrestlers. With the bright sun gleaming on the colorful uniforms, the playful participants and just the tranquility of this peaceful process in the midst of so much devilment outside. Kasper felt so serene for himself and everyone in these events today. Gone was any animosity or defensive abrasiveness that led him into the day. He could now watch Jimmy's race in the 110-meter hurdles in an entertainment mode.

The blast of the starter pistol bought Jimmy rotating his legs over ten hurdles in a pedestrian but safe 14:55 seconds with no accompanying flaws of step, no pivoting hurdles, while completing his qualifying. As always, Jimmy immediately set off to rest, because of the soon coming 400-meter qualifying followed.

In the 'bull pin', Jimmy stretched and conversed with his competitors as they waited. "Jimmy you still plan on joining the Army after graduation?" asked Henry Sprague.

"You bet," said Jimmy unhesitant.

"Ain't you scared of getting sent to Iraq or Afghanistan?" Henry asked seriously concerned. "Look at all the people dying over there. I used to dream about being a soldier, but I do not want to get killed."

Jimmy scooted closer to the boy, as he had a point to make. "Pal, Washington DC, New York City, and Boston have as many murders every year, year after year as the US has lost in those war zones."

"Is that so?"

"Yep, and I want to do my part and when I get out of service I want to run a boat garage," said Jimmy pleased to tell someone he had ambition. "I am going to sell and repair boats on Crimshead Lake."

"Okay fellows, let's head out," interrupted an official coaxing them toward the track. Escorted, assigned lanes and staggers they readied for the crack of the pistol.

"Easy plucking," offered Roy calling from the fence facing the start.

"Bang!" Jimmy started relatively slow, but worked the backstretch, floated the turn then powered eighty per cent to the finish. It was anti-climatic. There were no surprises, but Jimmy knew the 'honchos', as he called them, will be coming from northern Ohio. A couple of these principals he will meet with Saturday.

"I'll take a 49.7," assessed Thorpe, noting the ease of run. While Jimmy left for the 'bull pin' for his 200 meters, Thorpe rounded up the trio who would join Jimmy in the four by 400 meter relay.

"You got to run solid," warned the coach, "a couple schools could stay close to us and then Jimmy will have to run all out. He's running four races, so we do not want him hurt by over extending himself, okay?"

"We'll give him a pad coach," agreed Eli, "don't worry." Danny and Terry agreed, so they set off to get ready for the race. Kasper meanwhile was scanning a physics text and selecting some problems to solve for next week. Sitting next to

Katie and Zoe, the girls got the boy off this trend of thought soon enough with discussion of the Sheila affair. However, Jimmy was up again. The completion of the 200 meters event displayed why many would say it is his best event as he made a travesty of the field.

"Jimmy can hug that turn," commented Jayce. "Twenty-two flat looked easy."

"One more time guys," reminded Thorpe as the foursome proceeded toward the lineup for the relay, "one more time, people."

"Just do not think too much, dudes," suggested Jimmy, "just crank and fan it in baby." Crank they did; as Roy and gallantly and gave Eli a two meter led, Eli continued the rally issuing Terry a three-meter lead. Terry handed off to Jimmy after adding another five meters to the lead, whereupon, Jimmy cruised to an easy victory.

"Let's do it again tomorrow fellows," announced Thorpe after gathering everyone together, "Now let' get home and get some rest."

Kasper thought philosophically, "Look at what Jimmy did. Now, there is an example of what so few of us can accomplish. People like Jimmy evolved to reach out beyond their grasp; they do not rattle and tense up. Actually, the more the challenge the more they enjoy. Wish that was my nature."

CHAPTER 10

▼

Kasper awakened slowly. He came back to a position from which he could regard himself. Too much time had been scrutinizing his person in some dreamy way as if he had never before seen himself. "I started a cripple almost and now I have a ticket to the Regional tournament," he surmised, "I am somebody." How dare Kasper reasoned, to think he was without means beyond himself. The vague formidable difficulties of the exercise had passed; the boy thought methods of Thorpe begged his signature. Kasper felt he was a fine fellow creative ideal. The boy smiled in gratification.

Dawn creeps low and stealthy over the cornfields of Ohio, a haze of pale gray tinged with low sun light. Slowly, too, the boys rouse themselves. Along the line of beds, the boys yawn, scratch at the dry skin of their legs, and hugged the blankets that they had clutched to through the night.

"Get up sleepyheads," Kasper called to Danny and Greg, "you made it to the relays. Now we see what courage and manner of man you are on your own." Brother's comment was not taken in the humor it was delivered. This annoyed Greg, so as he rose from his bed he allowed Kasper to catch his scornful eyes.

"Come on dudes," said Eli sticking his head in the door. "Jimmy will be here in a few minutes then breakfast!" Thorpe had reservations at a restaurant for breakfast.

"There will be no eating again until after our races," reminded Danny

"That means not until the late afternoon for us," added Eli.

Upon Jimmy's arrival driving a van, they gave partings to mom and dad who would depart for the meet later. Setting off for the school Kasper beamed in fellowship and confidence. "Gee! A great day," he said affably.

"Yep!" said Jimmy behind the wheel, "I love it hot. That cold stuff plays with my muscles."

"I just hope this weather holds through next week as well," contemplated Danny.

Breakfast was delicious and short. Everyone ate voraciously and there was no talk about track. Sheila, Lacy, Nadine, and the girls were there, although only Sheila had qualified for the meet this day. Serenity with laughter capped off with friendly jollying parried seriousness for these moments, before Thorpe ended it all with a: "Come on girls and boys, let load-up, time to bear the brute." It was almost rude, and the kids felt interrupted as they filed silently from the restaurant to board their rides for DovScott High School again. Kasper eyes captured every sight today.

They traveled on under only occasional wisps of clouds. The sun shown bright and with the light breezy wind it made an idea morning perpetuating and heightening the excitement waiting for them. Passing the fields in these parts of Ohio is a disorienting experience, constantly beset with such slippages between the present and the past. Amish barns and buggies clashed with wide lane interstate highways between vanishing small farms and crossroads towns and newer landscape of megamalls and sprawling housing developments. Exactly at a time when America seemed more interested in diversity, special interest groups, patronage from countries Kasper held with revulsion, must of the culture he enjoyed in these scenes is in danger of being lost.

Nowhere is this truer, than in the Mid Ohio counties; these locations experienced controversy before. In pre-civil war years, this bucolic region found itself dean center between the warring factions for slavery and abolitionist. The Underground Railroad trekked through the lands where runaway slaves had to hide doing the day and travel at night in Ohio before finally crossing into Canada and freedom. The descendents of these very folks escorted these runaways across this land. Slaves prayed of reaching these grounds. These are hallowed grounds in history for black people, and these old Americans are extempore of a people's moral stance against an innate injustice of man. It would be a sad thing to witness the demise of this culture.

Kasper turned his thoughts to the housing developments and the populace occupying these abodes. His observations and summations produced a different venue. "They're going about everyday tasks…the same ole routines, jobs,…looking at the same ole TV programs…day after day…nothing exciting in their lives," the boy wondered what could they do to get a jar in this bland existence.

His mind cruised forward to the Regional meet, where all participants were as some sort of dutiful soldiers off to the defense of nobody-ness. Kasper exaggerated the endurance, the skill, and the valor of those at this meeting on the athletic field. He ennobled not just himself, but all present at these games. Kasper was conscious of his daydreaming and he wondered if all this serenity and compassionate camaraderie would survive, if he suffered a terrific failure of performance.

"On my return trip will I be cursing my being, resentful, and judgmental of the very people smile toward, now?" he surmised to comment on himself.

"Blam!"

Jimmy pounced from his stance. First to clear hurdle one, got his lead foot on the ground first and settled down to duplicate this sequence for nine more hurdles. He only wanted victory here; passing up the cocky style, he ran at Districts where he missed disaster in his trying to be a 'honcho'. Most the Lakeport family of fans was present and banded mostly in high bleachers near the middle of the stadium. Principal Stromberg and wife was an exception, as he had obligation toward graduation arrangements for the school. Accompanying Lakeport's crowd were many of the District meet fans; joined with many people from three other District meets. Relentless followers they were parents often wore large buttons with a picture of their child. Central about such devotion is a personal relationship to him or her, not athletic proneness; as some subjects were quite aware that their level of performance would not enable them to advance beyond this day. They knew all too clearly that this would be a final chapter in this theater of their life. Nevertheless, for mom, dad, a grandparent, or cousin there will be no belittlement of this occasion. Cameras, video recorders, binoculars made required gear with their person.

Already it was evident the screams are a pitch higher and demands more poignant than the Districts. Gone were the 'participant' entries; here the 'honchos' lay in feed on these fields, readying to pick the juicy plucking from the 'tree of victory'. Vision of grandeur, college letters of intent, and scholarships loomed in their imaginary. In this picture, pandemonium waited a chance for itself.

"13.94!" Katie screamed after Jimmy broke the white line with his lean across the finish line, "Poetry in motion, aha."

"That's a record!" exclaimed Jack, "According to this program."

"He looked smooth," said Jayce, "not jerky like last week." Jayce looked at the program, "Yea, he broke a record set eleven years ago."

The galley clapped with approval. "Ata boy," added Sophie Luke, "he made it look so easy."

"The second kid was just trying to get over the last hurdle," observed Jack

"That was just awesome," added Jaycee, "he's one of the best high school hurdlers in the nation."

"I see Sheila, Kasper, and Danny over there warming up," said Beth pointing to the other side of the field. No one of this group was far from thinking of Sheila's upheaval in her life.

"I understand her new family," said Sophie breaking the short silence, "well I guess that's what you call them. They are here somewhere. Sheila said they would come today along with the Brown's."

"Well, that's good," answered Beth, "Sheila doesn't need any continuing squabbles."

"More than I can say for our famous daughter," commented Jack with slow and carefully selected words. No one else choose to comment, they fixed on watching the boys and girl's 100 meters. Coach Thorpe was pleased Jimmy looked great in the hurdles. He hoped the day would continue to warm. If Jimmy cramped it would be so costly for the team.

The audience watched the 4 x 200 relays next. These events garnered the vigor of participation from supporters. From the explosion of the pistol, vigorous commands flooded toward the track urging on the athletes. Then, when there was a dropped baton or sloppy baton exchange, heighten comments slipped inadvertently from mouths. Always, they were enjoyable to watch as some runners would come from behind and snatch a victory. Often the supporters left feeling cheated. Their team would have won, if they had not had a bad handoff; we would have won if out third leg had been faster; we would have won it only…. Faces of disgust jutted from fans, but most would merely look defeated and dejected.

"Our school does not have enough kids to do all these sprint relays," stated Jack.

"And we don't have the quality, if we do field a squad," added Jayce, "the big city schools have times like 1:27. Numerous schools have times under 1:30. Fast times for here are like 1:32, and the likes."

"About five seconds difference!"

"Wow!"

The group groaned. They were anxious waiting for the 1600-meter runs. These relays required two heats; so Lakeport people fiddled around with small talk until: "Hey isn't that the ole track fan over there?" asked Jayce, "What's his name Roland?"

The small group looked to their left and indeed saw the ever-grinning face, watches and binocular hanging around his neck.

"Yea, that's him making his rounds," said Jack.

"The participants of the 1600 meters boys are…," the announcer started. Kasper, Danny, and the other fourteen runners followed a red-capped woman to assigned start positions on the wide eight-lane, red artificial surface running track.

"Here we go," said a concerned Jayce, "there's two kids, that's at 4:28 and 4:27. They may drop some time today as well. The fellows can't be off today."

"Bang!" There is seldom any delay unless the meet gets ahead of schedule.

As usual, the blast surprised most people. Runners sped around the turn to the backstretch.

"Can't wait for the last meters," thought Kasper moving swiftly into the stretch, "there are a couple guys besides Danny who can out sprint me." However, two runners to his left and two to his right closed around him like a sandwich and moved ahead. Danny was leading.

"You need to get out of there, Kasper!" Unmistaken he heard Thorpe fervent command. He had no chance, but to move gradually out to the second lane and try to pass to the outside. Danny was running where he should and Kasper knew he should be on his heels.

"Come on! Get up there, son!" Jayce commanded loudly with anger.

"Oh he's got three more laps," repulsed Beth equally displeased, but with her husband and not directed to Kasper.

"This is the State qualifications," shot Jayce, "these guys are not going to wait for anybody! They're not going to let up!" He stared at his wife as to say 'don't you understand'. Beth kept her eyes on the track and ignored him.

Jayce was actually scared. "Kasper let's go now; "he thought in desperation. He looked at the digital timer next to the start line as the pack of runners approached.

"63, 64…66 for Kasper!"

Into the second lap a pack of seven, some slight space then the remainder packed together. All slowed on this turn as Danny continued to dictate the pace.

"Where is Kasper?" Danny thought, "I am making an honest pace he should get up here soon."

Behind were Logansport's Bill Reise and Bob Munson of East Berlin. Both had followed the Lakeport pair in track and filed news pamphlets all season. So the two had dreamed of this moment where they could make some notoriety of themselves. The spectators were excited and chanted for the pace to maintain its brisk tempo.

"They're not falling off Danny fast clip," thought Kasper

"Kasper! Fifth place won't do!" again the voice of Thorpe thundered toward the boy. Completing the fourth turn, five were in trail like baby ducks following mother duck. As the turn straightened, Kasper moved outside toward lane two accelerating. Closing and closing toward the 800 meters. Kasper moved over just in time to past the halfway point in third place continuing his move to get with Danny. However, Munson looked over at Kasper and stepped up his tempo to fend Kasper off. Munson pulled up to Danny's heels as they leaned into the turn.

2:11 was the 800 time. "Kasper's back up there, but the kid in second looks strong. He's not working too hard," observed Jayce. "The boys will put him to work on these last two go rounds," suggested Jack.

"Kasper will get around him," said a petrified Beth making a rare comment.

Now four runners cleared themselves of the trailing field. Danny, Munson, Kasper, and Bill Reise raced the third lap displaying no stress or impediments of pace.

Approaching the end of 1200 meters the troop appeared to be moving faster…3:18…3:19…3:20; read the digital clock, located at the finish just inside the track, as they ran by.

"Here's where business gets done," said Jack just as Munson started moving to the outside so he could pass Danny.

"Watch it Danny, here he comes!" shouted Sophie, as Jayce and Beth watched ruefully scared, because Kasper did not respond to the movement up front.

Danny challenged Munson's move and kept him at bay. The pair pulled farther away from Kasper and Reise. Two meters, three meters, four meters, and then the growing space stopped. Kasper was moving for contention. His arm swing pumped higher. His knees lifted higher. Into the final turn, Danny continued his relentless gate. While Munson started slipping behind, Kasper was progressing to the red and white clan boy.

"Now he's making a move!" exclaimed Jayce, "but I think it's too late. He's got to sprint all the way to the finish." Howling came from all corners of the stadium as people cheered the runners on.

"Get him Kasper," yelled Thorpe.

"You got 'him! You got him!" added Jimmy.

At the top of the turn, Kasper was at Munson's heels. He moved to lane two for space. Danny was five meters up on them and starting into the final stretch run.

"Come on! Get second Kasper!" yelled little Zoe standing as everyone else.

Eighty meters out, Kasper pulled away from Munson's folding form. Danny sensing victory ceased pumping and went into a long stride glide. His mate too fearful of Munson continued his hard run until he crossed the finish line.

"Don't want to finish any farther behind," he decided.

"Great time, come on!" called out Katie looking at her watch.

"4:20.42!" her watch displayed.

"Click," Zoe stopped her watch on Kasper. "4:21.22," said she slowly reading.

The pair reeled to a stop. Munson followed in 4:27, Reise in at 4:28 nearly catching his rival.

"What a race!" Exclaimed Jayce relieved.

"Kasper showed his grit," reminded Jack, "he was in trouble but came through at the end."

"Everybody says Kasper does not have a fast finish; however, he actually was closing on Danny," revealed Sophie.

"I am so glad it's over," the peaceful voice of Beth, "I can breathe again."

"Hey those boys of yours look good," declared an unfamiliar voice. They looked in the voices direction and approaching through the crowd was the familiar face of Roland 'the fan'.

"How are you?" greeted Jack, "Yes, they knew their way around the track didn't they?"

While the other members of this common party paid their greeting, Roland probed. "Have you heard Steve Crestor of Hillsburg toured the 1600 in 4:22 with no one urging from behind."

Roland waited for some reaction of awe or concern from Jayce and Jack; but neither flicked an emotion detectable for the man.

"And then there's Ivan Holm of Lance Cruz, he went 9: 29 in the 3200."

"Impressive," responded Jayce.

The man could feel that he was not deriving any conversation so he switched the subject. "I was at the District meet in Delaware, watching Marlborough," Roland shook his head, "they can not pay quarter to your boys. They had no one advanced to the Regional."

"Is that right so," said Jayce acting interested.

"Coach Smith and Bell used to speak disparagingly of Coach Thorpe. Now when I remind them of some of your performances they become coy and want to get away from the subject," Roland reeled and smiled with the two men at his disclosure.

"Good," commented Jayce, "I hope we run against them in cross country next fall, so we can bury them."

There was rumbling of the crowd. They were directing conversation toward the girl's participants. Newspaper coverage of Sheila's drama was the prime subject in the bleachers; however, polite and humbled they were.

"Alright, Sheila stay focused," insisted Sophie.

"I am praying these factors do not impede her performance," interjected Roland, "but, such affairs historically are detrimental at this level on these young souls. That girl's got to be devastated," he continued, "and she's got to run against those sisters; both of which will probably run under five minutes at the North Regional today…and the South Regional has a few under five-ten."

"Yea, yea, yea," interrupted Jayce annoyed, "Sheila's got to run here with these girls. She can't run next weeks races today."

Roland felt the irritation coming from Jayce. Jack said nothing.

"Sheila's tear this group up," said Sophie, "she's fine about all that stuff. It's all behind her."

Roland thought his warning demanded attention as any expert of some discipline. However, he felt the sting from these supporters so he quickly made his exit for some like-minded fan as himself. Meanwhile everyone in the bleachers nearly turned their attention to the start about to take place. They watched officials line up the sixteen girls into the four staged lines on the turn, four to each line. Tiny creatures most were. As small as gymnasts some, others tall and lanky, a few were chunkier than what one would expect for distance runners. Petite figures garbed on an array of colors. Most looked younger than their age. Pony -tails, pig tails, French braids, spiked colored hair and page cuts; all presented a pretty sight at the stance.

Sheila looked toward her entourage and lit a smile, detectable even in the far bleachers. A couple minutes they had to shack the legs and gain some relaxation, as the meet was running slight ahead of schedule. The diversity of description they were, and the names of these girls were equally diverse: Jackie, Nicole, Melanie, Erin, Katy, Brittany, Stacie. Then there were Amanda, Molly, Carrie, Danielle, Kallesta…From the bleachers and track fence names sounded out wanting to leave encouragement, warnings, and suggestions toward their subjects.

Then the starter climbed to short stepladder on the infield, "Runners to your marks."

"Blam!" off swiftly, completing the turn they broke the stagger and gathered in a moving pack on the back straight.

"Take it out Sheila!" People yelled to the bobbing hair-dos. The girls ran with more deliberation than their male counterparts did, no erratic jostling observed.

Presently, the stillness was pregnant with meaning. Nervous was the on lookers, who could not help, but to wait for someone to trip and fall. The multicolored figures shifted and changed a trifle. However, they moved so ever carefully an anomaly to the chaos of the pack. The hush was solemn until they straightened in the stretch finishing lap one. Of the group, people seemed to discern the ones running with an aggression and began raining down all imaginable instructions toward the quick moving girls.

"71, 72…" Sheila led across the threshold moving confidently.

"Way to go Sheila," called out Sophie.

"Ata girl!" added Jayce. Then, they all reviewed her training with the fellows, the intrigue of the family matters, and predict her outcome today.

"She's running five minutes pace," said Jayce rocking in his seat nervously as he stared at the runners tracing the track.

Around the track muttered comments of, "That's the girl who was kidnapped when she was a baby…she had to go with her real family…her two families hate each other…No, the two families are getting along fine….etc.

Four girls stuck on Sheila's heels stubbornly as she strode fluidly toward the third lap.

"Looking good girl!" yelled somebody.

"2:28!" Katie muttered writing down the slit. "The second lap was 77," said she to herself.

Down the backstretch, two more girls joined the five up front.

"She appears to be slowing," said Jayce worried, "she's falling slowing too fast. Those girls behind caught up too quickly."

"We got to step down on it, the last lap Sheila!" yelled Thorpe from the sidelines.

Leaving the turn, Molly Truex of Libby Valley strode past Sheila. Sheila quickened her turnover and pulled right back onto the girl and moved with her.

"3:48!" said Katie.

Molly pulled Sheila and three more contenders around the next turn while increasing the tempo.

"Come on Sheila," Sophie, called after her.

"She'll out kick 'em; if she can hang on," said Jayce.

At another view on the backstretch, Thorpe could see his student strain with desperation and grimace cutting her face. "She's in trouble 300 meters out and she's hanging on for dear life," he said fearfully.

Space began to creep between Sheila and leader Molly; indeed Amanda Clert of Simone moved pass Sheila strongly, while Stacie Blakely ran on her right shoulder waiting.

About to reach the final turn, "Got to be tough Sheila, 200 meters to go," screamed Eli and Terry from the fence. "She's struggling," Terry observed, "in a bad manner."

On the middle of the turn, Amanda moves wide. Stacie moved in behind her. When the stretch showed itself, both girls began pumping arms and legs higher accelerating pass Sheila.

"Hold on to fourth!" Katie commanded, with Jayce, Sophie, Beth, Jack, and Zoe equality zealous.

To no effect however, Sheila's head reared back, her arms too relaxed had little rotation and the legs began to flounder uncontrolled.

"Golly!" exclaimed Katie, "there's someone else coming up fast!" Eighty meters out Sheila was several strides behind the leaders and losing ground rapidly. A gal in a blue and green stripped uniform and white ribbons tying her pig tails, Becky Howard of Mount Plier, a ninth grader moved firmly with no hesitation and just caught and passed Sheila like she knew it would happen. Sheila's form only begged to finish.

"Ahaa…" sounds came from though out the bleachers.

The posture child rescued by family after years of separation, whose popular appearance at these games prayed for the "Cinderella" outcome, suffered an untidy finish. The crowd moaned as luster faded from teary eyes. Jayce's smudged countenance sank to a profound dejection, as Sheila almost fell across the finish in fifth utterly exhausted. Sullen was the mood for a normally pompous crowd for these final seconds of a race.

The runners filed across the finish line with the normal accolades. Yet, in minutes the crowd fretted and complained. "Oh, it was really a long shot, after all the stress she's had to experience over the last several weeks…"

"Sheila's only a sophomore, she'll be back."

Zoe was crying. "Don't cry Zoe," pleaded Katie, "she ran 5:11, a school record and she'll be back next year."

Jack and Sophie Luke and the Wises's were still shocked by the last thirty seconds of the race.

"Where did these girls come from? 5:05! That girl came here with only a five sixteen."

"And that little tiny girl," added Sophie, "She came out of nowhere! And she looks to be about ten years old."

Down on the infield Sheila was whimpering. She was trying to drink a bottle of water given to all the finishers, but she was choking with emotion. Each girl from the race scattered after the finish; some crying and others tickled of their performance. Quickly everyone wanted to get to the emotional safety of supporters. Sheila however, wanted to hide from all who cheered for her.

"It's alright dear," said Sophie clasping the girl in her arms. The woman took it upon herself to leave her seat, trudged down the stadium steps and push her way through the mob of spectators hanging on the track's railing; then she nonchalantly walked through a gate to the track and to the infield to claim the affection of the wounded Sheila; quivering, sweaty, and white with fear. "Come on child," she led the girl toward an exit and they were seen being swallowed up by a glob of figures.

Kasper and Danny having witnessed the unfortunate Sheila, silently retreated to a relatively quite place on the far bleachers then stretched themselves out and tried to relax, if not nap while waiting for the 3200-meter run.

As he would, Kasper reflected. Sheila was undoubtedly a victim. An innocent child lacking audacity and thoughtful filled with courage. She was no swaggering babe, who strutted about her exploits. Why then did providence elude her deserving success?

Danny was thinking as well. "Well, Kasper," he said suddenly, "what do you think? Think we can make it all the way?

"You seemed pretty confident in the 1600, ran it like you owned it," replied Kasper.

"But it was a difficult race; my hardest ever, but next week the runner will be more aggressive than what we experienced today, already," admitted Danny.

Kasper considered for a moment, "We have to push the pace. I got trapped in the pack. I should have been up there forging the pace with you. I won't be able to catch people from behind next week, I know that for sure."

Danny looked a trifle amazed. "Push a faster pace?" He asked. He pondered. "Well perhaps I did let up the third lap," he decided while staring humbly at a cloud passing over them.

Kasper was quite disconcerted at this surprising reception of his remark "Oh, I didn't think you went out that fast," he said hastily trying to retrace his audacity.

Then Danny made a depreciating gesture. "Yea, actually the start was modest, that's why we covered the last lap so fast. Can't do that next week?" he asked.

There was a little pause, after the pair decided Jimmy was a shoe in for the 400 meters, being that no one else had broken 50 seconds, a feat Jimmy had accomplished several times.

"Why are we talking about next week?" questioned Kasper looking serious. "We got to qualify for the 3200 in about an hour."

"Hope there are no surprises there," said Danny

"Yea, and Eli and Terry may have a tough time, you think?" inquired Danny. "I hear a couple dudes didn't want to run against us, so they are just going to run the 800."

Surrounding Kasper and Danny conversations of similar subjects continued with the familiar seriousness. Parades of concern spoke between every pair of folks. The kids here had little history of losing in their events, so the effect was traumatic to them and supporters. Kinfolk fixed confused stares at the victors. Asking themselves what make of person this is who trounced their boy or girl: "How dare you beat my kid!" peering eyes would ask. Coaches knew better. They accepted the breaks and ride-out the letdowns; they understood how rare it was to make it this far and were prepared not to be here for another while, unless a break came in the form of another 'star'. Thorpe knew all too well of odds of he being at Regional, and attended each of his entries one for the other. In this time space, Thorpe sought out and found Sheila with Sophie.

"You got the school record," informed Thorpe patting the top of Sheila's head softly, "Everything had to be perfect to get five minutes. Her countenance begged for forgiveness; she thought her expectation diminished her effort.

"Be honest, have your mind been focused toward today for the last couple weeks?" inquired Thorpe with a consoling gaze.

"No sir."

"Of course you haven't," agreed Sophie holding the girl in her arms.

"All this stuff with my families has been bothering me most of the time."

"It had to," agreed Thorpe. "At this level of competition, if you're distracted you will not match up with the leaders. Now, your fellow teammates are waiting for you Sheila, they love you."

Sheila was quite disconcerted at this surprising reaction to her misadventure on the track. Paired up with Sophie, they deported toward the bleachers as Thorpe sort to find his 400 man, the public address had announced the last call for these participants.

"Jimmy's got a great day, for a fast run," said Jack standing and watching Jimmy adjusts himself in his blocks on the track along with the seven other starters. Jimmy had a last look at his challengers. Friend Henry Sprague was in lane one; Jimmy was in lane four seeded number one in the field. The announcer named all the participants, and old official in white shirt and red cap climbed a ladder partially, scanned all the runners as he leaned on the top stair and fired the gun.

"Bang!"

The boys shot out of each of the blocks and leaned into the turn to prevent centrifugal forces from throwing one to the outer lanes.

"Motor it!" commanded Jayce.

"Look at 'em truck!" exclaimed Jack.

On the backstretch, Jimmy make up the two staggers to his right he was moving so swiftly.

"47 and some change!" predicted Jayce.

"The fastest I've ever seen him breakout of the blocks," said Jack. Jack and Jayce were without their wives as the women sorted out both parent families of Sheila to offer support and satisfy their curiosities as well.

"Ah, man," shouted Jayce looking at his stopwatch, "he was about 24 flat at 200."

Jimmy negotiated the second turn maintaining a powerful form. Only lane two appeared even close. Then the turn straightened and the stagger disappeared, showing Jimmy in lane four ahead with one hundred meters remaining.

"Go to your arms, Jimmy…start pumping…bring those arms up!" Jayce commanded fearfully. Jimmy had always initiated these motions, but now Jayce saw a faint superficial effort from the boy.

Hoyt Waldo of Ricksburg in lane two commenced to perform just as Jimmy was not; the kid rapidly made up the four meters to catch Jimmy. Looking to his left slightly, Jimmy tried to lift, but to no avail, no strength in his motion.

"Come on boy!" Jack scolded; he had to watch Hoyt pull ahead with thirty meters to go. If one would check lane five, you would see Pip Gooch of Bakersfield running strong up to Jimmy and leaning into the finish.

"He barely savaged second," assented Jack.

"He was weary looking that last hundred, 49.84. Wonder what's wrong?" said Jayce staring at his watch. Jimmy had not stopped his watch that late since early in the season.

"He'll be weary next week as well l if he doesn't stop chugging beers Friday nights," revealed Jack.

"Can't be doing that, boy," Jaycee quipped.

"He's been doing it off and on all year."

Jayce Wise was not shocked at this disclosure. Jimmy's personality and his history of defiance would allow such behavior without any discomfort with his demeanor. However, Jayce did not have to hear this. He needed to believe for the best; hoping peer pressure would cease such activities. However, Jayce was dishonest with himself, "Jimmy's the top of the food chain around here. He looks up to no one and no one can pressure him," Jayce reasoned.

A specter of reproach came to mind, however. There loomed the dogging memory of his youthful indiscretions. He who had hustled the Detroit streets as a dope dealer's messenger boy, breaking in liquor stores with his little gang, selling the stolen ware and getting caught; then having the judge say 'jail or 'the army'. He even tried his 'I can hustle anyone' attitude on duty, until a stay in the stockade and demotion put a shift in his life's outlook. Only his marriage and Kasper's disabilities changed his from inside as to the lifestyle he pursued. So Jayce felt uncomfortable as Jack continued a diatribe about Jimmy and his scavenging methods to get by in life.

"Jack, maybe this experience will let him know he is vulnerable," suggested Jayce finally breaking into Jack's torrid tales of his grandson.

They watched Jimmy cross to the opposite side of the field. "I am going to have it out with him; he's got a whole team counting on him," said Jack.

"Jimmy got beat!" said Eli.

"Unreal," replied Terry. "Wonder what's wrong with him, he looked flat."

"Well now it's our turn, so let's not talk about Jimmy," Eli said, "it's going to be tough today."

The 300 hurdles cleanup crew of girls and boys in red shirts and white caps rushed to remove the obstacles as the red caped officials were escorting the 800-meter participants toward the struggle they chose. Thorpe intercepted the boys as they reported to the entry clerks. "Okay guys. Try not to give me any surprises now. Do not trap yourself, stay to the outside of the pack on the third turn. Good luck gentlemen."

"Have the rumors, got any great performance about to show up?" asked Eli.

"Yep," parlayed Thorpe, "I am looking at 'em," then with hesitation, he said to them, "I scratched Jimmy from the 200 meters." Then he walked away. Eli's mouth dropped open in shock as the coach walked away.

Then Thorpe sort a spot on the second turn as before to view and direct his runners. Jayce and Jack settled themselves in the bleachers ever anxious to rally their boys. Katie prepared her pad and watches, while Zoe departed to find Sheila and family. Nadine and Lacy sat nearby chatting with acquaintances.

"Let's run smart boys," said Jack, "Terry, my boy, stick with 'em."

As time approached for the race, exhibitions of sarcasm and fears appeared on the part of some athletes in the holding pen.

'I feel like a pig waiting its turn for the slaughter," said one.

"World beaters are here today; this is the last running life span," added another.

"It's too hot now, I won't run well," complained a third fellow.

"Next year, I am moving up to the 1600, too much speed here," revealed the first one.

Terry and Eli ignored these séances of distractions. They began to run this race in their minds. This would be the longest retention they would hold for the race; time being compressed doing the run. Mentally it will feel like a little more than a minute.

"Let's go boys!" ordered an official motioning the sixteen to follow him down the track for start positioning. "Gosh, I wouldn't want to be in your shoes for anything," the woman said without warning looking at Danny, "You boys must be scared to death. I know I would be." He looked around as if to check that no one noticed his comment, but kept walking mechanically toward the start area. Danny looked at Kasper as to say, 'Did you hear what she said to me.' Kasper heard and gave Danny a nod. Repeating routines took over the proceeding as had always before a start.

"What'll 'ya think will win this?" asked Jack.

"'bout 1:57," answered Jayce. "A couple kids have run, about 1:59."

"Terry hasn't broken 2:00 yet in an open race."

Talking stopped. The announcer had the runners go to their marks.

"Blam." The pack was sprinting. Eli pumped furiously into the turn, then slowed, but maintained his long stride on the stretch. Staying in the lanes assigned the colorful figures made a beautiful sight from the bleachers. Then the controlled mob swung into the second turn, nearly everyone remained up front. This was evident as the runners finished 300 meters and entered the straight. What appeared was a massive line of boys, only a few meters separated the front of the mass from the rear. With the stagger finished, the pack, all of them sort lanes closest to the curb.

"Stay outside! Stay to the outside!" screamed Jayce as if the boys could hear him. Eli was surging, he moved up to third. In the second lane, Terry without hesitation followed nearly tripping on his heels.

"53! 54! 55!..." Jayce called.

"55! For Eli! He's flying," cried Katie, "Terry stick with him!"

Eli took the turn confidently with Terry not releasing his position. "Those guys are too fast. I'll accelerate past them soon as they hit the straight," thought the boy.

Slowing too much, two runners slightly ahead of Eli saw the high steeping boy stride effortlessly by them. Then Eli pulled over to lane one. Terry was floating in close tow with the small group, just a few meters behind Eli. From the bleachers the side view showed flowing strides, many of them in sync with others. Slowly the pack began to unravel itself from both ends; while supporters screamed their orders.

"Make your move now, Randy!"

"You gotta pick it up Tommy!"

"There you go! There you go!"

"Terry move now!"

"200 to go! gotta move out!"

"There it is Eli! Finish it!"

"Move outside Lonnie!"

People kept drumming the bedlam, from all around the stadium.

"He's gotta start kicking it in now!"

"Look! That dude un yellow, looks strong!"

"Start driving the arms people, if you want it!"

"Sprint!...Sprint it in!"

Into the homestretch, Eli moved with high arm rotation, although the legs were reluctant to follow. Terry was fourth and on the shoulder of Lonnie Harris, he allowed himself to drift out to lane two for running room. Rand Said moved to the right of Eli and tried to accelerate. Eli and Randy moved away from Lonnie. Terry was two long strides back as number five, Tommy Sands of Fleetwood slowed.

This seen lasted for twenty meters; then Terry lifted and rotated arms and legs viciously. This carried him to Lonnie twenty meters from finish, where they started leaning and searching for the finish line.

"Lean Terry! Lean! Jack commanded.

Eli crossed, and then Randy, Terry leaned not that he heard anything, but on instinct and beat Lonnie to fourth.

"Now I've lost two of my nine lives," declared Jack smiling through his long beard and shaking his head.

"Make sure you save some for next week," replied Jayce, "you'll need 'em," and he laughed as well.

"First and third, they made it," a relieved Katie responded.

Everyone nearly was standing and the buzz of conversation droned unabated for minutes. The girls 800 meters usually provided an equally competitive race. Lakeport fans with Sheila out turned their attention to the 3200 meters run as Eli and Terry were gathering their gear and leaving the track area. Suddenly, the boys got, smothered by Beth, Sophie, Sheila, and Zoe. They clasped the pair, stole kisses and bathed them with congratulatory.

Sheila was on the receiving end from the boys. They consoled her and pushed off, the run they finished, as almost an after thought. The women then departed for refreshments. Terry and Eli found a place to rest.

"You know the best part of all this," a contemplative Terry, "is all the attention you get from your friends and family."

"Yep, even kids who lose or don't do so well; get a lot of support for the effort and work they had to apply to get this far."

"Except for people like my mom," Terry reminded Eli solemnly. "You know she did all that promising about coming to see me run; because she was so proud and all, but I haven't heard high or nigh from her since."

Eli did not know what to say for a second. "You're a number one guy, Terry; if anyone does not see that, they are not tuned into what's required for success. Let the dead go bury the dead pal; you have a world to conquer. Another thing Terry, have you noticed. At these meets, you see many of the same people all the time. You see these same people supporting their teams. Then you see some kids that never have any family come; you never see a parent of any sort. So forget the negatives man; hey, you got 1:58.8. You're down there with the thoroughbreds now, Terry."

Back in the bleachers, Beth and Sophie joined the men in waiting. The 200 meters was about to start with no Jimmy. Thorpe had informed them of his decision to withdraw Jimmy from this race. "He should have been in this race," said Sophie.

"Did you see what he did in the 400?" challenged Jack.

"He was fading at the finish," added Jayce, "he was hurting; but running the 200 then having to run another 400 in the relay is too much punishment."

Jack did not want to get into the Jimmy subject any farther. "By the way how's Sheila?"

"Fine," said Sophie, "and so is her father, real nice man."

"Blam!"

The 200 meters was off and running, but this group was interested in the 3200 meters and ignored this event. "How are Kasper and Danny feeling?" Beth asked Jayce.

"Haven't seen then, they're resting somewhere I hope." He said nothing of his concern about one challenger Gradsville's Jamie Dennis, who ran 9:30 some weeks before. Beth would be, just more stressed than normal.

Kasper, and Danny were checking in for the 3200 meters with Greg tagging alone to observe. "Take care of business guys," said Jimmy as the boys passed looking hazardous. The young tough fellow was feeling the effects of stress and fatigue.

"It's alright Jimmy," said Kasper seeing theses effects in his friend, "just cool out and relax." The pair continued there way to join the sixteen fresh faces at the end the track. Thorpe showed from nowhere.

"You guys are attempting the ultimate endurance test, running 1600 and now taking on the 3200. Search for your rhythm the now," warned Thorpe. "Float it until the last 400 and then push it in." Then just as sudden Thorpe took off to somewhere.

Kasper felt the gulf now between Thorpe and the calm pride he had for all: Sheila, Jimmy, and others who were not at their best at present. He felt vulnerable, but knew he could only push forward. It should not be a Shakespeare tragedy, if not all goes well, he felt. It bothered him; the high-pressure types, who could not 'cool out'. Greg standing by knew what was brewing in his brother's mind. "Gehen Sie Bruder vorbereitet sich, genug von diesen Ablenkungen (Go brother prepare yourself, enough of these distractions)," said he patting Kasper on the shoulder.

"Blam!" However, he planned when the blast from the starter's gun sounded; Kasper's adrenaline dictated his movement through the event. Both boys keyed on each other; secure in the knowledge of each other's abilities. The pair would resist losing contact however the tactics.

"There are the two guys from Lakeport who were first and second in the 1600," said a coach to a seatmate gazing down from a high perch in the bleachers.

"Jay's going to take 'em out real fast so those boys will drop off in the second half of the race," said this confident one, "their coach should know you can not double the 1600 and 3200 at the Regional the competition is too fast. Your boy is bound to blowup in the second race.

"I am not so sure that will happen," responded the seatmate, "Thorpe train those boys with high mileage, they may not weaken like you think."

"Ata boy Jay!" shouted the coach baring his attention to the aggressive running of Jay.

"67!" The men watched two boys lead the Lakeport pair. Red-white and purple lead the blue-gray pair. Tall and lean was the first boy, short but stocky was Jay Seymore, of Mullendorf.

Group one, consisted of six. Then a space of several strides and the remaining field followed in a tight pack strung out over just a few meters.

"Come on Stevie! Those guys are tired! Past them!" ordered someone near the track. The boy took the queue and raced past the twosome taking his position just off Jay's back. "Ata boy! Stevie!"

Cruising into the second lap, the digital reads 2:20…2:21…2:22…The first group pushes on with its crowd of six.

The second group strings out in file.

"The Lakeport Kids are slipping," said Jay's coach with growing confidence. His friend agreed.

"Stay relaxed! Stay relaxed!"

"Looking good young man," said someone else watching and leaning on top of the fence. "Hey that one kid's just moved right up there and teammate followed…they went one-two in the 1600…"

"Come on Jay! They're coming back on you!"

Continued pitching from the sidelines pelted the runners. Sometimes there was no reaction; sometimes there was a quick move to accommodate. Up front, the pace ignored comments the runners become more volatile and cruised into the second half of the race.

4:44…4:45…4:46… "Hood and Wise are back up there," said the mate sitting next to Jay's coach.

"Not for long," replied the cohort, "the second half will do 'em in."

That was when Stevie chugged up to the lead. Jay let him go, no response for his part. However, Danny and Kasper quickly stepped up the gate to set off after Stevie. The critics were without words. Stevie finished five laps in 5:58, pulling Kasper and Danny behind him. Jay and the other, 'almosts' had too much space to feel like contenders.

"Take over boys," Sophie said. She was never fearful of the boys losing.

Even Sophie had a say. "Go Kasper, Danny!" Rounding toward lap seven Kasper pulled by with Danny in tow.

"Those guys are strong," said coach, "they're picking up the tempo." His buddy said nothing.

"It ain't over yet," he said finally, "I've seen 'em chug it the last lap," reminded he.

"7:10! Two laps to go!" Katie exclaimed.

The Lakeport contingency was back in the glee mode. They could see Kasper leaning forward demanding pace. Danny with more arm movement in his rocking chair running style appeared to be laboring. The field gave up on the pair and could only suffer among themselves. Stevie deleted his adrenaline, tired rapidly, so Jay retained his distant third place, but the Mullendorf runner backed off pace allowing the second pack to reel him in.

Into the final lap "8:21," Katie disclosed.

"Run fast, Kasper! Danny!" added Zoe jumping up and down.

Standing room only, it was in the complex. The bleachers were full the track surrounded by fence leaning fans around the circuit. Tumultuous screaming with usual commands brought Kasper around with a 64-second lap, even Danny let up on him.

"I don't believe they did that," said the perplexed Mullendorf coach looking at his equally baffled pal.

"Best double I've ever seen," replied the humbled mate.

As the crowd rumbled about the race, Kasper and Danny completely exhausted, staggered around in the infield shaking hands, patting fellow finishers, then slowly moved from the finish area with the others. Organizers had the gathering for the next race forming and urged the boys from the area. A few competitors walked in a daze, perplexed, angry, without understanding as to what happened to the performance they had in them. Shocked they feared the approach of fans, coaches, and family. They could not understand it was over; no rerun, that was it, next year maybe if an underclassman, but none if not. Some fellows were accepting; ready to move forward with lives and plans and pleased this phase of life was over. "Better is the end of a thing than its beginning," they could agree.

Out on the track the girl's 3200-meter race got underway while teams began to reassemble around the complex for the four by 400 meter relay the grand finale of track and field. Jayce and Greg were on the field with the victors, as Thorpe came over. "Did a great job boys," said Jayce arms around both of them. "9:25, 9:29. I'd say you boys made my day; I've been sitting on needles all day. Thanks for the experience guys."

"I knew they would execute," said Thorpe, "I could see you guys were just setting those boys up."

"Well, they were running hard enough," Kasper, explained, "After passing the 1600 meters they slowed. I just let my momentum carry me. Felt strong at the end."

"You looked awesome, both of you," added Greg smiling.

"Not me," interrupted Danny, "I was feeling it the last lap."

"Boys, what am I going to do about Jimmy?" asked Thorpe surprisingly, "I pray I can get him through the relay, but what about next week? He seems to be gradually losing his conditioning."

"Yea, he's off," Kasper offered a timid comment.

Jayce thought a bit. He felt the coach did not know about the drinking thus some diplomacy. "Guys you need to talk to him and see what's going on if anything. A tough boy like Jimmy will not tell anybody if something is bothering him. He will just pretend nothing wrong."

"Definitely, you boys need to talk to him," agreed Thorpe, "Jimmy still hangs with his 'dudes', as he would put them. Therefore, I doubt if he is keeping away from the booze entirely. If I had hard facts, I would kick him off the team. However, he's clean at school and I do not know for sure, so it's up to you boys to have him come clean with you."

"You have got to tell him straight out, if you kids or others at the school have got any insight of any boozing around," Jayce took Thorpe's opening to drill in on the situation. "He needs to quit, otherwise there will be no victory next week, no write-ups from the papers to help get him into the Army tank school. Plus, we better tell him to straighten out, that Thorpe's about to can him."

"And he won't be invited out for the team his senior year either," added Thorpe.

"Coach we saw him briefly," interrupted Kasper. "He looked pretty bad. He knows he's in trouble for the State meet."

"Yea," added Danny, "he knows he dogged a bullet, staggering in the last meters on rubber legs, like that."

"Nothing like peer pressure to rattle a fellow," said Greg "we will set him straight Coach, Dad." Greg finished in at 'it's a done deal' attitude.

"We'll be on his case. Jimmy's a prideful cocky fellow; he'll have it together next week," Danny added in support in Jimmy's defense, "you can count on it."

"Okay, I'll hold you guys to get on his behind. Now let's get through this relay and pick up that team trophy boys."

Turning swiftly, the coach's heart seemed to wrench itself almost free from his body hearing this from the boys. He made a breath of relief and departed.

Greg could see how satisfied Thorpe was. He said to Kasper, "Das Englisch ist romantisch; sie sind so leicht, zu überzeugen. Sie sind, wie daß Sie wissen(The English are romantics; they are so easy to convince. They are like that you know)."

To which Kasper responded, "Bruderich dieser Fall, sollen wir auch für einen romantischen Verschluß bettein (Brother in this case, we too should beg for a romantic closure)." The boys moved to find a place to watch the upcoming race.

During the wait at the end of the track, the four x 400 teams jostled nervously among themselves. Kasper and Greg waited along the fence, a popular place of assembly for this race, in particular. They watched the assembly of teams readying. The ardor Jimmy usually displayed was lacking. Greg and Kasper question whether Jimmy had the opportunity to reflect on his responsibilities. Had he time in which to gather the muster to brute force this effort?

"Dad says, Mr. Luke told him Jimmy drinks beer and stuff sometimes. That is why he's a mess today," revealed Greg.

"Yea, he could get away with it until he gets into tough competition like today," answered the not surprised Kasper of the allegation.

"He's experienced some disillusionment about his invisibility."

They watched Jimmy stretched prone on the grass. His chest heaving up and down, his demeanor was quite, as there were no strutting and prancing around. Eli, Terry, Roy walked and stretched about in a small space, serious, and no talk contemplative in mood.

"Dies ist eine ernste Materie, der Laufen des 4 x 400 übertragen (This is a serious matter, the running of the four by 400 relay)." Greg said in a whisper to his brother playfully.

Then the officials proceeded to wave them forward toward the start positions. As Kasper and Greg claimed a place to watch the race, Danny showed up and took a spot with them. In the stands, Lakeport and crew including Sheila with her real father waited anxiously.

"Okay dudes," said Jimmy to Eli and Terry as they watched Roy being positioned for the first leg. "Just be focused and determined. We going to do this right now, guys!"

"Runners set!" announced the PA system.

"Bang!"

They kicked out of the blocks with the energy of racehorses. Spectators stood, no space was unoccupied along the circumference of the track. Screams, orders, commands rained the entire circuit as the eight runners remaining in the start lanes sprinted. Powerfully built Roy moved not as fast as his competitors did in the early meters. This changed as they sped into the second turn, as Roy's momentum revealed its superiority over those running on adrenaline issued by the desire to please parents and mates. Roy's strength seemed ominous on the turn and into the stretch. He struggled this finale, superior to all but two.

He extended to connect with Terry.

"About 50 flat!" Jayce screamed amongst the bedlam of constant accolades in the bleachers. Terry third at the baton exchange, in three strides was in a full sprint. Ben Tuck stayed in front of Terry and pulled up to Peter Seipel in first place. No changes occurred until 250 meters; there the almighty stork of pain made its claim. Terry's 800- meter strength came to play. Whereupon, he creped up on Ben, flowed to his right and then with a big move of legs and arm lift, he passed Ben. Forty meter out Terry was just one stride behind Jack. They both leaned for the exchange.

"'bout 1:41!" Katie announced as Eli snatched the baton.

"Go! Go!" screamed Zoe her pigtails flopping up and down with her bouncing.

"Chug it baby!" Jayce commanded. Everybody was standing in the stadium. Some were jumping up and down screaming demands and warnings, a few just staring in awe.

Eli was tearing around the turn, such was his acceleration that he drifted to the second lane and passed number one on the turn. Bedlam increased to a higher pitch. Most teams placed the slowest of their foursome on the third leg, but Eli was no slow leg.

"Gotta give Jimmy a lead," commanded Jack.

Sheila, Zoe, and all Lakeport supporters continued stomping, rooting and praying, all directed toward Eli. Stride after stride, Eli measured out a lot of space with each turnover. Second place was ten meters from him entering the second 200 meters. The other six teams warred over a space of seven meters.

"Stroke it in!" Eli," called out Kasper and Greg from the turn.

Eli made his last sessions of powerful arm and leg drives allowing him to pass off to Jimmy fifteen meters ahead of Peter. Jimmy received the baton at two-minutes-thirty-seconds into the race. Eli had blistered a 49-second leg. Jimmy had a good pad and normally would have double the lead in his effort; but everyone of his concern wondered this outcome.

"Lets do it big tough!" yelled Jayce drowned out among screaming crowd.

He looked like his usual self in his sped. Legs carried Jimmy on the backstretch as confidently as any Cheetah's early strides. Following Jimmy and gagging his pursuit carefully was Creepy River's Hoyt Waldo, the victor of the 400-meter race. Rounding the turn Hoyt had made up no space on Jimmy.

"Jimmy has rejuvenated his strength!" exclaimed Jack Luke.

"Yea but, here comes the tough part," warned Jayce, "Hoyt's gonna make a move about, now!"

Indeed Jimmy came off the turn into the final 100 meters and just as in the 400-meter race; his power started waning with every stride. Hoyt, to the contrary, went into a vicious attack. Stepping high and pumping the powerful closing, unseated everyone not already standing to their feet. Hoyt cut half the space to Jimmy, then to three strides. Jimmy tried to lift, he knew the action behind would happen.

"Get on with it Jimmy!" could be heard, but a crowd loves the 'come from behind kid' and witnessed they did. Hoyt collaring the weakening Jimmy twenty meters from finish and retracing his second victory of the day. Jimmy leaned and collapsed just beyond the finish line.

"He barely made it across the finish," declared Sophie, "but he got us second."

Jack looked sad, Jimmy was lucky he thought.

"Well, qualifying is Friday morning," stated an expressionless Katie, suggesting no immediate relief of responsibility in the few days ahead.

᚛ᚋᚐᚱᚃᚐᚂᚑᚒᚄ ᚐᚅᚇ ᚋᚐᚌᚅᚔᚃᚔᚉᚓᚅᚈ ᚔᚄ ᚈᚆᚓ ᚃᚔᚉᚈᚑᚱᚔᚑᚒᚄ
ᚉᚑᚋᚈᚓᚄᚈ᚜

The Wise family of boys closeted in the room for some hours on this Sunday evening, busied with study. Sounds emanating from within revealed the boys finishing assignments due the final week of the school year. Beth Wise, however, had to interrupt the session with her news.

"Boys!" said she excitedly. "Guess what? Bill Sweigert's on the phone, Johannes has just been arrested."

The boys stared amongst themselves for a second shocked. "You say Bill's on the phone?" a confused Kasper.

She nodded. "Come on talk to him, Kasper."

Kasper confused, could not understand why Bill did not accompany Johannes with the authorities. "What's up?" he queried when he spoke into the phone. Kasper did not know the boy personally and had hardly exchanged greeting with the Bill let alone having a conversation with him.

"The FBI came here and arrested my Johannes; it was far-out man!" Bill said with an excited demeanor. The boy knew Kasper amongst others thought he too was a cohort of Johannes, Bill enjoyed expanding on the details of these events and expound that he was a noble fellow all this while.

"To make a long story short, dude, the old man was with the SS during World War two. You know they hated Jews; so he supports the Arabs...so he came over here to money launder for the terrorist groups. He got me into it for a while. We were to appear as if we were just small scale buying and selling tourist materials. But, we received large sums of money from sleeper sells around the country and pass it to the overseas groups to finance their activities." Bill continued to describing how he would go to the city, collect, and mail the money. Sometimes they stuffed money in presents sent to Johannes great grand children or others.

"When I was in juvenile detention, I knew I couldn't hack real prison time and this was some serious stuff that could send you away, like forever. So man, I went to Sheriff Palooka and told him everything; after about a month, man I had to get out that crap."

"Now I get it," interrupted Kasper, "so the authorities had you continue…"

"Yea man, Shoot I been like an agent with the FBI; they gave me a code name and I had contacts to call. Dude it was exciting, man. Can you believe it ex Nazi dealing with Middle Easterners? Far-out man it was sweet, all the happenings and stuff."

"Yes I can. Most people do not know that near the end of the war. The SS formed a Muslim unit, along with other non Aryan units," replied Kasper then paused and said, "That's some story, sounds like a movie plot. How's Mrs. Sweigert?"

"Tearing her hair out, she's just frantic. Crying and stuff, mad at the old man to say the least," said Bill in a monotone voice. "But, she's glad I'm in no trouble," Then Bill's delivery changed to the gleeful. "I had everybody round here thinking I was a crook working for Johannes. Ya'll thought I was dealer and stuff," He chuckled denoting he was proud and he had gotten one over on everybody.

"Yea, we all thought you were a crook all right."

"Ha, ha, ha…" Bill was tickled and chuckled liberally.

Kasper was irritated. "Okay. Aha, have your mom call mine once she feels better, and I am glad you're a hero and all. Check with you later, dude."

"See you dude!"

Kasper placed the phone down, informed his mother of the conversation, then he dismissed himself to pass on these revelation to the waiting threesome. As these new events unfolded through his mind, he turned upon them and tried to thrust them away. Kasper denounced himself as a villain. He thought he was the most unutterably naïve person in existence. Out to the back yard bench and table he retreated to think.

"Here I am befriending old Nazi and labeling a local birdbrain as some drug lord," solemnly he thought himself, as foolish.

"Genug von diesem Kasper (Enough of this Kasper)," said Greg approaching, interrupting his moaning and thoughts, "ist das, was zu uns geschieht, wenn wir ins in Leuten nachgehen, von den wir kleine kenntnis haben (that's what happens to us when we indulge ourselves in people, of whom we have little knowledge)." Greg had not evolved himself outside the family to the extent of Kasper. Nevertheless, he knew brother was a leader figure at home as well as at school, so thus; he would suffer the pains for his role.

"Sie haben recht Bruder (You're right Brother)," agreed Kasper, "lassen Sie uns rufen es eine Nacht (lets call it a night). Ich will nur ein Problem in meinem Physikpaket anschauen (I want to just look at a problem in my physics packet). Ich habe nur zehn Tage, vor der Prüfung(I have only ten days, before the exam)."

The pair fled to their interests while Kasper bundled up on his bed with a reading light so he could scan through a book of problems. He was completely oblivious to others now, while he reflected:

"The thing about physics is that it purports to investigate those natural phenomena, which although elusive, is not evasive, not surreptitious and places itself for infinite scrutiny," thought he, feeling better of himself.

Then Kasper thought of Johannes and his deeds. How evasion, untruthful, and unrepentant of the crimes he committed. People, such as he are fundamentally wicked. Godless and conscienceless he had to keep up evil, just as a liar has to keep lying to stay ahead of the truth. If they repented, the cost will be self-conviction and that is against human nature. The carnal man thinks events and people bought his adverse experiences upon himself. If he denounced this persuasion, he and his tribe of family and fellows sank to the visionary that declared the existence of powers superior to man, a repugnant conclusion for such people.

"Hey! Why am I still thinking about that mess," he said out-loud. He needed something else on his brain. Quickly he got a headset, plug into his tape deck and instantly Sibalius's 'Korella Suite' flowed toward his ears. It was only a little while before Kasper dropped the text and his eyelids as well. His mind drifted toward the subject of that morning church service. Finally, those words claimed his present experience.

The pastor paraphrasing the great English Evangelist, Oswald Chambers, "…Disillusionment means that there are no more false judgments…You have no need to know the person they are all the same…. undecided by disillusionment may leave us cynical and unkindly severe in our judgment of others…Many cruel things in life spring from the fact that we suffer from illusions. We are not true to one another as facts we are true only to our ideas of one another. Everything is either delightful and fine or mean and dastardly, according to our idea...Our Lord revered no man, yet he was never suspicious, never condemning."

It was with these thoughts that Kasper drifted off to the unconsciousness of sleep. Upon awakening, his rejuvenated sprit would fuel his optimism for studies, and his running. Life, Kasper reasoned is just a long distance affair, not be distracted by events while in its progression.

Drudgery is a fine depiction of character. Drudgery is work not seen as essential for the average peasant, but to the Kasper Wises' of the world; it requires inspiration to go through drudgery. It hallows that thing and transfigures it to an activity pleasing to a person's inner being. Precisely at 6:00 am, Kasper and his drudgery of running erased the last remnants of despair from his countenance. With Danny joining his rousing silently, it was in a short time that they exited the home and set off in a jog. The route the runners take around the little community draws on a ceremony almost as they retraces the earlier runs started months before as novices of the sport.

Storm clouds from the night had given way to a rising sun, which will be a scorching noontime sun. The boys descended a hairpin trail into a small ravine of striated purple and yellow plants, heading toward a distant row of docks lined with tied up boats. They destined for the small road that followed the along the lake and settled into a graceful run, but not for long. On the edge of the road in short bushes, Danny saw a long black thing that moved. "Snake!" The boy yelled fearfully, and then took off to Kasper's shoulder as far away from the grass area as he could.

Kasper saw it too and just smiled not missing a stride. "It's just a big black rat snake they can get six to ten feet long almost."

"Crap! It scared the daylights out of me," said Danny increasing the pace. Kasper raced after him. "Lets crank it in," suggested the boy, "I thought I was tired. But that snake got my adrenaline pumping."

"See that's what we my do in a controlled manner, in competition," reminded Kasper. Continuing the trek around the lake edge shortened the usual winding paths through wildlife growth and bought them home.

"So you not scared of snakes, Kasper," Danny asked inquisitively as they walked to the house. The boy physically and emotionally affected by the encounter with the slimy creature.

"Naw, snakes are just an animal because of its nature are rarely seen," explained Kasper, "So they frighten people. Their long bodies take up too much space for the size. However most repulsive is they do not have a face and they crawl and they do not make any cute sounds. They're too silent, that's scary."

"Come on let's get ready for school, you give me the creeps as much as a snake."

"I have to look at several problems tonight," he said to Danny. Kasper expanded on his plans. "David is coming over and he's going to join us at the State meet Saturday. Everything is coming to head, so I need to hammer out as many problems as I can this week."

"All the classroom stuff is done, so is he coming over tonight?" asked Danny, surprised with this news, as Kasper usually would have such a visit planned.

"Early evening," said he.

"Well, I'm gonna go to Jimmy's place with Greg and Eli after practice. Terry will be there. We just going to cool out and talk about Friday qualifications and the 3200 meter relay final," said Danny letting Kasper know he wasn't about to make any last minute changes to his plans.

"You guys get a chance to 'jack him up' about the 'his problem'?" queried Kasper.

"Yea, but he knows what he's got to do," replied Danny. "Terry said Jack and Greg got on his case. They were mad as can be at him, but for a change he humbly accepted this admonition."

The boys strode inside the school and prepared for the school day. "It's time for us to act, Danny. The State meet, my physics exam," Kasper stopped to make eye contact with his cousin. "We make all these preparations and sometimes blame others for impeding our progress then we get scared when the task is upon us. I feel pressed Danny. Maybe we should not be trying this attempt for the double and maybe I am putting too much into this physics test. All the eggheads in the country will be competing for that scholarship, and for all of us rejected think of how wasteful and stupid we will appear. These tasks I have taken on myself require a savvy and tenacious character in both of these affairs."

Danny saw actual fear and doubt in Kasper to an extent he had never seen before. "Kasper, we can't back off now. This is where we have to prove our moment this is where you see if you are as good a student of physicist as you think."

"I suspect you are right. Correction, I know you are right Danny. Even if I don't get to the big ND; there's other good schools where we can get an excellent education," answered Kasper loaded up with reasoning that warrants a positive reason to go for the best. "We loose nothing by trying. Let's find out how hard we can work at trying to get there."

"Come on dude, let's just maul these situations and not worry," said Danny unusually aggressive in his delivery.

Kasper felt his rebuke, and accepted the chastisement as he continued his way. "Yep, let's get on with everything we have to do."

Five young men sat before Coach Thorpe on the bleachers of the football bleachers while he offered the rigorous workout. "I want ten 400's at 64, walk 200 between. Be conscience of your stride keep them long with a strong push-off. Then finish off with eight laps of straights, walk the curves, any questions?" He scanned the audience. "Okay, hit it!" then left for Roy and Jimmy.

It was a wicked assignment. "Tomorrow is the last hard workout; then we'll be on our own," said Eli. "Our heads will be on the blocks for the chopping." He laughed.

"Look at it this way, we'll be at our peak in existence, following our will with unimpeded," said Kasper philosophically, "we have created our fate," Kasper smiled.

Then after some stretching, they jogged toward the start and dropped the hand that gave Katie orders to start the controlling timepiece.

"Good float guys," Thorpe observed them speeding by as he directed Jimmy and Roy in sprint runs.

"63, 64, 65…," Katie watched them slow then walk. Kasper, Eli, Danny, Terry, and Greg finished within one second of each other.

"In the last couple years the race has been won around 4:22," said Kasper after a few strides walking.

"Well, it's quicker than that already," commented Danny.

"Charlie Hitchcock of Housenbeth and Ted Fox of Mt. Plier, have a 4:22 and 4:23, already," reminded Kasper.

They walked until it was time; then off with Eli, Terry, and Greg trailing. Nine more repeats to go. In the same timeframe, Thorpe and Jimmy were rubbing against each other. "…The lack of sleep will not allow your muscles to recover from a workout," warned Thorpe.

"You don't have to keep busting my chops, coach."

"I am busting on you. Last week is history. I am working on this week, Jimmy. The distance men are going to have a tough going. I have never heard of this Division having so many fast times from the 800 meters to the 3200 meters. We just need you at your best and this little school could win the state championships."

"Okay, all the dudes been at me already. I'll be there I'll be popping, okay?"

"65, 66...come on guys, that run was a bit slow!" Thorpe yelled from across the field. The scenario continued until it played itself out with the final painful run. With haste, Kasper cleaned up and cleared his way for home. He was excited with anticipation of what new onslaughts he would be required to tackle in his study session in physics.

"It appears I have an affinity for self imposed affliction," thought he, "I jump from the skillet to the frying pan with out a hitch." With such a conclusion of these matters surmised, the boy retreated to home for a busy evening scheduled.

CHAPTER 11

▼

Before the 'science of methods' would lay claim to this fellow, a fine dinner would intervene this event for some minutes of bless and delightful conversation with his mentor. David was the center of attention at the table. His short stories of some intrigues he had engaged were so entertaining. It was difficult to picture him getting into some escapades as normal rambunctious kid. One always want picture the outstanding of the genius as always had been.

"David you sound like you were a rascal," Beth chuckled, surly you are exaggerating."

"Nah, I got my share of spanking, deservingly I may add," said David ever smiling.

"David, you're alright," commented Jayce. "You give hope to us who had to dish out a whipping ever once and a while. Our hyper difficult kids can grow up to be physicists." The boys enjoyed just listening.

"Ah, he's just pulling you guy's leg," suggested Danny.

"He probably didn't tell you how he would fix the washing machine and TV when they were broken," everybody laughed.

"Nah, I wasn't helpful with anything like that. And I was a sophomore in high school, before I started having an interest in science," said David.

ᚷᚣᚠᛗᚳᛉᚣᚳᛗᛗᚳᚠᛗᚷᛗᚳᚣᚳᚣᚠᚳᚣᚷᚳᛗᚷᚷᚷᚠᚣ
ᚠᚳᚷᚣᚠᚳᚷᚣᚣᚣᚷᛗᚷᚣ

The early evening closed the dinner and led to the twosome, David and Kasper together gathering some material for a session of study alone. Danny, Eli, and Greg had various commitments of their own, while Mom and Dad were off for a visit to the Sweigert's.

"So you'll take the exam at Penn Community College. They have the exam already. Just be on time. You'll hear from the University in soon." David disclosed to Kasper the importance of studying the examples they had reviewed and emphasized how important it was to write down as much as possible. You get credit for work shown, as to how you arrive at the solutions. It's crucial that the team of professors grading your exam get a picture of how rigorous your thinking is."

"What if your method is good, but you're answer is not what they had," queried Kasper.

"The paths of the lost are many; but the road that leads to righteous are narrow and few," David answered a sermon delivery. "If you're using the few correct methods, you'll get most of the credit for the problem. So you want to write, write, write lots of steps toward the solution if you can."

"Okay, so what are we looking at this evening?"

Turning to a tab in his notebook, David paused. "Here's a typical problem in Relativity:

"How fast must a 40 meter space craft be moving, if its length is observed on Earth to have a length of 35 meters as it passes by?"

"Suggestions Kasper," David asked.

"Ah, this is a length contraction problem," answered Kasper.

"Precisely, so write down the relation. The length in the rest frame, 40 meters is equal to the length in the moving frame, 35 meters times gamma." Kasper started his script on the large page placed on the table:

$$L_0 = L\,\gamma$$

"Substituting, we have

$$40 = 35\gamma = 35/\sqrt{1-\beta\beta}$$

$$1.1428 = 1/\sqrt{1-\beta\beta}$$

"Square both sides

$$1.306 = 1/(1-\beta^2)$$

$$1.306 - 1.306\,\beta^2 = 1$$

"Solving for beta, β

$$\beta^2 = 0.234$$

"Since beta, is the velocity divided by the speed of light.

$$v^2/c^2 = 0.234$$

$$v = 0.484c$$

"Now we know the speed of light is $c = 3 \times 10^8$ meters per second. Therefore, we have the velocity of

$$v = 1.45 \times 10^8 \text{ m/s}$$

"The 40 meter space craft would have a speed of about half the speed of light for it to appear to have a length of 35 meters to someone watching it pass on the ground."

"We have nothing that remotely approaches such a speed," observed Kasper. "Only atomic particles in lab experiments moves that fast."

"So, in the real world we're not going to see the Lorentz transformation phenomena," added David then he looked up another problem.

"You know," suggested Kasper, "taking this concept to its limit, where an object could move at the speed of light, then the length contraction would go to zero. Hey, the object would disappear." He concluded perplexed.

"Yea, the object would be realized as only ball of light, maybe," added David.

"Genesis say there was first only 'light', reasoned Kasper, "then light was slowed, and thus matter was created."

"Exactly," replied David surprised at the quick application, "now here is another, must know problem....Compute the speed required to escape the gravitational pull of the Earth in meters per second."

"I think I can do this one, it's like a problem I've had before," stated the boy, starting to write. "Well, I can set centrifugal force equal to the force of gravity.

$$F_C = F_G$$

"I know what each of these is..."

$$m \, v^2/R = G \, M \, m/R^2$$

"Simplifying

$$v^2 = GM/R$$

$$v = \sqrt{GM/R}$$

"This will give you the speed of a satellite in orbit. Just plug in the universal gravitational constant, G the mass of the earth, M and the radius of the earth plus the altitude above ground, R." Kasper caught himself. "That's not the escape velocity is it?" said a disappointed Kasper.

"No its not, got another idea?" asked David smiling as if he knew the boy was stuck now. After a moment, he proposed, "what about setting potential energy equal to kinetic energy of the rocket leaving the earth."

"How's that?" asked a confused boy.

David leaned over and wrote: "We know kinetic and potential energies are:

$$KE = \frac{1}{2} mv^2$$

$$PE = mgh$$

"Is the gravitational constant g, a factor in our problem?" interjected David, "remember the rocket is leaving the earth's gravitational field, where g = 0. So PE = 0

"I see, but what can we do?"

"What we must do is compute the gravitational potential energy from the gravitational force equation. This form of potential energy does not have 'g' involved." He wrote:

$$F = GMm/R^2$$

"Okay, now you take the integral of that to find the potential," revealed Kasper.

Then he continued writing:

"We can derive potential by taking the integral of the force. That is:

$$U = \int FdR = \int (GMm\, dR)/R^2$$

$$= GMm \int R^{-2}\, dR$$

$$= GMm\, R^{-1}/ - 1$$

"Finally we have, we write the gravitational potential energy of an object above the Earth is

$$U = - GMm/R$$

"Way to go Kasper, great job," said David pleased and smiling. "Now, you must use the conservation of energy, noting the surface energy and the final energy far out in space,"

Kasper started:

$$\text{Initial} = \text{final}$$

$$K_i + U_i = K_f + U_f$$

"Now since we' are looking for the minimum escape velocity, then at infinity from the surface of earth, the final total energy is zero."

"So we have then

$$K + U = 0$$

$$\tfrac{1}{2} mv^2 - GMm/R = 0$$

$$\tfrac{1}{2} mv^2 = GMm/R$$

"This simplifies to

$$v = \sqrt{2GM / R}$$

"This is what I had before," Kasper realized, "except for the factor of two."

"Now Kasper we can simplify this, by noting; weight, mg, near the surface is equal to the force relation,

$$mg = GMm/R^2$$

"Solving for G

$$G = R^2 g/M$$

"Substitute this into your equation we get

$$v = \sqrt{2gR}$$

"See we don't even have to know the gravitational constant, G.

$$v = \sqrt{2(9.8)\ (6.4 \times 106)}$$

$$v = 11.2 \times 10^3 \text{ m/s} = 1.12 \times 10^4 \text{ meters per second}$$

"This is 11.2 km/s or about 25,000 miles per hour," added David.

"If a rocket left the earth's surface at a speed of 25,000 miles per hour, it would leave the earth forever," Kasper concluded.

"That's right. So we can calculate the escape velocity of any planet if we know its gravitational constant, g and its radius, R." David started flipping more pages. "Know how to use basic kinematics equations."

"The common constants will be given including most all of the fundamental equations, but I warn you; most of these equations will only get you started," he emphasized.

Another pause then, "You should know how Maxwell determined the speed of light mathematically. You may have to derive this, or understand its methods, so let's go through it, first:

"Experiment shows that a wire loop with an electric current flowing through it creates a magnetic field, B, depicted as concentric circles around the loop. The sum of all the little sections of B, $\Delta B\lambda$, fields equals the electric field times the speed of the current flow, v, times some constants, μ and ε, which are functions of some physical aspects of the wire; later I will derive these constants. All these concepts together we call Ampere's Law. Let us write and simplify:

$$\Sigma B\Delta\lambda = \mu\varepsilon E\lambda v$$

"Solving for B, magnetic field, we get

$$B\lambda = \mu\varepsilon E\lambda v$$

$$B = \mu\varepsilon E v$$

"Now Faraday's law says, the electric field develops from the speed,v, of the magnetic field, B, we can say. That is, E = vB. Substitute this for E in our B equation, we get

$$B = \mu\varepsilon(vB)v$$

"Thus,

$$B = \mu\varepsilon v^2 B$$

"Solving for velocity, v

$$v = 1/\sqrt{\mu\varepsilon}$$

"Now the values for the constants are given or looked up in any physics table of constants. So

$$V = (1/\sqrt{4\pi \times 10^{-7}})(8.85 \times 10^{-12})$$

$$V = 3.00 \times 10^8 \text{ meters per second}$$

"This is the speed of light; the speed of an electromagnetic wave. Maxwell computed the speed of light, before anyone measured the speed experimentally." David paused for effect; then he continued. "Maxwell's equation will be given; but in all these examples you must understand how to use them. Kasper you should make up your own examples to reinforce your understanding of the real physical applications of the concepts. Everybody is going to have this packet, but many are not going to recognize the concepts presented. They'll hesitate make wrong starts, loose confidence."

"How much time is allotted for the problems?"

"Half the problems are real fundamental stuff," David explained, "you should spend four or five minutes tops each problem. The second half of your time will cover the rigorous problems. There will be eight or ten problems, but these will take you on the average about fifteen minutes. So you want to give yourself at least two hours and some."

"I am a slow thinker," said Kasper, "I am going to start the second half first."

"Good idea," agreed David, "Yea, that's where the balance of the scoring comes from. See they do not expect most students will complete every problem. In the past, a tester who got fifty percent of the points received offers of scholarships."

"Are you kidding?" surprise was in Kasper's voice.

"No but," warned David, "there have been students who thought they were brilliant and could not complete but five or six problems of the second half."

Kasper gazed about the table. "I am definitely going to tackle the second half first."

"Good then, let's look at this one. You must understand the characteristics of a wave form." David flipped the large pad to a clean sheet.

"Suppose a particular wave is denoted as

$$y = (0.500\text{m}) \, Sin[(0.250/\text{m}) \, x - (9 \text{ rad/s}) \, t]$$

"Find (a) the amplitude of the wave, (b) the wave number, (c) the wavelength, (d) the angular frequency, (e) the frequency, (f) the period, (f) the velocity of the wave and (h) the displacement of the wave at x = 40.0 meters and time, t = 3.500 seconds.

"Now, Kasper write the standard form of a wave." Kasper wrote:

$$y = A \sin (kx - wt)$$

"Always write that down first," warned David. "So what's the amplitude?"

"By inspection of the equation, the amplitude is A, which equals 0.500 meter."

"Go on."

"The wave number is k, is the number of waves contained in the interval of 2π. That is, the number of wave in one circuit of a circle it's…" He wrote:

$$0.250/m$$

"That's one-forth a wave on loop of a circle," said he; then continued with the answers, "part © wants the wavelength which is the distance around a circle, 2π, divided by the number of waves, k, around that circle is

$$\lambda = 2\pi/k = 2\pi/0.250/m$$

$$= 25.13 \text{ meters}$$

"What's the angular frequency, ω, is given in the equation. Nine radians per second

$$\omega = 9 \text{ rad/s}$$

"We find frequency, using from the definition.

$$f = \omega/2\pi$$

$$= 9 \text{ rad/s}/2\pi$$

$$= 1.43 \text{ s}^{-1} = 1.43 \text{ Hz}$$

"The period is the time to complete one circuit,

$$T = 1/f = 1/1.43 \text{ s}^{-1} = 0.699 \text{ seconds}$$

"And the speed of the wave; that's angular frequency divided by the wave number,

$$v = \omega/k = 9 \text{ rad/s}/0.250/m$$

$$v = 36 \text{ meters per second}$$

"What is the direction of the wave, Kasper?" asked David pointedly.

"To the right since the sign in front of omega, ω is negative, "said he looking at the equation.

"Finally, the displacement of the wave at x = 40.0 meters at t = 3.500 seconds?"

Kasper substituted into the equation. Remember the argument of Sin is in radian units. So

$$y = (0.5000) \text{ Sin } [(0.250)(40) - (9)(3.5)]$$

$$y = 0.500 \text{ Sin } (-21.5 \text{ radians})$$

"Now one radian is equal to about 57.3 degrees," so Kasper with calculator in hand completed and arrived at…

$$y = 0.500 \text{ Sin}(-21.5 \times 57.3)$$

$$= 0.500 \text{ Sin}(-1232) = 0.500 \ (-0.470)$$

$$y = -0.235 \text{ meters}$$

"The displacement is below the equilibrium," said Kasper.

"Good, you'll be asked about waves and its components like this example," David mused as he looked at more material. "Kasper suppose an eight kilogram object is accelerated to half the speed of light. Find its kinetic energy,"

Kasper jumped right on this one. "I know total energy equals kinetic energy plus rest energy.

$$E = E_k + E_0$$

"Solving for kinetic energy

$$E_k = E - E_0$$

$$= mc^2 - m_0c^2$$

"We know E is equal to rest mass, m_0 times gamma, γ, thus

$$= m_0c^2/\sqrt{1 -v^2c^2} - m_0c^2$$

"Substituting, m_0 = 8.00 kg

$$E_k = 8.00 \ (3 \times 10^8)^2/\sqrt{1-(0.5c)^2/c^2} - 8.00 \ (3.0 \times 10^8)^2$$

Kasper simplified this to arrive at

$$E_k = 83.14 \times 10^{16} - 72 \times 10^{16}$$
$$= 11.14 \times 10^{16} \text{ Joules}$$

"Could you covert that to MeV for me?" asked David.
"No sweat! One

$$1 \text{ eV} = 1.60 \times 10^{-19} \text{ joules}$$

"So using this conversion factor, we convert to millions of electron volts, MeV

$$(11.14 \times 10^{16} \text{ J}) \times (6.24 \times 10^{18} \text{ eV}/1 \text{ J})$$
$$E_k = 69.5 \times 10^{34} \text{ eV} = 69.5 \times 10^{28} \text{ MeV}$$

"Now Kasper, tell me why didn't, we just use," David wrote:

$$E = \frac{1}{2} mv^2$$

"This is the kinetic energy equation. Why didn't you use it?"
With no hesitation, Kasper said, "For objects moving at speeds near the speed of light their mass increases as the speed increases. In the classical kinetic energy equation you have, the mass is a constant; it does not change with speed."
"Precisely! Good job, and I have one more," announced David reading the problem, "Derive Coulomb's Law from Gausses Law."
"Well Gauss's Law is that the Electric field surrounding a surface charge equals the charge density divided by the permittivity constant." He wrote:

$$\nabla E = \rho / \varepsilon$$

"Take the integral of both sides with respect to dV." He wrote:

$$\int \nabla E \, dV = \int \rho / \varepsilon \, dV = \int \rho \, dV / \varepsilon$$

"This gives the electric field through the surface area surrounding the charge and since a charge density on a volume gives a total charge, $q = \rho dV$, and $da = 4\pi r^2$, we may write...

$$\int E \, da = q / \varepsilon$$
$$E \, 4\pi \, r^2 = q / \varepsilon$$

"Finally we have

$$E_1 = q_1/4\pi r^2 \varepsilon$$

"Now the force derived from another charge, q_2 and if the first charge was labeled q_1; if they were placed next to each other

$$F = q_2 E_1$$

"Substituting, and adding a proportionality constant k, for units then we have

$$F = k \, q_1 q_2/4\pi \varepsilon r^2$$

"Done, we have Coulomb's Law." David closed his binder. Kasper dropped his pencil. They looked at each other.

"That was good," said Kasper, "just hope to see you Saturday, at the state meet."

"Oh, I wouldn't miss it," said David. "I know you have an outstanding mine. Now I want to see this great physical prowess of yours."

Kasper and David packed up the material before them. "How life otherwise been going for you?" asked David. Kasper for some reason felt, David knew of some affairs going on with the young man.

"Okay, but I did get involved with that German involved with that terrorist group, the papers have been writing about," Kasper disclosed.

"Ah, yea!" said David unsurprised as Kasper had figured.

"So you knew the SS man did you, ha, ha, ha," he chuckled.

"That's where my parents are now, visiting the Sweigert's. He is the Grandfather of Mrs. Sweigert," he explained, "Mrs. Sweigert described the arrest to my mom.

"My mom said: 'Mrs. Sweigert and I was in the kitchen talking about garden arrangement, then out of no where, the FBI just came through the front and back doors. They just busted in. They scared the daylights out of us. Quickly they filled the house and came out of the back room with Johannes. He was breathing hard with a stalwart FBI man on each side of him. I have never seen him with such an expression on his face, before. He had always shown me a smile, and seemed like just an elderly kind gentleman. Now I saw a tremendously virile and yet sinister face. His heavy eyebrow and quivering jaw formed a bitter line. He looked the part of a captured crook! I caught eye contact briefly. His cruel blue eyes, with their drooping, cynical lids, denoted aggression. He really did not eye me, but fixed his gaze upon a big FBI man standing before him. Johannes's face expressed hatred. 'It's the Zionists you should be arresting, you fools!' he blasted in a heavy German accent, 'you will be at war forever, unless you rid yourself of the Jewish tyranny controlling this country.' Johannes, pitched forward with a snarl of rage, but the agents dragged him back. The fury on his face was terrible to look at, said mom.'" Kasper finished.

"See the old man let the devil out," commented David, "one can never hold 'Ole Nick' inside you for long; he has to play his hand in the world."

"That's for sure," agreed David.

"So they hauled him off, did they?" affirmed David.

"Yep! Mom says, Mrs. Sweigert was mostly numb in shock, but later she seemed relieved as well."

"Then where is all this going?" asked David.

"Like the papers says the authorities are piercing together, who all were involved in the US and Germany," the boy accessed.

"They'll deport him, and let the German government prosecute him, I suppose."

"Yep! Mrs. Sweigert says he's going to be out of here in a few days." While speaking Kasper suspected David's mind was collating thoughts and that more questions were coming.

"I find it amazing people like that still exist and are continuing their wicked trades," David took a deep breath.

Kasper watched David absorb himself, then, "The Soviets hanged the SS they caught right off, but you Americans," Kasper shook his head, "are so forgiving, so gullible."

"The paper said he came to the US after the war as a rocket technician," commented David.

With that said Kasper bent his head and had a good chuckle, "Oh, please excuse me, but I could not contain myself. Let me tell you lot of those technicians," Kasper leaned over to emphasize his point, "When the last days closed upon them, many SS dressed themselves in white lab coats, joined up with real scientists and raced to get themselves captured by the Americans. The Americans were so obsessed with von Braun's V-2 rockets that they captured hundreds of the missiles at manufacturing sites, and then offered asylum to as many technicians and scientists as they could get. Johannes was a civil servant before the war. He had no technical training ever. He just faked it and the real scientists protected him and the others like him as fellow Germans."

"Yea," agreed David finding all this history preposterous if not shameful, "I can see there's no way you could detect their faking the job if everyone else around covered for you. Well, maybe he'll die in prison now and the world will be rid of him, finally."

With the conversation closed, the pair made their greeting and David departed for his home in Dayton. David always lived in an urban setting he found the trip to these areas as truly exploring a diverse culture. It struck him as strange at how the academically gifted black Americans were mostly from small towns and communities or like himself evolved from many communities as lived in while his father was in the Air Force. David figured people here had few concerns outside their own experiences, even Kasper and family; he was not sure he liked that. "Minorities should be aware of all the 'happenings'," he thought, "or should they?"

Lying on his back in bed in a dark bedroom, his arms folded behind his head on a pillow, eyes opened staring at the ceiling, his thoughts heavy. Kasper recognized events were culminating in his life the next week. He had finished a year filled with plans, anguishes, accusations, some degradations, injuries, and recovery from injuries. Time finished and brought forward the tests of the aspirations he held onto so grippingly. Raised to tread lightly, Kasper was not. Courage and innovation requires him to stride out on his own and the opposition realized was a measure of how far he was out there. "Just face it and be done," he thought. These efforts are what he chose to engage. He thought it peculiar how some people saw him as over extending himself or unhappy with these burdens. Kasper remembered last summer how he caught a man staring at him as he rested in the park after a long run.

"You're that Kasper fellow are you not? You look unhappy," the man said as he approached. Not bothering to excuse himself, no greeting, he just imposed his presence upon the young boy.

"Yea, I could have done better. I could have put more effort into this run," responded the boy parrying off any attempt the man had planned to feel sorry for him.

The man rubbed his mouth. "There's a diversity group meeting today at the Convention Center in Columbus. All sorts of people of many cultures will be there. Certainly not people you will see around here. I heard about you and your family. Ask your Dad to consider visiting this event it should be an uplifting for you and family."

"And you think we should all be there for this revealing experience?" Kasper repeated. Kasper knew what he was dealing with a liberal, rescuing poor minorities from the suffering prevailing in their existence. Upon the sight of Kasper, with his curly hair and light bronze hew 'there was rescuing to be done.' Kasper did not get upset, just combative with this condescendence. "Naw, none of us would have the slightest interest in such a gathering. We like the country people, the culture, the slow life style; it is quite tranquil, you know. We live here by choice, not by default, sir."

"I understand," responded the man, not understanding in the least, "the people around here they know you all." Then he retreated as unassumingly as he approached.

"Whew! I got to get home," he exclaimed out loud, "What was that about? Why don't people mind their own business?" The fellow jogged the short distance home to ready for a Wednesday church service.

"Hey! You about ready there, son?" Jayce asked standing in the doorway as Kasper laced his shoes.

"Be right there, Dad." When done with his last preparations, he joined his family in the packed van and they traveled to the church out in the middle of corn country. The parking lot filled near the entrances.

After the family found seats on a long pew, they quickly stood up and joined in the hymn underway. The worship here was vigorous and emotional, although tired Kasper was tranquil. Later sitting, he closed his eyes in the middle of the service while absorbing the message of the sermon. His mind drifter to his own personal experience illustrating the sermon message; Kasper recalled the road trips to Detroit, Washington DC, and Pittsburg. Ever so often, they saw three large telegram pole crosses together. In the display likened to 'The Crucifixion'. They were usually just some meters off the road. He learned later that some 'ole believer' had dedicated his life to constructing the signs along many interstate throughout of the United States.

"Golgotha, testimony to the Savior crucified," Kasper recognized, "What inspired such a testimony by this prophet, "What faith drove this man to declare Christ's eternal victory to people cruising along a highway?" Kasper thought then tried to imagine the mind he would require to dedicate himself to such a task. "What urgency must one have to allow so much of your life to be dedicated to something when you reasonably know only a few of thousands shall be affected to any serious extent." Scrutinizing himself, Kasper realized something: "That man did not care about the few who would value his great effort. Those few were well worth the effort."

He wondered about his resent self-serving whining. "Enough of that; I don't take back any of my work. If I finish first or last, I enjoyed the running, the struggle with my fellows. There's a value in that by itself." Kasper smiled he received the inspiration he sort. "I am going to enjoy pushing all out now."

𝄞𝄞𝄞𝄞𝄞𝄞𝄞𝄞𝄞𝄞𝄞𝄞𝄞𝄞𝄞𝄞𝄞𝄞

The time had arrived so it seemed. Like poker players with the last play of cards. Whatever capabilities realized now sat bundled up in sweatshirts and jerseys. The weather was warm soon to be hot, with welcomed erected breezes providing some relief. The thing about weather is it weighs on everyone differently. Some dine on it as the litmus test of their performance; most of the winning sort, never allow it to interfere with victory, whereas lesser participates accrues weather either as interfering with all their winning chances or they see it as essential for their success.

Swans of spectators left no empty spaces about the stadium. The fans came from every corner of the state of Ohio. Supporters three generations deep for some participants enjoyed the observation of a descent at these games. Elders in wheelchairs, to babies carried in arms; all these arrivals being spectators of the many athletes to for most the biggest and final athletic event of their lives.

Most senior athletes would graduate later in the evening or Sunday. A few will continue in athletics in college most will not. Some will blossom and see stardom in college, most will not. None, however, will regret nor forget the experience this day. Ohio athletic officials and hierarchy of all sports were present, along with many familiar past stars of these games. Although graying and providing middle age mid-section, some of these historic fellows were readily recognized. Others, showed not the faintest resemblance of the young-self and wondered about preferably incognito; that is for almost everyone except the "ole track fans' who could still sort them out from amongst the crowd.

With several thousand seated in the stadium, the public address system announced the participating schools in the Division II boy's 4 x 800 meter relay finals; the only finals of the day. Turning the state tournament program to this event revealed the teams and the regional times and placing.

"Our guys have the third best time out of sixteen qualifiers," observed Jayce speaking to Jack Luke, "but what's scary is there are two teams less than four seconds behind us."

"I'll say, everybody will, PR," answered Jack.

The men watched a mass of thirty-two runners, officials leading them toward the staggered start lanes. Amid this Jayce began to reflect upon various incidents throughout the year. He thought of workouts that bought arguments as to their value. He remembered how others knowledgeable of the sport would warn him of how difficult it would be to reach the college attention level of competition. However, Jayce had no choice other than to support his boys. Fear gripped him. He imagined others in Lakeport party of supporters felt the same. An ominous silent clutched a grip on all of them.

Kasper sat behind his dad near the top of the bleachers. Armed with a stopwatch he sat next to Katie. The teams' performance in this race should be a gage of how they would perform on Saturday, he suggested in his thought. "Danny and Eli will have to go one-hundred percent today. Their times over 800 meter will give enable me to figure what my 1600 and 3200 will be…come on dudes, surprise all of us…"

Kasper's armpits began to sweat, not from the weather, from anxiety. So much of his future he felt depended on his actions within this oval of space. "This isn't right," he thought, "so much importance shouldn't be withheld to a small time and space."

Thorpe was nearby. He did not want to be near anyone wanting of conversation. Overcome presently by a dragging weariness of all these matters he had to deal with in coaching this team. His head hung over the fence bordering the track. He held continuous arguments with himself as to whether he should have done a particular workout or not. He tried to dismiss his responsibility, but he ultimately felt what would occur these two days is mostly due to his issues of workouts. Thorpe's conscience nagged at him with every projected outcome of these events. However, this isolation had an un-welcomed interruption. He heard a cheery voice near his shoulder.

"Your boys ready coach? It's going to be a dandy today and Saturday." Thorpe turned to see the illustrious Roland May.

"Yep," Thorpe answered reluctantly.

"Alright," he said with a laugh, "I am pulling for you guys. I feel your boys have not really gone all out this season. But you'll have to in a few minutes," the man laughed, "Well, they're 'bout to start. I am going down closer, good luck coach." The man left as he said he would and Thorpe offered no greetings of departure.

On the track infield, one could see the holstered starter Frank Stamps slowly climb the several steps of the ladder podium and raise his arm. Thorpe watched the runners. Attentively, his eyes fixed on the boys. "The boys must be motionless or old Stamps will hold them forever," he accessed. The participants bent over with batons in hand, cocked and ready as they may; one foot forward just touching the start line, ready to spring into the run.

Both arms up now, red band on his gun arm. "Bang!" Eight colorful figures maintaining the lane positions they start in scurried around the first turn.

Then it started the screams, commands, and warning.

"Come on Joey!"

"Go with 'em Paul!"

"Stay outside…stay outside Stevie!"

Danny raced the back straightway. He hugged the line on his left leading the three others in his stagger," he thought. Trying to keep his breath deep faster than his normal, "What!" he was startled as they completed the turn, a runner moved to his right shoulder? Danny was a somewhat shocked, both to his right and to his left runners were in view.

"Look at that pack!" exclaimed Jack. He and Jayce watched the leaders spread across three lanes from the curb, moving at a reckless pace to complete the first lap. Danny was fourth with two runners to his inside and one on his right slightly ahead. The remaining twelve runners followed so closely that, the trailing runner was a mere four meters behind Danny.

"53! 54! 55!…" Jayce read his stopwatch as the pack crossed 400 meters and entered lap two. With runners on his heels and Danny surrounded, Jayce feared for a fall. "This is nerve racking! Look how close everyone is!"

"You telling me!" agreed Jack, "hope Danny can move away…"

At last, with a shift movement to his right he got clear and from thence took aim of the blue clad skin-headed fellow moving away three meters ahead.

"He's gotta die," Danny thought. He then forged ahead and pulled over to the curb lane ahead of two close followers. Now, the tight pack loosened out to cover ten meters with a few maneuvers at its rear exchanging positions.

"That's Bald East's Jay Sowell, he won't slow much," said Jayce, "Danny's got to get back on him."

"Roll 'em in Danny," said the unheard voice of Coach Thorpe from the fence as runners rolled into their final turn. Danny peaked in his effort, leaned into his final 100 meters. There he made progress on Sowell and Sean Arthur of Chancellorville, as they entered the hand-off zone.

"Give 'em the stick!"

"1:54! 1:55!" Write 1:57.0, Zoe," ordered Katie watching Danny's pass to Greg. The young freshman took off as fast as could five meters behind Chancellorville.

Chancellorville's number two man pulled away from Greg with ease and Hale Frank overhauled the boy leaving the curve. By the end of the straight, another runner passed Greg. At the end of his first lap, he was thirty meters behind and fending off another challenger from behind.

"You're alright Greg! Hang in there, son!" screamed Jayce.

"Its okay!" consoled Jack, "Terry and Eli will make up all that space."

Jayce did not say anything, because he could not see the boys making up that much ground. Sowell's second runner had all the intensity as Jay on the first leg. However, Randy Quaid of Wikesville moved up and around Greg followed by Lonnie Harris of Toberstown. All Lakeport supporters begged Greg to hurry up and get the baton to Terry, who was bouncing in the exchange zone nervously from one foot to the other. Chancellorville ran particularly strong in his finish, as Sowell remain helpless ten meters back while Harris maintained position. Greg lifted and his face strained, as he demanded his legs and arms to turn over quicker.

"Ata boy Greg!" Praised Jayce, his heart was beating madly as sweat poured down his face and from his armpits. He saw Terry snatch the baton from his exhausted younger brother. Jayce signed with relief, as Terry set off twenty meters behind the lead.

The stadium was riveting, as every person it seemed had a favorite on the track. Rancor ruled. Indifferent spectators could not discern the source of such excitement. They stood mute, captivated by the enthusiasm. Orders, commands, and anguish channeled itself toward the recipients scurrying around the oval. There would be no letup until all was finished.

"'bout 4:01 flat," Katie announced to Zoe almost quietly, "that's a couple seconds faster than last week, Zoe."

"Terry's going to catch those guys, I bet," the little girl said, matter-of-factly.

Terry had made-up ten of the twenty-five meters ending the backstretch. He latched onto Toberstown's Bodo Trum, who trailed Ricky Bolt of Wikersville, who trailed Chancellorsville's Harry Smith leading and not letting up.

"4:56," announced Katie.

"Way to go Terry!"

"Reel 'em in Terry!" screamed Jack and Jayce.

"Get back up there!" yelled a man setting behind them.

Terry followed around the curve then accelerated past Bodo.

"Crank it Terry! Crank it!" demanded Jimmy from the bullpen waiting for his 400 trials with other qualifiers. "Come on dude!" Not so, responded the Wilkesville runner; increasing his tempo at the middle of the turn. The boy continued his effort into the straight leading Terry with his ten-meter pad, but down another five meters behind Chancellorville.

"Pull, pull Terry!" Jack called frantically.

As the crowd's pitch increased for the exchange; so did every athlete roll into their final meters with a vigorous pump action draining the last of adrenaline.

"5:53! 5:54! 5:55!" bellowed Katie trying to hear herself over the bedlam of screams surrounding her.

Eli snatched his implement at 5:56 in third place, three seconds behind leader Damian Leight. Between them, were Mickey Bell and Frankie LaMay. Damian was tall, bronze, long legged with shaved head. He negotiated the first turn with confident high stepping strides that seemed easy. As if running at half-effort, most spectators thought the boy appeared invincible.

"Damian is the state runner-up in the 800, 1:56 man," revealed the Roland showing up just behind Jayce and Jack. "He looks like a gazelle doesn't he? He can step," grinned Roland.

At issue for Eli was the space before him. "Can't loose any ground to him," he thought. "The second lap maybe my endurance…maybe he'll come back…"

"Come on son!" yelled Jayce high up in the stands.

"Keep 'em in your sights!" hollered Jack, backing up his neighbor.

Eli however, had more then problems up front; behind him Moe Stevens last year's 1600 champ from Churchill latched onto him. Eli looked at the red head and fixed his gaze ahead.

"He ain't going to beat Eli from behind," commented Jayce observing Moe's progress. Meanwhile, Damian strode by the main bleachers in his fluid easy gate.

"He's so smooth," stated Roland leaning over toward the men, "doesn't look like he's moving very fast with those long strides."

"6:49!"

The eyes followed Eli passing Bell then LaMay. Moe had come from too far behind to catch up with Eli, now he was paying his way to the rear of the leaders.

"That was about 54!" said Jayce looking at his stopwatch.

Frantic calls increased. They inundated the strung-out runners the entire circuit.

"Come on! Push it Sammy!"

"Take 'em Pat! You can do it!…"

"Reel them in Jerry!"

Eli's mind was turning over thoughts as quick as his feet were switching positions. "…I am second…someone is still on my rear…I have got to hold this…if they pass I'll never bring 'em back…"

The final turn saw Damian cruising comfortably followed by Eli then Moe just a stride behind Eli and appearing anxious to pass. The next following team was twenty meters behind.

"Fight him off Eli!" A fearful Jayce commanded.

Watching them file into the backstretch, all people considered final efforts forthcoming.

"Don't let him pass…," thought Eli, "he's coming back to me!…"

Spectators would see Damian slowing. His form seemed effortless and most thought he would run vigorously the last meters. Instead, Damian's long form appeared to be weakening. The gangly legs hampered any attempt to turn over faster. Gone was the high lift and easy gate. His push off was strength-less and a faint attempt to check over his left shoulder only hastened his demise.

"Come on Eli make an effort at him.

Moe ran out of his effort and stopped his progress toward Eli. With Damian appeared weakening up front, Eli started his last bid to close the space behind Damian.

From the stands, it was evident when Eli's effort took effect. "That's it Son!" screamed Jayce among the standing fans, spectators, and team members hollering at the top of their voices.

"I think he can get him!" stated Jack seeing the cut the distance to half.

"Damian's been injured most of the season," said Roland sitting behind Jayce, "looks like he's short on strength. Your boy is pulling him back." Into the final space to the finish, Eli moved out to lane two for passing space.

Three meters behind, two meters but Damian looked to his right caught Eli in the corner of his eye and started an attempt to rotate faster. Eli appeared to cease his attack fifty meters to finish, as Damian held onto his two-meter lead. The yelling and screaming was deafening. The finish was set, or was it? Twenty meters out Damian's head went farther back as he slowed completely exhausted. Eli flared up for another effort. Fanning his arms, he leaned forward and nabbed his foe by a foot. Entirely spent, Eli flopped off the track to hug the ground.

"Yeaa!" screamed Jayce and Jack in unison, raising clinched fists. Even Roland exclaimed. "You can't stand up near the finish or someone will catch you every time."

"7:51.55," Jayce announced, "that's a record!"

"What a race! What a race!" Jack affirmed in his drawl. "Hey you have any more lives left in you? I know I've got 'bout one left myself to get me through tomorrow."

All around the track campus the grumble of conversation of congratulation permeated throughout the stadium. Clapping and cheering continued minutes after the athletes scattered amongst the masses. Jayce and Jack disappeared trying to find the boys.

Elsewhere, teams were assembling as if for a conference. They gathered for other relay events, and the boys and girl's 400-meter runs. In contestant are two heat races. The first four from each heat would advance to Saturday's final.

The foursome from Lakeport had walked over to the second curve near the holding tent for competitors, reporting for a race. "Way to go, guys," said Coach Thorpe, "you guys were awesome. All you guys PR'd, and you got the record too!"

Thorpe had figured a third for his boys. "Now, Jimmy's about to go in the hurdles, let's rally him boys," suggested Thorpe, motioning them to follow. They complied, but kept up the conversation detailing all feeling and fears during the race.

"My nervous energy carried me through," said Terry.

"That Damian dude," related Eli, "I never thought I would catch him, but the dude just fell apart the last 200 meters."

Presently on the track, Jimmy was adjusting his start blocks, readying for Heat 2. Next to him in lane four, was Gregory Hines of Lincoln. Slated for some college in Texas, he logged a 14.45 at his Regional. On his right was Bull Run's Simon Bett with a 14.60 to his credit. Jayce and Jack visited the boy briefly, expressing confidence, and allowing Jimmy to realize the support he had without regard to the previous week's efforts. Now Thorpe and some pals overlooked his preparations.

"The top four in this race are faced with a 14.55 and 14.41 a seconds in Heat 1," warned Thorpe.

"Where did all these guys come from?" asked Danny.

"I know Jimmy is asking himself the same thing, so he's got to be on form in this race." Replied Eli, thinking of how intense his effort was just minutes before.

"Yea all sprinters have got to be confident before their races," stated Thorpe, "any hesitation in the start they will be out of the race at this level of competition."

Jayce and Jack had resumed their seats in the stadium, after placing a cell-phone call to the wives back home disclosing the results of the boy's performances. "Now, if Jimmy can take his best shot," said Jack standing looking down at the lineup of starters.

"He'll be clicking," said Jayce matter-of-factly.

On the track starter Frank Stamps had perched himself on his stepladder to the left side of the row of eight runners in various positions of readiness. The girl's races were over and this would finish the boy's hurdles. Preparations for the 4 x 400 relay would begin for Jimmy and crew after he finishes the 110 meters high hurdles. Parents, relatives of several generations, and fans moved to their favorite rest spots in the stands and waited.

Kasper made these few minutes before start to reflect his perceptive observations toward the magnificent order and somewhat pageantry, taking place. "These sporting events are the nearest the Americans can get in approaching a Royal affair," thought he.

The boy watched some aged figures take varied positions about the field. Armed with a red and a white flag, these dignified fellows move stoically waiting for the 'stage curtains' to be lofted so they apply the eye of judgment toward the cherish implementation of 'fairness'. "If we only had such goals for all public institutions," he thought. The integrity of orderliness, sportsmanship, and uncompromising issuance of conformity of events they cosseted about as well as any infringement upon the constitution of the United States at these games.

"Bang!"

Like in three steps, Jimmy was ahead and his left leg was reaching for hurdle number one.

"All right Jimmy!"

Everyone watched him step over number two, then number three, and leaving one meter, two meters and three meters ahead of Hines. Jimmy continued the steady unbroken rhythm. Hines hit number seven in his desperation to keep Jimmy from continuing to throw distance between them to no avail. 14.05 seconds was the automatic time given to Jimmy, Hines was14.40 seconds and Bett was in 14.52 seconds. Henry Storm took the last qualifying spot with 14.75 seconds.

While everyone with Lakeport was with congratulations, Thorpe mumbled dire concern looking ruefully at his stopwatch. "First right now on time," he thought, "He was high over four hurdles, a bit off balance over four and five as well, could have tripped fallen." Supercritical maybe, but Thorpe saw tough goings for the distance boys on Saturday as well.

However, time for more contemplation was short. A couple relay races and Jimmy was due for the 400-meter rounds and then a sudden interruption.

"Hey coach, you got an impressive troop of boys," said some voice. He thought he recognized. Thorpe turned to see Andy Bell of Marlborough.

"Yea, they're getting it done but it's a struggle," answered Thorpe shaking hands as Bell stood before him smiling admirably.

"I hear you really put the mileage on 'em," then he paused slightly, "I'll increase my boys running their senior year." Bell delivered his conviction with somewhat of a melancholy repose. Thorpe felt immensely superior to him but he inclined to condescension. He adopted toward the coach an air of patronization.

"Well I am sure what they miss these days it will be there for next year," said Thorpe, not the least sincere, knowing that Marlborough were not getting anyone to the Saturday finals.

The man smiled and excused himself coyly. Thorpe beamed with self-pride. In the shade of what the team accomplished, he strode with self-confidence. He had already defied the expectations of all his critics. Every new qualification for Saturday would be gravy. He would not shrink from an encounter with anyone again. Indeed, when reminded of his fortunes today, Thorpe looked at colleagues from retrospect began to see something fine with his young fellows and all the adverse experiences. He had license to be pompous. "Gosh I am hungry," said he realizing he had not eaten all day, so off he was for the canteens.

"Coach," a familiar voice of Katie called. "They're getting ready for the 400. Jimmy's in heat one." His little assistant discovered Thorpe walking amongst a small group leaving the concessions booths. Time had sneaked away from his conscientiousness briefly. The pair made their way to seats in the stands, still munching on a bag of popcorn. For a change, Thorpe would not be trackside for this race.

"Is he confident? Did you talk to him?"

"He's pumped," answered Katie, "this is his favorite event. He wants to show something, after last week's pitiful run."

Frank Stamps was at his trade once more with the majesty of a priest moving toward his altar to make grace upon his subjects. The announcer would set the runners in their start and waited to observe them motionless. Only then shall he fire the pistol to set the blessed off to an exercise that glorifies this whole event. Stamps held time in abeyance; no way did the man not know this. His motions were slow and deliberate like a conductor of an orchestra. Wiping his braw, retrieving his pistol, Frank Stamps straightened his arms above his head.

"Blam!" This sound sending the first eight runners scrambling for one of the first four places across the finish. Jimmy in lane five moved conservatively away from his blocks.

Farther toward the center of the bleachers, Jayce and Jack rallied Jimmy on. "It's the last one-hundred meters that separates the men from the boys. We'll see where Jimmy's at then," said Jaycee standing as everyone else in the stands watching the run unfold.

"Well he better be where he wants," added Jack, "there's another guy that's right at 50 seconds flat." As the line of boy' neared the second curve, Jimmy appeared comfortable, but so did the boys on either side of him.

"His form looks good, but let's see," questioned Thorpe with Katie.

"Come on Jimmy!" yelled Katie with a rare display of hurrah. "Start kicking now!"

The runners filed around the turn defying positioning until the curve started straightening. Then it appeared three were nearly shoulder-to-shoulder until Jimmy started the pumping action.

"There it is!"

"Go to your arms Jimmy!"

"Rotate dude!"

Jimmy in lane five entered the straight two strides ahead of lane three with the remaining field in multiples of two and three strides farther behind. With his head leaning back ever so slightly, and his arms slowing, Jimmy appeared relaxed and cruised across the finish.

"48.6!" Katie said writing the time down.

"He looked decent," commented Thorpe, "I've got to catch-up with Roy, send Eli and Terry to the tent, if you see them." Thorpe needed to get his 4 x 400 together for the last trials of the day.

Back higher up in the stands, "Jimmy looked 'bout ninety per cent," assessed Jack.

"Well, he's got the 4 x 400 coming," Jayce submitted.

"Northeastern Ohio will always show up with the horses," the pair saw Roland filing their way, "the relays are a tradition up there and the talent that goes with it."

"And plentiful," said a man from below them.

"Roland, how you doing?" greeted Jack.

"Been taking everyone's hopes away have you Roland?" asked Jayce.

"Aha, naw," responded the man, "quite the contrary. I have instilled optimism on most folks. I'll tell them pointedly what they're up against."

Other spectators began contributing to the conversation, a usual occurrence in the dictums of track and field polite society.

"Erie City's got three runners besides their 49 man, who can beat 52 seconds," said one elderly man dressed down in Ohio State red and gray.

"I like Bedford Trace they have been going, 3:25 to 3:21 all season…they are ready to drop a few seconds Saturday…"

"…Lakeport has been under 3:25…"

With the sun blazing overhead, and a slight cooling breeze pulling and withdrawing its effect over the crowd, the final scene was set. It was a day that people conversed straightforwardly and time withdrew it talons allowing events to pass quickly. Popcorn, hot dogs, cheese dips, drinks and the toiletries taken care of; the crowd readied for the finale of the day the 4 x 400 meter relay.

Now the runners of the 4 x 400 meters are a particular sort of people, somewhat unlike other athletes in their demeanor. Here the group, clan, gang, mentality was realized foremost. The foursome displayed behavior quite independent from the each individual in its makeup. Identity of such a group was readily apparent, much like their counter parts making up the 4 x 200 meters and 4 x 100 meters relays. This clan of runners is the biggest and tallest fellows on the track and they made the conversation, because most were football talents as well.

"You hear? Sammy Sikes is going to Georgia Tech; he visited Ohio State, but nothing happen there…"

"Well he ain't going to get much playing time with Milt Fylow aboard…"

"…That Kid from Bakersfield is leaning to Michigan…"

"There's a talent there, he'll be playing on Sundays…"

"Yea, no way he'll ever graduate…he'll go early in the draft…"

Then the time arrived. Colors and combinations of colors filled the track with the teams of four runners. Some minutes later all team members exited the track leaving eight fidgeting with starter blocks. A couple starters did not use the blocks, they will make a standing start. The first of two heat races this was; the fastest four from each heat will advance to the final Saturday.

Frank Stamps assumed his position, while Roy assumed his in lane two with no blocks. He liked the standing position for his start. Big even for a 400 runner, it was not ideal him being in an inside lane, where the turn was tighter than the outer lanes. Roy would have to work hard to keep his bulk close to the inside of this turn.

"Bang!" Roy powered away with the seven others in sight in outer lanes. He looked ungainly as usual in the turn. As the turn relaxed and straightened his stride increased and the boy floored his speed on the stretch, making up the stagger on lane two. However, the middle lanes raced away from him. Roy negotiated some fine running of his second turn; then the big fellow chugged his thick arms up and down with all his vigor.

"Come on Roy! Ata boy!"

He was the fourth to hand off his baton as the lane two runner passed Roy in his final meters. Terry grabbed the implement, busted forth in pursuit of Beggswell, Chappieville and Stoneybrook all within two seconds of each other. Terry strode out a pressing run, but made no progress toward his leads. Into the turn his 800 strength brought back some footage allowing the boy to slowly move to lane two and pass on the turn.

"Be brave boy! Be brave." Jack encouraged. Passing on the turn was discouraged, but the two in lead were slowing too rapidly, while Stoneybrook's strong runner increased his lead further. Terry aimed for Eli coming into the stretch; already a stride ahead over Beggswell, he collared Chappieville. Stoneybrook passed to their number three runner, eight meters up on Terry. Eli bounced in place with anxiousness before he made his snatch and accelerated, cutting over to hug the curb lane.

"Here goes our two strong legs," predicted Jayce, "now we see what we're made of."

"Yea, but this is our strong legs too!" said a man from below them and looking over his right shoulder to make his point to the Lakeport pair. One must be careful in any adverse comments of predicts at such occurrences as these.

"Oh boy!" acknowledged Jayce, "We'll have a match-up then."

By this time, Eli and the leader were midway on the backstretch. Both had long ground sweeping strides with powerful rotation, undoubtedly, the fastest running seen so far. Beggswell and Chappieville were running in tandem five meters back and slipping slowly further in arrears of Eli.

"Stay smooth, don't let go...we're moving...got to drag in a few meters...okay, start now, pump the arms, lift Terry lift!"

"Good job son! Good job!"

"Way to go Eli!"

They watched the boy close, and then watched him lose his gain as Shadybrook's flared desperately the last few meters. Eli leaned and passed to Jimmy nine meters behind, anchor Tommy Sands the winner of heat two of the 400 meters.

"That kid ran 48.8," Jack reminded Jayce.

"It's going to be tough goings."

Indeed spectators observed these runners make the fastest negotiation around the turn all day. Tommy, however, began to slow after the turn ended. Jimmy with no hesitation pulled Tommy toward him in powerful thrusts of the hips and sweeping strides.

"He made up that space awfully quick," warned Jack.

"Yea, he's got to have something for the last hundred," said Jayce concerned.

The two leaders were entering the final turn of the race. Formidable, both boys rotated legs and arms in unison as they finished the turn and started the straight.

"Swing wide Jimmy!"

Jimmy tried that, but Tommy Sands had it figured to the meter. He figured Jimmy was near exhaustion having closed so much space between them, the boy thus saved his big move for the last hundred meters.

"Finish it Tommy!" yelled the Shadybrook fan below. Tommy started pumping with fresh vigor. Seeing Tommy obviously had been waiting for him, Jimmy allowed himself to float to the finish behind Tommy.

"Just three strides," Jack exclaimed, "he missed catching that guy by a few strides."

"3:21.53, for us," Jayce read his stopwatch, "3:20.22, for Shadybrook. We have got to go faster Saturday, if we want to make the top three."

"Agreed, I think the top two are going to break 3:20," affirmed the man from below.

On the infield, the foursome strode slowly to the other side of the track to retrieve their gear, with Kasper and Danny trailing. Jayce and Jack intercepted the group and walked along with them. Heat 2 was being lead out to the start. Jimmy and clan ignored them. No time for sentimentalizing, the next group of eight would fight it out for the remaining four positions on Saturday's final.

"I decided not to keep up the crank on," explained Jimmy, "he was waiting for me, gotta save something for tomorrow."

"You did right," said Jayce.

"Great job, Jimmy, I am proud of you," stated Jack placing a comforting arm around him.

"Let's head to the bus, everybody," suggested Jimmy.

"Don't you want to see what they do in Heat 2?" asked Jack.

"Not really," answered Jimmy, "whether they run fast or slow; I have got to pop it all out. It is all one can do. Today has nothing to do with tomorrow."

The group acted on Jimmy's suggestion and departed for the school bus. Thorpe, Katie, and Zoe, were in the stadium somewhere.

"You know coach," said Kasper, "he's probably watching Heat 2. He would be at the score board copying down results of all our events."

Kasper agreed with Jimmy as far as their going to the bus. "Jimmy's good at taking things day by day," he thought. "He's no worry worm. A healthy and confident outlook to have about anything, he has. Nothing in a day will dampen Jimmy's spirit for long."

"I must find the simplicity of these problems; that is the secret of seeing the solution methods clearly. In trying to focus on details we see nothing, we must digest that thing until we see the simple major steps to a solution. That's it!" thought Kasper after having flipped through his physics packet. He was reviewing the thought process he recognized as being common in successfully finding solutions in problems. "Most difficult problems, when completed disclose an overall simplicity."

He remembered how David had inferred this reasoning. "…like an artist. You first want to sketch your subject briefly; initially it looks simplistic, like something a child would accomplish, then you start filling in the details." Sitting at the back yard table alone, Kasper ceased a little time to reflect on his long effort to claim proficiency on the subject of Physics. He in the process of reviewing his text of problems, and examples; thought this digestion of his methods was an enlightening and necessary. Expanding this exploration, Kasper suggested this simplicity should be sort further and applied to those biting social thorns. Grasping at air, he understood better. "Observation and disclosure is one aspect. Agreement and cooperation applied to a social problem is entirely another thing." With all this contemplation, he accepted that Saturday would bring the culmination of his physical designs for the year and the following Wednesday Kasper had to place his head to the block for the sake of physics.

"I must have imagination, be enthusiastic and my fate will be inexpressibly bright." He surmised.

"Kasper!" He looked to see his mother leaning partially out the back door calling for him.

"Yes 'ma'am."

"David called. He said he would be at the stadium early. He said he would try to find us. Your Dad spoke to him as well."

"Thanks."

Kasper grabbed his material from the table. His day was at hand and he was upbeat. "What did I expect my work must be tried at some point," he thought as he departed for bed. Kasper had to go through spells of unsealed isolation. He made an sublime utterance before he fell asleep. "Obwohl Er mich erschlägt, warden Sie noch ich habe gestoßen Ihn(Though He slays me, yet will I trust Him)."

CHAPTER 12

▼

Every minute from 9:30 a.m. on this day was on the schedule. The Ohio State Track and Field Tournaments events were starting. Located on the campus of the Ohio State University, in the center of Columbus, the trip to this sight consisted of the twisted and turns over asphalt and concrete roadways. Bumper to bumper traffic it was for fifteen thousand plus people who would visit the tournaments this day, not counting the hundreds of competitors, coaches, and officials.

Colorful dressed spectators and athletes crisscrossed the sidewalks and grass-ways leading to the Jesse Owens Memorial Stadium. The day is warm approaching hot. People wore shorts and caps to block out the beaming sun. Small brothers and sisters of the participants dotted the grounds shirking with excitement. Vendors selling T-shirts, sweatshirts and caps baring the tournament logos realized long lines for their ware.

The athletes and spectators received the national anthem most respectfully as the whole campus stood attentively for the occasion. After which, every minute on the clock became somebody's ultimatum. The events were on and moving as a plane racing down a runway, not having the option of stopping. "We have to go on, we have to go on!" One could imagine Frank Stamps issuing the word to his army of officials. That is what everyone knew was the destiny of the day.

Jayce chatted nervously with the Lakeport contingency sitting midway in the stadium of people donning caps to block the sunrays, as already the day was sunny and warm. He scanned the crowd inconspicuously, not wanting to appear as nervous as he was, but he did not get away; He made eye contact with Principal Stromberg and his wife Patricia higher up the bleachers. They waved to him. He returned the gesture; in this crowd, Jayce figured they probably could not get any closer to their group. He saw many faces he had seen the last couple of weeks; the man wondered whether they were as anxious as he was with the approaching dramas.

"Why am I so nervous, Jimmy's running now?" Jayce thought, "...who am I kidding Kasper and Danny will be toeing the line in just minutes."

"Y'all say he looked good yesterday did you?" asked Sophie.

"Yes, but two guys were faster in the other Heat race?"

"Okay, they're getting set!" warned Jayce.

All eyes throughout the bleachers on both sides of the track focused on the line of eight facing ten hurdles in their lanes. The contestants were fidgeting around with the starting blocks making everyone watching them more apprehensive.

"Guns up!" someone in the near crowd said.

"Bang!"

In two seconds, four heads from the middle of the line simultaneously stretched and bent themselves over the first line of hurdles. Jimmy was in lane three running neck to neck at hurdle two and three with Willard Reinstein in lane four. Willard struck wood at hurdle five. Jimmy forged ahead, cleared hurdle six cleared, increasing his effort to get his feet on the ground quicker. Jimmy skimmed the obstacles, a foot lead, then two feet, over number ten...very quick drives of the arms...finally...leaning, leaning.

"Yea!" exclaimed Jack and Jayce fists clinched over their heads. Most of the onlookers in the stadium were all standing after the pistol fired and cheered madly during the seconds of time of the race. The crowd buzzed with people questioning each other as to what occurred in the race; it was a minute there about before people sat down.

"Alright Jimmy," said an ecstatic Sophie, "that's my Jimmy. He can take care of his business when he has to."

"That was sweet," said Jayce, "hope he sets the stage for the others." He looked at his wife peevishly.

"What was the time Kate?"

"13.88,"said the girl sitting behind him.

"And that's a record," added Zoe.

While Jimmy left the track with the other competitors, the 4 x 3200 meters relay finishers were taking their places on the eight-tiered awards stand at a corner of the stadium. Lakeport's foursome received their medals on the top step. After pictures, Kasper and Danny spirited away to get ready for the 1600 meter run coming up in twenty minutes.

"There's Coach Thorpe over there," said Katie pointing across the track. She saw his figure moving near the check in tent. No doubt, he was anxious for his 1600 boys, but first the girls and boy's 4 x 200 meter event was set to start. After the awards ceremony, Kasper and Danny checked in for lane assignments and attempted some last minute relaxation.

The race would be fast, Kasper surmised. It would be a record he was sure. Well rested with two days of doing nothing, but warming up and stretching, he was ready to run. Danny had run on the relay, but it only served to loosen him up for today, he was equally prepared, for the fastest 1600 meters of his life.

Kasper reasoned that every race he had before was irrelevant. Those runs meant little; today's race meant everything. He became nostalgic, while watching the 100 dashes. Ceasing these few moments he reflected. The running of the mile run, a truly historic event as it is. The1600 meters was just a few meters short of the English statue distance, but Kasper thought it close enough to substitute for the 'real' mile. This was the event of Paavo Nurmi, Glen Cunningham, and Roger Bannister. These gentlemen were heroes in their day. Bannister the medical student, who was first to beat four minutes for the mile; accomplished the feat as a part-time athlete by today's standard. Those were the days of the gentlemen athletes.

"Ja, wenn das Englisch macht etwas für eine lange Zeit, es wird historisch oder eine königliche Angelegenheit (Yes, when the English does something for a long time, it becomes historic or a royal affair)," he has said on occasions. Now he was a principal participate in this noble event.

"Here they come, "Beth announced watching the group of sixteen colorful clad runners moving down the track from the far end, following several officials.

If Jayce was nervous before, now he was frantic. Beth was not so untidy as her husband; nonetheless, she was glad this was the last day of the season. However, this day was not much different from all the others; they all had been stressful to her.

The crowd was buzzing as many took their positions around the track. Armed with video cameras and photo equipment, the spectators readied themselves for the event.

"Ah, David," Jayce called out, "Glad you made it." He said as David worked his way through people clogging the aisles in the stadium.

"Sorry, I didn't spot you all, before," said David moving up the steps. Shoulder to shoulder the crowded stadium was, but many were still looking for seats and their family, track friends, sons and daughters.

They made room for David, and after being introduced to everyone, they resumed their attention to the track. "There the boys are," said Jack watching the boys standing erect at their staggers.

"I see Kasper and Danny have the third and fourth fastest times," observed David looking at the tournament program.

"Yea," answered Jayce, "but they held back last week to qualify. It's going one-hundred percent today for this race." Jayce's face was wet. There was a slight breeze from their left and the temperature was warm.

Looking down on the infield the audience observed the red-banded arm of interest raised. Then the blast issued from the pistol sending the four lines of competitors running around the turn. The movement was in such haste it would appear they were running a much shorter distance than 1600 meters. Enthusiasm of unequaled intent evolved as the group did not string out quickly as in previous contests. All here were championship caliber. Unless, injured or ill these fellows did not surrender a challenge without opponents tasting their vigor.

Negotiating around the second turn, the group bunched and spread-out into lane three moved carefully forward. Kasper's fuzzy head was amongst the first six. Staying to the outside and into the stretch, Kasper with Danny a stride back moved uncomfortably fast in the group from front to rear only measured eight meters.

"This is scary," exclaimed Beth, "somebody could trip."

"I agree," said Jayce, "this makes me nervous."

"61, 62, 63…," Katie called out the times as the troop of runners passed 400 meters. A tall, longhaired fellow in green and white lead slightly, then a muscular skin-headed young man to his right followed. Kasper in the second lane and passing forged toward the leaders at the top of the turn.

"Come on Kasper! Move out!"

Into the backstretch, Kasper surged ahead. From his parent's view, three bobbing heads protruded barely ahead of a close group of five. Then they could see the figure of Kasper accessed his situation. "62…I should hit 2:07 at 800. I am okay…got to hammer it out on the last 400…." he thought on, "…where's Danny?…It is so quite."

Danny followed in fourth, "Kasper is running tough," he thought, "I've got get on him after the turn." Touring the turn, four in single file moved majestically, but then some daylight grew behind runner number five. The remaining runners slowly fell back, unable to make pace with the lead four."

"Move up there, Danny!" ordered Jayce.

Danny was running wide on the turn. As Kasper got to the straight, Danny was in lane two and attempted to move up to his mate's shoulder. Red and white clad Ricky O'Neal, of South Eastern, wouldn't allow Danny's repositioning; so he moved up to Kasper and ran tandem with him as they passed the 800 meters of the race.

"2:06, 2:07!" Katie called, "2:07 for Kasper."

Danny and Patrice Henry of Moulendorf ran nearly shoulder-to-shoulder two strides behind the pair.

"Its going to be fast!" exclaimed Jayce.

"They're so athletic," said David looking perplexed.

The next pack's four seconds behind," said Zoe looking at her watch. "Come on guys! Run the race fast!"

"Come on Bill!" called someone near, "don't lose contact now!"

"Those guys are running too fast," someone else was stating behind the Lakeport crew. "Pat's a great kicker, he'll be on them after they slow."

"Look! Lead's 'slowing already. The third and fourth guys caught up...right on their heels..."

"It's a four man race, look like they're waiting," said someone else below.

"They slowing, Patrick will get 'em at the finish."

"Gun lap! 3:15!"

"Hey! They're running hard now!" exclaimed a female voice.

"Watch the leader is going to be passed at the end of the turn," said someone else.

"Look at the arm movement the leader has really picked up the pace. He hasn't given up yet."

The galley watched Danny move past Patrick while O'Neal appeared to be struggling and losing ground to the trio ahead.

"Here comes Danny," warned Jack, "starting his regular run at Kasper's back."

"Come on Ricky! Stay up there!"

"Crank now Kasper! Crank son!"

Crank he did, knees lifting increasingly higher as he closed toward the finish. Danny had lost ground while trying to get by Patrick on the backstretch. He was three meters in arrears out of the turn when he set off with confidence he set off to catch his pal.

"What's happening to Patrick?" said a supporter, "he's tying up! Look at him!"

"The other Lakeport kid's coming!"

"Ricky! Come on! Come on!"

"Danny's closing, but he's not going to have enough room today," declared Jack.

"He did it!" yelled Jayce, "4:18.33! I don't remember the last time he beat Danny."

"Danny was 4:19.55." announced Katie calmly.

The women mused at the results. They did not understand the concern about who won. The boys went first and second and the time was meaningless to these women.

"Fantastic!" Jayce was floating nearly, "I love those boys. What a job they did!"

"That was awesome alright," David rolled his head with amazement.

"4:25.5, for Patrick," whined someone nearby, "he ran 4:19 a few weeks ago. What was wrong with him today?"

On the infield, the finishers drank a sport drink offered by officials as they tried to recover from their efforts. All of them were sweating profusely and exhausted. Most appeared dazed and sat on the grass or walked slowly as they consumed some liquid. As usual, those finishing in the rear were in worst shape than the early finishers. Kasper and Danny dared not to get too relaxed; they had the 3200 meters to run in less than an hour.

"I couldn't catch you," admitted Danny, "you raced smart. You were so fast at 1200 and I had a time trying to get around Pat Henry."

"Yea, I was afraid I'd end up third of fourth, if the race was slow," revealed Kasper, "but, what matters are the one-two finish and the fast time. Maybe we will attract some colleges."

"Well maybe I'll have a chance to get an athletic scholarship at Howard University."

"Your SAT score is above average," reminded Kasper, "have coach give them a call," Kasper was pleased to praise his cousin. "And by next year this time maybe we can get times like the California kids."

"It'll be nice. Hey they're calling us for the awards!"

"Come on let's get our picture taken. We will then be in next year's tournament program. I wouldn't miss it," said Kasper. Moreover, he would not have. To Kasper this is history and he is part of it now. The normally unsentimental young man saw such an event as this as required for all the nostalgic values. He wanted to follow the traditions of the mile and be part of that history of high school participants. Jim Ryun set all standards with his 3:58 English statue mile back in the early 60's on a cinder track.

"Hey! We got twenty seconds to go to catch Jim Ryun," chuckled, Kasper. They both laughed in mockery of themselves and set off for them awards tent.

No way will the officials allow the track to get cold from competition. As Kasper, Danny, and the other finishers stalked off the infield and track, the 1600 meters girls were ushered up the track toward the start. Sheila and Jenny joined Thorpe at the fenced area on the first turn.

"I need to checkout the Tweedle sisters, Dee and Bee and the others that I may run against in cross country," said Sheila in a bubbly mood.

"You've got two more years," added Thorpe, "they're going to get to know you real well, Sheila."

"I think that girl from Gettysburg is going to win," said Jenny.

The girls were at their positions, bouncing around, rotating the arms attempting to stay relaxed and loose.

"There she is," said Sheila, "in blue and gold."

"Jodi Bonney will be the only one under five minutes today, I bet," added Jenny.

"She's going to have company today, I think," corrected Sheila.

"The winner should be in the low four-fifties," stated Coach Thorpe.

'Bang!"

The girls scuttled out aggressively. The crowd packed along all 400 meters of the bordering fence and banisters. More than the boy events, these audiences had the added populace of three tiers of family. Grandparents, parents, and guardians, brothers and sisters, while many competitors may additionally, had small nieces and or nephews present. As they scurried around the oval, the stadium mostly stood to enroll all the commands, suggestions, and warnings. Few runners could hear anything, but it did not matter. This participation relieved the nervousness and projected virtual control.

Subjects consisted of small, tall, medium sized young girls with bouncing braids, ponytails, arrayed in an assortment of color and combinations. Quite expectantly, these announced names of the contestants spanned the alphabet.

"Go Kallie!"

"Way to go Becky!"

"Stay up there Jodi!"

"That's good Jackie!"

"Hang in there Whitney. You can run with them."

Finishing the first lap, "70, 71…" called Sheila reading her stopwatch as the girls sped by 400 meters.

"That's Sara Moran in first," declared Jenny, "she could win it. She's done 5:05."

"Seldom does the leader at lap one win the race," pointed out Thorpe. "Besides 70 seconds is too fast for the first lap."

"There's Dee Tweedle in third," observed Sheila, "...there's her sister, Bee," she pointed toward the pack.

"Watch Tina George, she will be up there," said Thorpe again. "She's got a 5:02 to her credit."

Touring the second circuit little pixie Sara was over taken by the redheaded Sallie Triggs, of Frankfort. Following her is Jackie Waters in all blue, then Dee Tweedle looking relaxed and un-pressed, and finally Jodi Bunny. Then there was a gap of three meters. Bee Tweedle led a band of five while the remaining girls were already falling out of contention. The leaders passed 800 meters in 2:25 with Sallie forging the pace.

"Get up there Dee!" someone yelled.

On the backstretch, Sallie slowed and Dee passed the three ahead of her dragging Sara with her. Bee's group closed on the lead group around the turn. Suddenly as they entered the stretch, Jackie moved in lane two and proceeded to overtake everyone. She crossed 1200 meters in the lead.

"3:42!" said Thorpe to his group, "they were slow on that third lap, Jackie could win it she's a fast finisher."

Yelling commands and warnings swamped the stadium grounds, as the pack strung-out with no changing of positions on the third backstretch.

"Jackie's stringing them out!" said Thorpe.

"Sara's not finished with her though," warned Sheila. Then watched the pint sized girl move pass Dee and latch onto Jackie, with Dee reacting by moving up to Sara's right as they started into the final turn.

"Three girl race," Thorpe called out rocking himself with excitement.

Rounding out of the turn the tall figure of Dee appeared on Jackie's right shoulder, having moved pass Sara who reacted by settling between Jackie and Dee.

"Come on Jackie!"

"Sprint around her Sara!"

However, Sara surged carrying her to Dee's shoulder. This sent Dee into her final effort after Jackie. The lanky brunette went into her own overdrive which put any threat from behind out of reach. Dee had to defend herself from Sara's onslaught by requiring a quicker turnover a lean forward. Such was the finish. Jackie, Dee, and Sara pulling up slightly seeing she could not out lean Dee.

"4:51!" announced Thorpe, "fantastic!"

"What a race," Sheila said solemnly, "second, third, and fourth broke five."

"Yea," added Jenny, "like 4:52, 4:54, and 4:58. And the next two were under 5:06."

"Golly, I would have been blow away today," suggested Sheila, "they were awesome."

"You would have been up in that lead pack, Sheila," added Thorpe, "no doubt in my mind."

"Yep! Sheila," added Jenny, "look how much time most of them dropped today," with that the group headed back up to the stands.

While the tournament raced the 4 x 100 relays, Kasper and Danny poised for pictures recorded into Ohio track and field history. At the same time, Jimmy and the 400- meter run competitors gathered in the big tent.

How imposing these fellows are the 400-meter runners. The most physically impressive young men to take to the track, many are football players whose long strides and power can maintain speed for 50 seconds or less. The stallions of track and field arrived to the stage.

Lift up your eyes on high and behold, who has created these things, says the judge. Raise your heads and be seen, while stiffening your neck in our direction. No boy here, behold the man and take heed of this fellow. Gentlemen, women, boys and girls - the principals of the 400 meters!

At the crack of the gun, one experienced the awe—long sweeping strides took only several of them to negotiate the turn. Jimmy's rate of turn was somewhat faster than his competitors and his leg-lift was not as high as the boys sandwiching him. Staying in their lanes, one could see that the middle lanes held the faster runners, as they moved passed the competitors in the outer lanes. Jimmy in lane three caught up with lane four's Jo Jo May before entering the second turn. Such was the speed that all these figures appeared to be fighting to keep from running into the lane to their right. Now it was as if the race was in abeyance until these final seconds as the spread of runners finished the turn and entered the straight.

"Let's go to the arms, Jimmy!" Jayce ordered, "gotta start a bit earlier today boy!"

"Move those legs Jimmy!" screamed Sophie.

"Come on boy! Move!" yelled Jack.

The eight arrive from the turn, and then everyone started the finale flare. Like the championship caliber they were, all these fellows shifted to a higher gear over that last 100 meter. Only lane one, and lane seven was off pace as they all powered in nearly even. Separations were slow. These boys just did not allow anyone to get away without a stress move. Obliged to the task, lane five's runner started pulling ahead slightly while lane four's Jo Jo May followed with faster turnover. Jimmy hesitated, then pumped vigorously to collar Jo Jo and began trucking up to leader Ben Samson in lane five.

"Jimmy's taking it!" The boy decreased the distance in the gap to Samson, "All the way!"

"Keep chugging!"

Then it was over.

"47.7! Alright," screamed Katie as Jimmy slowed.

"Way to go Jimmy," said Zoe in an unsurprised tone her face beamed with a smile.

Jack and Sophie grabbed and hugged each other in glee. Then they exchanged hugs, with Jayce and Beth.

"Man, you guys dominating everything, here?" asked David, "I didn't know your school was a power in track."

"No we're not," disclosed Sophie, "we just have some great boys this year."

The Luke pair left the stands so they could snap pictures doing the awards presentation. Left alone with Jayce, David took the opportunity to ask questions as to the performance of Kasper, as he did not know how to judge them. Jayce gave him some idea as to how rare such times are. "So he's ranking amongst the best in the country is he now," David concluded.

"Correct." Jayce smiled and said, "There are only a couple dozen or so runners in the country that will be faster than four minutes–twenty-seconds; and he's got his senior year ahead, as well."

"Great! Kasper's an outstanding scholar and athlete as well, it's just a matter of where he wants to go to school at," David suggested.

In other sections of the bleachers, some discussions evolved.

"I didn't think the Lakeport pair would run that fast," said a coach to another coach in the stands.

"Not for the 1600 meters," agreed the other coach. "And they're supposed to be in the 3200 meters as well."

"Before that they have the 800 meters," replied the first coach, "they were the fastest pair on that 4 x 800 relay, you know."

The pair thought some between themselves. "Huh," started the second coach, "I thought Cleveland Bakersfield with their sprinters would win the team championships, but Lakeport could be the team, they have forty-eight points already."

"Well, they're about to start the 300 hurdles. Bakersfield should score here."

Correct in this assessment, the team from Bakersfield expected no challenge today; presently wary with some despair of their circumstance, the team hoped to seize the opportunity to score a win in the hurdles. Jimmy had snatched victory from one of their star athletes in the 110 meters hurdles. It had begun to seem to them that events were trying to prove that they were impotent to stop a band of country boys, for they had no distance men to challenge Lakeport in today's events.

Thorpe had his mind on Bakersfield as well; not too many days before he feared this confrontation, now he endeavored to demonstrate that his few boys could resist the onslaught from the notable historic track powers from Northeast Ohio.

"Let's see what they do here," Thorpe said to himself from the top row of the bleachers and raising his stopwatch while watching the starter about to fire the gun for the 300 hurdles. Confident, he felt like a conquering hero at the pentacle of his acclaim.

"Blam!" After start, by hurdle three the Bakersfield entry was stepping over and reaching the ground before his chief adversary hit number four and stutter stepped to get over number five. Harry Jones took three big strides and then launched himself toward the waiting hurdle; with this rhythm, he continued unchallenged to the finish.

Thorpe complexion was white. "38.4! That was a milk run," he credited somberly, "Ten easy points for them. Now they have forty-eight points, this ties us. Come on Eli, Terry got to score big on your run boys."

However, the team's fans including Sheila, Jenny, and Zoe continued to hoot unabashed for Jimmy. The leader of the 'clan' was clicking. Everyone else had no choice but to perform. The 'Boss' had made his statement. Nothing could break their resolve, now. The little school and community had never been in contention for a state championship of any sport in its history.

Behold the hour cometh. Inner desolations were scattered and the two boys acknowledged that circumstances is engineering their reckoning moment laid before them. Eli and Terry felt the pressure from the successes from their fellows. Now, it is their turn to stamp the ground with success once more.

"Be of good cheer, Terry," Eli reminded his mate, "grit is our armor now. We prepared this script Terry. Now on to the stage, we must perform."

Terry parried Eli's bolstering, unnecessary. He would be facing four other runners listed under two minutes, thus he was committed to run the first 400 meters faster than he had ever before. "I am focused on what I have to do, Eli. I just want to see you out front. We have got to take control after 400 meters."

"Follow me gentlemen," ordered an official waving to the sixteen hyped young men in the tent. They followed the woman steering them to the start lineup.

"Come unto me," Eli quoted the old command. Beckoned by the words they should spring into action ready in the preparation they have sowed.

"It's going to be tough alright, Terry," said Eli as they approached the start. "So we get to see if we're any good. The height of the mountain top is measured from the valley."

"Yea, I am in the valley alright," Terry countered wondering how Eli became so philosophical these last moments, "but I am game to make that peak."

"That's the attitude, let's pop now babe."

Talk, pompous generalities, with optimism and elation would last mere minutes before the time and space for boy's 800-meter run would occupy its reality.

"Bang!"

Stampede would be the term applied to the sight of runners rushing around.

"Ease up guys, this is not the 400 meters," warned Jayce amongst all the boy's supporters.

"Watch the cut-in!" yelled Thorpe calling from the fence on the backstretch. "Stay outside!"

"Come on Eli, Terry!" called the very immature voice of Zoe, who was back to her spot with Katie and the Lakeport group.

"Eli's moving right with 'em," observed David feeling acknowledged with his comments.

As the spread of runners finished the second turn and finished the staggers. They weaved toward the curb lanes. Stan Groth, of Hattiesburg, medium build and muscular for a runner strode to the lead two strides ahead of Tony Bono, then Eli on his shoulder with Terry trailing. The remaining runners bunched up only five meters behind.

"55!" yelled Katie, "Eli and Terry was 56."

"They're flying!" Jayce said standing, as everyone nearly started rising from their seat as the runners entered the final lap. Around the turn, Eli followed Groth and Bono. Groth stayed a couple strides ahead of them. As they rolled to the backstretch Bona and Eli started reeling Groth back; suddenly, from their rear Damian Lee over took Terry, Eli, and Bono. After the assault, he relaxed with long strides and unusual forward body lean.

Eli had wanted to overtake Groth before the final turn. Jayce could see the situation. "With so little space left he's got to pass that kid on the turn," he exclaimed.

Just at that moment from the turn, "You got to move now!" ordered the familiar voice of Thorpe. The four however, appeared to ease off. Terry stubbornly held on the pace one stride behind Eli. These boys were still moving too fast for any assault attempt to pass during the run on this turn. As the turn started to relax its hold, Eli allowed himself to flow outside to lane two. However, Damian saw his goal ahead, so the tough guy started lifting arms and legs for his finishing run to victory. Groth followed. Eli not quite ready for his finale move had three long strides to catch Lee. Moving inside seventy meters, in his fatigue, Eli started to pull up on Groth's shoulder as Terry was slipping off a bit from his mate. His stubbornness to maintain contact was wearing.

"Move Eli! Move now!" insisted Jayce.

"Come on Terry," said Jack barely audible through Sophie's screaming.

Groth was flat out with his awkward lean and could add no more to his effort. Eli was closing on Damian, when Bono came to life and surged overtaking Eli, then he caught Damian ten meters to finish.

"All the way Eli," is all Jayce could say in the scene before him. "Fight him off Terry."

Terry could not hold off the strong senior Peter Mayo. Bono, Damian, Eli, Groth, Mayo, and Terry completed the order.

"1:55.73 for Eli and 157.54 was Terry's time, so for third and sixth we got nine points. That gives us fifty-seven points for the team," announced Katie. "What was the time for first and second, Zoe?"

"1:54.35 and 1:55.13," said the girl unimpressed.

The group watched the finishers gather. Eli and Terry exchanged high-fives. Then they filed from the track to the awards area.

"Can you believe they went that fast?" Jayce asked still stunned and rolling his head in disbelief, "I thought it would be won in about 1:56."

"Compared to the other races I've seen," Jack explained, "they just ran that second lap so fast.

"Yea, the 800 meters is always like that," commented a fan from the row of seats below them, "people will drop a couple seconds from their best. And the girls in particular, will drop a lot of time as well."

True to the word the girls 800 meter run was consistently the most competitive race of the tournament events. Evidenced is by the crowded pack running over the distance and the lack of a spread at finish. Such would be the effort of these young girls. Several had run the 1600-meter run; confident of speed and stamina, that last final turn and finish required grit.

Bets were off in these entries. A toss up among four, maybe five different girls could win this one. Six competitors have a difference of only two seconds for their 800 meters times from the Regional. Thorpe and the girls would not make a quest as to who would win this contest. Kasper and crew favored the 1600-meter winner Jackie Waters. "I like how she stayed back and ran strong that last 200 meters," commented Kasper.

"Yea, and she's a senior," added Danny, "she's more plentiful than the others."

"What's that word?" the all-precise Kasper asked.

"Plentiful."

"She plans her races more," quipped Danny, "how's that?"

The boys had to observe the race from the report tent. After the girl's 800 meters, there were the 200-meter runs, and then finally the 3200-meter run.

"There they go," cried Danny as the gun blasted. Half minute later, the pair had sight of the solid spread of runners maintaining their lanes. As they passed, the boys observed bouncing ponytails swaying side to side in rhythm with their rapid strides. Two girls were sporting braids that reached the neck.

"Oh gosh, look how fast they're moving," Sheila said. "I think this may be a record."

"See why you need those 200-meter speed workouts?" Thorpe queried. Sheila just stared as the wave of runners finished the turn and left their lanes to get as close as they could to the curb.

"Run it Jessica!"

"Mandy! Looking good girl!"

"Stay right there Nicole!"

Forging past the mostly standing crowd the girls was three abreast.

"64, 65, 66…" Katie called out times, "65 for the lead group."

"Erin Madison's leads slightly," said Jayce, looking at the participant's index in the back of the program.

"I didn't know girls could run like I've seen today," said David who knew little of track and field.

"Yea, it's amazing how athletic they are," said Beth.

"And some of them as so small," exclaimed Sophie.

The moment had not arrived yet. The three abreast running continued through the turn. "Jackie's in the second group of three," observed Kasper watching the pack advancing toward them at the final turn.

"The tall Tina Boyer is coming around them," said Danny watching Tina move into the lead in lane two, then the girl moved over to the curb lane.

"Jackie responded to Tina's movement," Kasper said excited, "she's going right with her." But Mandy List, of Sycamore didn't mind staying almost in lane three to pass four girls to get just off Jackie's right shoulder.

"Ata girl Mandy!" screamed frantically a man to the upper left of Katie and crew. "Ata girl!"

"That must be her Daddy," said Zoe looking up there.

Tina continued her tow of strung-out girls in pursuit. Jackie stayed just some feet behind and off Tina's shoulder with Mandy in file. Not a full stride behind, three others girls maintained close contact.

As the turn started straightening out, decisions bore fruit to actions. Jessica Walker in the second group of three swung outside of Jackie and started aggressive arm and leg action. Jackie caught Jessica in her periphery and rotated quicker. Mandy was in between trying to stay up with them. Tina was inside on the curb.

"Jackie's moving ahead!"

"Tina! Hang on girl!"

Everyone watched as Jessica far to the outside made another surge, which managed to get her pass Jackie. Mandy Sharpe made a quick move to pull up to the inside even with Jackie.

"Lean Jessica! Lean!"

"Tina's going to get her!"

"That's a girl Jackie she's coming back!"

No more space left, Tina first, then Jessica, Jackie, and Mandy crossed the 800- meter finish in the style of stampede.

"Gee wiz! 2:11.5!" Katie cried.

"Is that real good?" asked Zoe licking an ice cone.

"Yes. It's a record for Division II," Katie disclosed while whooping and all the modes of exhilaration continued for minutes.

"It was as tight as I thought," a man below Katie said. "From first to fourth was three seconds."

"Yea, the girl who come in sixth was about 2:16," said a woman's voice.

"Lady's and gentlemen," said the announcer on the public address system, "please bring your attention to the awards stand for the 800 meter boys."

Sophie and Jack and the Wise's had already departed to take pictures of Danny and Terry on the awards stand. David sat with Katie and Zoe asking an assortment of questions about events.

Kasper and Danny had taken positions of relaxation, as preparations for the 200 meters were underway. However, this close to race time Kasper's adrenaline was building, so was Danny's; their bodies were getting anxious to relieve itself of the hormone.

Thorpe showed with the bustling ways of a concerned mother. Kasper thought it peculiar that coaches felt they were priming their athletes with the bickering and warning. In reality, they only transferred their anxiety to the subjects, who knew all too well, what was on the line. Bakersfield should score fourteen to eighteen points in the 200 meters. His duo needed to score equally or more. He grabbed the boys at the back of the neck and then patted them on the head.

"There," he said moving off and surveying them, "you guys can dominate, just go for it. Forget about the 1600." The two youths made no reply but offered high-fives.

"Well now," continued Thorpe, "I'll be on the second turn. God speed fellows."

After coach left, the two ignored the 200 events and thought only of their soon coming efforts. The body of male and females jocks rustled around them. There was the general buzz of activity. A constant murmuring of voices broke only into accolades for some on going contests.

Finally, it was their time. They could not help but hearing that Bakersfield had taken first and third, sixteen points in the 200 meters.

In the stands, Jayce was chewing a mouth full of gum with much vigor. He was satisfied with the 1600 meters, but Kasper had dropped so much time in the event that some may think it was a flute. A good time here would solidify his performance as legit.

"Between these runs and a good job on that physics test, maybe my boy can make it to one of those Ivy League schools, I hope," He said to David.

"I don't think you have any worry about that," reassured David.

While these conversations were issuing down on the track, the 3200-meter run was readying while Terry, Roy, Eli, and Jimmy were meeting in the 'tent' for the final event, the 4 x 400 relay. Jimmy pumped exclaimed, "Come on homies, we can take these dudes. I know it's a strain, but strain in the strength, dudes. If there is no strain, there is no strength, let's pop it!"

𝒳𝓀𝓀 𝓀𝓀 𝓀 𝓀 𝓀𝓀 𝓀𝓀𝓀 𝓀𝓀𝓀𝒳𝓀𝓀 𝓀𝓀𝓀𝓀 𝓀𝓀𝓀 𝒳

"Bestreiten Sie dieses, dass ich werde (Contest this I will)," thought Kasper as he stood his position waiting at the start. "Finsh dieses das ich muss (Finish this I must)." He was not just thinking of this contest. Kasper would be reviewing physics for the next few days. He wondered what would ultimately be the most difficult, today or Wednesday. Both days are crucial to where the future will take him. The boy asked "Why now" at such a time in his young life. One is born into this world by no know means of our own. "Shouldn't persons be given by default certain things in life essential to full development?"

"Was ein unkluger Vorschlag (What a foolish proposition)," Kasper thought more clearly. "Nichts ist zu einer lebenden Seele, nein nichts geschuldet (Nothing is owed to a living soul, no not anything)."

For a time this pursuing reflection took all elation from the boy's disposition. Then he realized the majesty and selectivity was an honor that few would ever participate. "Let me rejoice and enjoy these events, however the outcome."

"Runners set!"

"Blam!"

"How many laps do they have to run?" asked David mystically.

"Eight," answered Jayce, "just short of two miles by a few yards."

"I am amazed at how fast they're going for two miles?"

So they watched with several thousands as the boys trudged from their rest. David smiled, for he saw and enjoyed this intensity of these efforts though they of grunts and muscular flexing and not through mental assessment. He wondered how many others were like Kasper smart in the sciences and athletics. David always thought you were competent in one or the other, seldom both.

"That's it Kasper, Danny!" cried Jayce watching them stream by. "66, 67…good clip son, keep it up." Ending lap one, Kasper led the anxious runners. Patrick Dundoff followed with Danny in third. Patrick was fresh, choosing not to run the 1600 meters although he had qualified for the race. Close behind was a pack of Dick Starkey, of Moulendorf, then Jamie Dentist and Beebe Stuart. The reminders fell back quickly.

"There is the race, already," observed Jack staring at the bunched runners.

Kasper moved in a smooth even gate. "Behalten Sie diese Bemü hung bis den letzten Schoß (Keep this effort until the last lap)," thought he.

Danny was in a precarious position, because Patrick was between him and Kasper. "Kasper is setting a wicked pace," he thought, "I'll wait until this guy let go."

"Stay with that rotation guys!" Thorpe called out from his stakeout on the far turn, "very fast Kasper, very fast."

"Slug it out, Patrick," said a voice from nearby, "stick with him!" Thorpe paid him no mind. Patrick several inches taller than Kasper and more than thirty pounds heavier was to maintain his position on Kasper regardless of pace.

"He'll tire," said the voice as earlier. "Those two Lakeport guys ran a fast 1600, they'll crunch soon."

"2:17, 2:18…" called Katie up in the middle of the huge bleaches and packed crowd, as the trio passed.

"Go Kasper! Go Danny!" yelled Zoe next to her sister barely visible, "that guy can't stay with them very long I bet." She was amongst the usual contingency of Lakeport fans huddled close together in the thong of people.

"He looks to be really running fast," observed David next to Jayce, "hey, that guy in red is moving up to the front." Indeed, Moulendorf's Dick Starkey moved around the trio to barge into the lead.

"Yea that kid ran 9:19 awhile back," reminded Jayce, "he's for real," his voice trailing off with concern and his face rolled with the accompanying fronds.

"Take care of business dudes, now!" called out Jimmy with equal greetings from Eli, Terry, and Roy as Kasper latched onto Dick while the pack cruised by the tent.

"Ata boy, Sharky!" someone called out apparently addressing Dick's pet name. "Go on do your thing." The voice finished.

Thorpe paced in a small space getting nervous. "I told them to latch onto Dick when he moved out, but the guy is chugging out under 9: 20 pace. They got to be careful not to blowup and finish poorly because of the torrid pace."

Thorpe saw Jimmy and crew leaning against the fence watching the race. "Hey, Jimmy, you guys should be relaxing," said he trying to relieve some tension, "the guys are alright, you boys go cool out now!"

Then Thorpe turned his attention to the race as Jimmy and mates drifted reluctantly away from the area. The single file of runners all very good athletes struggled to maintain an all too fast race. Dick finished the third lap, Kasper just one stride back sweating profusely as it was quite warm and his bronze complexion made this observation apparent. In spite of this, Danny moved past Patrick and took his place right behind Kasper. Jamie Dennis and Beebe were running together ten meters back.

"Be careful son, got a good pace as it is," warned Jayce with a little pause then. "Danny don't lose it too,"

David stood mute not knowing what the proper mode of vocalization he should display. Beth was biting her fingernails, while Sophie and Jack muttered encouragement in a low voice.

"4:35, 4:36…" said Jayce, "ease off boys." He insisted speaking more to himself than to anyone else.

"Ease back a bit," thought Kasper, "he's fresh and pushing a record pace." The boy was suffering trying to maintain the long stride. His feet plants were getting flatter. "Keep them out there…where's Danny?" His breaths were short and not deep. He had become more conscience of trying to maintain control. "Relax the next 600 meters then push again…he's moving out from me…can't do a thing."

Another completed lap and Kasper was three meters behind Dick as the skinny crew-cut blond eased from his onslaught on the lap. It was then also that Danny swept by Kasper to latch onto Dick's rear.

"Way to go Danny!" Jayce yelled out.

"Kasper ran himself out in the first race, maybe Danny can stay with this guy," suggested Jack.

"Hope so," answered Jayce.

"Think he'll finish?" asked Beth.

Jayce glanced at the woman briefly displeased with the comment. "Definitely he'll finish." He shook his head side to side.

Approaching two laps to go it was Dick and Danny, Kasper ten meters behind.

"Stay with them Pat!"

"7:01, 7:02…"

Kasper as if given a cue, rushed forward to catch Danny. Then there were three up front together. Seeing the quick movement of Kasper, Patrick was disheartened and let up chasing the trio. He turned to check the field behind him. Patrick's race changed to guarding his fourth place.

"That's it guys!" yelled Jayce as the group clapped and urged them on.

"The two-three punch is in position," said David smiling and clapping.

Sensing activity behind him, Starkey went back to work and the boys found themselves strained with exhaustion once more. Kasper in particular suffered from the intense effort. Coming around the far turn, he lost ground slowly behind Danny.

"Stay in there Kasper!" Jayce yelled.

"Never seen Danny pull away form Kasper in this race before," commented Jack.

"Kasper gave all he had in that, 1600 meters," Jayce finalized.

"He still's doing good," said Sophie, "look at the lead they have over the others."

"You're alright Kasper," said Beth defensively.

There was no music playing in his head. Kasper's breathing rate increased while he gradually lessened his long stride involuntarily. "Behalten Sie meinen Rhythmus, Reichweite aus so weit wie ich kann bei (Maintain my rhythm, reach as far out as I can)," he demanded of himself. However, onlookers could see Kasper's shortening stride and increasing laboring effort.

"Take it away from them, Sharky!"

Thorpe heard the familiar voice as the runners approached his position on the far turn.

"Stay with him Danny! Come on hang tough Kasper!" The coach commanded warmly toward his battered subjects. "Dick is hammering on them now," he thought acceptingly.

Approaching the final lap Dick rotated arms and legs with an aggression that enabled him to pile ten meters in front of Danny with Kasper. Normal accolades rained toward the two runners as they streamed by but with little registry for the boys as their brains processed no such sounds anymore. Every bodily function temporarily slowed for the convenience of directing all energy to the legs and arms movement.

"Sharky is something is he not?" announce a nearby voice from a galley of several onlookers.

"He's only a junior, too," reminded another voice from that crowd.

"8:10, 8:11, 8:12…," calls from an assortment of sources while the stream of runners sped into lap eight.

"8:14! Come on Danny! One more time hang in there!" yelled Jayce. "You're alright Kasper!…8:19!…Second and third…still got a great time going!"

Dick looked over his left shoulder quickly to check his pursuers, a wasteful motion looking behind. Danny was straining not too lose any more ground to the high stepping, fast rotating, and confident fellow up front.

"Patrick just let go with three laps to go," said a concerned voice near, "pity, now hope he survive to finish the race."

Dick Starky was inside 300 meters to the finish when Danny shifted his form and started serious arm pumping.

"Ata Boy! Danny," Thorpe screamed at him, "Pull him back!…Come on Kasper! You're not finished yet!" The trackside spectators were in bedlam with commands and warnings, then urgings. Danny's head rolled, grimace gripped his face. Out of the turn and into the final straightaway. The crowd stood, if they were not already up, and pilfered the runners with commands as they struggled to get to the finish. Dick pulled away from Danny, whose white teeth shown bright as he grimaced behind while the third follower, Kasper, appeared in dire need of help to make it on his own to the finish line.

"Come on Kasper," Beth called out urgently toward her son; however the stronger voices all around drowned her out.

"Come on Danny, Kasper," repeated Sophie. The men were hollering all sorts of accolades with each stride of the boys toward the finish line.

"Chug it in baby! Chug it in!" said a settled and confident voice as Dick crossed the finish looking just delightful with a little grimace of a smile. Danny approached the finish with arms flaring uncontrollably nearly staggering. Kasper followed in what seen like minutes floating weakly with no flare and slowing almost walking across the line. Totally spent he was, and looked it.

"9:13.33," said Katie is business manner, "was the winner. Danny was in at 9:18.42 and Kasper got a 9: 27.67." She logged in her times.

"I never seen them get beat," said Zoe. "But Danny and Kasper they did well didn't they?"

"Yes they did," big sister, agreed, "They got fourteen points for us. All together Lakeport has seventy-one points. Bakersfield can't catch us now."

While the stands buzzed with comments and swelled toward the track to get near the finishers. The Wise and the Luke couples, tugging David along, headed for trackside to get to the boys.

"Can you believe it," asked a coach to another, "ole Thorpe's boys really performed beyond anything I would have guessed."

"Well they were prepared," answered the other, "I figured they were passed their peak, but I was proved wrong big time."

"And those guys are just juniors!" interrupted a third voice from near.

While the girl's race was in preparation, the awards area was crowded with supporters of the first eight finishers waiting for the picture taking sessions. Their family's present and school fans gathered close by to snap pictures, tape video recordings while pillaging congratulations upon their proud subjects.

Kasper spoke apologetically to Danny, "Well, I panned out. I just could not stick with Dick's increasing pace. Now, you did well Danny. You had a great 3200 and got the school record. I just couldn't double today."

"Yea but look at your mile, you were super. This is my first time running a fast 3200 meters," consoled Danny, "shoot, those other dudes none of them attempted the double and came out decent"

"Thanks, but that's water under the bridge now," said a tired Kasper, "I wish they would hurry up. I want to see the 4 x 400." The two strode toward the awards area and waved to Jayce and Beth when they spotted the pair waving and smiling as they were making their way through the crowd, to get to the boys. It was then that Danny saw him trailing behind Jayce.

"Hey!" Danny shouted pointing, "There's my Dad!"

"Yep, I see him," answered Kasper, "I bet your dad knew he was coming."

Now they sped across the track to meet up with the family, pushing through a packed thorn of people. As they met, his Dad, Benny Hood, smothered Danny with hugs.

"I had to be here for my boy," said the emotional Benny Hood. Jayce had gone to court and gotten an early release after a meeting with the judge. Benny was in jail for the better part of a year for driving without a license. It was his second time in jail for the offense. That and other minor scraps with the law, provide little sympathy from the law. However, Jayce showed the judge the newspaper write-ups of Danny's running and grade reports of his excellent schoolwork. Additionally, Jayce assured the Judge that Benny could work at the trucking company where he worked. With such reassuring, Benny received a release under probation terms from the judge.

Benny had arrived to the meet late, arriving with a friend who dropped him off then left. "We thought we knew exactly how to get here, but we got lost briefly; but I saw the entire race from the fence," said the Benny, "but I didn't call out to you. I didn't want to shock you in the middle of a race," they all chuckled a bit.

Elsewhere from this setting, young men and women were parting the stadium premises. Accompanied with family, coaches, and fans these were sober moments for many. They made the State meet, but just as non-qualifiers for Districts, and Regional; it was now time for them to retire. For the seniors, many will attend college, fewer will participate intercollegiate athletics. Of these, fewer still will compete at the large school divisions.

Some participants observed leaving the stadium carried drooping heads while arms of support rested on shoulders from their supporters. At the same moment on the awards stands, others draped with medals around the necks received the cheers and homage's directed toward them. In the background, there were the cheers directed for the girls 3200 meters, already underway, and forming its own drama of movements.

Time crawled so slowly for the participating principals; but quartered with the sedentary, the ten to twelve minutes required for the girls 3200 meters was all too soon finished. Preparation for the 4 x 400 meters sent all the crowds attention back to the grand finale of track and field events. The eight foursomes gathered on the track. First leg runners set in their staggered lanes readying for the orders that would send them off. Finished with picture taking and the deluge of greet-ings toward Kasper's and Danny's race. Lakeport supporters moved back to their places in the bleachers.

These events had an effect like a revelation to Jayce as one gets when the sun breaks through after a period of cloud cover. It seemed to him everything was clear. The competitors with their sweating face running wildly hopping about, or crying, all comprehended. Before they all seemed as an enemy he needs to squash, humiliated, and or ignore. His mind at present was tranquil with every soul he saw. He had a smile for every eye contact he made. Jayce wished the best for everyone and wished for the gloomy faces and distraught looking parents that they had a chance for another event in some time soon; he was unhappy for them. Jayce was elated that Benny was present to see his Danny perform so mag-nificently. What an impetus, not to do anything that would embarrass his son again. To see Benny with his arms around Danny was a sight he would cherish for a long time from this day.

They had all just made it to their seats when they heard the start gun crack "Bang!"

Ray was the first leg. In lane six he looked smoother than his run the previous week from lane one.

"He's going to run with 'em today," commented Jack.

"We got the meet won with the 3200 meters," said Jayce, "this is just gravy."

Cleveland Bakersfield in lane 4 charged the turn and backstretch. Haysfort appeared to maintain contact. Roy looked as fluid as he ever; nevertheless, he was losing ground to those two and a bean-headed boy in lane two.

"Come on Ray!" yelled Sophie, "Lay it on the line now!"

"Chug it Roy! Chug it!"

Into the home stretch, Bakersfield led by three meters over Haysfort and Falls Creek's bean-headed Pat Movine. Roy's big arms and legs strutted as never before, in the fastest 400 meters the boy had ever run. Then the handoffs started. Roy leaned and handed off to Eli. Such was the speed the boys carried, that in a two-second span all eight teams had passed into the second 400 meters.

"Roy was about 49.5 seconds!" claimed Jayce looking at his watch and turning toward Benny, "that's his fastest split ever."

"They are moving," said Benny smiling agreeably impressed with the speed, "and they're so good at passing the baton while moving so fast."

Roy was pass history, now Eli was rapidly touring into the turn. Almost every-one was standing and screaming toward their favorites traversing madly on the backstretch single filed for these first four teams. Bakersfield's runner was in a full sprint for a distance that required some pacing; then followed Falls Creek, Haysfort, and Lakeport in close contention.

"We'll see on the top of the turn who can run," challenged Jayce again, while Beth gripped herself with anxiousness at his side. Addressing Benny, his unknowledgeable guess, "Those guys are running full-out. Eli will get 'em coming off the turn, just watch," he finished assertively.

Was Jayce presumptuous? From behind, Jake Van Horn of Weiland pulled to Eli's right shoulder, and continued to pass. Eli would have none of this move. He had to dip his head slightly to help get his rotation, and the boy was at one-hundred percent effort. Shoulder to shoulder, they entered the second turn; however, Jake fell in tandem behind Eli as both began gaining on Haysfort. Such was their closing speed, that both drifted to lane two, posed to pass Haysfort.

"That's right! You got him!" exclaimed Jack.

"Get us back in the race Eli!"

Eli was passing Haysfort as did Jake. Both set to fanning arms as hard as they could with the accompanying leg push-off. Bakersfield exchanged the baton with their third runner. Two seconds later Fallsworth, Lakeport, Weiland and Hayworth arrived. Three remaining teams followed not close enough to get into the fray up front.

After he snatched the baton from Eli, Terry used his Luke speed to pull right up to the Fallsworth man as they sped around the first turn, both in a near reckless effort. Mid way on the backstretch, Terry increased his pace and drove pass Fallsworth, then trailed Bakersfield closely. Weiland's Jake matched Terry's every move taking position just a stride behind the boy.

"That a boy Terry!" screamed Sophie with Jack echoing.

The entire circuit of the track had people leaning over the guard fence issuing the all assortments of calls toward the speeding athletes.

"All right Wilson! You can take him!"

"Step on it Nick!"

Terry followed closely in trail not attempting to pass the Bakersfield runner, but Weiland remained attached to Terry's rear. The three entered the second turn while Haysworth lost contact. Coming into the stretch, Terry suddenly ran wide as the Bakersfield runner was now running wide legged with weakening arm action, tiring in the struggle to reach his mate still one hundred meters away.

"Go Terry go!"

They yelled seeing Terry head rolling dragging the lead back to him while Weiland fell back from pace.

"Only Terry is running strong in the stretch!" commented Jayce. Jack and Sophie were frantic in glee. Beth held onto herself tighter and tighter.

With the usual bedlam of commotion from the crowds with the final hand-offs, absolute turmoil raged the stands.

All this, uncontrolled fray on the track was watched with stoic professionals, stationed about the track. Non-emotional close peering by the official was every present. Sometimes they walked dangerously close to the speeding runners watching for any infraction causing the interference of any impedance of another participant. They gazed vehemently, while holding a red and a white flag, which they were prepared to pop up for any infraction or clean pass observed. Sometimes the official would run next to the flow of traffic for a few meters for scrutiny.

"Go Jimmy go!" A chorus of screams rained toward the boy three meters behind Bakersfield's, Abe Green.

"2:30!" Jayce shouted, "It's going to be under 3:20."

With the snatch, Jimmy broke into a torrid almost reckless effort behind lead. They both took their first turn so fast that the leans into the turn had the pair looking like bent trees in a high wind.

"Look at 'em book!" the otherwise silent Benny broke out.

"Nothing going to happen until the second turn," said Jayce to Jack and Benny. Watching he could see the Weiland was getting nowhere on Jimmy.

"Go to the arms, now," Jack insisted seeing the side view on the turn revealed Jimmy had started at his man early. "Come on! Use that power!"

"He's going after him, now!" Jayce called. Barely anyone was sitting. Most stood on the bleachers rallying for their favorites.

Two meters, one meter behind was Jimmy as he and Abe left the turn. Abe reached higher as he straightened, but his rotation slowed as was Jimmy's. However, the game was who would outlast the other, so both bore down. As the highway adage warns, 'speed kills', indeed both athletes had multiple races in their legs before this confrontation. Now, it would be which can hold up for a 400-meter struggle.

"Pull up on him Jimmy!"

"He's got him!"

"No, I think he's running out of space!"

"Keep pumping Jimmy!"

At 30 meters, Jimmy led by one foot; 20 meters, three feet; finish, Jimmy ahead by about five feet. Cheering, yelling, some crying continued to bring in the other six teams.

"3:17.3," said Katie to Zoe, "that's a record!"

"Jimmy was speeding!" cried out the little girl.

"He ran 46 and some change!" declared Jayce his head swiveling around as he beamed at everyone with a proud smile.

Following hours witnessed tumultuous celebrations for the Lakeport High School band of supporters. Team championship Division II, records runs, with a crew of boys that will all return for another year, these people were in a dream of a sort of existence. All the clan, upon announcement of the victory took to the track and toured the circuit waving the school flags and attires above their heads. Then came the team awards; where each team member received a medal and ribbon around the necks; after which the presentation of the large shinning trophy. It was the ultimate accolade, putting to rest all the sorted scenarios imagined for both individuals and the team over the prior months.

Short lived were these pompous activities for Kasper, as he suddenly felt like he was only halfway to where he needed to be. "I need to go over and over all those example problems until the test Wednesday," he mused.

"After my test, we must go back to our training, Danny," suggested Kasper to his cousin as they were leaving the stadium.

"Don't pressure yourself so much Kasper," replied Danny, "you did good and you will do good on the physics test, I have no doubt you will."

"Yea, but Danny, 'good 'is the enemy of the 'best'," prompted Kasper, "All the pomp we have experienced in the last hour will blunt our focus on big picture. We must tread with diligence. We must not think everything is downhill from here; if we stumble, there are no promises out there for us Danny. So forward we tread, but with careful deliberation."

𝕏⚹𝕏⚹⚹ 𝕜⚹⚹𝕜⚹⚹⚹⚹⚹𝕜⚹𝕜⚹⚹𝕜 𝕜⚹
𝕏⚹⚹⚹⚹⚹𝕜 ⚹⚹⚹𝕏 ⚹⚹⚹⚹ ⚹⚹⚹⚹⚹ 𝕜⚹

The next early afternoon, Kasper found himself alone except for the riveting stanzas of Beethoven's fifth. Morning church services and a big lunch let him isolated in his small room, as family had departed to their varied interests. Reclined on his bed he followed the movements of the music waving his arms.

Dad made some road trip for the company, taking Benny with along as a driver. "Since I have been unavailable the last several weekends; I need to put in some heavy time on the road," his Dad had disclosed to Kasper displaying inadvertent relief. Kasper's mom was visiting the Sweigerts after expressing that Helga was free of the deported Johannes. Beth surprised her son however, by disclosing that Bill received an award, a tidy sum for his 'undercover' participation and aid to the nation's security against terrorism.

He allowed his mood to saver with Beethoven a bit; then he scoffed at the thought of Bill, "Ist eine Sorts des Helden er jetzt (some sort of hero, is he now)?" Just some days before, some firm adherents of his views, held Bill as a misfit. However, the boy used good judgment in getting the authorities involved in his activities. Moreover, with ole Johannes, Kasper should have known better than to think friendly with an old generation German as he.

Kasper felt, however, that his problem was in no wise lifted from him. There was, on the contrary, an irritating prolongation. The escapade had created in him a great concern for himself. Now, he was compelled to sink back to his old with-drawn personage, thereby not demonstrate such lack of judgment as he had recently displayed. Such recourse led him to his 'art of physics' his withdrawal, he had his study to retreat to.

"If one calculated enough, you may arrive at some wondrously satisfactory result, or one could establish nothing. In either case, it is acceptable. Figuren sind nicht trügerisch auseinander von uns (Figures are not deceitful apart from us)," thought he.

Thus, he fretted for the opportunity that awaited him in three days. With his music going in the background, he sorts out his materials to review. Reassurance propped up his demeanor.

Arriving an hour early, there was a time of waiting. Kasper bore no notes or texts with him. Only identification and a letter of presentation for the exam accompanied him. David and Kasper accompanied with Danny made the five hour drive to the Notre Dame University for the exam, rather than take it locally. Coach Thorpe had informed the Notre Dame coach Keith Mahoney, of Kasper's performance at the State tournaments and took the opportunity of disclosing Kasper scheduled test. Ah, ha, now Kasper could meet with him and check out the track program without violating any recruiting rules.

While David and Danny relaxed in the Morris Inn, Kasper made his way to his destiny. The aura of the University humbled Kasper just as his first trip to the extent that he felt vulnerable to failure. He saw the people who looked like par-ents. They smelled like money, he thought. Dads looked like they owned where they worked, or if not, they were certainly in charge of the place. Was he being uppity? Was he biting off more than he could chew, would he fit in here? Maybe not, but he wanted to show who he was by showing his proficiency on this exam.

"Remember tackle the essay problems first," suggested David, "that's where you gather the most points and make the best impression on the judges."

At his arrival, he showed his identification and invite letter to a clerk at the door of a large lecture classroom. Directed to find any seat, Kasper climbed a lane of rising stairs and placed himself in the middle of a row of folding seats. As others arrived, they voluntarily spread themselves throughout the room Kasper counted forty-two students including himself were present when the clerks came in closing the door behind them. He was surprised to see five girls.

"Huh, only two other brown people," thought Kasper, "and they don't look like they're originally from the US."

The same self-taunting sarcasm, "minorities can't do math or run the distances, everybody knows that." He was getting nervous. He observed the various personages around the room. Kasper would have liked an acquaintance with someone like himself. "What did they do with their spare time?" The boy queried.

After a short briefing, proctors quickly issued test material Materials were breached and the exam was in progress. Kasper said a prayer, "Ich bin Ihnen, Sie zu liefern, hat den Herrn gesagt.(I am with thee to deliver thee, said the Lord.)" Then he went to work.

"How was it?" asked David who had arrived outside the doorway only minutes before Kasper made his departure, "I thought you would still be working. You still have more than a half-an-hour time remaining."

Finishing early David knew usually revealed that the student found the exam easy or it was so difficult for them that they gave up attempting to solve the problems.

"Ah, not too bad," responded Kasper with relief, "I worked on the long problems first, like you suggested. The multiple choices didn't take much work."

"I can tell," interrupted David, "you did well."

"Like you said, the examples we've been working on were valueless," Kasper exhaled, "the calculus was trying but I felt confident of my answers because they were all close to my rough estimates."

"Fantastic! Come on let's go to the Inn and relax a bit. You deserve it."

"Actually, Danny and I plan on going for a run around the campus before dinner. I will feel better after a long run."

"As you would have it," agreed David not amazed of this "strange fellow'.

THE END

978-0-595-37199-0
0-595-37199-X